PRAISE FOR SULEENA BIBRA

"Bibra debuts with a sparkling, hilarious rom-com about rival art auctioneers. …laugh-out-loud banter and sensitive heart-to-hearts that will make readers swoon. This enemies-to-lovers tale hits all the right notes."

— *PUBLISHERS WEEKLY* (STARRED REVIEW)

"Fans of Sonya Lalli will love Bibra's impressive and hilarious debut. The witty banter of this feel-good romance will delight readers and have them looking for more from this author in the future."

— *LIBRARY JOURNAL* (STARRED REVIEW)

"Bibra's assured debut is an immensely fun enemies-to-lovers story of two auctioneers at rival New York auction houses, Loot and Carlyle's. A fabulous recommendation for fans of *The Hating Game* (2016) by Sally Thorne."

— *BOOKLIST*

ALSO BY SULEENA BIBRA

Love At Auction Series

Two Houses

Two Christmases

Road to Romance Series

The Road to Gretna

Magic in The Museum Series

An American Desi in Queen Victoria's Court

For additional books by Suleena Bibra, visit her website, suleenabibra.com.

AN AMERICAN DESI IN QUEEN VICTORIA'S COURT

SULEENA BIBRA

ISBN 978-1-967839-03-2 (paperback)

ISBN 978-1-967839-02-5 (ebook)

An American Desi in Queen Victoria's Court

Copyright © 2026 by Suleena Bibra

All rights reserved. No part of this book may be used or reproduced in any manner whatsoever without written permission except in the case of brief quotations embodied in critical articles and reviews.

Any use of this book to train generative artificial intelligence (AI) technologies is expressly prohibited.

This is a work of fiction. Names, characters, places and incidents are either the product of the author's imagination or are used fictitiously. Any resemblance to actual persons, living or dead, businesses, companies, events or locales is entirely coincidental.

Cover: Ink and Laurel

Editing: Mackenzie Walton

To those whose stories have been ignored or hidden. And to those who do the work to uncover them.

As he talked along, softly, pleasantly, glowingly, he seemed to drift away imperceptibly out of this world and time, and into some remote era and old forgotten country; and so he gradually wove such a spell about me that I seemed to move along the specters and shadows and dust and mold of a gray antiquity, holding speech with a relic of it!
– *A Connecticut Yankee in King Arthur's Court*, Mark Twain

CHAPTER 1

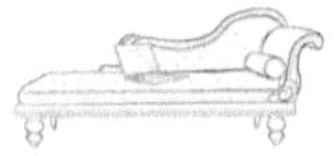

resent Day, July 3, 2025

"But there were barely any Indian people in English history," Heather laughs when I tell her my area of research, her whole body shaking and sending the layers of her dress bouncing with the movement. Great, even her Victorian-style costume is mocking me.

I grit my teeth and clench my fists, the familiar frustration welling up at the woman in front of me. The woman with, against all odds, a PhD in history. From a well-known school, no less.

I knew coming to the conference was going to be an exercise in frustration. I knew it, because it always is when I gather with other history professors. The constant dismissals, the light condescension, the outright confusion. But I wasn't going to give up a chance for an all-expenses paid trip to England, where I could do more research in my concentration: Indians in England, specializing in the Victorian Period.

And however exhausting it is, I do feel like I have a responsibility to talk on as many panels as they'll let me on so some people have to hear the history. (It was one panel, which is one more than the last conference.)

Plus, they planned this costume dinner and ball for the last night, and the opportunity to dress up like a Victorian in one of Queen Victoria's actual houses (Osborne House on the Isle of Wight), was too good to pass up. The opportunity to see Victoria's Durbar Room, a room designed by an Indian architect with Indian decorative motifs like scalloped arches and peacocks, and see her hallway of portraits of Indians from her time, was very compelling.

Even with this company.

Which is how I find myself in Victorian clothes outside the back of Osborne House, its formal gardens with statues surrounded by strict lines and curves of grass and plants behind me and the Italian Renaissance-style palazzo in front of me, its tall belvedere tower just in the edge of my view.

I wish I was in the tower right now. Or anywhere that didn't involve talking to Heather.

"And they were all servants and sailors, if they even had jobs. They couldn't be happy, wealthy, or influential. How much could there possibly be to research?" she continues before I have a chance to respond.

Not that I know what I'm going to say. From past experience, any argument I use, no matter how backed by primary and secondary sources, won't fit in with her perception of what history is. So she'll ignore it. And I'll get even more frustrated than I am now.

Before I can make the decision, Heather makes it for me.

"Oh, is that Professor Andrews? I'll catch up with you later." She leaves me without hearing any of my meticulously researched points on why she's wrong.

"Actually, turns out, ships need crews and sailing is one of the most dangerous professions with a lot of sailors dying on trade trips, so a large number of Indian lascars were employed for the return voyages then dumped in England with no way back so they had to find a way restart their lives there. And once Indians were traveling for trade, they started travelling for other reasons too. Not just sailors, but scholars, doctors, spouses of British citizens, aggrieved princes and domestic workers, among others. As the English moved on to straight-up colonizing, more and more Indians came to England. So. There were Indians of all socio-economic strata in England from 1600 CE on," I say to the spot where Heather was. The empty spot.

"Meera, there you are. Are you talking to yourself?" My friend and fellow historian Luis hands me a glass of wine that I accept with alacrity.

"Just trying to educate Heather on some salient facts about Indians in England since the seventeenth century that she doesn't want to hear." She's already across the room, talking to the professor she mentioned, conversation with me probably long forgotten. Not by me, but definitely by her.

Luis nudges me with his shoulder. We've known each other for years, bonding over our slightly overlapping specialty areas: Brazil in the eighteenth to twentieth centuries for him, and Indians in England during the same period for me.

Okay, so we have entirely different specialties, but we gravitated to each other because we were some of the few professors of color studying the history of people of color at the conferences we've been to.

"The conference is almost over. You won't see much of her after that," Luis says.

I take a sip of the drink; it's much more comforting than Luis's words. "No. But there will be so many more people like her wherever I go."

From L.A. to London and every other city, most people do not care about my area of study. It's a conversation I've had to have a lot since I started college, with professional historians and amateurs alike. They've never heard of Maharajah Duleep Singh or the Munshi, which is fine; people can't know everything. The problem is they have no interest in finding out, and even outright deny, that the routes of colonization were a two-way street.

A two-way ocean.

"I mean, there have been ships since the Phoenicians made them back in 1300 BCE. Humanity has been sailing long distances for quite some time now."

Luis holds his hands up. "I know."

"And since boats are going from England to India, the chances are very high that boats will also need to go back from India to England. You know, to transfer the spices, tea and racism back home."

"Yes, you're preaching to the choir here."

I sigh. "I know."

It's frustrating to be in the minority, pun very much intended, studying a topic no one has any interest in. I thought that by me studying and publishing on the subject, I would be able to make people outside of academia, if not care about it, at least acknowledge that people of color existed in the Regency, and all the periods that followed, and some that came before.

"Do you want to come back in?" Luis points to the mansion with his cane, really getting into the costume part of this party.

I fix my period-appropriate gloves and take a deep breath, restricted by the elaborate Victorian corset and gown I rented for the party. "I'm just going to walk in the gardens for a bit. I need a second before going back into that."

"Okay. I'll save you a dance."

I nod. "See you soon."

Luis walks back into the historic house, where a hundred of our peers are dressed up in costumes and a little buzzed as they enjoy the last night and get in their last-minute networking, while I try to remind myself that despite the downsides, this is an amazing opportunity.

Since I'm usually reading, writing, teaching or working my

way through the entirety of Netflix's catalogue, it's nice to get out of my routine. Or it would be, if I could focus on the historic building and all the research in England I don't have access to in California, and ignore the Heathers of the world.

I take one last look at the out-of-place Italian architecture that found its way to the rainy shores of an English island, and then turn away from it, starting my walk through the formal gardens. Maybe I'll walk all the way to the beach—it's only about half a mile away. Then I can look out over the same sea that Victoria looked at for inspiration on my next article.

Maybe *this* article will be the one that makes people care about the history of Indians in England.

I walk down the stairs leading to the lower terrace, wanting to see the putti who are riding sea-monsters lining the Andromeda fountain, and the woman at the center, forever waiting for Perseus to save her.

On my way down the stairs, mind already on a potential next article, I trip on one of my many layers and fall. The world spins during my dizzying descent, the lights of the estate grounds blurring in my vision. My body makes painful contact with the hard stairs as I roll down them.

This is all because I cared too much about making people acknowledge brown people in history. Now I'll never get to write the article that would have made people see.

On that depressing thought, the world goes dark.

CHAPTER 2

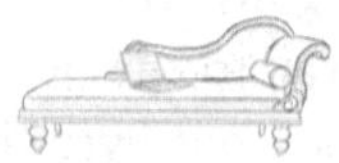

$\mathcal{A}$s I slowly start coming back to consciousness, every body part fights with the others to see what's in the most pain. Whatever wins, I'm the loser.

I slowly sit up, glad to be able to do that at least. Even though everything is on fire down to my bones, nothing seems to have permanent damage.

Everything is different now. The sounds of the party are louder, like the guests multiplied and everyone moved outside while I was knocked out. And the lights seem dimmer, with more flickering, like they added real candles to the mix.

How long was I out? Did they set up for another party? Did no one look for me? I'm not even that far from the main house; that's just sloppy event management.

I try getting up completely with help from the stone banister, making it to my feet for an embarrassingly short three seconds before I sit back down on the stairs. This is as good a spot as any to check for injuries. It's somehow darker than it was before I fell down, but maybe I knocked out some lights with my windmilling limbs.

I run my hands over particularly sore areas but don't see any blood on my fingers when I'm done. I'm sure I'm going to see bruises tomorrow and this hairstyle's a lost cause, but at least I won't have to pay the costume rental place to get blood out of silk.

So I've got that going for me.

"What are you doing out here?" an annoyed man asks in an Indian accent. A tall man in a white-and-gold turban, a red tunic, and loose pants under a long white jacket, all made of a shimmering, very touchable-looking silk, approaches me, the thunderous look on his face a stark contrast to his beautiful clothes. He looks familiar, a bit like Mohammed Abdul Karim, one of Queen Victoria's attendants. But it's the wrong century for that.

"Excuse me?" How hard did I hit my head? No one was dressed like this when I left the party. And I think I would have noticed another brown person at the conference, especially one dressed in historic Indian clothes who looks like someone from history. But also, I need to know where he got his costume, because its quality is blowing mine out of the water. Even after whatever happened to all the light, I can't stop staring at the way his clothes are reflecting what little light there still is.

"You should be inside. And why aren't you dressed in Indian clothes? You know how much Her Majesty likes it when we wear traditional garb."

"Excuse me?" I ask again, this time with a good deal more anger. "I'm not a circus bear. I can wear whatever I want at any given moment." Also, the costume rental place I went to didn't have any period Indian clothes. I checked.

"This is Her Majesty's birthday and she requested that all the Indians dress in Indian clothes. This is not a hard a request to follow. Especially after all she does for us."

"What is...Who do you think you are?" I sputter, now just as angry as the man was when he found me. "I've just fallen down your stairs; you'll be lucky I don't sue you for...unsafe stair conditions."

"Sue me?" The man puts his hand on his chest, taken aback. "It is an honor for you to even be invited here. But your fall explains your insolence."

I open and close my mouth a few times, so angry I can't even form words anymore. But I can think them.

"Come. I'll present you to the Queen and we can all hope you don't offend her."

That takes the wind out of my sails, to be replaced with confusion. "The Queen?" Did they appoint a queen in there while I was out here? Or hire an actress for us?

Even though we are in England, I doubt it's a real royal. They probably have more pressing things to do than show up at an academic conference hosted in the country.

"Show some respect for your monarch." A vein throbs in his forehead. This guy needs to relax, maybe do some meditation. Because being this high strung can't be good for anyone. Even if he is only acting.

"I paid good money for this conference." I look around my person to find the badge, but I can't see it. It must have fallen off in my tumble. I'm about to go into all the reasons I personally don't have a monarch as an Indian-American woman, including an ancestry of one war and another ancestry of long-term resistance against the Empire, when the man cuts me off.

"You are so strange. Be quiet when I present you to Her Majesty. Nod and bow and don't look her in the eye. She wants to meet all of the Indian royals before the night is over."

Indian royals? What is happening? Did they add an event about the history of Indians in England? And not ask for my input as an expert in the field? The only expert in the field at this event.

The uptight man piques my interest enough that I follow him without further complaints about his attitude. If he's playing some sort of royal servant, he is very good at this acting business.

The man takes me up the stairs, this time without incident,

and through the garden. The light still looks different, and I make a mental note to get my vision checked out tomorrow. Can changing vision be a part of a concussion?

I wish I had my phone on me to check right now, but I left it in my purse with my jacket in the coat room. I didn't want to mess with the appearance of the Victorian clothes, and it's not like I have pockets where I could bring a phone anyway. I'll look it up at the end of the night.

The man takes me through a crowd of people I don't recognize. Whose costumes have gotten more realistic since I've been out of the room. The rooms, however, are just as obnoxiously decorated, bright gilt surrounding beautiful paintings and silk-upholstered furniture, showing off a lifestyle all paid for by colonialism.

He leads me back to the Durbar Room, with its beautiful white wall carvings showing Indian decorative elements amid dark wood accents, until we stop at a group in front of the fireplace, a giant carved peacock above the mantel looking down at me.

"Your Majesty, I found another of our Indian guests," the man beside me says.

A short woman turns, her black dress so wide around it keeps people at a distance. She stands out in the crowded room, the dress embellished with white lace as well as silver- and gold-threaded embroidery in floral and other decorative motifs. She's an older white woman, with lace widow's cap over her grey hair, a small crown resting on top of the lace. Although she has an air of command around her, there's a slight droop in her shoulders and a paleness to her face.

The man turns to me. "This is Her Majesty, Queen Victoria."

CHAPTER 3

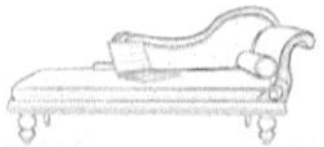

"Victoria? Queen Victoria? They've got the queen here?" I smile and look around. This is taking fancy dress party to a new level. And congratulations to whoever did casting for this party, because this woman is the spitting image of the queen, and the man is the spitting image of Karim.

"Respect. Your. Monarch," the man says through gritted teeth, looking like he would throttle me a little if we weren't in a crowded room.

"The act is getting to be a bit much." But he's committed to his role, I guess.

"Don't speak to Her Royal Highness in that manner," says another imperious man, this one white and much older than the first man who annoyed me.

Three other men step forward, in sharp red jackets with gleaming medals over pressed black pants, and semi-ridiculous fuzzy, tall hats like they wear outside Buckingham palace. They're all armed like we're about to go to war. But war where they only use swords. They put their hands on those fake weapons and look at me with a frightening focus in their eyes. Actors a little *too* committed to their role. And those weapons look a little too real. This feels like an immersive dinner gone way too intense.

I will be writing a review for this company when I get my phone back, taking off one star for a little too much realism.

"Forsyth. Abdul." Victoria gives the men who told me to behave a hard look. "She is our guest from India. We cannot expect her to understand royal protocol." Then she faces me. "Come, walk with me."

Before I can accept the invitation (although that's generous since it sounded more like a command than anything else), she starts walking around the large room we're in. Whose furniture might be different, and in different places, than before my fall. Mainly, the table where we had dinner has been removed to make space for a dance floor.

I rub my head, wondering if this is part of a concussion. Maybe I'm remembering the room wrong because of my fall.

But being around this woman does seem like a better option than all the suffocating masculinity behind me. I hurry behind her since she's already started the walk without me.

"Which family are you with? Cooch Behar? Maratha? Baroda?" she asks.

Wow. I haven't heard those names come from someone else's mouth in casual conversation before. Or even at a conference like this with historians of all different time periods together. They have really stepped it up this year.

But only for the last event, apparently.

"Yeah. I'm in the Cooch Behar family." This roleplay aspect of the costume party is kind of fun.

"I know the daughters, so you must be a niece. But didn't the family leave early? Suniti Devi said something about wanting to get back to India to handle some issue with her women's school."

"You know about Suniti Devi and her school? You do better research for your roles than the historians I interact with."

"Pardon me?" She looks confused now, and someone please

give these people an acting award already. Their refusal to break character, even when maybe they should have to give me medical attention, should be studied by actors everywhere.

"You're all very committed to the job."

"Oh. I do think there is a little being lost in translation. And your strange accent. Why don't you have a dance with the young Marquess of Basildon and he can tell you more about England? Leopold." The actress grabs an attractive tanned man walking toward us.

A really attractive man. Too attractive for me to not have noticed him at the convention before tonight's party. There weren't enough books around to distract me from noticing him. He must be an actor as well, then.

His black hair is thick, falling haphazardly across his tanned forehead and around his ears, and then playing with the nape of his neck. Warm brown eyes twinkle at me charmingly as he takes my hand and raises it to his lips that are surrounded by a beard, not breaking eye contact with me, with an arm that fills out his fine black jacket with what looks like hard muscle. He stands again and smooths his hand down his pleated white shirt and dark waistcoat.

And, for the sake of historical accuracy, it should be noted his clothes are impeccable reproductions, down to his white bowtie. Because as a historian, that should have been the first thing I noticed.

It wasn't, though.

"Basildon, may I present... actually, I didn't get your name." The actress playing Victoria looks at me expectantly.

"Meera. My name's Meera Chopra."

"Of the Cooch Behar family. Must be one of the nieces. And this is Leopold Clifford-Alston, Marquess of Basildon, Baron Chelmsford. He's half-Indian, so you have that in common."

"It is a pleasure to meet you." Great, his voice is just as suggestive of sex as his face and body. A body that's currently bowing over my hand.

"You…" I clear my throat. "You as well."

Silence fills the space between us. I look around but can't see any of the academics I've attended panels with during the past week. Or any of the presenters. Or any of the organizers. And all of the lights in here have dimmed and turned into candles too. And again, an entire table seems to have been moved while I was outside.

What is going on?

"May I have this dance?" Leopold asks.

"Sure." The angry men the actress playing Victoria saved me from earlier are looking my way, still glowering. I'll say yes to anything that takes me away from them.

I take the gloved hand in front of me, shivering in relief that I'm not getting direct skin contact. It's been a year since my last relationship and I'm usually surrounded by much older, married colleagues, so even the slight physical contact with someone potentially eligible might have made me combust with all the lust.

Only one problem, though. "I don't really know how to dance. Well, not these dances. I can sway to a beat, but this looks more complicated than my repertoire."

"Ah. Not a problem. It is a waltz and I have been forced to learn the steps under penalty of no pudding. And nothing can stop me in the pursuit of pudding. I shall take care of you." He winks at me, apparently reading my mind about the glove barrier and determined to make me combust despite it, a challenge I didn't even know I was throwing out there.

I clear my throat. "I appreciate that."

We're silent the first few minutes of the dance. I'm concentrating on not stepping on his feet or bumping into anyone else and enjoying the wall of muscle under my hand. Which makes concentrating on the first two tasks more difficult. I have no idea why he's so quiet. Probably mad to have an amateur foisted on him. He does keep looking around, probably scouting for the next woman to dance with. One who knows her way around a waltz.

"I hear India is lovely this time of year," Leopold, Marquess of Posh-Sounding-Place, says. In a pretty posh accent, actually. It's all too fancy. I'm going to start thinking of him as Leo.

"It's monsooning right now," I say before remembering it was just polite small talk.

"Right. I've never actually been or that's probably something I would know. You have a curious accent, though. Doesn't sound like anyone else in the Indian delegations that come here."

"Because I'm from America."

"The former colonies? How did you end up there?" He's focused on me now, no longer looking for greener pastures.

"The former colonies? That's cute." Did these actors have to prove they had at least a master's degree in the history of the Victorian era before they could be here? Are they just that committed to a one-night gig? If I ever need period actors, I'm calling the conference organizer to see who they are.

"It wasn't cute when we were fighting and dying in the mud over there."

"*You* were fighting there?" I look him over, from his shiny black shoes to his impeccably tied ascot necktie. Also, it was well before his time, if the actors are pretending to be in the Victorian era. Late Victorian era by the looks of the costumes I'm seeing.

"No. I want to say someone in the family did fight over there. A great-great-uncle who was a second son and drew the genetic short straw, so he ended up with an Army commission and got shot in some field in Massachusetts. Don't worry; he survived." He tilts his head with an easy grace. "Why are you there?"

"I was born there."

"How was a member of the Cooch Behar family born in America?"

I look around yet again. This is *really* weird. "Are there multiple events here tonight? To be honest, I might be in the wrong place. I hit my head earlier, and everything is…off." As nice as this conference is, they didn't even spring for coffee. I can't see them spending this much for actors to entertain us on the last night.

"This is one of Queen Victoria's homes. The only events here are the ones she hosts. Like this ball at the end of her birthday celebrations," Leo says carefully, like he's confronting a wild animal with a hungry look in their eyes and he's the only meat within a mile radius.

And while he is an appealing piece of meat, I may have bigger problems on my hands.

"No." I stop dancing. "This doesn't make any sense." I break of out of his arms. "If you'll excuse me, I…I think I need to leave." Or at least find my phone and call Luis. Because panic is starting to set in at how confused I am.

I turn abruptly and walk out of the ballroom. Relying on my very probably concussed brain, I go down hallways and look through doors, trying to find the coat check.

"Where are you going?" Leo asks me from behind. Following me. Why is he following me? Can't he take a hint?

"I'm trying to leave." But I don't know my way around. This is a giant house with more rooms than I have books, and the party was only in a few of them. I can't even take the time to appreciate the historic furniture, because nothing is right, damn it!

"Right. And I do support you in your endeavors. It is only that the front door is in the opposite direction," Lord So-Helpful says. "Here, if you give me your arm, I can lead us out of this labyrinth."

That sounds better than me being forever lost in a house museum, a warning for docents to give visitors in the future. Although as places to be trapped in goes, a palace isn't that bad. Still, the whole situation is less than ideal, and the way he's treating me, like I'm a small child who's lost in a mall on a back-to-school shopping trip, is grating. "Sure. Let's do that."

Much more efficiently than I was doing it, Leo leads me to the front door. I'm about to thank him so he knows I'm fine and he can leave me alone, but I get distracted when I realize there's no coat room.

"Where's our coats? My purse?" I look around the giant foyer, my stomach dropping when I don't see it.

A white plaster cast Victoria and Albert sculpture, the figures dressed in medieval garb, looks down at me. Mocking me. Because I don't remember that there this evening. In fact, it should be in the Victoria and Albert Museum, where I saw it two weeks ago when I was playing tourist in London. And there should be a small table and racks set up for coats in its place, which was there at the beginning of the party.

I drop Leo's arm and push through the massive front doors. Outside is no more helpful than the interior. Our shuttle is gone and replaced by some horses and carriages along the drive. Which is no longer a paved road. I can't see any of the bright lights of the town that was just past the trees when I got to this party.

The vague feeling of panic intensifies as the evidence mounts that something is very wrong.

"None of this is right," I whisper to myself, for the hundredth time tonight. "What's the date today?" I ask desperately.

Time travel isn't real. But what other explanation is there for all the strange things happening here? It's either time travel, a concussion, or a really elaborate *Punk'd* prank.

And that show hasn't been on the air since 2007.

He looks at me like he's worried about me, but answers, "It is May 25, 1895."

CHAPTER 4

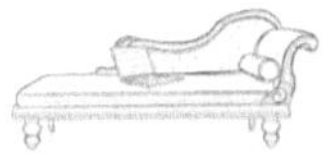

*N*o. This isn't real. Time travel isn't real. And if it was, it would involve complicated physics that I don't even know well enough to casually throw out. Maybe something to do with quantum or quasars… something with a Q for sure. And elaborate machines that spin or whirl, with buttons that say *Do Not Touch*.

I'm just a girl who's clumsy enough to fall down some stairs. There were no machines! Quantum or otherwise.

No. We still have the explanations of this being an elaborate coma-dream resulting from the fall and too many nights falling asleep while doing research on this very period of time, or it being a joke.

If this is a dream, no one will admit to it or be aware of it, but as for the other… "Am I being pranked? You have to tell me if I ask; I'm pretty sure that's the rules of pranks." It would be the worst time for historians to develop a sense of humor, and a kind of cruel one that's making me doubt my sanity, but it would be a relief right now to find out I wasn't imagining the impossible.

"No. Unfortunately, if you want this to be a prank." Leo is looking at me like I'm a candidate for Bedlam.

Shit. Bedlam. What society does for mental health isn't great in the present, but it was even worse in the past. I should try not to get sent there, on the off chance that this isn't a dream and I have somehow figured out time travel.

I sit down at the bottom of the stairs leading up to the house and hold my head in my hands, which is pounding with confusion and frustration. And a lack of hydration.

Tears I don't need right now leak out of my eyes. Because I want my mom, and she's at least an ocean and maybe a lot of years away.

"What do you want to do now?" Leo kneels in front of me, using a voice so careful, calmer and softer than any he's used so far tonight, that I know I must look on the brink of a panic attack right now.

"I don't know," I say hopelessly, sniffing so I don't outright bawl in front of him. Usually, most of my problems, questions, or general boredom can be solved in the pages of a book. But I don't think there's a manual for this. Nor do I know where the closest library is.

So it's a bad day on all fronts.

"You don't have to stay here with me. I'm sure you want to rejoin the party." I know I want him to. Because I don't need an audience to my misery.

"I do like a good party." Despite his words, Leo takes a seat on the stairs next to me.

"Then why are you still here?" Really, bro. I can't hold the flood of tears back much longer, so it's going to be wet here in a second. Not in a happy, sexual way.

"Ah. Well…" He pauses dramatically, piquing my interest. "You look very sad. And it doesn't feel right to leave you here, alone. Whilst so sad. I have often found that happiness is the preferable state, so you should try that."

I laugh at him, a small one, but a sound that qualifies. Because who in the Pollyanna is this guy? "Excuse me? I don't think I can will myself to be happy. Especially not right now. When I have no idea what's happening to me and no idea what I need to do next."

I haven't been this rudderless in my entire life. Or at least not since elementary school, when I vacillated between wanting to be a princess and professional reader when I grew up. Then I learned that those weren't really feasible job opportunities, but I could spend my life studying about princesses (and everyone else living in the past) while reading books, and never looked back.

Since then, I may not always be able to achieve my goals, but I know what I want them to be. And I always have a plan on how to achieve them; I've always known what my next steps needed to be.

Now, I don't even know where I'm going to sleep tonight. Oh, that thought has me burying my head deeper into my hands as I hunch over my knees, rocking back and forth a bit.

Leo sighs beside me. I don't know what his damage is. He wasn't transported against his will to another time, so I have no idea why he's so aggrieved. "Come back inside the ball? I will procure some weak Madeira for you and show you why having a good time is much better than...this."

"But I don't know where I'm supposed to sleep tonight. Or how I'm supposed to get home," I end on a wail. I'm aware that'll raise more questions than it answers for him, but I need to vent to someone.

He's taken aback, probably wondering how I got into the ball in the first place. "Hmm. I do not know how to help with that. But if I leave you here, you are not likely to find somewhere to sleep either. Unless you bivouac in Her Majesty's hallway. If you come inside and dance with me, you can be drunk and you still will not have somewhere to sleep, but you will be happier about it. You have nothing to lose."

I open my mouth and close it a few times. "You've lived a very different life than me." Also a good piece of evidence for why

France guillotined their nobles. How is this avoidance of responsibility or problems sustainable?

"Probably. But we are both here now, Your Royal Highness Meera Chopra, of the American Cooch Behars."

"What the hell?" I throw my arms up. "I have no other plans. Might as well eat and get drunk."

"Her Majesty does a fantastic supper. And it will all work out, in the end."

"Great." Because it always works out for rich people. But I am not in that club, so I don't think it'll apply to me.

But since I don't have any other plans, I might as well try to brazen it out.

Leo extends his arm again and I take it, trying to do what he would do in this situation and push the worries to the back of my mind.

Despite me telling Leo I can enjoy the party on my own, he stays close to me, pointing out which drinks and food I might like. If anyone gives me an assessing look, he charms them, telling them I'm from India, explaining my "curious accent" with my many travels. He makes me sound more like a woman of the world than a lost woman with no idea what's going on, which I appreciate.

I should probably be offended that he explains all my eccentricities as being because I'm a "simple girl" from India and can't possibly understand the "complicated" Western world (*gag*) but it does keep me out of jail and Bedlam, so I guess I'll have to grin and bear that condescension from the masses at this party.

Leo also stays away from any topic that could possibly be stressful for me, like family, where I grew up, or anything about me, really. Instead, he walks around the ballroom with me, trying to distract me by telling the scandalous gossip about the people we pass.

Well, it's meant to be scandalous. But when you're from the twenty-first century, some adultery and intrigue are not shocking, and even kind of expected, studying this crowd like I have. I know a few of the people in this room, and well…let's just say I've read their love letters and seen the pornography they tried to hide.

The Prince of Wales is at this party, and he's had so many affairs, I could write a book about just that topic, if other authors hadn't already beaten me to it. Two of his mistresses are actually here: Daisy Greville, the Countess of Warwick, and Alice Keppel (the great-grandmother of Camilla, who's queen in my time). There are also other members of the Marlborough House set, the name for the Prince of Wales's group of friends who got together to carouse and cheat, it seemed like.

But I don't tell Leo that. Instead, I pretend to be appropriately shocked that the "quality" would ever stoop to something as pedestrian as lust.

Tonight is a new party experience for me. Usually at parties I stick close to the people I know and we stay in our bubble, and *not* knowing anyone at an event is my nightmare. Because then I'm either going to stand awkwardly alone in the corner or be forced to meet people. And both are unpleasant choices.

But it's different with Leo. He's clearly well-liked in this crowd, and everyone has a smile and a kind word ready for him. Some even seek him out. Meanwhile, I get confused glances from everyone that we encounter. But he handles the more curious among them, saying that the Queen told him to take care of me for the night and he takes his responsibilities seriously.

That always gets a laugh, so I guess Leo isn't known for his responsibility. I guess he really does love fun. It's hard for me to understand, because my joy has always been tied to my work. Which means it has also been tied to the frustration of not getting a grant, or not being chosen to be included in a journal. Some happiness, and some heartache, where the stakes are giving the ignored of the past their voice back. And when I fail, it's not just me I'm disappointing, but them as well.

But Leo's frivolity is…well, helpful for me, in this moment. So I guess I can't judge him too much for it, even if it is completely foreign to me.

I don't tell Leo that I'm a little starstruck by some of these names. Like the aforementioned countess, Daisy Greville, who became a socialist and advocated for policies that would address income inequality, including education and food insecurity for women and children. And had a bunch of affairs, wrote love letters, and then later blackmailed her former partners with them so she could continue to entertain herself lavishly and support her causes.

So kind of a champagne socialist, if that exists. Either way, her autobiography is very entertaining.

But I definitely don't tell any of them about my excitement to meet them; their egos don't need the boost. My history books are coming alive in a way that every historian wishes but I don't think any have gotten up till now (not that I can be sure about it, since apparently time travel *is* a thing).

I'm slowly getting used to the idea, and with the distraction the party provides, I'm less despondent than I was an hour ago.

I ask a few too many probing questions to some of the highest aristocracy in this country, but Leo soothes any ruffled feathers with a reminder that I'm from India. How could I possibly understand the rules of *polite* society?

The same polite society that is, in the time I'm in, stealing land and resources from India with reckless abandon, while looking down on the people they're exploiting. But I choke that down, because this crowd does not want to hear that, and I don't want to be sent to the Tower of London.

Once Leo and I have made a lap around the dancefloor, we loiter by the French doors on one side of the ballroom, watching the crowd of couples in their intricate clothing, doing their complicated dances in front of us. I'm glad to be with a professional partier right now, because the ballroom is getting hot with all the people and the open flames, and the open doors are letting in a little bit of a breeze. Our tactical position also helps lessen the smell of the ballroom. As nice as these people look, and even though they have access to warm water for baths and perfumes, they don't have access to the good chemical-filled deodorants, and it shows.

I knew I would miss my phone if I ever went to the past; I didn't realize how quickly I would miss modern deodorant.

I *almost* forget I'm screwed when a presence creeps up next to me. Creeps so subtly that I first get goose bumps warning me something is near, and then jump a half of a foot in the air when I realize a person has materialized next to me.

"Oh, hello." I put my hand to my chest to keep my heart from beating out of my chest. Don't need to draw any more attention to myself.

It's the man from earlier who demanded I respect Victoria, who I now believe is the actual Queen Victoria. A dream wouldn't have lasted this long. Or been this detailed.

Leo is less shocked at the man's sudden appearance, and jumps in to introduce us. "May I present Charles Forsyth, Lord Wellesley, and the Secretary of State for India. Lord Wellesley, this is Her Royal Highness Meera Chopra of the Cooch Behar family."

Ah. I know him. The man is awful as he uses his position to promote polices that will exploit and not develop India like cutting public programs such as irrigation projects and famine relief for a larger army presence, lives beyond his means, and cheats on his wife. And he's rude.

"I found it odd that one of the Cooch Behar contingent was still here, and a woman no less. One who acts like neither an Indian woman nor an Englishwoman. I would not be attending to my duties if I didn't find out more about you." What a fancy accent and innocuous words for such a threatening tone. And not even a "hello," or "nice to meet you" before he dives right in to subtly accusing me of lying.

Which I am. But still, he doesn't know that. My heart rate roars back up, when I had just gotten it back under control after realizing *when* I was. It doesn't help that Leo got distracted by someone saying hello to him and isn't doing his usual smoothing over for me.

"When you put it like that, I guess it does sound odd. But here I am. How would I have gotten here if I wasn't part of the group?" Answering a question with a question is good evasion. One of the first thing they teach lawyers, in a class called "How to Be Annoying," probably.

"Then why are you still here? The Maharajah and his retinue left a few days ago. Why would they leave you behind? Unless you aren't with them, and you are lying to all of us?" He arches an eyebrow, making him look like a villain. Probably the look he's going for. I bet he practices the look in the mirror while being mean to puppies, the monster. "We do not need more of you people taking advantage."

I immediately grit my teeth and lock my muscles to hold my body back from flying at him like a wailing banshee at the "you people" remark. "Yes, they have left." I don't offer an excuse for why I'm still here. Not because I made a conscious decision to evade his questions, but because I have no idea what to say—no idea what will get me in the least amount of trouble while I'm still trying not to physically fight him.

And the Madeira is not helping. I've had a lot of it tonight, and I'm not even normally that quick on my feet. I need time to process information and write out a well-reasoned response that I can edit before submitting. It's why I'm a scholar and not a lawyer.

Although being quicker on my feet would have helped scholar-me when my professor tore apart my thesis proposal during undergrad. He was the first in a long line of people who don't think there's any value to studying people of color in English history, or anyone other than the aristocrats, really. And the reason I didn't bother trying to study it myself until grad school when another professor encouraged me to research whatever I wanted, as long as my papers cited legitimate sources and were well-analyzed.

"Why are you still here?" Charles isn't letting this go anytime soon.

"I…am…" Going to take a damn improv class when I get back to the correct time period. "Here to study. England does have some of the best tutors." There's no way he's going to argue with me on that fact; he seems the type to be very certain of England's superiority. And I am studying these people, whether they know it or not.

"Tutors can travel to India. Why would your family leave you here?" he asks, not as flattered as I thought he would be.

"I…I…" Shit. This is it. I'm going to be caught and *dealt* with. Which now means hard labor, and that does not sound fun.

If they don't hang me outright for lying to the queen.

Lucky for me, Leo rejoins the conversation. "Her Majesty said that she would take care of Her Royal Highness while she is here, as a ward. Did she not tell you that?"

I don't know if she actually made me her ward, but I'll take the lifeline. And Victoria has acted as guardian to many colonial subjects who wound up in England, like Duleep Singh, Sarah Forbes Bonetta, Princess Gouramma, and Prince Alemayehu. Although they did not live with her directly, she became their godmother and directed their lives, whether they wanted her to or not. She has a soft spot that maybe bordered on a little weird for them, along with a very strong maternal instinct, so it isn't out of the realm of possibility that she would do it for me.

Plus, this guy is a pompous prat, so I don't see him wanting to admit the Queen kept him out of the loop on anything. Hopefully we can ride his arrogance right through the end of this party.

I send him a placid, I'm-definitely-*not*-up-to-anything smile. I heard from a show about heists that confidence really sells an outrageous lie, so I try that on for size. And although I'm not a great actor, I've never been this motivated to sell a lie.

Charles sputters. "Yes. Well. Of course I have the Queen's ear on all important matters. She must not have thought enough of you to mention your stay." Charles looks down his nose at me, wanting me to know we're not even in the same stratosphere.

If he meant to hurt my feelings, he doesn't understand that keeping to myself is preferable, not only in daily life but in this precarious situation. If he wants to suggest he's morally superior to me, he doesn't know that *I* know he's having an extramarital affair with his best friend's wife, Lady Dumfries. No one will find out in his lifetime, but a historian finds the letters in about eighty years.

The man is an ass in person, and even more awkward when it comes to seducing a woman in writing. I don't even feel bad that I laughed at him in the future when I read them. In fact, when I get back, I might need to write a paper on the letters, just to publicize them some more. Maybe someone will make a movie about how bad he is at seduction, and how disloyal a friend he is.

But even though I can't tell him that or I'll face very uncomfortable questions, it does calm down my panic slightly. No one here is perfect, and I know more about them than just about everyone else now or in the future.

I can use this to keep me safe.

Or get me burned at the stake. Sure, they've stopped doing that, but I don't want to be the reason they start it up again.

"Yes. That must be it. I am supremely unimportant." I smile at him like an amenable pod person, trying to look as harmless and unimportant as we just established I was. He's taken aback by my easy agreement.

Charles clears his throat. "Still, unimportant though you are—"

Great, I am definitely going to need to talk to a therapist after this. Not only because I thought I time travelled, but because my self-esteem is suffering here.

"It is very unusual for the Queen to make arrangements without telling her staff. Perhaps we should call her over and verify some of the particulars of this…story." He sniffs derisively after the word, leaving me no doubt as to what he thinks about me and my story, as he turns to call Victoria over.

That would be bad. Why did Leo have to name-drop the Queen? Maybe he thought the audacity of the lie would carry me through, but it's not working out that way.

"How is Lady Dumfries these days?" I say in a panic, tossing out anything that will stop him from looking at me.

What the hell? I'm not usually so reckless and mean, but it's desperate times. And, Madiera. It might be watered down, but you can just drink more and then it's like it was a normal strength. Which is what I did.

The man turns an interesting shade of red. And puffs up like a balloon. It's fascinating to watch. "Why would you ask me that? Go ask her husband if you want to know."

"My mistake. I thought you two were *friendly*." I say the last word with as much lascivious implication as I can, like my life depends on how salacious I can make this word sound. And it might.

And people say there's no use for history. How do you like me now?

"You are mistaken. And I'll thank you to not mention our names together again. It could only hurt the good lady." He rushes off without getting my promise that I won't say anything else, and without asking me any more questions.

Oh, could it hurt *her*? You're so concerned with her? Or could it hurt *your* image as a family man when you try to run for Prime Minister in this morally conservative time?

"What mischief was that about?" Leo asks, not understanding what happened in the last minute.

"I thought I saw him talking to her earlier, that's all. I don't do mischief," I say. Although if you'd asked me ten minutes ago, I would have said I don't do blackmail either. Yet here we are. My morals the first thing to go in a desperate situation.

"You just need more practice."

"That I do not need. What I need is a place to stay." Charles did remind me that I have no idea what to do when this party ends. He's also still glaring at me from across the room. But away from Victoria, so I don't think he confronted her about my lie. Yet.

The walls of this situation are slowly closing in on me, and the smart course of action would be to get out of the room.

Leo sighs. "I thought we were going to ignore worries for the night?"

"That might be easy for you to do, but my quickly upcoming future is about to punch me in the face if I don't figure this out."

"Yes, I suppose my own worries are getting harder and harder to ignore as well." He looks around like whatever caused that cryptic comment is going to jump out at him from behind some silk curtains and club him with responsibility. Then he snaps his eyes back to me. "But we shall fix this for you. If you refuse to have any more fun until your present problems are solved, we shall solve them. I have an idea."

"It's not going to be that easy."

"Of course it is." Leo takes my hand without any input from me and tugs me where he wants to go.

Which appears to be right toward Victoria.

CHAPTER 5

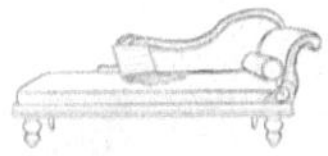

I try to put the brakes on, backpedaling so we don't go toward the most powerful person in the room. The person I've already lied to and about tonight. And the person who can throw me in a dungeon. Because she has multiple dungeons.

She wouldn't do it herself obviously. She's a pixie grandmother who is about four inches shorter than me, but she can order an entire armed guard to do it. A whole country, if it comes to it.

"I don't think we need to bother her," I say.

"It is fine. I'm named after her son; she is exceedingly fond of me." Leo continues on his path past laughing aristocrats twirling in large gowns and tuxedo tails, and stoic servants standing by refreshment tables ready to make any request a reality for the guests of this party. He's undeterred by my attempts to have us go in any other direction.

From everything I've seen tonight, Leo has all the indicators of a real-life rake. It can't be that hard to sway him from his path.

"Don't you want something to drink? We could get that instead. I promise I'll have fun."

Nothing.

"There's a rousing game of something card-like in the drawing room. Don't you want to play?" I ask.

He doesn't even slow.

"There's a very attractive woman over there in a low-cut frock. Don't you want to see what'll happen if you go over there?"

That does cause him to finally stop. "Excuse me? Are you suggesting licentious contact?"

Oh yeah, they cared about that sort of thing back then. Cared about women talking about it, that is, and not the premarital sex itself, which people have been having in all time periods since forever. But he doesn't look one breath from a scandalized heart attack. More like he's trying not to laugh at me in public.

"I want to say no. Marriage. You should see if she wants to get married. Unless you already are married?" I know nothing about this man.

Leo gives up trying to hold it in and laughs at me outright. "I am not married. And you are more forward than any woman I have ever met. More entertaining than any, too."

Oh boy, just you wait a hundred and fifty years. I am probably shyer than everyone I have ever known. An actual walking stereotype of the academic who would rather spend time with books than people.

"I'm so glad you're entertained. Why don't we go over there" —I point in the opposite direction from the Queen—"and I can be even more forward, probably."

"But then you will still be worried about this lodging situation. Which will inhibit our fun. And I cannot have that."

He starts walking in that direction again and I get more physical with my deterrents, digging my heels in.

"You'll make a scene," Leo says.

I give in. I've already attracted enough attention in this room.

"Your Majesty," Leo calls out when we get closer to the

woman. He bows in front of her and I belatedly follow with a curtsey.

"Are you still taking care of my guest?" she asks.

"Of course, Your Majesty. I live to serve."

She raises a grey eyebrow. "You did not abandon her because you got distracted by a young woman?"

"I would never." He brings the hand not holding mine to his heart, suggesting that he very much would, and has, probably regularly.

None of this is my business. If an attractive man wants to fuck every woman in this town, or in this country, that's not any of my business. Because this would be robbing the grave. In that he was in a grave before I was even born.

And for a long time, too. Decomposition will have started, for sure. Finished, probably.

Even if he certainly looks alive from this angle, I need to remember I'm a time anomaly, or whatever, and I don't think time anomalies should be making out with people in the past. I think I'm okay to lust after him from afar, though. It's like lusting after a fictional character or the Roman Emperor Augustus.

He has very flattering statues.

"We have a slight problem—"

"If you already got her gambling debts, I will not be amused."

"No debts. Not from lack of trying, but she is irritatingly responsible. However, she does seem to be left behind by her family, the Cooch Behars."

"They left you behind?" Victoria looks at me with kind eyes. Maternal eyes. But she asks the question directly of me, forcing me to answer instead of leaving it up to Leo to lie for me.

This is a woman who buried the first love of her life, Albert, at forty-two. Then, she fell in love with a Scotsman and her servant, John Brown, who called her "woman" in a Scottish brogue, and she buried him too, at sixty-three. She feels isolated because of her position, and her nine children cause her a lot of stress.

That man in the turban I met before must be Abdul Karim, her Urdu tutor, so she's in the process of finding a friend again. But she's lonely. And a bit starved for affection. I would be a bad person to take advantage of everything I know about her personal life. Then again, I don't want to go to jail. Also, however nice she is to some Indians…it's still in a very colonizer way. That makes me feel slightly better about what I'm going to do.

I take her hand in mine, a breach of decorum considering Leo's sharply indrawn breath, but affective when I see the shock in her eyes be replaced by warmth. She did love John because he didn't treat her like a monarch; he treated her like a woman. So I'll treat her like a family member.

"I think it was a case of poor communication. I was supposed to stay longer to experience England, but the people I was supposed to stay with left too, probably thinking someone else was staying with me. You've been so kind to invite me to this assembly, and I'm having such a nice time. But I don't have anywhere to stay and I'm afraid of being alone here. And honestly, I miss my mother. I hate to impose further, but if you know of anywhere…" I hope she finishes that sentence herself. I channel the family dog while I wait, making sure my eyes are turned up to full puppy-dog-looking-at-you-eating status.

Victoria squeezes my hand. "You must stay with me. We certainly cannot kick a member of royalty out in the streets."

I smile in gratitude and relief, finding the English's genuine love of royalty, even from areas they've colonized, stranger in person than it was when I read about it. And I wasn't even expecting her to take me in; I thought she's make someone else do it like she has with other Indians. I'm not complaining, though. "Thank you. That's very kind of you."

"Of course. Do you have your things? We can move them up to a room." Victoria looks around for someone to order to take care of it.

"They actually took all my things with them. Because of the miscommunication."

Victoria raises her eyebrow. "That's quite the miscommunication."

"You know what the last day before international travel is like, Your Majesty. Always a mess of wondering if the servants have packed and arranged everything they need to," Leo says.

"Yes. That is so stressful for *you*." I hope no one's discovered sarcasm yet, because if they have, I might have just sarcasmed my way out of a room in a palace.

I even agreed with him until he mentioned the servants. Because I was worried about making sure I had my passport, credit cards, chargers and good walking shoes the night before I came to England. All I'm saying is, I can see how the McCallisters left Kevin behind in the rush of pre-travel in *Home Alone*.

It's stressful.

"That's settled then." Victoria looks delighted to have solved my problem, and I am too. Half of a giant weight has been lifted from my shoulders as I figure out where I'll sleep tonight, but not how I'll get home.

Charles chooses this moment to slither toward us. "Ma'am, is there anything I can help you with?"

"No, I've taken care of it. I will have a guest for a little while."

Charles scrunches up his face is distaste. "This is most irregular—"

"She is royal. We cannot allow her to struggle when we could easily render assistance," Victoria says.

"But what if she is not with the party? No one has verified that bit of information and it is quite convenient that no one can verify it right now, Your Majesty," Charles says. He motions to some people behind him. "Maybe we should detain her until we sort out the truth."

That gives Victoria pause, and the panic, which had just receded, kicks up again. "Are you saying Her Majesty's guards would let an imposter in? How would I get into the palace if I wasn't meant to be here?" I hope they can't hear the tremble in my voice at the lie.

Victoria nods and waves off the guards. "We will verify the story, of course, but in the meantime, I will not allow a royal family member to have nowhere to stay. And this is my house, therefore it is my decision," Victoria says firmly. "But thank you for your concern. Please, do enjoy the rest of the party."

My eyes bounce back and forth between them like I'm watching a tennis match. Although in this situation I may *be* the tennis ball flying between the two leaders. On one side is a royal who wants to rule in a constitutional monarchy when the monarch is losing power, and on the other, a government official, albeit an aristocratic one, who is getting more power to actually govern.

I know who wins in the long run, and the push for more democracy is a good thing, but in this case I'm glad Victoria could put her foot down, the way she does for Abdul Karim when people complain about him.

She only knew him for a few days as one of the Indian men brought to help serve her meals during her Golden Jubilee celebration when she made him her Urdu teacher and companion. I'm glad she's doing the same thing for me now.

"We should take our leave. I want to introduce Her Royal Highness to some university friends." Leo, astute as he is charming, doesn't want to be around the power struggle any more than I do.

"See, did I not say that things would work themselves out?" Leo bends down to gloat quietly in my ear.

I roll my eyes in response. Sure, this one time, because of his connections and my omniscient knowledge from the future, this one crisis is okay.

But there's still the next day to worry about.

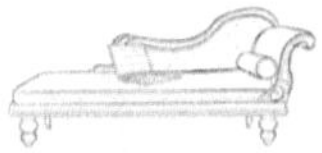

$\mathcal{I}$ snuggle deeper into the bedcovers the next morning, relieved all over again that I'm not spending the night in jail. Instead, I'm waking up in what is probably the exact opposite of jail: a palace. A bit sore from falling down some steps, but in one piece and in a nice bed.

The rest of the night was surprisingly fun. Without the stress of where I was going to sleep, I was able to enjoy the party. Because of Leo, because without him standing next to me, I would have melted into the floor under the intense scrutiny of everyone in the room.

I couldn't make a move without over twenty eyes staring at me, wondering about me so intently I could feel their thoughts. Who is she? What is she doing here? How did she talk to the Queen twice? Why is Leo glued to her side? Who does she think she is?

Usually, that would be a trial by fire for me. Not only to be the center of all that attention, but to know it's negative attention, would make me want to throw myself against the nearest hard surface, hoping that it knocks me back into the present. Or to another time if that's what the universe wants. As long as it gets me away from all the eyes.

But it wasn't so bad with Leo next to me.

Then at the end of the night, I was taken to the nicest room I've ever stayed in. Old Masters paintings hang on my walls (although I guess they aren't quite as old right now), while the walls themselves are plastered with a pink silk Damask wallpaper that is so soft to the touch. And yes, while I do not touch things in museums, these pieces are not historic yet, so I didn't feel guilty taking a pet.

I lay under a canopy of thick, embroidered, floral fabric in a dark blue, green and silver pattern, enjoying the fireplace that had been lit before I even got in here, wearing a soft white cotton nightgown that had been laid out for me.

I got a better sleep than I have in a long while. Even with all my current problems, I was no match for a royal mattress, which was luxuriously filled with feathers and sheep's wool, allowing me to sink into it and feel very cradled. And if I ever get back to my time, I will try not to gloat at my curator friends for being able to spend a night on one of their historic beds, which would only lead to them asking when and where that happened, and then not believing me when I answer.

Even the bathroom down the hall has plumbing. Rudimentary plumbing, but it works well enough to make me glad I didn't go to an even earlier time.

Now that my immediate needs are taken care of (food, clothing, shelter, priceless art, and a royal party with a charming rake), I need to focus on how to get home. Last night I cried, but today I need to focus on next steps, because a plan has always served me well in the past.

I open the drapes to let in light and sit at the writing desk in the corner of the room, grabbing some paper and a fountain pen from a drawer.

Whenever I'm stuck on a problem with an article or lesson

plan, writing by hand helps me brainstorm. It's a little harder to do with a fountain pen and inkwell, but the principle must still be the same. But I'll have to burn it later so people don't find this and jump to the absolute accurate conclusion.

After an hour of doodling, all I have is that I should go back to the steps and try to recreate the fall. I don't look forward to getting another concussion, but it's the only idea I have for getting home, since I still don't know exactly how I got here in the first place.

And I can't stay here forever. I have a life to get back to; a life that I already miss desperately. Like my mom who usually sends me any and every social media post she thinks I might like, which end up ranging from hilarious to adorable to slightly passive aggressive suggestions for my life. And the books I usually spend my days with, as well as the neighborhood dogs I see on my evening walks. Especially the hours of pre-bedtime scrolling I do before looking at the time and realizing I won't be getting my recommended eight hours of sleep, and I have no one to blame but myself.

It's only been half a day, but it feels worse since I have no idea how or when I'll make it home, or if I'll even see any of those things again.

A knock at the door interrupts my useless brainstorming session/ homesick pity party. "Come in." I fold up the paper with all the heresy on it and hide it in a drawer.

A woman comes in, and her plain but finely made black dress covered in a white apron with simple lace frills along the straps, her hair pulled back and topped with a white lace hair covering for maximum efficiency suggests she may be one of Victoria's maids. "Good morning, Miss. Her Majesty sent me to help you dress for the day," she says.

"Hello," I say awkwardly, getting up from the desk. "There's no need…" But then my eyes drop to the giant lump of material I assume is a dress that she's holding in her arms. There's actually very much a need. There's no way I can get into any of those layers by myself. "Thank you. That would be very appreciated. My name's Meera." The woman looks at me without responding. "What's yours?"

"It's Anne, Ma'am."

"Nice to meet you."

The woman gives me a nod and then helps me get ready for my first day in Victorian England. The dress is much more authentic (and even more uncomfortable) than the costume I rented for the convention party (but that I could get into by myself). But I can't argue with the craftsmanship of it. Anne gives me looks as I gaze with a little too much wonder at each garment she tries to put on me, and let my hands linger a little too long at the different textures of the soft undergarments to the heavily embroidered and heavily beaded (and just plain heavy) dress itself.

When Anne is done, I can't stop staring at myself in the tall mirror. I look...Victorian. My clothes are exquisite, my hair is piled on top of my head, and Anne is looking at me like I shouldn't be this amused to be dressed (and not so awkward when someone is trying to dress me, but in my defense, it's been a while since I had help in that department.) I also can't stop staring at the butt this dress gives me. It's so big I'm going to knock things over with it if I'm not careful and I turn too fast. I'm glad bustles aren't a thing anymore.

"Breakfast is served informally in the morning room. Then you can have use of the library or hall for entertainment, and luncheon will be served at one o'clock. Before dinner I will have the rest of your new clothes waiting for you here and you can change into something more formal for the meal," Anne says.

If my plan works, I won't be here for any of that. But that's a lot to explain to a stranger, so I nod in gratitude. "That sounds lovely. May I take a walk around the gardens?"

She looks taken aback that I'm asking her for permission,

probably not something the nobles she works for would do. Right. I hope I'm not here too long, because I do not have the temperament for this. "That would be fine. I can show you down to the morning room or outside, if you'd like?"

"Yes, please. I think I'll go outside right now. Work up an appetite." And if I'm successful, I can be back to present-day England with a sausage roll in my hand on the way to the airport before lunch.

"All right. We'll head there now."

The route is long and winding, through rooms filled with marble columns, gilt on everything, luxurious curtains, and walking on thick carpets. Copious amounts of paintings fill the walls, complemented by the army of statues standing in front of them. I gawk at it all in historian, but Anne doesn't blink an eye. Either everyone gets this starstruck in front of all this conspicuous consumption, or they expect it from a foreigner.

Anne leaves me in the same verdant garden I was in yesterday (or a hundred and thirty years in the future), and I walk to the stairs.

"Okay, Meera. This is it. Just fall. You did it once; it can't be that hard." Except that it kind of *is* that hard. Every time I get close to the edge of the stairs, my brain orders my feet to freeze, not wanting that pain again. The few times I get past the first step, my feet move quickly down the rest to stop me from tumbling down.

Where was all this athleticism when I was trying out for middle school soccer?

"You barely have any bruises from the last time. Just do it and it might hurt for a bit, but then you'll be back home where there's adequate pain management options. Or back in England where you can catch a plane home. Because planes will exist."

I try to throw myself down the stairs one more time, but my arm shoots out to catch the railing and clutch it like it's the last copy of a book I need for research at my university's library, and I see another historian from the department heading for it.

"Damn it, woman! If you don't do this, you'll never get back, and you'll have to wear a corset and bustle every day for the rest of your life. Although, on the bright side, I will be actual living proof that there were brown people in European history."

Honesty compels me to finish the thought with the cons list. "Counterpoint, I won't be around in the future to tell anyone about it, and I'll fade into the pages of history, lucky to be a footnote like all the other people of color in the West."

"Are you all right?" a voice asks from behind me.

A voice that startles me enough that I turn to it without realizing I'm on the edge of the steps. My right foot doesn't find the step behind me, instead getting tangled up in my many layers.

The last thing I see before the world turns into a blur is Leo's too-handsome face.

CHAPTER 7

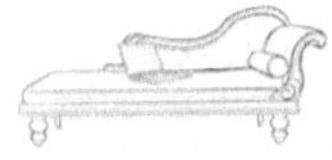

"Oh my god!" Leo says as my feet fly over my head and my already angry back (from all the time I spend hunched over books and my laptop) finds the sharp edge of every stair.

I try to remind myself that this is what I wanted. That it's a good thing and this is my very painful ride back to the future (I really should watch that movie now…) but my body and under-used muscles, overwhelmed with pain, don't care to hear it.

"I'm coming!" I vaguely see his shiny shoes move rapidly down the stairs above me.

No, I have to go now. But when I get back to real life, I'm going to look up how your life went. Maybe I'll even write a little paper about how kind you were one night to a stranger. Put flowers on your grave.

Fantasize about what could have been if I met you at a faculty party or on one of my research trips to England.

But the same blackness that overtook me the first time isn't happening, and I keep getting flashes of the blue sky, the tan-colored building material, and Leo's legs encased in black pants as I tumble.

And then I stop in a heap at the landing of the stairs, on my back, still very awake, and very confused. And in lots of pain. More than the first time, actually.

As I'm trying to suss out whether I succeeded in getting to the right year, Leo's head blocks out the sun, his short curls framing his face, looking kind of like an angel since he's backlit.

Even though he helped me yesterday, this is not a comforting sight and my heart sinks at my plan's failure.

"Are you all right?" Leo kneels down next to me, taking my hand in his strong one and gently helping me up to a sitting position. I would appreciate the warm hand on my back much more if there wasn't so much happening right now.

No, that's a lie. So much is happening, but my brain is still taking the time to notice a tingle where his hand is firmly touching my back. Through layers of clothing, no less.

Horniness finds a way.

It's not my fault; he's looking so concerned about me while he's touching me. It's sweet.

"I—I'm fine." More disappointed than hurt, even though the pain is not an insignificant factor right now.

"That was quite the fall. I heard you speaking to someone, but they must have run off." His voice is imbued with derision over the person who abandoned me in my time of need and he drops his hands, which disappoints me more than I care to admit.

"No. Just talking to myself."

He arches an eyebrow up in a way that makes my two eyebrows that only ever act in unison jealous. Probably because without threading, they are one. "To yourself?"

Eventually, he's going to realize how strange I am, and he's going to tell the palace guards I need to be locked up for the safety of the country. And that moment is going to come sooner rather than later if he thinks I'm talking to myself, but I already went with honesty, so it's too late to backtrack now. I'll try to mitigate instead.

"Yes," I hiss in pain at the end of the one-word answer. And take a few more deep breathes before trying to talk more. "Just thinking out loud. Everyone's doing it in America. Helps stimulate the brain by stimulating the body."

"Well, they did want to leave our superior care and governance, so I would expect them to be a bit mad."

"Yes. Completely irrational to want autonomy. Taxation *with* representation and all that." As someone with the heritage of two former colonies (India and the US), I put a lot more sarcasm in there than is strictly necessary, considering my survival depends on the kindness of him and other people here.

But something about Leo makes me forget I'm shy. He's so easy to talk to that the things I would normally keep to myself come out without permission until he's laughing with me, genuine warmth in his eyes. He charms it out of me.

And he's never made me regret it, like other people have when I say what I'm really thinking. So far. In our short acquaintance.

But he also doesn't know the truth, either.

"No one *wants* to take the time and effort to vote; you must have hit your head harder than you think. Can you remember my name?" He slows his voice down and raises his volume in a way that he might think helps, but I doubt would even if I had an actual brain injury.

"People do so want to vote. Leopold Too-Many-Last-Names-hyphen-That-Are-Pretentious. Marquess of Eliteness."

He quirks one side of his mouth in a smile. "Close enough, I suppose. Let's get you up." He gently retakes my arm and lifts me all the way up with little input from me. The tingle returns at the easy way he helps me to standing. It's been too long since I've been on a date if a simple touch is sending me into these levels of lust.

"What are you doing here?" I resign myself to the fact that I'm stuck in this time for another day at least.

Maybe I need to hit my head harder. That's not a pleasant thought.

"I came to check on you. Make sure you made it through the night you were so worried about." A pause as a furrow forms between his eyebrows. That's unusual. Sure, I've only known him one night, but he doesn't seem the type to be worried about anything, living that rake life and all. "And I have a proposition for you."

"Me?" My voice gets so high on that question that I suspect only dogs can hear it.

"Yes." He takes my arm. "Let's call for some refreshments and a doctor, and I will tell you all about it."

"I don't need the doctor." I don't need another person questioning me, even if they're concerned with my physical well-being. Better to lay low and talk to as few people as possible. And not get the attention of Victoria's court. I think I'd rather just soak in a warm bath and hope nothing's broken. "But I'll take some food."

Leo nods in agreement, willing to compromise on the doctor since I am walking on my own-albeit slowly. Too slow considering how impatient I am to find out why he's here.

"What is the proposition about?" I ask as we make the long trek through the same hallways I walked this morning. I never thought of the logistics of having a mansion; it's kind of exhausting to walk around all the square footage doing daily tasks. At least this is not a problem that modern me has to deal with. No, when I forget my water bottle, it takes seconds to get it from the other room.

"I will tell you soon. Once we obtain food," Leo says, and he sounds kind of nervous. Which is not helping my curiosity at all.

Leo ignores any other attempts to get him to tell me sooner, making us walk in silence, and then sit in silence waiting for an entire plate of snacks to be brought in. He waits to long that Anne reappears and hovers in the corner of the room. I'm about to tell her she doesn't have to stand there, when I realize she might be…chaperoning me.

I don't like it, but I don't think I can tell her to leave.

"About that proposition..." I begin.

He swallows a bite of scone on a sigh, then puts the rest of it back down on his plate. "Can you please get us some more tea?" Leo asks Anne.

She looks uncertain. "I can call for—"

"I tried the bell, but no one responded," Leo motions vaguely to where the bell system must be, and I don't remember seeing him actually do that.

Anne chews on her lip, apparently not convinced, but must not want to contradict a peer. "I'll go arrange for the tea." She rushes out of the room.

"We will have to be quick, she will be back soon." Well, I am intrigued now, if this is evade-the-chaperone serious. "I know I did not mention much last night about my personal history, but I have recently inherited a title." He looks at me expectantly.

"Um. Congratulations on all the hard work that must have taken." Hard work waiting for your relations to die, you ghoul involved in a ghoulish system. You're just one of the lucky ghouls.

But this is confusing. I thought I would have known if there was a half-Indian titled man running around Victoria's court. I didn't realize last night because of...everything. But I should know his name. And I don't.

"Thank you." Wow, he does not pick up on sarcasm at all. Guess they don't teach that at the Oxbridge schools. "Unfortunately, we are rather title and land rich, but money poor."

"That must be so sad. For you." Not the thousands of people you've taken advantage of over hundreds of years, extracting labor out of them to build your fortunes on while you do nothing but live in a big house and party in London, while they struggle in shacks.

"Yes, it is." He looks relieved that I understand. Poor, simple man. Hot, but simple. And kind, I suppose. But also a little bit of a parasite.

"Oh. The influx of cheap corn from America and the resulting agricultural depression can't be helping you any," I say as I realize exactly what's happening right now. Desperate to distract myself from my revelations about him and his character.

"Well, yes. Actually." Now he looks puzzled, head cocked like a confused puppy. "How does a woman know about that?"

"Oh, no." I pause to take a breath to prepare for my rebuttal to this dinosaur, both in his age in comparison to me and his outlook on life. "There are these things called newspapers and books. I read them, occasionally." Or all the time. In fact, I spend all my time reading books and newspapers from and about this particular era. "Sometimes, I even understand what they say. Even with this woman's brain, I somehow manage to hold a coherent thought about the world around me. Because it turns out that women have brains and they won't faint if they have to use them to have a thought or two."

Leo holds his hands out, not wanting to poke the bear any more than he already has. "Most ladies of my acquaintance do not exactly bother themselves with the newspapers. *I* don't even want to read the blasted things. Constantly giving me depressing information," Leo grumbles.

"I'm confused as to what you think *I* can do about your money problem." I can't fix him. He's a relic and I have to find a way home. I can't get distracted teaching this man than women can have value outside of the roles society has assigned them.

As tempting as that is.

"Ah, yes. The bit you can help with. I need rather a lot of cash. Normally I would not talk about anything as vulgar as money with a lady—" Okay. But your problem seems to be you don't talk about money with *anyone*. "But I did think that you should know the background for what I am about to ask of you."

"I don't have any money," I say before he can ask for a loan. "Sorry."

"I did rather assume that. What with you being worried about where you were going to sleep last night."

"Then I'm still not sure what I can do to help your cash-flow problems."

"Right. Fathers mostly understand the world, and they are keeping their heiress daughters away from me. Heiresses I need if I am going to give duty and responsibility a go and save the estate. For my family and all the people working it. I might not perfect but I am better than a lot of people who could buy the estate after we lose it. Or those who want to buy the land to mine it, displacing everyone who has lived there for generations."

Is he, though? Mr. I Love Fun and Hate Responsibility over here.

"But you have a title. The fathers shouldn't care about the debts as long as they get the title for their family." I know how this works. Rich industrialists, sometimes American ones, give their daughters and fortunes to poor aristocrats that didn't plan well enough for the shift from an agrarian society to an industrial one, and they get proximity to the "upper class" out of it. Win-win.

Tale as old as time. Older than the idea of a love match, at any rate.

"Yes. Unfortunately, my father, a gambler I could respect for the amount of time he devoted to the game if it had not affected me so badly, created a bit of scandal throughout his life and especially on his way out. That coupled with the giant debts we have and the taxes we owe, have the richer fathers steering their daughters out of my path and to less complicated options. And the daughters that remain don't quite come with enough blunt to get me debt-free."

"Why can't you sell the land?"

"I could. And it may come to that. But it is my home. The home of all Alstons for generations, and I would like to keep it if possible."

"What was that scandal?" I can't stop myself from asking. I've spent my entire career poking around in dead people's lives: their houses, their stuff, their letters, their finances, their graves. I'm not going to pass up a chance to get more information out of them now. And whatever the last Marquess of Basildon did wasn't enough to get my notice in the future, so I don't already know. And I hate not knowing, especially about a half-Indian peer.

It just goes to show how many gaps in history there are. So much we've lost out on because no one recorded it in any way.

"I suppose it would not be sporting to get you involved and not tell you everything. But good to know news of the scandal has not reached America or India yet."

Leo finds the scone in his lap very interesting all of a sudden. So much that his eyes and all his intense charm and focus are directed at it.

Lucky scone.

"Are you stalling?" I ask.

A faint red slashes across his cheekbones. Then he takes a deep breath.

"He publicly left us to live with his mistress. When the debts and the drinking and the gambling were all overwhelming, he threw his hands up and decided if he was going to be ruined financially, he may as well become morally ruined as well and live with who he really wanted to. No one faulted him for having a mistress, of course, or even the gambling, but everyone faulted him for being tacky enough to want to live with her. He died shortly after leaving us. From injuries sustained after a beating regarding some of those debts. And now they fall to me along with the title and the estate. Mother passed shortly after that, whether from grief or embarrassment, the doctor would not say."

"I'm sorry for your loss." I think I remember the scandal, now that he mentions it. In the heightened mortality of the Victorian period, many of the rich and powerful were still having their affairs and living their vices, but they were forced to be quieter about it than in previous times, with society being harsher to those that were caught. The irony is, Leo's dad might have been fine if it had happened in an earlier era.

But I certainly didn't know the man's wife was Indian, or I would have paid more attention to the whole family and dug deeper. Her experiences must have been so interesting.

But it sounds like this man needs a therapist and a PR team. I still don't know what I can do to help. I have a Ph.D. so unless he wants me to write an article about his family in the context of a changing Britain, I don't know how I can contribute.

"Your presence has sparked interest among the ton. Yesterday, people came to me, asking about you and how you were acquainted with the Queen. Talking to her and then standing next to you who spoke to her multiple times, reminded people how close my family was to the Queen before the scandal. Some of those rich industrialist fathers looked at me a little closer last night, even speaking to me before the night was over."

"So you want to…what?"

"I want to court you."

CHAPTER 8

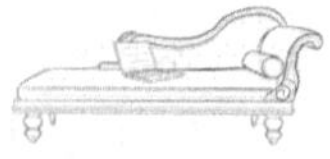

"$\mathcal{I}$ want to court you as a ruse," Leo rushes to clarify when he sees my frozen face. "I will call on you, like this. Show you around London, once we get back. Dance with you at balls. And I think it will help you too, if I can be so bold. You were curious last night, different from us. I do not think that is a bad thing, but people noticed. And wondered and talked. I got the impression you did not want people asking questions about you. If you were always close to me, I could redirect people if they ask questions. Despite my father's actions, mine is still an old name capable of some protection, and I know how to distract these people."

"I..." I shouldn't even be around long enough to help with this. I want to go home. But as today proved, that isn't going to be as easy as I hoped. Having someone around from this time, with the protection of a title, who doesn't mind how odd I am and has something to lose if I'm found out as a liar, wouldn't be the worst thing.

I have nothing else to count on here, and no way to get home.

When I don't finish that sentence, Leo says, "You do not have to decide now. I realize that I am asking quite a bit, and you may wish to court someone else while you're here." Leo gets stiffer than he's been in our entire one-day acquaintance.

"No. I'll do it. On one condition."

"Yes. Anything."

I raise my eyebrows. "Don't you want to know what the condition is?"

"I am very close to losing the family seat. And the London residence. You have the superior bargaining position at the moment."

"You shouldn't tell me that." If only he knew how dire my own situation was. But still, I'm curious. As he pointed out. "What if *I* wanted your family seat?"

"I would direct you to any other building in England. It is draughty and has not been updated in generations, which means it is uncomfortable and out of style. But sentimental, if you're a Clifford-Alston." Always ready with a flip remark, this one.

"It's a good thing that is not what I want then." He looks relieved, even though his response was casual. "When you're with me, I may say or do strange things. May ask you to take me to strange places. I want to make sure that whatever I say or do is only between us, no matter how… curious, or odd, it sounds. And no questions when I do something strange."

"Now that is intriguing. Of course, the answer is still yes. I will not tell anyone anything that happens between us. But the no questions part might be more difficult for me to follow. Are you a spy? An Indian revolutionary who wants freedom?" He doesn't sound particularly upset at the prospect.

"Doesn't everyone want freedom? You want money, to make everyone go away so you can keep enjoying life. What's that if not freedom?"

"Touché." He's not offended by my estimation of his character. "*Are* you an Indian revolutionary?"

Even though I said no questions, I still answer. If anyone

understands curiosity, it's me. After all, I made a career of being nosy. "No."

The good I could do if I wanted to get involved—but no. That would be changing history. I'm not sure what the rules are for this time travel experience, but all the TV shows and books on the subject say I can't change the past or it would Butterfly Effect the present in ways that could be very bad. And if that's the *one* thing they agree on regarding time travel, I should take it seriously.

And I'm not a hundred percent sure the men of this time would take me seriously enough to let me help. So there's that, too.

"Excellent! We're courting then." Leo raises his teacup to me in congratulations, a carefree, boyish smile back on his lips.

I'm sure he would have found an heiress anyway. So this meddling into history doesn't count. But really, if the universe didn't want me to meddle at all, it shouldn't have sent me here in the first place. Me breathing is probably enough to change something.

I raise my teacup back at him. "Fake courting." We both take a sip. "What do we do now?"

"This visit will be noted by the gossips here for the Queen's birthday, so it is a good start," Leo says. Her birthday is probably the only reason I'm having a chance to pull this off; the chaos of all the different people coming and going is serving as helpful cover. "We wll find Her Majesty to get her permission for courting and then maybe I can take you out on an excursion tomorrow."

"I don't need permission to da...court." Oh wait, I *do* need her permission. My modern sensibilities don't like this and are immediately trying to deny it, but my historian brain knows I don't have the luxury of independence anymore.

"Then America is a truly wild, liberated place. But in England, we are still very much bound by propriety. And the Queen's blessing can only help both of us in our plan."

I stand up before I do a treason by rolling my eyes at all this nonsense. "Let's see if she's around."

"Excellent. I appreciate your enthusiasm for our courtship. Illusory though it may be."

"Well. Fake relationship, fake enthusiasm." I don't need him getting any amorous ideas. This is all complicated enough, with me being from the future and now lying about a courtship. I'm still thinking amorous ideas, but I am trying to limit them.

I don't need him to know about them. I allow myself one last little look before I try to shut down the lust. Unsuccessfully.

Leo puts his hand on his heart and staggers back into the couch he's sitting on. "My lady, I am wounded."

"Stiff upper lip, old chap. Needs must," I say with the most obnoxious English accent I can summon. Tea-and-crumpets-on-my-sailing-yacht-in-my-red-pants-and-bow-tie-on-holiday-from-Oxford obnoxious. I stand up and motion for the door, an exaggerated movement that includes a bow.

"I do believe I am being mocked."

"I would never mock the solemnity of the English aristocracy." Not out loud, usually. I reserve that for my articles. Especially the footnotes. You can get wild in the footnotes.

"Yes. I can see how seriously you take us."

Oh, sarcasm must have already been invented, because it was just used on me. In a royal drawing room while I'm wearing a corset within shouting distance of Queen Victoria.

No one is going to believe this if I do get back to the right time. But that squashes any joy I just found, because what if I never get back?

Anne returns as I contemplate the future, a little out of breath, and I feel bad we sent her on a wild goose chase to the kitchens that are probably far in this oversized mansion.

"The tea is coming," she says.

"Excellent. But we are going to see Her Majesty now." Leo stands and holds his arm out for me as Anne purses her lips in frustration that her rushing is now pointless and her chaperoning was evaded. "She is usually out in the garden doing her correspondence or learning Urdu with the Munshi right about now."

I could tell him I already know that. But I don't want to explain *how* I know that. "You know so much about her." I even flutter my eyelashes, practicing being besotted with someone. Practicing flirting with someone. I need it, being out of practice myself.

I feel like this was easier with fans. Wait, this *is* when they flirted with fans! Finally, something I studied might come in handy, so I don't accidentally say, "Kiss me," when I mean, "I wish to get rid of you."

Take that, Mom; I *am* using my history degree in my daily life.

"Your Majesty, it is a beautiful day," Leo calls out in greeting when we approach Victoria and her outdoor office. I don't know who had to lug the table, boxes with papers and pens, chairs, tent and carpet out here, but they should get a raise, because this is not like when I work out in nature. I usually balance my laptop on my stomach on the grass and try not to position my hands in a way that offends ergonomics too much. But this is better, if you have someone to set it up for you.

Today, Victoria is wearing a simple but luxurious black dress, still mourning Albert even after all these years. Abdul is standing behind her in a white-and-gold silk turban and a long, deep red Indian tunic and pants, while she's bent over some paper on the table in front of her. A quick peek shows all English, so it's correspondence and not her Urdu lessons.

Unfortunately, the peek isn't long enough to read the documents, even though the historian in me wants to, so much. But I think that might be against the law, and I'm already breaking enough laws already.

"Yes, it is. I hope you had a good night's sleep," Victoria says to me.

"Yes, thank you, Your Majesty. The room and the clothes are lovely. You're too generous." No one is immune to flattery.

"Good. I do not know if you met at the assembly, but this is Abdul Karim." Victoria's Urdu teacher and general companion/helper with her correspondence. Who Victoria's son will try to erase from the written record after Victoria passes, because he didn't approve of the closeness of their relationship. But he won't succeed, and I will learn about him. And write about him, to boot. Take that, Prince of Wales.

"The Munshi. Of course. It's an honor to meet you in person. I've heard so much about you." Victoria values his opinion, so I should use his legendary ego and try to get on his good side.

Abdul nods a regal head with a disapproving frown. So, he is still holding a grudge from last night. With how cruel Victoria's family and household are to him, you think he would welcome an ally, but he apparently doesn't think I'm worth having as one. This is not the solidarity I wish we could have. But I think his loyalty to Victoria is going to override our shared ancestry.

"Where are you from in India?" Yup, he's still suspicious.

"I'm from Cooch Behar." Now I'm committed to that, a claim I threw out as a joke. At least he's from Agra and not royal himself, so I doubt he knows everyone in the Cooch Behar royal family personally. Especially since Victoria thinks I'm one of the nieces.

I'll apologize later to my parents for not saying I was from Punjab, where they're actually from, but considering that royal family is currently living in London, I'm really glad I didn't.

If I see my parents again. Well, that is a depressing thought.

"It is odd that you are not with them," Abdul says.

As everyone has already pointed out, thank you very much. "I was meant to do some studying here. You know how much the Maharani is an advocate for education, especially for women, as she has opened a school back home. But there was a miscommunication with the exact time and details of my trip, and they left without me, including my escort. Her Majesty's birthday has been so big and busy, I think they got confused. Her Majesty was kind enough to offer me shelter."

I combine a few of the lies I've told in the past day into one. Now hopefully I can remember this new, refined version.

"Hmm. They must be worried about you."

"I've written to them already. We should sort this out soon." It's a point in my favor that letters take forever right now and there's no e-mail. I never thought I'd be happy about a lack of e-mail, but it has bought me some time. And I'm being saved from getting hundreds of marketing e-mails asking me to buy things from a store I shopped at once.

Oh god, I'm going to have so many e-mails to get through when I get back.

"You have a strange accent." Is everyone going to be interrogating me until I leave this time? Why are people so untrusting? Probably because I'm lying to them, but still. Why is the world so cynical?

"I was taught by American teachers. And I travel often, especially in America, and meet a lot of different people. I suppose it's a mix of all those influences."

"Hmm." Abdul purses his lips. Not entirely convinced but he doesn't have enough evidence or desire to make a bigger stink about it right now. But I need to be careful in the future.

"What are you doing here?" Victoria turns her attention back to Leo.

"I am here to see your lovely guest, Your Majesty." I snap my head at him, wondering despite myself if he means the "lovely" comment or if it's just part of the ploy. Then reminding myself I have no business caring either way, because this is not a real relationship. As long as Victoria buys it.

"Are you now?" Victoria's sharp eyes, the intelligence in them not dulled by age, bounce back and forth between us, lingering on my hand still on his arm, and his other hand covering mine. This is the woman who tried to set up all of her children, grandchildren, and godchildren. And probably a lot more people whose documents didn't survive to tell about it.

She's a bit of a romantic, from all I've researched. And now she's turned her motherly attitude and matchmaking toward me.

"Yes. She is hard to forget." He looks at me fondly and I stop myself from turning to check if he's talking about someone behind me. Because while I would one day like to be the recipient of that look, I would like it to be from someone I've known for longer than one day. And who is from the same century as me.

But I still soak it up, because I haven't gotten that look from someone in my century in a long time.

"Indeed." Victoria's eyes are sparkling.

"You may know where this is going, but in light of how last night went, and since she does not have any family immediately accessible, I was hoping you—"

"Yes!" Victoria says. "You were going to ask if you could court her, correct?"

Okay then. I knew Victoria loved to matchmake, but being on the receiving end of it is another story. And even though it grates that I apparently need permission to date someone, I'm glad to have this excuse to spend more time with Leo while I'm still here.

For the ruse, of course. The ruse that benefits both of us. And nothing else. Because even if we didn't live in different centuries, he's still unsuitable for me. He's an aristocrat, part of a system that shouldn't even exist. And because he has all that power, if he decides he wants to out me as a fraud, he can. Even if we're supposed to be helping each other, he might decide it's not worth it if he finds out the truth.

"Yes," Leo says.

"Fantastic! We have an assembly tonight since we're leaving Osborne tomorrow, and you can spend some time with her there. Then we'll be back to London. You are welcome to travel back with us." She turns to me. "You can come stay with me at Buckingham Palace until we sort out where you are supposed to be. If we cannot get in touch with your family soon and need a more long-term option, I know there are many families that would welcome you into their homes."

Just like with Victoria Gouramma, whose father, the rule of Coorg, brought her to England after he surrendered to the British and left her in the care of Victoria. Victoria then placed her with a major and took an avid interest in the details of her upbringing.

While it is terrifying to have that much interest of a monarch used to getting her way, I am excited about seeing more of the past.

"Thank you so much, Your Majesty." I have a ball to go to. One that I am actually excited for, despite the gravity of my situation.

I blame too much Cinderella as a child for that.

And I have the chance to see Victorian London in person. Not in the pages of a book, and not a reconstruction. Not even a historic building with velvet ropes meant to keep tourists away from the furniture.

I get to see history. Live it. Touch, taste, smell, hear and see it.

I'm not going to pass that up. Even if I have to do it in a corset.

CHAPTER 9

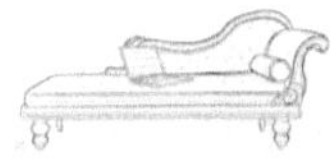

"Which dress would you like to wear tonight?" Anne pulls options out of a hefty wooden trunk someone delivered to my room while I spent the day snooping around Osborne House with Anne following close behind.

"All of these are beautiful. I can choose any of these?" Every time I go to touch them I pull back. I need to remind myself that they aren't history yet, and I can touch to my heart's content. It's strange if I don't, actually.

Anne nods at me, pulling even more out while I get dazed by all the choices. But then she takes out *the one.*

"This dark blue one is fine," I say.

Sure, it's just fine. It shines like the midnight sky illuminated with sparkling stars embroidered in shining thread, and there's a delicate black velvet floral pattern along the bottom. The neckline is low and the waist is impossibly tiny. It's the most beautiful thing I've ever seen, but sure; it's *fine.*

"That's a beautiful choice," Anne says as she sets it down to take out matching accessories.

"Thank you. How did you get all these dresses at such short notice?"

"With the right corset, you have roughly the same measurements as Princess Louise."

My hands, in the process of gently stroking the soft silk still feeling like I'm getting away with something illicit by touching history, clench into it at the news. "I'm going to wear the dress of a princess?" I whisper the question.

"You already are," Anne whispers back to me, eyes dipping down to the dress I'm wearing.

I gasp and clutch the cloth already on me, abandoning the gorgeous dress in front of me. This is a bit more than a historian getting to just see history; I'm literally clothed in it. I give it a discreet sniff to find out if royals smell better than the rest of us. It's just kind of musty, so Louise must not have worn it in a while.

"And they're last season's clothes, so the princess won't be needing them again," Anne says.

Of course. The princess wouldn't be an outfit repeater.

Anne gets me ready for the evening without me fangirling over any more of the items around me. At least on the outside. The only thing that would make this better is being able to document this visually, but cameras can't fit in these tiny Victorian beaded purses just yet.

Anne leads me down to the drawing room before dinner, a smaller event with Victoria and some aristocracy I barely get introduced to. Victoria assures me with a twinkle in her eyes that Leo is coming to the assembly itself later.

"Like I even care," I mumble when Victoria has safely looked away and is talking to someone else. I feel like I need to put out into the world that I am *not* interested in the spoiled man.

Or maybe I need to tell myself.

Aside from Victoria's short aside, no one thinks I'm important enough to talk to, which I'll take since I don't have to answer any awkward or dangerous questions like where I'm from or my name. They do think I'm interesting enough to openly stare at like I'm a museum piece. Like I'm a painting and don't feel discomfort at the intense scrutiny. Like they're entitled to watch me openly. And I don't want to draw attention to myself so I swallow down the discomfort and silently stare at the antique rug in front of me.

It's thick, with an intricate pattern of intertwined flowers organized around geometric shapes. The bright reds tie into the upholstery of the chairs and couches in this room, but that's all I can see from studiously looking down. The historian in me wants to look up and investigate the room more, but I don't need to make eye contact with anyone here or draw any more of their attention.

The butler announces dinner, and a well-dressed man in a tuxedo I don't know approaches to walk me into dining room. As if I would get lost going across the elegantly decorated hall. But the British do love any opportunity to reinforce social hierarchy, even for the ridiculously short walk from one room to another.

Conversation flows around me but not to me, and I take the time to brainstorm ways to get home in my head. Maybe someone in London knows how to time travel? If they do, they're great at keeping it secret from everyone else.

I also take the time to look at Victoria. I don't see the same woman who talked to me, Leo and Abdul. This woman is showing every one of her years. Tired and bored with everyone around her. And a little sad.

But then she turns to me and Abdul, face lighting up. "I have a curry coming. We usually have them for lunch daily, but I thought you would like to eat it more often. A taste of home while you are so far away."

"Thank you, Your Majesty." I mean, since my parents are Punjabi, they make dals and sabjis and the always delicious and similarly named kadhi, while curry is actually a British dish that is meant to westernize northern Indian food in general. But sure, taste of home.

It's extra ironic that since I moved out of my parents' home, the taste of home is whatever takeout place is most convenient between the university and my apartment.

After a meal so rich Leo would marry it, Victoria leads us to the ball room. Just like she promised, Leo is already waiting for us in the same Durbar room from yesterday, his elegant tuxedo creating sleek lines that make him look good.

"Good evening," I say with a genuine smile. This dinner has proven him right; getting along with all these people, and their judgmental, openly curious, and sometimes hostile stares, is easier with him near. I almost give him a hug, an action I would have taken if I had a fake suitor in my time. But these are Victorian times. Where we are suppressing our immoral tendencies.

"Good evening." Leo takes my hand and bows over it. "Our plan seems to be working. Multiple women have accepted dances with me tonight. But I saved the best ones for you, of course. And when everyone heard I was invited on the royal yacht to go back to London tomorrow, multiple mothers suggested they would be amenable to me calling on their daughters when we are back in town."

"That's great." I dim in excitement, remembering that Leo is using me to get at other women. It's fine; I know about it in advance and I'm using him too. I need to remember this is a transaction and I have no right to be disappointed when he mentions other women. "Who's in our sights tonight?"

"Railroad money is most likely out of my league even with the Queen's association. So Miss Ogborn is the most promising candidate."

"Tell me about her. Or tell me about her money, if we're getting to the good stuff right away."

Leo walks me around the ballroom, the faint strains of the orchestra starting up their music as couples slowly make their way to the dance floor. "And it is 'good stuff.' Her father was a merchant who worked his way up in the ranks of the East India Com—"

"No." I try to snatch my arm back, but Leo has a firm grasp on it.

"What's the matter?"

"If you want to marry an heiress whose family has engaged in exploitative economic policies and outright colonialism toward your and my ancestral country, as well as all the racism, you can do that without my help."

"Ah." Leo looks right and left, not sure how to handle this. "You know the British Empire rules India now? Instead of the East India Company?"

"I'm trying to forget it because I haven't figured out any other options yet. But actual East India Company members are a bit too far for me to accept." If anything, I'm engaging in fraud against the Empress of India to get things from her, so from a moral standpoint, I think I'm good. But either way, I won't actively help one of them get a title with their money.

"You know I could have money from the East India Company," Leo says.

"But you don't have *any* money."

"Yes, true. Though unpleasant. But we could have had it, long ago."

"You clearly aren't exploiting Indians currently, and honestly, your family didn't do such a great job of doing it in the past, or you wouldn't need an heiress so much now. Plus, you are half-Indian, so only half of your parentage is problematic in a colonial sense. It's easier to handle."

"Damned by faint praise; my family is too incompetent to take advantage of people."

I rub his shoulder. "Just the brown ones. Don't worry, I'm sure your white tenants don't like you very much."

"That does not make me feel better, actually."

"Hey, maybe there is a decent person under all that champagne."

"I would not go that far. But all right. No Miss Ogborn. What about Miss Presley?"

"Tell me about her." I'm wary. What fresh hell will her father have done to make their fortune?

"Her father owns a coal mine. "

"Truly terrible labor conditions. But without the colonialism, so there's that, I guess."

"There's also Miss Chilcott, whose father is a brewer. His beer is in almost every pub in the north, and he is expanding daily, it seems. He's even in a few London pubs this season."

"I still doubt anyone's labor conditions at this time, but it must be better than a literal coal mine."

"We will put Miss Chilcott at the top of our list." He directs me gently to the drinks table. "That was hard work. Let's toast to celebrate."

"You and I have different definitions of work." I refrain from saying that this may be why he has no money and has to marry an heiress, because I do need his goodwill. But I do note it for myself, so I remember we are two very different people. "Do you have any money at all?" I'm still curious about him.

"Such a frank question. Very curious for a woman."

"I just mean that if you have some, maybe you can look into hiring a business manager, who can help with some investments or someone to help look for new agricultural opportunities."

I could just tell him which companies to invest in, but I think that would be affecting the timeline a little too much. I can rationalize helping him with the wife because it was his idea and I'm sure he would have found someone eventually. And telling him to hire a professional seems fine because someone else would make the final business decisions.

Ugh. This accidental time travel business is fraught.

"I should go claim those dances. But I shall be back to collect ours presently," Leo says.

"Sure. Yeah. Have fun. Woo some bank accounts." I pump my fist in the best *go get 'em, tiger* way that I can as he walks away from me to take the hand of a beautiful woman in a pale pink silk dress.

Again, I have no right to be disappointed that I'm going to be on my own. He's too old for me by over a hundred years, we're completely wrong for one another, and, oh yeah, I might destroy the future if I get involved with him. Like there could be no airplanes. Or maybe the polio vaccine won't be invented. Or maybe everyone will have a pet squirrel.

Okay, I could probably adapt to the last one. But still, that's a lot to put on me.

I'll just use my event skills and fade into the wallpaper. I don't have a phone with me to help provide a distraction, but being a wallflower is more a state of mind than props, and I just need to channel the wallflower way.

The vintage wallflower way.

And not glare daggers at the woman who gets to dance with Leo. And laugh with him. And flutter her fan at him.

It's fine.

CHAPTER 10

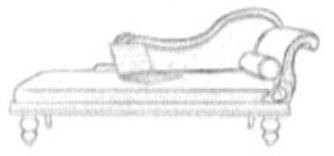

The ground pitches and rolls as I stumble on the top deck of Victoria's royal yacht, holding on tighter to Leo for balance. He tucks the muscular arm I'm holding tighter against his solid torso and extends his other hand in case my stumbles turn into full-on falls. A very real danger.

Although the risk of a fall might be worth it to be wrapped in Leo's arms again. I'm in so many layers I don't think I can physically bruise from the fall, and I missed him last night. His banter, his touch (through layers of clothes), and his carefree approach to life (even when it annoys me) were all things I got used to at our first ball, and all things I missed at the second. Since he was busy enjoying the fruits of our plan. And I was busy keeping a plant company.

A few men might have looked for me to dance, but I avoided them all with the expertise of someone who knows a subpoena is coming, dodging everyone like they're potential process servers.

"Not quite used to sea travel?" he asks.

"No."

"That must make the voyages between India, America and England torture." His tone isn't accusatory, but the statement tells me I'm being suspicious again. Or "curious," as he likes to call me.

And I can't exactly tell him that I'm not used to boats because I travel on planes.

"My body adapts eventually during a trip and then immediately forgets everything it learned about the motion of the ocean about ten seconds after I'm back on dry land." I do always get butterflies in my stomach when I take off and land in planes, no matter how many times I fly. That must be the same principal.

"Let's get you seated. There is a topside lounge. If you can make it another twenty feet."

"I'll manage." But I tighten my hand around his bicep anyway. For stability. Completely ignoring the smooth wooden railings along the luxury boat.

Leo opens the door to the lounge, and I brush past him to get inside, followed by Anne, who has been following me like a shadow. There are a few members of the royal household already in the lounge, and they give us judgmental looks but return to their conversations.

I sit down on the closest surface, a blue tufted bench. The same bench goes along the entire edge of the room, with a gleaming wooden dining table in the middle. Windows cover the walls above the couches, so I can still enjoy the view while not being sprayed by the sea.

If only my stomach wasn't trying to stage a rebellion to rival the one that happened in the US in 1775. Instead, I lean back and close my eyes as Leo sits down next to me.

"It will not be a long trip, Your Highness."

It's so weird to be addressed as a princess. And reminds me that I'm a liar. "Thanks. But please call me Meera."

"That's very familiar."

"I'm odd, remember?"

"Not odd. But curious, I would say."

"What's the difference?"

"Odd implies something I should probably avoid. Curious makes me want to investigate further."

His voice is low when he says that, making me strain to hear him over the water crashing against the side of the boat. Sitting down, I feel stable enough to raise my head, open my eyes, and look at him again.

He's looking back at me, attentive even though I was practically having a nap on the bench. His wavy hair looks especially soft in the filtered light of the lounge, making me want to run my hand through it not only to see how soft it is, but to watch it move and bounce as I straighten it then let it go. Right now it's flopping over one eye. Rakishly. A fitting attribute for my first ever, real life rake.

It's no longer just a concept I've read about in historic romances.

"I want to know more about you," he says. "The truth. Where you are from. What you do there. How you think. You already know everything there is to know about me. Anything worth reporting in the papers, at any rate." The last two sentences are said in a tone so bitter it gives me whiplash from the cheerful, demanding tone of the first few. And from his general *I love life* outlook.

But my real story would make his head explode. "There's more to people than what's fit for newspapers."

It's why I love diaries so much. The big events are reported in history, written about and analyzed by contemporaries and modern historians. But in a diary, I get to see what someone actually thought when no one else was looking, about every day, ordinary subjects. It's intimate. It makes me feel close to them.

Not too many people keep them. Not even me, even though I've started one approximately twelve times at various stages of my life, never to be kept up for more than a few weeks each time. I should probably start one now. Except if someone read it, I would be locked away. Maybe not then.

But I don't just want to know about the big moments in famous people's lives. I want to connect to those people, see how they thought about what was happening to them. Get a peek into what their daily life looked like. Ideally, I would be able to read them from more people in the past, from the aristocrat who lived in the country house, to the builder who built it, to the maid who worked in it, to the coal miner who supplied fuel for it. But it doesn't really work that way, unfortunately.

"It is the only thing that lasts."

"Maybe." This historian can't argue with that. "But who cares what people a hundred, or even two hundred, years from now think? The people who are close to you know you in a way the papers never will. And that's special too."

"I want to know you."

He's persistent. Not so much of a careless rake then. "I'm a scholar. I study history and then write about it and teach it." There, I can give him part of my story, without any unnecessary details. Like geography, or time period.

"What do you study?"

"Mostly the history of Indian immigrants and those with Indian heritage in the United Kingdom."

"Ah, you find me worthy of study." He takes a second to preen, and I think this is where I'm supposed to fawn over him. I don't. Not because I disagree with him, because I do think he's worthy of study. But because it'll make his already inflated ego burst. So I fawn on the inside. "Why that area specifically?" he asks.

"It's close to home—my parents are immigrants, and I've moved around for my education. So I find the immigrant experience here an interesting reflection of my own, with its own differences which are also fascinating."

"America must be a very progressive place."

"Weeeeell, let's just say I'm lucky and have opportunities that not many people here"—more like now—"have."

I hold my breath but he accepts it without asking for more

details. "Are you being courted in your home? Is someone going to be jealous of me and our fake courtship when you return?"

"No. I've been busy, with studying and work. There haven't been any serious…suitors." And they would laugh themselves out of my office if they heard me call them suitors.

"Why?"

"The…courtships never seen to go anywhere. And I have work anyway, so I don't have time to court." That's not just it. I just haven't found someone who wanted to be with me, and everything tends to fizzle out before it gets serious. I'm not fun like Leo; most of my free time is spent ranting that no one respects my field of study. That's hard to deal with, maybe.

"You are dedicated."

"I guess. I have good friends through work and my family doesn't live near me but I'm able to caaa…write letters to them. On paper." The telephone has been invented, but it's use isn't widespread right now, especially in England. "What about you? Tell me about yourself." I order before he can wonder too much at what I was going to say.

"Much less exciting than you, I'm afraid. Eton, then Cambridge. Then enjoying life in London and the family seat when Father inherited, until he died and I realized just how badly he was doing. And how I had not been helping with my own activities. The drinking, gambling, hunting, et cetera."

"I would have loved to go to Eton and then Cambridge. Not to be unappreciative to my own schools, which at least let women in." I send him a pointed look, despite it not really being his fault. "But there would be something really special learning about history *in* history." My campus was mostly built in the 1920s, which is basically ancient for California, but not quite the same as Cambridge.

"I never thought of it like that. I can take you, if you want to go. It will not be as exciting as studying there, but at least no one will flog you."

"Oh, god. No thanks on floggings." I cross my arms then ruin the effect my leaning forward to whisper, "But I will take that trip to the schools."

"No corporal punishment for you?"

"No. A teacher who needs to beat their students isn't very good at their job."

"That is not the prevailing outlook here, I'm afraid."

"Well, they're wrong."

"Probably." The agreement is easy, no fervent defense of the way things are done just because that's how they've always been done. Impressive from this dinosaur. "Where else would you like to go in London?"

I smile slowly and widely, like the Grinch does when he thinks of stealing Christmas. "You don't know what you're offering me." I take a deep breath. "But I'd love to go to the British Museum, and all the palaces and Westminster Abbey and Parliament and all the country houses that let polite tourists in, and honestly, any house I could get into—" I progressively bounce higher and higher in my seat, the seasickness forgotten, or at least pushed aside, at the prospect of seeing all those places I've studied. "Anywhere and everywhere, basically."

But I keep some of the places off the list, because if I try complete honesty, like mentioning I also want to visit the Indian community in Limehouse, I don't think he'll react well to it. And even though he seems nice enough, he's still an aristocrat who can turn me in if I annoy him too much, because he has a lot more power than me here and people who have been given everything can have fickle natures, even if we're supposed to be in this together. I need to remember that, and keep distance between us.

"All right, all right." Leo laughs at me. "I will take you to all of the places that propriety lets me take you."

"Thank you." I settle back in. "Can I also add a blank notebook to the list of things I want out of this agreement?"

"Yes, I shall procure you a notebook. Is there anything else you would like?"

"Writing tools would be great."

I don't know how this all works, but I know I'll want a written recollection of this adventure. It might be the first diary I stick to.

Even if I can't share it, or this experience with anyone else, I can still have it for me.

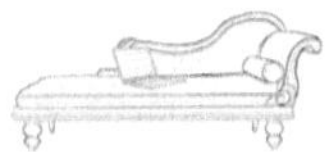

$\mathcal{L}$eo is right about the trip being short, and I'm grateful to be back on land since my stomach never got used to the sea. The rest of the trip has us in a royal train, which is like a regular train but much more expensive to build, with furniture upholstered in the same cobalt blue of the yacht, thick carpet covering the floor and enough furniture and decorative arts to fill an entire sale at an auction house in my time.

I end up in the train lounge with Leo, Anne, and Abdul, who thankfully doesn't go out of his way to find out more about his fellow country-person. Mostly, he wants to talk about himself. It's a nice break from the rest of the household, who send me hostile looks or aggressive questions whenever I exist near them.

Lucky for me Victoria has decided she likes having me around, and all the cold shoulders from the household can't take away from the fact that the monarch is throwing her warmth and protection over me. It makes my feelings about her even more complicated than they were before I met her.

She has genuine interest and affection for everything Indian, but it's always a little condescending, and her empire is exploiting the country. An exploitation whose effects will still be there in my time. And the racism that intensified during the period of the British Raj in order to justify the colonization is a whole different issue.

Not that Victoria even has that much power now, since the power of the monarch has been slowly decreasing through her reign and Parliament is really responsible for a lot of the policies that are negatively affecting India.

Finally, I'm shuffled into a horse-drawn carriage for the last leg of travel, like I've just done *The Amazing Race* but in Victorian times. And as a rest stop, I end up at Buckingham Palace.

"I hope I can call on you tomorrow?" Leo asks.

"Our plan won't work unless we're seen out and about." Even though he's been a nice distraction, I need to find a way home, and I can't exactly go around asking about time travel with him in tow.

But I can't exactly alienate an ally here either. So I grit my teeth and smile at him, part of me still giddy at the thought of more time with him, and another part hoping he gets distracted by an heiress and forgets me.

And then another part disappointed at the thought of him with an heiress instead of spending time with me.

All adding up to a very confused me.

"Excellent. I look forward to seeing you."

But despite us having concluded all the business we could have, Leo stays where he is. So I get to burn this picture into my memory, of Leo, dressed in his complicated suit, standing in front of the entrance to Buckingham Palace. Looking at me.

Looking like a damn romance novel cover model. Or someone in my history books. Either way, I'm turned on.

But just like a picture in a book, he's not for me. I can't trust him with the truth, and one slip up could lead to him exposing me to the others. Maybe he would even get more credibility if he revealed me as an imposter, and no one will believe me when I say he's in on it, because I'm the foreigner. I'm not going to test it, either way. I need to focus on getting back home (primary goal) and soaking in as much history as I can before I leave (secondary goal).

A wild affair with a British aristocrat is *not* on that list.

So I force myself to nod, turn away, and not look back as Anne leads me inside the palace, who is probably satisfied that Leo didn't ruin me on the journey over.

She's twelve years too late, and simultaneously a hundred and eighteen years too early, to guard my virtue. But I appreciate the thought.

I walk into Buckingham Palace, trying to prepare myself for the sight. I've studied it, in theory. And even visited the modern building. But like Osborne House, everything is different and despite generally knowing the floorplan, I would be lost without Anne leading me.

She takes me to an exquisite room, but all I can see is the giant four-poster bed with curtains hanging off each side, pulled back to make an inviting bed fort I want to spend all day reading in. Or as tired as I am, just have the best sleep of my life in. The gleaming neoclassical desk, the Louis XIV chairs and matching couch, the plush rugs that are so thick my feet are sinking in with every step I take, and the flickering candles nestled in wall sconces reflecting off a giant mirror hung over a fireplace all get ignored for the splendor of that bed.

After time travel, two balls, not knowing where I would sleep, wandering through historic buildings and trying every form of Victorian transportation except early cars, I'm exhausted and I'm going to collapse. Anne helps me take off layers of clothing but puts a few more back on for good measure.

After letting her know I want to skip dinner, I sink into the covers as she pulls the thick window curtains closed, the room slowing turning dark. I fall asleep before the last of the light can leave the room.

~

"MA'AM YOU HAVE A CALLER."

"Hmm." I raise my head slowly and look around. Nope, no chance this was all a dream and I'm back to real life, despite how much I wish I was home. The physical proof of that is right under me, where I drooled on Queen Victoria's fine pillows.

And how many historians get to say that?

But just in case anyone eventually DNA tests these, I try to wipe up the drool as best as I can. Preferably without Anne seeing what I'm doing.

"Who would call on me?"

"The Marquess of Basildon."

That gets me up and moving. "Leo's here? To see me? Do I have anything to wear?" Not just a question that anyone asks before they see someone hot and wonder if anything they have is appealing; a literal question I'm asking because I'm a royal squatter.

But at least I'm distracted from brooding over how homesick I am.

"Yes, miss. Her Majesty made sure of it." She indicates a trunk that I didn't notice before, the same one from Osborne.

"Thank you so much."

Anne nods at me. "The privy's just down the hall and you have warm water in the basin here."

If I didn't have Leo waiting for me, I would be disappointed in myself for how spoiled I'm getting. I can get ready by myself; I've done it for actual decades. But I do usually have modern conveniences like reliable running water and zippers.

So instead, I stand still, body awash in anticipation for seeing Leo, while Anne floats around me, pulling and prodding and generally getting me ready for the day. And every time I try to help, I get a deep sigh that tells me I'm making this harder for her, so I channel a mannequin and let her work.

Finally, Anne steps back and nods approvingly at me. "I'll lead you to the drawing room."

I follow behind, ignoring the rare opportunity to gawk more at Queen Victoria's Buckingham Palace in its original style, ignoring a prime research opportunity, to think about what Leo has in store for me today. He's breaking me as a historian.

And I'm so broken I don't even care. Nor do I care about the fact that nothing can happen with this historic artifact and in fact it can all go terribly wrong, so it would be smarter to stay away from him completely. But my feet follow Anne happily.

"Good morning, Leo," I say as I sail into the drawing room. Or I feel like I'm sailing along. I'm surrounded by enough fabric and bustle that I feel like a large ship coming into harbor, hoping to not hit anything with my stern on the way. Leo, on the other hand, gets to wear a black suit with a lot less fabric, one that he can move around in with a little more agility than me.

"Good morning." He stands and bows. I, not having cotillion training, awkwardly half squat/bow down, keeping my eyes on his to gauge if it passes muster.

He doesn't look disgusted, so that was probably okay. Or he doesn't care.

"Are you ready for your first official day of being courted?" he asks.

"I'm ready...for whatever that means." I don't think he means that he wants to feel me up in a dark movie theater. Maybe in a real *theatre*, although I've no idea how dark they keep those. Probably pretty dark, lighting being what it is now.

"I thought we might do a compromise. We can go to the British Museum first and then take a stroll in Hyde Park. The museum is for your enjoyment, and the park is to be seen by everyone, as part of our agreement."

"Sounds great."

"I also brought you this." He lifts a brown-paper wrapped package from his side.

"Oh, a present!"

"Part of our deal," Leo says.

"Right. Because this is a mutually beneficial deal and not a real courtship." It is surprisingly easy to get distracted from that fact. Something about these damn clothes makes it all very…romantic. Like a fairytale. Damn it.

"Open it," Leo says.

I follow directions and tear into the paper. "A notebook. And pens!" I run my hand over the scarlet-red leather cover embossed in gold with a scene of a monk writing in a monastery. I open the clasp and flip through some of the pages. It's almost too pretty to write in. I wish I had one of the hundreds of empty notebooks I have sitting at home instead of this work of art. I thought they were too pretty to use but they're garbage compared to this.

"That is not all." Leo gently places his hands on mine and opens the book, gathering the pages together like he's about to flip through them. The motion reveals a hidden scene on the edge, in what looks like some landmarks from London: Buckingham Palace, St. Paul's, and the Houses of Parliament.

I gasp in delight. "This is amazing." And now it is *definitely* too pretty to write in.

"I'm glad you like it." Leo looks satisfied, patting my hand as he retracts his.

I clear my throat at the touch, which is through gloves, and still too much for me to handle.

This is the best present I've ever gotten, even if it is part of a deal. There are a lot easier ways to get me a notebook; this one looks expensive and special. Maybe he has a stash of exquisite notebooks to woo nerds, but I doubt it. I hug the book to me.

Leo laughs. "I am not going to take it away from you."

"I'm not taking any chances. But, well, can you…afford this?

I'm supposed to be helping you, not hurrying your descent into debt."

"It is so little compared to the mess Father left. And soon it will not be a problem at all, because we are going to solve the problem. Honestly, even if I do not find an heiress, it also stops being a problem. When they take my estate away. And the London house. And everything in them."

"At least they don't put people in debtor's prison anymore." Small consolation for him, probably.

"There is that. Shall we?" Leo extends his arm.

"Yes, please." I take his arm before I can put my foot in my mouth and remind him about his problems more.

Leo leads me out of the palace and to the front where his carriage and footmen are waiting. Anne follows us out, and joins us in the carriage, which is made of the finest materials, but is on the older side. I can tell in the fading paint, in the wood chipped along the frame, in the velvet seats that are fraying along the edges, that Leo has not been able to upgrade his family carriage in a while. There are flecks of gold on the family crest carved into the door, a horse rearing on the top portion, and a set of trees on the bottom, cut in half diagonally by a silver strip.

While we bump along the pre-modern road, I stare at Leo across from me. Watching the way the light comes in and highlights his black hair before moving on to his high cheekbones. Watching him smile as he points out London landmarks to me as we pass them.

Then I do tear my eyes off him to look outside, because while he's gorgeous, this is my life's work and I can only be induced to ignore it for so long. But my head bounces back and forth outside the carriage and inside, taking in all that the past has to offer.

In between looking at history, I take the time to regret that Anne is here so I can't find out if Leo's hair is as soft as it looks.

I'm too curious for my own good, but once I find out if it is that soft, I'm sure I'll be able to focus on the history in front of me.

And after I find out if his plump lips are as kissable as they look.

And after I find out if his chest is as broad as the layers of clothes he's wearing make it out to be.

Or maybe all of that would only make me want more, something I can't have.

CHAPTER 12

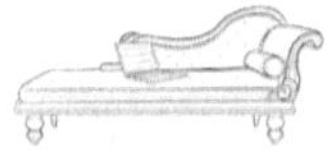

When we get to the British Museum, the allure of historic buildings in their prime outweighs Leo, and after the brief tingles I feel when he helps me out of the carriage, I focus on the history.

Since I've already been to the museum (albeit on a lot later date) I'm able to focus on how everything is presented when I am, and the reactions the presentation gets from the Victorian visitors.

Some enjoy the novelty of seeing and learning about things they weren't aware of before. Others are more interested in the beauty. Some just want to stand before the items from all over the world and remember how far the British Empire extends. Some are interested in finding new motifs and designs to copy for their furnishings to show how worldly they are. And others are here not to see, but to be seen. They want people to know they are intellectual with intellectual pursuits, even if they spend more time focusing on who else is here rather than the art in front of them.

Absolute gold.

Despite still being a bit in awe of the pretty journal Leo gave me, I push past the feeling and take notes during the museum trip.

Then we get to the Parthenon Marbles. Leo looks excited about my reaction to the room and the items in it, keeping his eyes on me instead of the beauty and history surrounding him.

"Is there something I can help you with?" I'm beginning to feel like I'm a museum display.

"No. Only trying to see if you are going to faint. And if so, making sure to be ready to do my duty and catch you before you injure yourself."

"I'm sorry. Not following. Why would I faint?"

"Because of all the sights you are surrounded by." He looks around to make sure we're alone. "Who are unclothed," he says the last word so low I can't hear it, only knowing what he said because I watched his mouth move.

"Thank you, for your concern. But I do think I'll be able to manage."

"This room has affected many women. It is allowed in the name of education, these being very classical, heroic unclothed men." The word *unclothed* comes out easier this time. "But we do have to look out for the fragile sensibilities of the fairer sex."

I laugh directly in his face, not knowing how else to respond to that. Or knowing how, but not wanting to spend all my time in the museum explaining to him why he's wrong, just for him to ignore me.

I'm still shaking my head at him while I walk around the room. But I can't stop the judgement that replaces some of the mirth. "Thieves. The lot of you."

From the sculptures taken out of Assyrian palaces, to the Egyptian funerary goods, to the sculptures in front of me that used to sit on the Acropolis in Athens, most of the pieces of the British Museum do not come from the shores of Britain. And they were often taken against the wishes of the local population, who had no say because of the mechanics of colonialism that meant lords could cart off as many national treasures as they could move.

The Parthenon Marbles in front of me, or the Elgin Marbles depending on who you think should have them, were taken from Greece in the early 1800s, when the Earl of Elgin asked the Ottomans if he could remove the pieces from the Acropolis, and the Ottomans, who were in control of Greece at the time and had used the Parthenon for, among other things, ammunition storage (and yes, it did explode the one time), agreed. Greece has since argued that the removal was illegal and unethical, and have requested them back, building a museum right outside the Acropolis where the pieces could be housed if they're returned.

I may be angry at the theft, but I don't waste the opportunity to see the younger versions of the friezes from the Acropolis. Earlier than the last time I saw them, maybe, but still too late to see them without the museum's unfortunate "cleanings" with metal instruments and too-harsh acids which go against all art conservation guidelines.

"Not me, remember? I am too poor and irrelevant to be the problem," Leo says. He's been letting me work in silence without rushing or distracting me, despite the fact that it must be a little boring for him. It must be even more boring for Anne, but I comfort myself thinking this must be better than cleaning a palace. But I might only think that because I hate cleaning, and love history.

"The problem is everywhere here." I wave my arms around sadly. Encompassing the museum, the city, the country. "At least one of your ancestors must have been part of the problem. My lord." The title drips with sarcasm.

He inclines his head. "I cannot deny that. Probably more than a few of them were problems to a great quantity of people. But we did *get* the title without any bloodshed or exploitation, when a particularly…enthusiastic king made us marquesses."

"Please explain." I turn away from the art and other tourists for the first time in the hours we've already been here.

Leo looks mischievous, so I know this is going to be a great story. I get my notebook ready as he shifts so we're a little further and no longer facing Anne, and he lowers his voice.

"Great-great-some more greats-grandfather Cecil Clifford, a country squire who owned a very modest amount of land, met Henry VIII while on a trip into London. Cecil was charming and got invited by a duke to a hunt in Hyde Park, which was Henry VIII's private hunting grounds at the time. That's when he saw Henry on a horse, doing things with a lady that are unacceptable to mention in a lady's presence. He directed the rest of the party away tactfully, and Henry saw the heroic deed. From then on, Cecil caroused with the young monarch around London, becoming one of his closest friends and advisors."

"Those things are fine to *do* to a lady but not to *say* to one?" I raise my eyebrows.

"Yes." Leo nods gravely, just a hint of a smile on his lips. "It is the talking about them that's the real danger to young ladies."

"Makes complete sense. So your ancestor was on unacceptable actions watch once, and then the king made him a marquess?"

"Yes. There was some bit about making him Treasurer or something government related, but he knew what his real job was—to carouse with the king and get paid for it."

Head fuckboy in charge of a good time, apparently. Leo comes by his raking legitimately. "That is a fascinating story." That is going in a book one day, when I get back home. I make note of it now so I don't forget.

"I think the official line is the title was granted for heroic actions that imply a military bent and some paintings that outright lie about him being a military hero, but if you look closely, Cecil never fought in any of Henry's wars. I usually do not tell it to ladies, on account of it being so unacceptable, but I did think you would enjoy it." His eyes are sparkling, and yes, I enjoy both the lascivious story and the bright brown eyes.

"Because I'm so curious," I finish for him.

"Curious is a good thing." He's looking at me too intently again. "An interesting, unique thing."

I clear my throat at the intensity in those eyes. Aren't rakes supposed to be purely surface? How is he able to command that much focus on one thing? Although I guess if that one thing is a woman...

But still, there are a lot of women in London who are easier to deal with than me and my baggage. Women who don't have to lie about almost every facet of their life. Women who can solve his money problems. Women who are actually interesting and not just in the wrong time period.

And none of that is me.

He can't mean to flirt. It's probably a reflex whenever there are breasts near him. And I can't get drawn in, or I could end up in a Victorian jail.

I clear my throat and get back to his personal history. "Victoria mentioned that you were half-Indian. Can you tell me about that?" Since he's so ready to share. And because as a scholar in this field, I should know about him. But I don't, and that's bugging me.

Leo shrugs. "If you'd like. It is less interesting than the title story, though. Dear Father was visiting a friend from university who was posted in India. He met a local woman from Mysore who came from a family that was quite important in the time before the British Raj. He fell in love, he said. Or lust, the gossips said. Or saw the perfect opportunity to irritate Grandfather, my mother said. Whatever the reason, he proposed. Her father agreed, because he hoped the British would give them back status they had before, which didn't happen. But the new couple moved to England and had me."

"What was it like? Growing up half-Indian here."

"A lot easier for me than it would be for a half-Indian servant. Class is everything, so aside from the snide comments from some people that never really went away, I was mostly treated like any other young lord. Eton, Cambridge, London, hunting parties, the balls and the country estate."

"Interesting. What about your mother? What was her life like?"

"I think it was harder for her, since it was more obvious that she was from India. There was always talk but she had the family money and then when Father inherited, she had the title too. But the women of her circle never really accepted her like their children did me. I do think it was easier at the country estate because she outranked everyone there, and harder in London because there are so many aristocrats here. She learned English and I think she eventually got more comfortable at parties. And then it got worse again after Father left, especially the way he did. She moved to the country permanently after that."

"That must have been hard, to move and make a new life here then have her life upended again."

"Yes. I think most people ignored that we were Indian. Mother, whose name is Eshika, became Eliza."

Maybe that's why I hadn't heard about them. Some people were hidden to history because they changed names and no one wrote down what the gossips were saying about them or the places where they were written about were destroyed, so the information was lost. Or no one looked at that particular newspaper that held the information, and it's still hidden somewhere, waiting for a historian to find it.

"Thank you for sharing," I say.

"But I am not allowed to ask about your life, correct?"

"Um. You know my parents were immigrants, and very supportive, and loving." I don't think I can add any more details. Time for a subject change. "Do you want to know one of the many tragedies in this room?"

"You do know how I feel about sad things…"

"Yes. But this is also a piece of information that no one else has here, that you aren't allowed to tell anyone." It's a bit of future knowledge, but I need to distract him from my personal story.

"I do love a bit of gossip. All right, what is it?"

"All of these sculptures"—I lean closer as I indicate the Parthenon frieze and pediments, and the galleries beyond that hold antiquities—"would have all been colorfully painted back in the classical period." I cross my arms now that the bombshell is dropped.

"No! Everyone knows white sculptures are a sign of antiquity. We decorate our houses with replica white marble sculptures."

"Now they're white, but back in the day, the Greeks and Romans liked things painted. Brightly. Garishly."

Leo looks at me like I said the sky was green, then back at the art, getting closer like he can see remnants of paint. "How do you know that?"

"Ummm…" I can't very well tell him I know that because someone used a high intensity UV light on them in the future. "Some people have seen traces of paint on things that are coming out of the ground right now. Before they're 'cleaned' by archaeologists and museums. And they're suggesting that it's not dirt; it's paint."

"That is amazing. I studied classics and no one said a word of it to me."

"It's all very new. That's why you can't tell anyone." I shush him.

Leo shakes his head. "Curious," he says with a slight smile, in that soft tone that says he can't figure me out.

"You don't even know the half of it." And he won't ever if I have anything to do with it. I'm physically uncomfortable with the fact that he's being so open with me about his life, and I'm lying to him about every detail of mine, but there's nothing that can be done about it.

And there's no reason for him to know the real me, anyway. No matter how much I wish it was different. He just sees me as a unique woman because he's never met anyone like me, but if he lived in my time, he would realize I'm not special.

"Is there anything else you want to see?" Leo asks.

"I could spend a week in here." Leo doesn't look as enamored with that idea as I am. He opens his mouth, but I interrupt him. "But it's fine. We can leave now."

"I can bring you back again, if you would like."

I take his offered arm and then shrug. "There's a lot to do in London, and I don't know how long I'll be here." Understatement. "I'd like to see as much as I can. And help you, of course."

And get home, at some point. Somehow.

"Then you will love Hyde Park. There's history, for my family and London, and it will help both of us, for our future security."

All of that is true, but I'm nervous about being back in front of large groups of people who make a sport out of tearing people down with a sharp word and some scandal. And me lying about everything, to the queen and everyone, seems like a juicy bit of gossip that no one would leave alone if they found out.

The only person not looking to tear me down is Leo. Only because he sees me as useful now; I doubt he would if he found out the scope of my lying. The sooner I help him, the sooner I can stop spending so much time with him and reduce the danger of discovery.

I'm going to find him the most ethical, richest heiress I can in this city. And then I'm going to smile while he flirts and courts her; I'm going to be gracious.

Even if on the inside, I'm imagining scratching her perfect, kind, intelligent, rich eyes out.

∾

THE WEATHER IS nice at the park. Or nice for England; it's not the Southern California weather I'm used to. But rain is only a suggestion today, in the form of warning gray clouds in the distance instead of a steady presence, so that's a win.

Leo helps me down from the carriage and then starts the walk next to Rotten Row, Anne trailing an appropriate chaperone distance right behind us. I leave the journal behind, even though every instinct in me wants to pick it up and take notes while we walk. But that's weird, in this time and my own.

The first half hour of the walk is mostly just exercise. Leo keeps conversation light and the pace average. People look at us with speculation, and a few respond to greetings from Leo, but none stop and chat with us.

The air's so thick with pollution from the ongoing Industrial Revolution that I can't stop the cough that bubbles up in reaction. Which can't be making us more appealing to talk to.

"Leo. Good afternoon!" A laughing brown woman with the same black hair and the same sparkling brown eyes as Leo waves as her giant horse runs at us with no indication that they'll stop anytime soon. The rider doesn't seem like she wants to stop anyway, graceful on top of the majestic animal that she moves easily with, curly hair blowing under what I assume is a fashionable hat.

This could be a relative of his. Or a potential heiress. Or both, damn this pervy time.

Leo stands there, like a bowling pin waiting for the ball to knock it over, while the rider and horse approach us. I start to tug at his arm, willing to abandon the man if he wants to get trampled in Hyde Park. But at the last minute, the rider commands the horse to stop, and it does.

Kicking up some unnecessary dust in our direction, just like in a movie. But I guess dirty is better than trampled.

"Good afternoon, Lydia. You have gotten better at stopping," Leo says to the new arrival.

Lydia, whoever she is, tosses her hair back in a movement not unlike one the horse she's on would do. "I told you I could learn myself. And that I do not need useless riding lessons from pompous men who will not let me go fast."

"Good, because we cannot afford lessons from anyone, pompous or otherwise," Leo says. "Your Royal Highness, may I present my sister, Lydia Clifford-Alston? Little Pest, this is Her Royal Highness Meera Chopra, of the Cooch Behar royal family. One of the nieces."

"Oh, Indian royalty! So you are spending time with Victoria's newest ward?"

"If even you have heard about it, pest, news must be travelling swiftly." He gives me a wink, excited that our plan is working.

"Do you know he's poor?" Lydia asks, getting back at Leo for the pest comments.

"I heard." I get on my tiptoes to whisper-talk the next part. "I am too."

"Such a shame for us all." Lydia clicks her tongue in disappointment and dismounts off the horse as gracefully as she rode him. "So I shall have to marry a rich old man then?" The words are glib but there's a tension in her shoulders and around her mouth.

Leo sighs, rubbing his forehead with the arm not holding mine. "I am working on our finances. I think we have time before we have to resort to rich, old men. It is not like they are in short supply."

"Unfortunately." Whatever else Lydia was going to say is cut off by a disheveled-looking woman on horseback, calling Lydia's name. Going much slower than Lydia was when she approached us.

"Can you please stop irritating your chaperone?" Leo asks.

"Probably not. Got to dash, Leo. Love you." Lydia gets back on her horse and gallops off, followed by the beleaguered chaperone. Anne must be happy that at least we're not on horseback, although after making her walk for probably more than ten thousand steps today, she might prefer the horseback option.

"Love you too, Little Pest." Leo waves after his sister.

"Your sister seems nice."

The obvious affection between the two is making me miss home. I'm an only child, but I miss my family and friends. All of whom haven't even been born yet. I don't even live close to my family since they're in San Jose where I grew up, and I moved to L.A. for college and then my job. But the fact that they're *this* far away, geographically and temporally, makes missing them even worse. It intensifies the ache that I've had since I realized when I was.

When will they notice I'm gone? Mom calls every few days, so it should be soon. And then she'll worry. Which makes me feel worse.

But there's nothing I can do about that now.

Leo snorts. "That is kind of you to say."

"No kindness about it. She's sassy and I like it."

"That is not usually seen as a positive. Mother blames me for it, for spending so much time with Lydia and teaching her to be like me, but when we were in the country, there were not many others to play with. And no one else can understand what it is like to be different. I might have had friends, but I could not speak to them about wanting to visit India or feeling like I missed out never having seen it."

"Where I'm from it..." Nope. Can't go into those details. "Well, some people can empathize with that feeling." I want to tell him more about me, that I've got complicated feelings about the thousand directions immigrants and their children are pulled in, from not wanting to forget their past but trying to embrace their future, and how what that balance ends up being looks different for every person. And then everyone has opinions on that balance, from those outside and even those inside the community. It's what made me want to study historic immigrants in the first place. But that might get complicated if I start going into details.

"Then we should get on a ship and all go to where you are from. Because I do not think anyone here appreciates her finer points or understands us." Leo casts a dark look around at the people walking in the park.

We keep walking, making light conversation until we've seen and been seen by what seems like everyone in the English aristocracy.

Near the end of the walk, back by the carriage, we're stopped by an elegantly dressed young woman, thick brown hair piled atop her head, showing a long and graceful neck, her back as stiff as a board which she unbends slightly to do the absolute minimum to classify as a bow. She's covered in the finest clothes and dripping in the shiniest jewelry, so whoever she is, she's rich. "Lord Basildon."

"Miss Vanderbilt." Leo bows back at her and I awkwardly do the half bow thing I did to Victoria. If it was good enough for a queen...

"I keep hearing your name wherever I go lately," she says, in an American accent. Miss Vanderbilt...at this time, with her appearance...that's Consuelo Vanderbilt! She's about to enter into one of the most famous and most scandalous (and most unhappy, unfortunately) cash-for-title marriages of all time when she marries the Duke of Marlborough later this year. She's actually named after her godmother Consuelo Yznaga, who was also an American socialite that got married to a nobleman who needed money. This happened so many times between rich Gilded Age Americans and poor but titled European families (over 400 times) that people called them dollar princesses.

For the hundredth time, I wish I had my journal.

"Hopefully only good things," Leo says with a charming smile.

"Not entirely terrible ones. You've been at the palace twice in two days."

Wow. Hanging around this circle makes London feel like the biggest small town I've ever been in. And apparently even the Americans aren't immune to the snobbery.

"Her Majesty is kind." Leo avoids giving any information like why he was there, how he got invited twice and if he's going to be invited a third time.

Consuelo looks me up and down instead of grilling Leo more about the visits. "You're the Indian aristocrat."

Yup, definite small-town vibes. "I guess so."

That surprises her, as her brows draw down. "But you sound American. Well, almost American."

Maybe not everything gets around. "I get that a lot. I pick up languages and accents well, and I travel often." I say it, changing between an English accent, an Indian accent and an Irish one every few words to show my skill, but by the look Leo gives me, I'm not pulling it off. I clear my throat and go back to my modern-day, Californian accent. "Her Majesty has been kind enough to help me while I'm in London."

"And why are you in London?"

"It is a lovely city, is it not? So many people are always visiting our fair town from all over the globe," Leo says, and then checks his pocket watch. "Ah. We regret we must leave, but Her Majesty did want us back for tea. We better go before we become late and anger Her Majesty. I hope you have a good day." Leo tugs me away and I start breathing normally again.

I have a lot of powerful people protecting me, but it's still stressful to have people looking at me with such open curiosity and asking me all sorts of questions. Running into another American really emphasizes how precarious my position here is, and how much I rely on Leo. And how much a disaster it would be if he knew I wasn't who I said I was.

Once we're safely inside, with only Anne to overhear anything we might say, I melt into the seat, head against the windowsill. "This is exhausting."

Leo smiles at me. "Being courted by me is exhausting? It is not exactly what I hoped my effect would be on women, but I suppose it is best to know the truth, however unflattering it may be."

"No!" I jerk up with a little too much energy, then force myself to relax against the seat again. "The subterfuge is exhausting. You're only mildly tiring."

Leo leans closer. "That, although a small step in the right direction, does leave room for improvement."

I lean in as well, the swaying of the carriage encouraging my body to move closer with each rocking motion. "I think you should be happy with your current level of wearing on women. Any more would take a lot of work."

"Ah, but haven't you heard? I am now fully responsible and ready to work."

"I had heard something to that effect."

"It is true. I only think of others now. And work."

I can only think about how close he suddenly is in the enclosed space of the carriage. So close we could kiss, with a few quick adjustments of our heads and a small shift forward from both of us. Then I could find out if his lips are as talented at kissing as they are at charming everyone around him. If kissing him is as fun as just talking to him is.

If his kiss can convince me that I need to experience some things instead of just reading about them.

Our heads are making the micro movements that would bring our lips together when Anne delicately clears her throat. We both jerk back, cheeks as red as the leather of the seats we're on. Anne has been so quiet today, I sometimes forgot we weren't alone. But she did her job and chaperoned when she needed to, protecting our virtue.

Leo's much realer after today. He's not just a spoiled but poor aristocrat who wants to continue his lifestyle. He's a spoiled but poor aristocrat who wants to look out for his sister.

And, okay, he also wants to continue his lifestyle.

Leo drops me and Anne off at the palace, getting out of the carriage first to help both of us out. He lingers with my hand in his when it's my turn.

"I have not looked through my correspondence yet, but I think my name is still enough to get me invitations to dinners and balls despite my many scandals. If I see something promising, I can send word for tonight," Leo says.

"Right. We need to get you to the altar." And it won't be with me. Even if my position here wasn't so dependent on the lies I'm telling to everyone, including this man, I'm sure time would have things to say about me marrying a man in the past. Something negative, which would maybe stop an entire city from being in existence.

Hey, if a butterfly's wings can cause a hurricane, I can stop a city from existing with my vagina.

So no more lusting after Leo. And yes more trying to figure out how to get back to the right time.

CHAPTER 13

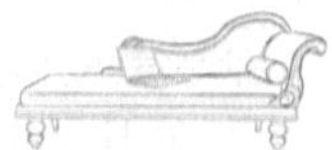

"Good afternoon. Did you have a good day?" The Queen of England walks into the library where I'm brainstorming ways to get home, Abdul trailing behind her.

"Yes, Your Majesty. Thank you for the clothes. And the chaperone. And your general hospitality."

She waves away the thanks. "You are very welcome. The Duke of Norfolk has invited us to his home for an assembly at Norfolk House tonight. Would you like to come?"

Well, not particularly. I'm kind of exhausted from pretending all day to Leo and pretending with him to everyone else. I was hoping for a quiet night where I could regroup and think of ways to get home.

"Thank you for thinking of me. I've had such a busy few days. I was wondering if maybe I should rest?"

"Nonsense. You shall feel better once you get out. I know it."

I really don't think I will, and would give anything to just get out of this very heavy Victorian dress for the rest of the night and be alone to recharge my social battery, but I can't really refuse a monarch whose house I'm living in, so I grit my teeth. "That does sound lovely. Thank you, Your Majesty."

At least I'll get to see Norfolk House. The house's plan became the blueprint for the London townhouse and townhouse parties since it was built in the mid-eighteenth century, with its circuit of decorated rooms for guests to meander through instead of just one main salon where an event would be held.

A groundbreaking, historic house that didn't make it until my time, torn down for office space before I was even born.

"Of course. A few of my godchildren will be in attendance, and maybe speaking to them can help you in navigating London. Charles tells me that he's sent word to the Cooch Behars as well, and we can sort out what happened. But we do enjoy having you here with us in the meantime."

Oh, shit. The smile freezes on my face. That letter will undoubtedly say they have no idea who I am, showing I'm definitely a liar. And as kind as Victoria is to an alleged fellow royal, she would be decidedly less kind to a liar. A common liar.

Less than ideal, this letter.

Charles probably sent a telegram, which is much quicker than a letter by mail. The telegram still has to get to the right person, and then they have to travel to Cooch Behar to get a response, and then travel back to where the telegram machine is with the answer. That gives me maybe a week or a few weeks, tops. If anyone in the process feels there's more to say than a telegram allows, they'll send a letter, which won't get anywhere for about two to three weeks. Although the most likely response, "They don't know her," is simple enough to be telegrammed.

There was always a limit on my time here. And whether it ends with me back in LA in the twenty-first century or me thrown in a pit of lions for lying to Queen Victoria, this isn't going to last forever.

I need to stop getting deeper entwined in the lives around here.

"And I will invite Basildon." Despite the fact that this is not a good start to distancing myself from Leo, I'm relieved at this part of the queen's news.

~

THAT EVENING, the royal carriage (and I will never get tired of this mode of transportation, because what it lacks in speed, heated seats, and a sound system to play my audiobooks, it makes up for in historic atmosphere), drives Victoria, Abdul and me to St. James's Square.

We pull up to the façade which takes up more space than any other plot in the square but is surprisingly understated with its simple columns and pediment design. But they can't trick me, I know what's inside. I've seen the black and white pictures.

I trail the group into the hall. Victoria is immediately surrounded by people, and I fade further into the background, happy to be ignored. I left the journal at home, despite every scholarly instinct telling me to take the book, but compromised by tearing some papers loose and slipping them into my bag with a pencil.

I walk the intended circuit, making a circle through the rooms of the ground floor and then moving upstairs to do the circuit there. Each room is decorated in different themes and color schemes, the only thing they have in common that everything is blindingly expensive.

I walk past furniture, paintings, and other decorative arts, pieces that must be in museums in my time, that are now brand new. And some that are already old even now, like all the intricate gold covered wooden molding and panels from the Music Room that in my time are installed in the Victoria and Albert Museum as a room you can walk through. It feels very different to walk through that same room now, with people in Victorian clothes milling about, instead of modern tourists with their cameras trying to capture the grandeur of the rooms and selfies as well.

Others are wandering through the rooms with me, admiring the wealth, good taste and power of the Duke of Norfolk, just as he intended.

"Hello," a woman's voice says from close behind me.

I freeze, my hopes of getting through this night completely unnoticed destroyed. "Hello?" I turn, trying to prepare myself for whatever might be coming towards me.

But I didn't prepare for the sight walking toward me. Like normal people meeting Pedro Pascal or Taylor Swift, my eyes get big, my jaw drops open and I start hyperventilating. The Indian woman and the Nigerian woman in Victorian dresses in front of me look concerned, but I can't force myself to have chill. These women are both children of those displaced by the Empire: Sophia's father from the Sikh Empire in India and Victoria's mother was Yoruba from West Africa. As the children of immigrants, they made their way in London with the help of Queen Victoria, and while one chose to stay here, the other returned to Lagos.

And I have spent a lot of my adult life reading and writing about them.

"Sophia Singh? Victoria Davies Randle?"

"Yes," they both say. They don't look as concerned about me knowing them as they do about my general demeanor, but apparently that's how life is when you live in the world's largest small town.

"It's so nice to meet you! So nice! I'm Meera Chopra."

"Related to the Chooch Behar royal family, right?" Victoria asks.

"Yes," I say with a grimace. Lying to women I admire isn't the easiest thing I've done, but the alternative is jail in a nineteenth century prison, so I'm going to dig deep. At least they haven't asked why my accent is strange.

"Her Majesty sent us over here to help you navigate London society. I've grown up in it and Mrs. Randle visits often from Nigeria. We're also both godchildren of Her Majesty's," Sophia says.

Oh, I know. In the least creepy way possible. "How has your experience been in London?"

"Some people will be excited about you because you are 'exotic,' like a zebra or an Egyptian sarcophagus. Some people will think you're simultaneously much stupider than them *and* somehow successfully conning them out of what's rightfully theirs. Others will try to find out everything about you, the same way they would with anyone who gets invited into this tiny circle, and it won't have anything to do with where you come from, but because you're different, and these people do not enjoy change," Sophia says.

"Fun. I think so far people are mostly in the staring phase. And the occasional rude comment."

Victoria shrugs. "It is not that bad. There are worse places for a woman to be."

That's depressing. "Yes. I'm very grateful to Her Majesty for taking me in on such short notice."

"That's Her Majesty," Sophia says. The woman lives in a grace and favor house near Hampton Court, so she's well acquainted with the Queen's hospitality. Even though she wouldn't need the queen's hospitality if she were the sister of the Maharaja of Punjab, instead of in exile.

See, complicated.

"But be careful of the people around her. She might have a soft spot for you as an Indian royal, but Parliament gets more powerful every day. They are much less enamored with you, and if they think you are a danger to the Empire, you will be dealt with as a threat. And her household will not appreciate you taking the attention they feel they deserve," Sophia says.

The two women tell me stories about their very different

experiences in England, from debuting in front of Queen Victoria, catching her attention, and getting lavish presents from her, but also sometimes dealing with her feeling she knows exactly what's best for them and how hard it is to do what they want in light of Victoria's "suggestions" for them. And dealing with jealous courtiers and those who used them to get close to the queen.

Then too soon, Victoria sees her husband and excuses herself. Alone with Sophia, I bite my lip to stop myself from asking her all the questions I have. Victoria's experiences are amazing and I've studied them, but Sophia is my actual thesis. The subject of my graduate thesis.

Princess Sophia Duleep Singh: Punjabi, German and Ethiopian, and one of the daughters of the last Maharaja of Punjab. Not that she's been to visit there yet. She was born in an English country house called Elveden in Suffolk, with a decidedly Indian interior full of scalloped arches, peacock fireplaces, plush Indian rugs and Indian furniture.

My parents are both from Punjab, so I can't help but feel connected to the woman in front of me, not only because we're from the same place, but because we were born and grew up somewhere else, only visiting the birthplace of our parents later in life.

But I have a feeling if I asked her all the questions I really wanted to, she would get a little scared and encourage those people who are already suspicious of me to look closer at the strange woman with no filter and too much knowledge of people's personal lives.

Still… "How do you feel about being in England, if you don't mind me asking? Instead of India?"

"It is complicated, I suppose. It is strange to miss a place I have never been, or a life I never lived. Father became a ruler at five and then two years later the British declared war. He came here at sixteen, but he could never decide if he wanted to be an

Englishman or if he wanted to be a Maharaja. But he knew he wanted to live an extravagant life, so his spending probably didn't help anything. I have never known anything else. None of his children even know Punjabi. But lately I do connect with Indians who have moved to London or are visiting, and that has felt nice, to hear them speak of this place. I would like to visit it one day."

The grief is thick in her voice, and I do some mental math to realize he passed two years ago. In Paris with his second wife, an English hotel maid he started an affair with before his first wife died. Duleep certainly made some…choices. And the English didn't live up to their own treaty with him either. Also, they stole a kid from his mother. And the Koh-i-Noor diamond from that kid's treasury. And then cut it up to place it on one of their crowns. Very rude.

"Your Royal Highness," another voice calls out from behind me, dragging me from the past into…well, still the past. This time it's a man's voice.

"Leo…I mean Lord Basildon. Good evening."

Leo bends low over my hand as he bows, touching his lips to my hand like I wished his lips had touched mine earlier. Even now, the stupid glove gets in the way of me feeling his actual lips on my skin.

"It is lovely to see you again." Leo bows over Sophia's hand too. But with less lingering, thankfully.

"Lord Basildon. It is always a pleasure." Right, they must know each other. Victoria does have a habit of seeing two brown people and try to marry them off to each other. Case in point. Although that is helping me, so I shouldn't complain about it.

"If you'll excuse me, I see some friends. It was a pleasure to meet you, and please do call on me if you need any help while you are here," Sophia says.

"Thank you." I belatedly look up at Sophia, only to see her smiling at me. Then she walks away, leaving me alone with Leo.

"You got Her Majesty's letter?" I ask, even though he must have, because he's here.

"Yes. I received it just as I was getting ready for the evening, so I thought I would answer in person." He extends his hands out as if presenting himself. "I would be delighted to come."

"Good. Although it would have been awkward if you showed up just to tell me you weren't coming."

"Hmm. I could see how that would be. Since I am here, would you like to dance?" He extends his arm to me.

"Yes." I tuck my hand in the offered elbow. "Wait. Is it an easy one?"

"I will pay the orchestra to change it, if it isn't."

"All right then." Leo walks me down the stairs and past the room with refreshments, and one that has been taken over as a card room, until we get to the ballroom.

Leo stands with me while the current song finishes, and then tugs my arm when the music starts up again. "Perfect. It is indeed an easy one."

In theory, I know the steps for these dances. But only in theory, not in practice. My books are very different from this dance floor with music, which takes the steps and translates them to the groups of dancers moving together like waves in the ocean.

Maybe I need to start going to events that do this type of dancing, just to fill the gap in my historical knowledge. There are probably some groups in England who are keeping the tradition alive.

Like the last time, Leo is confident and graceful. I, on the other hand, have all the confidence and grace of a newborn baby giraffe. To give baby giraffes their due, it is impressive what they can do so soon after entering the world, but they don't do it with either confidence or grace.

But like the baby giraffe, I persevere until the music stops. When it does, I breath out a sigh of relief and move faster than I ever have to walk back to the outer edges of the dance floor.

"You are in such a rush to get away from me. I think I should be offended," Leo says from behind me.

"No. In a rush to be done with the dancing part." But when I turn around he's smiling. I should have known it would be almost impossible to insult Leo. He lives encased in a hard shell of his privilege, where almost nothing can touch him.

Except debt. But even then, he continues on with a smile, going to parties and ready to sacrifice his body to find the solution.

I can't fully understand his cheerful attitude. It just seems frivolous, when my work has always been so serious. Even though I do find it fun, it's never been this carefree. I always have to worry about getting published in the next journal or getting tenure.

It's hard not to get swept away with Leo's always good mood. I'm in an awful place right now, trapped in this time, no way home, could be exposed at any second, yet when I'm with him, I'm…lighter. It's nice.

"Then you will be happy with my news: rich heiresses have agreed to dance with me. Our plan is working. Are you going to be all right alone for a while?"

I scoff at the through that I can't handle some alone time. Not only did I have two parents working full-time growing up, I've lived alone since college. So I think I can handle a ball. Plus, now that Leo's going away, I can direct my attention to what matters: the Duke of Norfolk's wallpaper, decoration, and furniture combinations and how they're received by contemporaries.

But even though that makes a good distraction, it isn't perfect. My eyes keep shifting to look at whatever items mean that Leo is still in my peripherals. And whatever beautiful (and rich) woman is in his arms.

Leo starts a waltz with one of his admirers, and I immediately turn into a Victorian chaperone, concerned that they're too close for propriety and he's going to ruin himself on this damn dance floor. Forced to marry someone who can't even help his money problems.

I move with Leo, forced to if I want to keep in him my line of sight. I'm so focused on the décor and Leo that I don't notice Charles until I almost bowl him over.

"Oh. Hello, Lord Wellesley." He can't even let me enjoy this beautiful, if dimly lit and hot, room in peace.

"Miss Chopra." He inclines his head, lips turned down in a pout. And he didn't use my title. My fake title. Rude.

"How are you enjoying your evening?"

"It is fine. I hope you're enjoying your time as the shiny new object that the *ton* shall soon get bored with."

My smile, already fake as hell, become more teeth than lips, more snarl than sunshine. "It's great. Thanks for your concern."

"Enjoy it for now. There is still the matter of the telegram we've sent to India regarding you. I personally made sure it was expedited, so we will not be waiting long for the response."

Lucky for me steam's still not the most reliable method of transportation, carriages are always slow, and the only thing reliable about wind is it does what it wants, which is rarely what a ship captain wants. And maybe the people in a telegram office lose the message or it gets misfiled or sent to the wrong place. A lot of things have to go right for him to get a fast response. And a lot can go wrong to delay it.

"You're ever so kind to check for Her Majesty."

Charles narrows his eyes at me, not getting the reaction he wants. It's irritating him that I'm not terrified of him, and it makes me even more resolved to be strong. Pettiness is a great motivator. "The penalty for lying to our monarch is a hefty one."

I feign innocent earnestness, eyes so wide I'm channeling Bambi. Who doesn't like Bambi?

"Of course." My voice raises a few octaves to levels of neutral customer service employee, ready to agree with everything so I can get off the call and get to my fifteen-minute break. "We have to make sure that liars are punished."

Then I look at him with knowledge. Knowledge of everything he's done wrong in his life, all available to me in my crystal ball— or more like my crystal book. He's going to become prime minister. An accomplishment for him and a tragedy for England, but a boon for me. Because prime ministers get written about in a lot more depth than if they had stayed the Secretary of State. Who get written about a lot more than if they had stayed an anonymous aristocrat.

"Shall I ask Lady Dumfries how she feels about liars?" I ask quietly.

"You will stop speaking to me about the good lady. I'm sure I have no knowledge of her." But he's scared. He thought he was hiding his secret, and to be fair, he is to everyone in this time. He doesn't know if I know or how I could even know, but it's stressing him out that I might.

He mumbles something about seeing a friend and flees. I watch with satisfaction; glad I paid attention in my history classes to people other than my maharajas.

Leo dances back into my line of sight. He didn't seek public office, or any other highly publicized position. He also didn't make enough of a splash that I could see the ripples in the twenty-first century.

My life would be easier if he had.

Maybe knowing he's going to marry some heiress and save his house, sister, and tenants would help me keep my distance. It would be hard to lust after the man if I had studied him and his family in detail. Or if I had analyzed all the negative traits he had and the bad choices he made. Watch his children squabble over his estate when he died.

But he's a mystery to me. And in a place where I know a lot about everyone, that's...refreshing.

CHAPTER 14

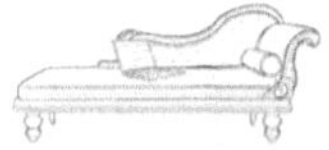

Charles was right about one thing: I am the shiny new object. Now that I've been at multiple events with Her Majesty and her godchildren, and been seen doing fashionable things with Leo, people feel much more comfortable coming up to me and talking.

So. Much. Talking.

"Are you the Hindoo princess?"

"Sure. Yeah. Umm-hmm." Why not?

"You don't talk funny."

"Some would say you do talk funny."

"I say…" *unintelligible sounds of British affront*

"No, yeah. Like that is funny."

That man goes off in a huff, mumbling further British sounds of indignance. But I can't understand what he's saying, beyond general unhappiness at me, so I don't think it's as effective as he thinks it is.

"Do you have tigers?"

"No." But I can't be mad at that one, because, honestly, if having Rajah was a safe, ethical option, I would have a cuddly big cat.

"Why aren't you wearing Hindoo clothes? They're so pretty."

"They fell off the boat." I'm getting so good at lying. And talking to strangers.

In the meantime, Leo has danced with three other women who aren't named Meera. But after that he remembers he's courting someone and comes back to me. All flushed with excitement. Over other women.

Great.

"This night is going so well." He reclaims my hand and walks me around the room.

"Yeah." Because it is, if you judge it by the metrics of our deal. No one has outed me as a fraud from the future and he's getting the attention he needs to marry rich.

I have no reason to be upset.

Which makes me *more* upset, actually.

"Want to play cards?" Leo asks when we find ourselves in the card room.

"Sure." These shoes do pinch. Some things haven't changed after all, despite the giant advancements in other arenas.

In the card room, Leo teaches me whist, another thing I know only in theory. I'm delighted that it goes better than him trying to teach me how to dance. Not that it could have gone worse than that, as I am very uncoordinated. But like every time I go out with Leo, this is the most fun I've had in a while, and he even makes losing easy to take.

Not that we lose much; we do surprisingly well. And even win some money by the end of the night. But then one of the footmen tells me that the queen wants to leave, and I say my goodbyes.

"My lady." Leo elaborately bows to me in front of the carriage while Queen Victoria is finishing her goodbyes.

"I'm not a lady." I'm getting sick of the lying to him, even though it's an important component of my survival in the past.

"You are in my eyes," Leo says, putting his hand on his chest.

I roll my eyes. Charming rake, even if it is an act.

Then Leo extends our winnings out to me.

"No. You take it." I push the money back to him. He did spot us the original amount, and I don't need any money right now. What with the Queen of England sponsoring me, living in a palace, and wearing a princess's clothes.

He divides the amount. "At least take half. You never know when you will need cash. I speak from experience."

I accept this time. He's right. I should have a little bit of money, especially since that letter is making its way back to the Queen while I get no closer to finding out how to get home.

"Thank you." I tuck the money in my purse.

Leo's brown eyes get brighter. Or maybe they just get closer and I can see them better in the dim light of the night, only illuminated by the flickering candles on the exterior of the house. "I enjoyed—"

"Good evening, Lord Basildon. Lovely night. So glad you could come." Victoria sweeps between us, forcing us apart as she gets into the carriage.

"I should go. Can't keep the Queen of England waiting." I just said that without any irony.

"Probably for the best. I will call on you tomorrow."

"I look forward to it."

As the carriage gets going, I peek out the window to see Leo still standing outside the house, watching us get eaten up by the London evening fog.

Which happens after about twenty feet, because the London evening fog is no joke.

"He's a good boy, that one. Shame about his father. But a lovely boy." Victoria drags my attention inside the carriage instead of trying to see through fog to catch a few more glances at Leo.

"Yes. He is rather lovely." But I don't want her to think badly of him when he inevitably dumps me and marries an heiress. So the least I can do is some preemptive damage control. "But he does have responsibilities to his title. I won't be surprised if he ends up with...well, you know." I hope she can pick up on my subtext while I avoid saying "a rich bitch."

"I do know. But I do not like it. Any of it. You two get along so well, and you are perfectly matched." I'm reminded again of how lonely Victoria felt throughout her life, after Albert's death of course, but even before she met him. It's hard to have friends when you're meant to be above everyone, I guess.

"It's probably better this way." What with me being a future-lady.

"Hmm. Well, we will not give up. I am certain we can find someone for you. Victor, Duleep Singh's son, is unmarried. That would be a good match."

I laugh nervously. "That is incredibly generous, Your Majesty." But he is going to marry Lady Anne Coventry in three years, and I think that would qualify as changing history if I married him instead. Also, she knows nothing about him other than we're both Indian and sort of royal, which might be enough for these people, but I would like to get to know my partner better than that. Maybe share some interests. Maybe enjoy spending time with them, before I marry them for life.

Like I have been with Leo. But no, that is not an option for so many reasons. For one thing, he needs money and I have nothing. For another, any interest he has in me is solely because I'm so different from everyone else he knows. There's nothing special about me.

I'm going to have to have to avoid matchmaking, while not offending Victoria who is housing and feeding me.

She smiles at me, the same smile I've seen directed at me that doesn't quite reach her eyes. It probably gets closest to a full smile around Abdul. The way it probably did around John and Albert.

The way I'm worried mine does around Leo, damn it.

~

THE NEXT MORNING, I wake up with a plan. I need to walk around London.

Okay, it's not the most specific of plans. But I defy anyone else to come up with a more specific plan on how to figure out time travel.

Maybe I can find someone who won't think I need to go to Bedlam. Maybe this is something that happens more than everyone thinks. Of course, no one knows about it, so any time travelers are good at hiding their secrets. That'll be a hard point to get around.

But I have a plan which, despite how vague it is, is more than I had last night. And if I get to see some more of Victorian London, then the trip won't be a waste no matter what I find. Or don't find.

Anne comes into my room to help me dress.

"Do you have anything…not as nice?" I ask.

Anne replies with a look full of meaning. Mostly judgment, wondering why I would turn down the beauty in front of me.

Because I have places to be. Places I want to blend into.

I answer her unasked question, because I'm a people pleaser at heart. "I want to take a walk, and I'd feel bad if I got dirt on the princess's clothes."

That reduces the judgement. "But miss, you have a lot of callers. Maybe we can put on one of the nicer dresses first, and later I can find something for you to walk around in?"

"I'm sorry. *Callers?* More than one?"

"Many more than one."

"What is going on?" The plan might be working *too* well if people feel the need to visit me. Unless callers is a ruse, and it's people coming to arrest me.

"Everyone is excited to meet you, miss. What with you stayin' with Her Majesty, and…"

Being more exotic than a box of chai. Yeah, she doesn't need to finish that one for me; I can get there myself. And it won't help to piss anyone off, at least not at this stage.

Unless that person is Charles. Seriously, fuck that guy.

But I do look out the window to gaze longingly at the trees and sigh, thwarted again from my plan to find a way home by this gilded cage I'm trapped in.

"Let's do your plan." I let Anne work her magic, my own fairy godmother transforming me into a respectable Victorian lady. She's very good at it and doesn't comment at all when I get giddy at being able to touch the items she brings forward.

Like the shoes. Not only are there no gloves between me and the material, but I also get to put my feet in them! And then walk around in them! A historian's dream. Minus being trapped in the past and in danger of being found out every second. And my period will happen at some point, and I would prefer not to experience diaper-like belt contraptions or rudimentary tampons.

Even this historian has a line on how real she wants to get in the name of research.

I follow Anne down the stairs and into the drawing room, where a small crowd of people are waiting to chat with me, all in various states of getting tea from a tray or drinking said tea.

"Good morning," I say tentatively. A sea of feathered and floral hats turns toward me as one, letting me know all my visitors are women today. I stifle my disappointment that Leo isn't here. He isn't actually courting me; he's allowed to sleep in. "It's so nice to see you all," I say, despite me wishing they would all go away so I could get shit done.

The seven people in the room all start talking at once, giving me a headache from trying to figure out who I should be paying attention too. Probably the one with the biggest, oldest title is the one I need to make sure is on my side.

Where's a copy of *Debrett's Peerage & Baronetage* when you

need it? Even if it would be considered tacky to read it on front of said titles.

"Excuse me." I step around long skirts and feet on my way to get my own cup of tea.

I really need something to focus on while they eye me like I'm prey, and they haven't eaten for a while.

"Your bustle is so big. It's not in this season's style," one woman says after the introductions.

"*Her Majesty* gave me these clothes. So, if it's good enough for Her Majesty, it's good enough for me." I smile with all my teeth at the woman trying to shame me for not having taste.

"What's India like?" another asks me.

They're all looking towards me still, so many faces, with various levels of interest; some hostile, some curious; most in between.

"Hot. Sometimes rainy and hot. The food is good. With like spices and stuff. Um. There's nice architecture. Lots of domes and sculptural reliefs. A lot of monkeys. And cows." I try to remember my last trip to India, which was when I was in high school. Mom's been wanting to go back, especially during Diwali or maybe Holi, but there never seems to be any time. Also, it is very difficult to distill an entire country into a succinct answer. "Lots of interesting history. The first civilization with a plumbing system."

The women continue to grill me like a prosecutor in a highly publicized murder trial. I can feel the handcuffs tightening around my wrists with all of their questions, but then they finally get bored and leave.

None of them yelled "fraud" at me, and I only wanted to punch one of them when she smugly told me about her uncle in the military who was stationed in India. Instead, I ground out a "Good for him" through clenched teeth and a hint of a snarl.

But now they're finally gone. I run back up the stairs to my room, then freeze when I realize that I can't get undressed without help. Anne, a paragon of maids, appears before I can frustrated cry at my lack of ability to be independent.

I'm grateful. It would have sucked to have kept it mostly together through actual time travel and then have a breakdown over a dress.

Anne helps me into another dress, this one still not what I would have picked if someone had told *me* they were going to go traipsing through the dirt, but at least it's not made of silk.

Anne walks with me through the palace hallways until we make it the patio overlooking the back garden. Lush green trees sway in the gentle breeze and provide privacy for the outdoor space in the middle of a city while a lake in the background draws birds to the area. Dense shrubberies dot the landscape, and the focus is a more naturalistic looking garden than the formal gardens of the eighteenth century.

"You don't need to come with me. I'm just going on a walk in the gardens. And it's gated around here, so I think I should be safe." I slowly back away from Anne and toward the garden space. "How much trouble could I possibly get in while I'm in the gardens?"

It's a good thing TV hasn't been invented yet, because if Anne had ever seen a sitcom, she would know that is the cue to *not* leave me alone. That would be the cue to lock me up in a tower and throw the key away, because I just signaled to her that I was most definitely going to be getting into some trouble.

Luckily for me, Anne isn't up on her sitcoms, so she shrugs and stays where she is while I walk into the gardens. I give her a few more minutes to make sure she's not going to change her mind and come back out, and then I sneak around the side of the palace, running as quietly as I can.

But it's a giant building, with very long sides. And I'm wearing so many layers. Which means my sneaky run quickly descends into a fast walk. And even quicker, that deteriorates into a regular walk where I'm panting but still trying very hard not to make too much noise. Which makes the panting louder, because of course it does.

I'm in academia. I do not break out of palaces or evade the Queen's Guard; I read books. This is new to me.

But I shouldn't have been worried. I passed some guards and they didn't even bat an eye at me wandering around the place. I can see how that kid snuck in and sat on the throne, early in Victoria's reign. Then again, I would assume news has spread that I'm a guest, and guests can walk around the gardens when they want.

When step one of the escape plan is done, I turn to step two: finding transportation.

I could lie to the stable workers and say Victoria gave me permission to take a carriage out. I'm getting so good at lying lately.

Then I remember that the stables are *behind* the palace. Closer to where I started from. I turn to make the slow walk back, sad at the unnecessary cardio, when someone grabs my arm from behind. I scream and throw both hands up as I turn, ready to defend myself from whatever fresh hell this time wants to throw at me now.

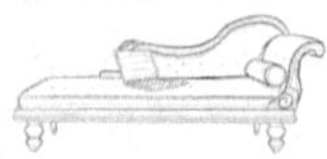

"Oh, Leo. It's you." My hands, grateful they don't have to protect me anymore, go to my chest in an effort to calm my pounding heart.

"Steady on." Leo removes his hand and holds both of his arms up, apparently worried about my fighting ability (which he really shouldn't be).

"You shouldn't grab women, all creepy-like."

"I am sorry. Next time I grab a woman, I shall endeavor to be less creepy about it."

"Maybe don't grab women unexpectedly at all."

"Also a path I could take." He takes in my appearance, my hair askew from the aforementioned running, my slightly puffy sleeves sticking to my arms because of sweat from, again, the running. "Where are you off to?"

"Nowhere. Just having a nice, very normal walk." Yes, Meera. Totally normal walks are usually described as normal. No more questions needed.

"Well, I was coming to call on you. May I walk with you?"

"I..." What would be a legitimate reason to tell him to get lost?

It's already getting late, and if I walk with him, that's even less time to be out exploring for my way home.

But he is my partner. And I've gotten him enough dances in the past few days that I think I can start getting into the weirder requests I mentioned as part of the deal. This could be the red flag that makes him rethink our deal, but I can't continue lying like this, so I have to take the chance.

"Did you come by carriage?" I ask.

"Yes."

"Great. Let's get in it."

"Although I do approve of taking walks in a carriage, does that not somewhat defeat the purpose?"

"This is one of those times I'm going to need your help, without question or judgement." I cross my arms over my chest so he knows I mean business. Even though I have nothing to bargain or threaten him with if he decides he wants out of the strange requests.

"Then by all means, we shall go." Leo calls for his carriage back from the groom who was about to take it away. "Out of curiosity, how many of these requests will you make?"

I hold my chin up. "You did not specify a number when we were negotiating the proposition. Therefore, it's unlimited until you're married and/or I'm home. But I will try to not abuse it."

Leo snaps his fingers good-naturedly. "This is why the family fortune is in shambles. Are you sure you cannot take over as my business manager? Then maybe I could put off marriage for a few more years. Not that we have very much to manage at this point that hasn't already been auctioned off."

I laugh awkwardly, knowing I could save his entire fortune if I became his business manager. I certainly know the trends of the time period, and even remember some the biggest businesses. I could make him so much money if he had some time.

But I think that would change the timeline too much. Not that I got a manual when all this happened.

A manual would be so nice.

"I shall send for Anne," Leo says.

I glare at him. Another person is not what I need. Especially one that can report back to Victoria that I'm being suspicious. "Why don't we just go the two of us?"

Leo laughs. "Whilst I would enjoy nothing more than thumbing my nose at society, I do think this is not the time for either of us to draw negative attention to ourselves."

He's right. I don't like it, but he's right. We wait while his coachman fetches Anne, and then finally we can get in the carriage. I would have liked to be on this trip without a spy, albeit a nice one so far, but it is not looking like that is an option. I'll have to watch what I say and do on this trip. This trip to figure out time travel.

"Where would you like to go? No questioning or judging you, just because we need to know how to get there," Leo says.

"Bedford College, in York Place, please."

"All right. You heard her," Leo calls out to his coachman. "Wherever she wants to go."

He's so obliging it's a shame I can't ask to go to Osbourne House in the year 2025.

"You *want* to go to a school? I cannot say I enjoyed the concept much the first time around, but I did say we could go where you wanted."

"I need information. There's no better place for information than a school."

"Maybe a school library would be the absolute best." Leo purses his lips in thought.

"Don't threaten me with a good time." But the thought of all those books isn't the only thing making me warm under all the layers I'm wearing. It's the potent combination of the ideas of Leo *and* books, Leo *near* the books, Leo *in front of bookshelves* that really makes me a little wild.

"What kind of information do you need?"

Right, the task at hand. "Information about faraway places and how to get to them."

"Then we should be going to the docks for a ship."

"Places that can't be reached with a ship."

Leo scoffs. "What kind of place cannot be reached by a ship?"

Of course a citizen of the British Empire can't fathom a place that can't be reached by ship. Just you wait. Even though you've already seen the height of the Industrial Revolution and all the changes it brought, just you wait for the future that's going to blow your mind.

I miss those mind-blowing conveniences that I took for granted. Reliable electricity and plumbing. A pocket computer that helps me answer any question I could have and provides entertainment. But also the necessities. My parents. My friends. My students.

I'm alone here. Even with Leo, no matter how much fun I have with him, it's not the same.

I want my mommy.

And I know I don't get to see my family that much. They're a six-hour drive on a good day, but with California traffic, that could easily be ten. But they're only a call away. A text. A WhatsApp thread.

And now they're not even that close.

"There are places outside the reach of the Empire," I say.

"I shall have to take your word for it. Even though this tangent has done nothing to answer my original query."

"You wouldn't believe me if I told you." But the urge to share with him, unburden myself of my secret, is strong. Especially as the silence lingers. And then stretches.

A very potent weapon, the silence. Begging to be filled. Begging for me to say anything to break the unending nothingness. I try to distract myself with the views of London outside my window, and it kind of works. I see people going in and out of buildings, finishing their business for the day and meeting acquaintances. People in extravagant clothes who are visiting these buildings and those in more functional, less expensive ones who work inside them, all mingling on the city streets. All the hustle and noise of a Victorian city, people yelling, wheels turning over cobblestones, and horses pulling carriages, is interesting. But it's not quite enough to distract from the man across from me.

So I'm grateful when the carriage finally stops.

"We're here," I say, hoping but also a little sad that this could be my last day living in the past. Which means there's not going to be any more Leo. It's very confusing.

I don't wait for him as I jump out of the carriage and onto the busy nineteenth century London street. I dodge horse poo, street sweepers and finely dressed women to get to the building's entrance. Then I stop. I don't know if this is a place I can just walk into.

History teaches about the general: this is Bedford College, founded in 1849, and one of the first colleges for women in the U.K. A few years from now, it'll become part of the University of London. Notable alumni include: Sarah Redmond, one of the first Black women to speak about abolishing slavery in America during the 1800s; George Eliot, author; Elizabeth Blackwell, the first woman to earn a medical degree in America; and plenty of other scientists, politicians and historians.

But I don't know the particulars. Like: do they have a front desk or some sort of guard system? Frankly, that would be more useful than any other fact I know about it. At least right now.

"Are we going in?" Leo whispers from beside me, having snuck up on my while I was lost in confusion. "Or does the door have all the information we need?"

Like anything's that easy. "In."

Taking a deep breath, I twist the doorknob. It gives easily, opening inward into a silent room. The stillness is a shock after the chaos of the street, especially when Leo and Anne come in and he closes the door behind them, leaving us in the quiet and dark entryway. Once my ears and eyes adjust to the new space, I wander deeper in.

"Can I help you?" a man asks. He's dressed in a suit and walks with perfect posture and an assertiveness that says he's supposed to be here. A guard, maybe.

"We're trying to find…" No, I don't think the truth will serve anyone here. But I didn't think of a suitable lie, either. "Umm."

"You cannot just come in and wander around the woman's college unless you're authorized to be here." He takes a threatening step forward. To throw me out? That would be a first, getting thrown out of a school. A first I do not want to achieve.

"This is the Marquess of Basildon, Baron Chelmsford. He's looking for suitable colleges for his sister and I'm her tutor. We'd like to look around. Speak to the women here about their experiences."

Leo jumps right into the ruse and ups his arrogance to at least double intensity. "Yes, we need to see if they have been improved by your tutelage, and if it is worth the fees. Thank you for your assistance."

Then he sails past the security man like he owns the college, without waiting for approval. The guard sputters, but notes Leo's expensive clothes and very proper chaperone, and lets us pass with a glare.

Fucking aristocrats. I channel all that frustration into a shrug I share with the man and then run after Leo. The arrogance can be helpful, on occasion. Weaponizing his worst characteristics for my gain, as it were.

We pass dark, wood-paneled student spaces, a dining hall, a chapel, and a few classes led by lecturers that aren't too keen on being interrupted by a stranger opening the door with a hasty apology.

"I know you do not want to tell me what information you need, but do you want to tell me who or what we are looking for to get the information? I have a pair of eyes that can be made a slight more useful if they knew what to look for," Leo says.

"Like you said: the library. Librarians know everything. We need to get to a library and then they can help us to the next step."

"I never found anything useful in the library," Leo mumbles.

"Did you try reading any of the books *in* the library?"

"Touché, madame." He has no regret in his voice for all the books he didn't read.

I roll my eyes and refrain from saying he might not be in the position he's in if he had read some of those lovely, useful books.

After we've opened enough doors that we must be in danger of running out of rooms soon, we find the room we're looking for. A magic space of towering dark wood bookshelves, desks and comfortable chairs meant to invite long study, and thick rugs to muffle the sounds of other patrons seeking their knowledge. Windows were an afterthought, a few planes of glass here and there letting in slivers of light, some already covered by bookshelves.

The lack of light isn't the best for reading, but it sure does give the room atmosphere. Along with the smell of books that are old even in this time.

"Anne, why don't you wait at one of the tables? We might be here a while reading and finding books, and there are people around anyway." I don't need her listening in on my talk with the librarian.

"Oh, I don't think that would be proper…"

"What can be more proper than a library? A repository of knowledge. You know, when the library of Alexandria—"

"All right then. I'll stay right here." She sits on an overstuffed chair in front of a desk, already knowing, even in our short acquaintance, that I can really yap about history. And she doesn't want to hear more of it.

"Great. We'll see you soon," I say.

"Hi." I approach the first woman I see, a woman behind a desk. She's wearing a plain dress, without any of the ornamentation that I've gotten used to being around aristocrats. It's comforting to be around people who don't need to dress up, because they're going to be surrounded by books. And books don't judge if you go for comfort over style. "Sorry to disturb you. I'm looking for the librarian."

"You have just found her." Then she slides a look past me to my companion. "Are you a student here?"

"No. But we heard this is one of the best libraries in London."

The woman snorts, not believing anyone would give the women's college its due. Which, to be fair, no one during this time has said that. But *I* have said it, albeit in 2025. So it's also not a complete lie.

I try again. "I would really appreciate any help you could give us."

The woman looks back and forth at us. I smile and try to step in front of Leo, thinking tall thoughts as if I can will myself more inches to hide him. Any smart woman would realize he's full of shit, and I need her to believe we are earnest humans who deserve her help.

Not rakes.

Whether we present a trustworthy appearance, or she doesn't have anything else to do, she closes the book in front of her. "What can I help you with?"

Now that the easy part is over, I have to explain the next bit. I take a seat across the table from the librarian. "I would like to learn about..." I look around, sure that this is when I get arrested for being a heretic. I lean in closer to the woman and Leo leans in closer to me from behind until his breath is making my hair flutter. "...time travel."

CHAPTER 16

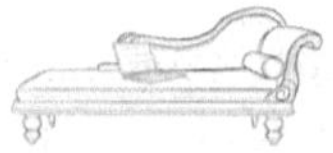

I feel more than see Leo's sharp breath. There goes any attraction he might have had for me, now that I'm going around suggesting the impossible.

And there's still a chance he'll tell on me. But I'm desperate now, with no way home in sight. So I'm going to have to trust him. And from the time we've spent together, he doesn't seem malicious. A little frivolous and irresponsible, sure.

But he cares about his sister, and about his tenants too.

And I'm running out of time as that letter saying I'm no royal gets closer.

But I can't worry about any of that right now. It's the reaction in front of me that I need to focus on. Because if she doesn't take this seriously or know how to help, then even sort of admitting I'm a time traveler in front of Leo was a waste.

The librarian sits back in her seat, crossing her arms and considering me. She's not even looking at Leo anymore, focusing all her curiosity on me.

"H.G. Wells has recently published a book on time travel called *The Time Machine*. And he's already written a short story on the subject called 'The Chronic Argonauts.'"

"Yes. In fiction." But he focuses more on the critique of his industrial society, using time travel as a literary device more than a scientific theory. Just like Mark Twain did in *A Connecticut Yankee in King Arthur's Court*, published six years before the date I'm in now. "Do you know if anyone's studying it or thinking of it as a *scientific* concept?"

"Time travel doesn't exist."

"No. Of course not." I force a laugh past my lips that I think might sound more maniacal than comforting. "Wouldn't that be wild?" I keep up the tight smile and attempt to throw a look at Leo, who is looking back at me without any expression on his face. I didn't even know the usually expressive man could do that. Again, no time to worry about that.

"It's interesting. And we've got to study something before we can completely rule it out. Maybe we'll discover something else. Electricity seemed like a wild concept at one time and now we can light rooms without fire," I say. They're not well lit, but points for trying.

The people around me respond to my babbling about as well as expected. More blank stares. So I fix a smile on my lips and hope the librarian says something helpful. Something that will send me home and make this trip and awkwardness worth it.

"You're incredibly lucky," she says. Well, the universe tore me out of the comfortable present and into the corsets of the past (both as a metaphor for what this time does to women and also, actual corsets). So, I'll reserve judgment vis a vis my alleged luck. "I think I might know someone who is studying physics and has an interest in time travel. Up at King's College, in Cambridge."

"That's fantastic," I breathe out in relief.

"I cannot guarantee he's accomplished anything. No one believes he will find anything, but we are all watching and gossiping about his attempts."

"Can you give me his name? Maybe I can visit him and talk about his findings."

The librarian writes something down and then hands me the paper. "Here's his full name." The paper says *Andrew Huxley.* "Good luck with your search."

"Thank you," I say.

I slip the sheet with a possible solution into my purse and turn to Leo, but his face reveals nothing. Instead of walking back to the entrance and to Anne, I take a few turns through book-shelves until we've gone deeper into the library, where even less light gets in and the smell of old books overtakes everything.

A comforting smell for an uncomfortable situation. At least Leo can't yell in the library. It's against the rules.

"So..." I avoid looking at him by instead focusing on the leather-bound books next to his head. Leo doesn't say anything, and I'm too cowardly to look him directly in his face to find out what he thinks. "You probably have questions?"

"Time travel?" His voice sounds shocked and a bit incredu-lous. "That is not possible. It is only in stories."

"Come on, you have to have noticed how strange I am. Doesn't this explain everything?"

Leo hits the back of his head on the bookshelf and then keeps it there, closing his eyes. "You are just...you..."

"I'm a product of another time."

"I cannot believe I am thinking this. But *when* do you think are you from?"

"The year 2025," I whisper. It's the first time I've said it out loud. I'm still half convinced someone is going to jump out of the stacks and commit me to Bedlam, but it feels good to get it out to someone. To get it out to *Leo*.

It may stop feeling good depending on what he does with the information. But for the time being, it's nice to be honest with someone who's been so honest to me.

"Where are you from, in 2025?"

"America. California, to be precise. Although I bet it looks different now than it does when I'm from it. I was in England for a conference, with an event at Osborne House, when this all happened. I am really a historian back home and I teach at a university. I study Indians in England in this particular time, actually. And you met me the first night I was in this time. The first hour."

"Are you royalty?"

Even though the British aristocracy looked down on Indians and half-Indians, they still felt a begrudging respect, or maybe more a tolerance, of Indians with royal blood. Or at least to the idea of royalty, from any place.

But while still taking their lands.

It makes little sense, but I'm not going to tell them that. It's why I'm glad I responded to Victoria's question with a yes that night, even if I thought it was a joke. Who knows where I would have ended up if it wasn't for that one question?

But even understanding the history, my heart sinks that it would be important to him. "No. I'm very common."

"I don't know that you are particularly common." He isn't yelling at me or calling for help to restrain me, so I risk a peek at his face. I can't see disgust, so maybe he isn't only obsessed with royalty. "Did you come in a...machine, or was it more a Rip Van Winkle type of transportation?"

"I hit my head falling down some stairs, so probably more the second one."

He nods, like this is a perfectly reasonable conversation to be having. His face still gives nothing away.

"Do you believe me?" I want him to. Not just because it bodes well for my safety if he does, but because I want him to trust me. Because I like him, and I trust him.

Leo shakes his head. "I do not think I can. It's too impossible."

"Oh." That's not exactly what I want to hear.

"Can you prove it?"

"Probably." I turn my hard-fought degree into a sideshow

trick and think back on what's happening right now. It's hard to do when the stakes are this high.

This is the worst history test I've ever taken and I feel a little bad for my students.

"On June 13, Emile Lavassor will come first in the first auto-mobile race, from Paris to Bordeaux to Paris at a whopping twenty-four kph. But he doesn't win because he's disqualified for having a two-seater instead of a four-seater, so Paul Keochlin is the official winner. But you have to wait for the thirteenth to verify that. And Charles, your Secretary of State for India and future Prime Minister, is having an affair with his best friend's wife. But I don't know how you'd verify that either."

This was easier in Twain's *A Connecticut Yankee in King Arthur's Court*. There was a convenient eclipse that the titular Yankee knew about happening in a matter of days. But I never paid attention to the weather patterns; unless something happened to derail crops and lose fortunes, it wasn't in the books I read.

"What? Forsyth and Lady Dumfries? That *is* news." He's distracted out of his emotionless response at the gossip. Now he has a look of delight on his face to know a thing that no one else does. Aside from me.

"Please don't tell anyone about the affair. I've been sort of lightly threatening him by alluding to it, and if you say something he'll know I'm talking and I'll lose the leverage."

Leo shakes his head. "I will not. I don't know if I believe you or not, but I suppose we can wait to find out. At least until June 13."

The letter must be coming before then, but it's the best I'll get. "Will you tell anyone in the meantime, about the time travel?" I ask.

He shakes his head. "No one would believe me if I did. I do not even know if I do. But while some will easily believe you have been lying, they will not believe you are from the future.

Then I will be branded a liar or insane and lose any benefit from our deal. And the deal is working for both of us, so we should keep it as is."

"Thank you," I mumble.

"It is at least half self-interest." Then he looks at me with sharp eyes. "What knowledge that beautiful head must hold, if this is true."

"Nothing more than what anyone else in my time knows." As a historian I might retain more of these facts, but everyone in the future at least has the opportunity to know them. It's probably not an important distinction for the sake of this conversation, but I don't want him to think I'm more unique than I am.

"Do you know what will to happen to me?" He asks it as a half joke, like he doesn't believe me but on the off chance this is true, he wants to know what happens to him.

"No." I don't point out that's probably because he doesn't do anything of note. "I don't know information on everyone here. Just the people who..." I don't know a non-offensive way to say the next part.

"Just the people who distinguished themselves. Good or bad. Enough to be remembered in the annals of history."

"Something like that."

"It's all right. I never expected to change the world. I never thought so much about the future in general, I guess. Maybe I should have." The last part is a mumble, more to himself than me, I think.

"Well, thank you for not abandoning me. That's pretty monumental and world changing to me." I'm so grateful this is how he's choosing to respond to my news. I would like him to completely believe me and support me, but that's too much to ask for and I'll take begrudging silence.

And the opportunity to spend more time with him.

If I have to go without Netflix and Instagram, at least I get to look at Leo. Like I am now. He's got a thoughtful look on his face, like he's still not sure he's being pranked, but he's going along for the ride until it stops being fun for him.

I smile back at him in thanks and he blinks in confusion. Probably wondering why I suddenly turned on that big a smile, so I dim it to what I hope is a normal level.

He stops the frequent blinking, but his eyes are now locked on my lips. And I realize I left my chaperone behind and I'm alone with Leo.

CHAPTER 17

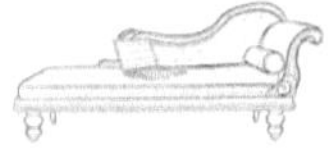

"I guess we should head back," I whisper. "I hope the queen doesn't get mad that I left. Not that she'll probably notice." But I don't want to piss her off before she even gets the letter.

"You're hard not to notice." Leo extends his fingers and plays with a curl that's sprung free from Anne's artfully arranged hairstyle. He tugs on it lightly, the slight sting dragging me back into this moment. Back from thoughts of what I'm going to do if the Cooch Behar royals say they don't know me. Back from thoughts on how to get home.

Then he uses that curl to tug me closer, and I go willingly.

"I'm usually very easy to ignore," I tell him because it's impossible to keep anything from him in this temple to knowledge. Lying, or lying by omission in letting him think I'm someone interesting and not just interesting because I'm from the future, feels wrong here. "Other historians do it all the time. And the general population doesn't care about my research either."

And I let it go. Because at worst, they'll be like the professor who laughed at me when I said I wanted to study Indian immigrants in England, and mock me, so sure they're right with their pre-conceived notions and biases of what "western" history is. At best, they'll just ignore me, or scoff every time a person of color is represented in western history, sure that history wasn't diverse because the one survey history class they had to take for their degree never mentioned it. And since it never gets through, I don't even want to try, because then I'll just fail again. Same as with dating.

But not now. Now I'll tell them with complete confidence that I know of at least one Indian royal(ish) who slept at Buckingham fucking Palace.

If I ever get home.

"It's just because I'm so different to everyone you know. Because I'm from…you know." Even though I don't say it, I feel a little thrill that I don't have to lie to Leo anymore. I've been so worried about what would happen if the truth got out, and now at least one person knows and I haven't been arrested. It's very freeing.

Leo doesn't dismiss the idea right away. He tilts his head and *considers*. I don't know if I would have preferred an instant and probably disingenuous denial over him actually considering if I'm boring in front of me.

Then he shakes his head. "I do not think so. This is London, and people come here from all over the world for business, pleasure, or a new start. And they have been coming for a while. Take my family as an example. Yes, London has never had anyone from the future to my knowledge. But I still do not think my interest is just because you are from a different place."

"You can't know that unless you meet more women like me! Then you'd see there's way more interesting people out there." I don't know why I'm trying to sell other future women to Leo so bad. I just don't want him to have the wrong idea about me. If he is interested, I want it to be because of *me*, not my strange future personality.

Not that this is going anywhere, regardless.

Leo snorts softly, respecting the silence of the library. "I do not think I could handle any more women like you."

As I open my mouth to tell him *again* that he just doesn't know what he's missing, he steps forward, so I step back. We keep up the dance until my back hits the hard leather spines on the bookshelf behind me.

"But I am very grateful, for however or to whatever brought you here, that you did come. And that I met you at that ball." He raises his hand to touch my cheek and I lean into it despite my resolution to stay away from Leo.

Then he closes the distance between our mouths, his full lips softly caressingly mine in little butterfly touches that make contact, withdraw and make contact again, repeating the process until I'm half-wild with wanting more. But, because he's irritating, he keeps it light.

I make a sound of frustration that doubles as a demand for more, abandoning all my principles of not getting involved in the past while I pull his shoulders in.

I slip my tongue past his lips, deepening the kiss as I drag him closer. His kiss warms me from my lips out to my extremities, giving me contentment and making me ravenous for more at the same time.

I don't feel like a boring option right now. With the way Leo reciprocates with enthusiasm, wrapping his strong arms around my waist so I'm surrounded by the feel of a wall of books on one side, and a wall of man on my other, it makes me feel like I'm as exciting as the people I read about, doing daring things and changing history. If I had any doubt that Leo's frenzied movements were a lie, the hard length he presses against me is impossible to refute.

The scents of the leather-bound books swirl with Leo's faint smell of bergamot, making a very specific catnip of my now two favorite things: books and kissing Leo.

We shift and slide against each other, trying to get more

contact in the embrace, in the process accidentally knocking a book off the shelf. The sound of heavy object hitting the rug in the quiet space, although muted, is enough to make me jerk my head up and away.

Leo reacts slower, and when denied access to my mouth, leaves a trail of kisses on my chin and neck while one firm hand grips my neck to stop my retreat, and the other on my breast. Making me forget why I was pulling away but making me feel even more desirable. Not even the threat of scandal and his new attempts at responsibility can drag him away.

But then other sounds filter in, and I think I hear footsteps. Or I'm paranoid about them and everything sounds like footsteps, so I push Leo away, almost knocking him into the opposite shelf. He resists for a half-second, before he makes a sound of frustration and pulls himself completely away.

Well, I've never done that in a library before.

Instead of saying anything, and because I have no idea what I even would say after that amazing kiss, I turn and walk out of the library, telling Anne we're ready to go on the way, and then leave the school. Once outside, Leo silently signals for his carriage, and we get into it. Leo tries to make conversation, but I take the coward's way and keep my responses monosyllabic. Even some nods and grunts.

Because even though he makes me feel more wanted than anyone in my time, things can't go further. I have to go back to that time; I can't be attached to the handsome rake in the past. Who is actively trying to marry someone who is not me.

Also: condoms? They've moved on from animal intestine and bladder "skin" condoms, so at least there's that. But I don't know where to get the rubber ones. And what if he prefers the skin condoms? Because initial market research on myself says no, I'm not ready for nineteenth-century condoms.

And what if time travel interfered with my IUD? Like antibiotics and the pill.

Nope. This is all too much for me to handle. So, I won't.

Leo is letting me have my delusion that the kiss in the library didn't happen, but he's not going to let me forget he exists. "I could take you to Cambridge," he says in a whisper.

"I don't know if that's such a good idea." Sure, I need to go. But with Leo? That's too much temptation.

"No, most likely not. But at least you do not have to tell me why…" He looks at Anne and clears his throat. "And my family seat is out that way, so it would be natural for me to go."

"Not with me," I whisper.

"No, most likely not." He has a decidedly rakish smile on now. "But if you find your answers, it will not matter what people are saying about you. And we could do it quietly."

I don't have many options. I don't have the money or resources to get there any other way. Still. If I do have to stay, that will ruin me. "We'll see what the queen thinks about it." Or if I can think of a way to do this without becoming London's most scandalous woman. Which is not something I thought I would ever have to worry about, frankly. "But thank you for the offer."

"I shall be here should you change your mind."

"Thank you, again." The kiss has made things awkward between us. I don't regret it, even though I should. Maybe Leo is having a bigger effect on me than I thought.

Because all I hear now is the newly discovered irresponsible side of me, telling me forcefully to tear off my multiple layers of clothes and throw myself at the arrogant marquess. Right in this carriage. Anne be damned.

I could use some of my responsible side, throwing cold water on me with statistics and well-reasoned arguments and maybe a pie chart about why this is a bad idea. Even my irresponsible side can't argue with a well-executed pie chart.

But the responsible coward is nowhere to be found, leaving me watching Leo warily and hungrily out of my peripherals in this carriage.

"I will see you tomorrow," Leo says when we stop in front of the palace and get out of the carriage, after Anne has already made her way inside, probably assuming I would be right behind her.

"You don't have to come every day. The plan is already working; you must have rich heiresses to call on too. Before they can be swooped up by someone else."

"They are not mice, and I am not a hawk."

"Sorry. Should I add more romance to the marriage mart?"

"Just the illusion of it, thank you. So I do not feel like all I have to offer this world is my name and seed." He looks at me expectantly—to see if I'll faint at his crudeness? Good luck with that; I teach college.

But it does feel like I hit on a sensitive issue. I've written a lot about how trapped the women must have felt in some of these cash for title arrangements, but at least some men resented the need for them as well, apparently. I don't feel *too* bad for them, though, because in this arrangement, they have more choices and more power.

"Well. You still need to move with haste before the fair maidens lose their hearts, and purses, to other fair suitors."

Leo tilts his head at me. "You do not have a high opinion on romance?"

"You're literally trying to marry a woman because of her fortune. Do *you* have a high opinion on romance?"

"I did not used to. Mother and Father began as a love match, and that love did not seem to last much longer than us children being born, if even that long. But my father genuinely loved his mistress. Not just as a diversion but as someone he *needed* to spend time with. So much that he sacrificed everything just to be with her all the time. Not that he had a lot to sacrifice since he went through most of his fortune and Mother's by the time he left. But he did sacrifice his reputation and family for her. Since he did it, I wondered what it would be like to feel so strongly for someone. To love someone to the point of ruin. Dangerous, but intriguing."

"That's unexpectedly romantic, in a messed up way. When we met, I thought you said you were only concerned with a good time. What happened to that?"

"Father made being in love, true love, seem like a good time. The ultimate good time if he was willing to sacrifice his lifestyle for it. Not that best time for us, but he seemed happy enough walking out the door to his new life. I want to love someone like that. And I would like to be loved like that. Although without all the destruction, preferably."

"So, you're not a rake?"

That makes him laugh. "I never said I was."

"I assumed. What with the loving of good times and the flirting with everything that moves."

Leo tilts his head. "And who else, aside from rich heiresses, have I flirted with?"

"Well, you know." I don't want to say it out loud. My cheeks are already starting to burn at just the thought of it.

"I don't."

"*Me.*"

"I like you."

I clear my throat and shift. "And the heiresses." I focus on the fact that he is pre-spoken for.

"That is necessity."

I hold his gaze for longer than I'm comfortable with, wishing for more than is reasonable right now.

We've been standing outside the palace for the entire conversation. Anne will wonder what's taking so long and come get me soon. She'd be wrong if she thought licentious things were happening.

Not that both of us aren't *thinking* licentious things, but even in the Victorian era, thinking about sex isn't illegal. Just frowned upon. And even that only publicly. I've seen your private pornography, Victorians. I know the secrets you keep. Filthy, naked, hot and sometimes confusing secrets.

"I really should go." But I don't move toward the palace door.

"Yes." Leo doesn't move either. Until I reach for the doorknob, then he jumps into action, opening it before I or the guard can get to it.

"There's a ball tonight," Leo says.

"Another one?" I'm aghast. When do these people find time to run the country, or take all those resources from India if they're constantly drinking Madeira and dancing in formation? It's mind-boggling.

"We are committed to balls."

I snicker. "I bet you just love the balls." I can't help myself. None of my students would respect me if I had just let it sit there. *I* wouldn't respect me.

Leo looks confused and I wave him away. I don't have the energy to explain that I have a dirty mind.

"If Her Majesty wants to go, I'll see you there." I turn and walk inside before we spend another hour saying goodbye. I'm getting worse than my mother, who has to say bye to my aunts or her friends about twelve times over the course of fourty-five minutes before she means it. I know; I've timed it, sitting in the car ready to go because I believed her when she said we were leaving a family party.

Like an amateur.

"Wait, were you laughing because I accidentally said the English like bollocks?"

I hear the question from behind me but don't stop to answer it because I'll probably lose it if I do.

That'll definitely make people talk about me.

And they won't be saying good things.

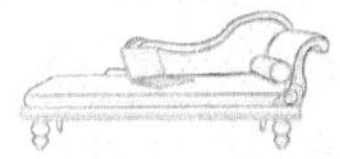

Victoria doesn't want to go out tonight. Not surprising; she doesn't go out much since Albert passed. I'm more surprised that she's gone out to the three balls we've been to in the past week, but two of those were at her house as part of her birthday celebrations, and the most recent was to introduce me to her godchildren, so maybe it isn't so hard to believe.

I'm more than happy with her decision. Even though it would have been nice to see Leo again, it's good to have time away from his magnetic presence. To build up some defenses against him, since he keeps making me forget why getting involved with someone from the past is a bad idea.

And he does need to work on those heiresses, despite what he thinks. A task I'd rather not see happening.

Victoria's decision also gives me more time with the longest-reigning monarch until 2015 when Elizabeth II takes that title from her. We have a nice dinner of curry, since I keep leaving during the lunch curries and Victoria doesn't want me to miss out, and some elaborately molded jellies for dessert.

She also agrees that I should go to Cambridge, after I said it would be good to see the university. Since I am here to learn. She's going to send Anne as a chaperone, and let me go with Leo, who she trusts implicitly.

A statement I would perhaps believe more if there wasn't a tinkle in her eye when she said it. A matchmaking twinkle.

Victoria is surprisingly chill about it.

Then again, maybe it wasn't so surprising. This is the same woman who took John Brown and Abdul the Munshi to Glassalt, the secluded lodge on the Balmoral Estate, which she called her "widow's house." Took both men there without any other people on the trips. I don't know what she did with them there, and no one but the parties involved ever will, but it is a fact they were alone, and it made tongues wag.

And women are travelling alone more at this time than they ever had, exploring the world around them with more and more freedom.

The rest of the meal is taken up with Abdul talking about India. Victoria's not the only one soaking up every word; this historian is glad to hear about what it's like in India at the time, through his perspective of living in Agra.

Another plus of the small dinner is there's less people to worry about. No odious Charles or overly curious aristocrats I have to perform for.

And no Leo to worry about for different, more lust-based reasons. Although he hasn't been far from my mind since I got here.

That night I go to bed with hope. I'm getting too involved with the marquess, but I have a next step that can lead to home. And that's more than I've had in a while.

"I HAVE HOW MANY VISITORS? *STILL*?" I ask Anne as she helps me get dressed for the day in my room.

I've never been this popular and I wish I could tell sixteen-year-old Meera how fucking exhausting popularity is.

And inconvenient. How am I supposed to soak up everything in Victorian London while trying to avoid how attracted I am to an actual aristocrat, *and* find a way home? All while serving as entertainment for bored rich people? Who I have to *socialize* with? No.

This is worse than the end of every semester, when students are panicking about how they did on finals and I have to grade like the wind while attending all the end-of-year wrap up events.

"Can we tell them I'm not in? And then shuffle me out of some secret passageway, maybe?" I ask as Anne finishes tightening my corset.

Anne suppresses a smile so quickly I don't know if I imagined it, and then nods. "Yes. We can do that. If you're sure you want to? It's a compliment that they want to see you."

"I can see why that is. But yes. Please."

"Her Majesty would approve. Except for the going out part." She opens my door to say something to a footman, and then comes back. "But I have to do everything in my power to stay with you this time. I have my instructions."

"That's all right." I could use someone who knows London. "Wait. Does she want you to report back to her? Have you been reporting back to her?"

Anne hesitates, the first moment of uncertainty I've seen from the woman. "Yes. You haven't done anything to worry about, though. A trip to the museum, a walk in the park, and a visit to a library are all appropriate activities."

I force my face to remain neutral when I remember exactly what we did in the library.

"But I am also to bring money for you and help you with whatever you want to see," she says.

It may be less than ideal, but I can't keep wandering around the city alone and penniless. Nor can I piss off a queen. "Thank you for your honesty. I won't leave you behind."

Anne finishes getting me ready, picking the least conspicuous dress she can. Sure, it's made of silk, but it's gray and only has a little bit of lace. And it's the best I'm getting in this palace.

"Is Lord Basildon one of the visitors?" I ask while Anne's distracted by making me presentable.

"He's not among those in the drawing room."

Well, good. That's what I want. I hope he's off charming some woman's bank account. And that it's going well for him, so he can live the outrageously spoiled lifestyle he's grown accustomed to.

True to her word, Anne sneaks me through the backstairs and other secret passages until I'm out in the British sun, this time in the front of Buckingham Palace. I only take a minute breathing in the atmosphere, because along with the morning air, there's the strong smell of coal, horse poop and sewage. The trifecta of Victorian London smells.

A very real, but less glamorous, part of history.

Smarter than the last time I did this, I turn to head to the stables, but Anne clears her throat and looks in the opposite direction. "Why don't we go this way?"

"But can't we use one of the queen's..." Then I see Leo, leaning against his carriage.

Today he's wearing a black suit, a green vest and a black coat showing the shape of his tapered torso. He leans nonchalantly, like he doesn't have anything else to do but wait for me, when I know for a fact he does.

"I thought you said he wasn't here," I murmur to Anne.

"I said he wasn't in the drawing room. He wanted to surprise you." I can tell by her affectionate tone that she thinks it's the height of romance. And since I can't exactly run around the gated area yelling "It's all a ruse!" I guess I'll have to play charmed courtee.

"Hi, Leo. Ur, I mean Lord Basildon," I say when we're close

enough that I don't have to yell anymore. This title thing takes a long time to get used to, especially since I've been using his first name in my head this entire time.

"Good morning, Your Royal Highness. But you know you can call me Leo if you want." Oh good; we've kissed and now we can move on to a first name basis. Even though we'll probably cause a scandal with all our public first-naming.

"Call me Meera, then. What are you doing here? I thought you were going to be *busier* from now on." I put emphasis on *busier*, because we both know what he should be doing.

"What kind of man would I be if I left the woman I was courting to the wilds of London with no guide?" He winks at me. He's recovered from me being a future-lady rather well. Or he just doesn't believe me.

"I don't know if either of you want to go where I'm going today," I say. "And there's no use in stopping me; I need to go."

"I had a nice outing planned as well, but we can do what you would like. Where to?" Leo asks while he helps me up into the carriage.

"Limehouse, please," I say once I'm in. I don't acknowledge the shock that my words cause. Leo stops in the process of helping Anne in, and she stops with one foot on the stair and the other hovering just off the ground.

"Devil take it, we cannot possibly go there," Leo says. Anne cuts grateful eyes over to him, glad to have an ally in controlling me and my wild ideas.

"I assure you, we can. We just take the Strand or Embankment and then just keep going east past the Tower until we hit it. Simple, really."

"Pedantic," Leo says through gritted teeth. "But *why* would we go there?"

"I have to see it." I have relatives, great-great-whatever-greats-relatives who came to London. As lascars; not as pretend or real nobility. They didn't stay, making the voyage back and forth as often as they could to make a living as sailors. And the British sure did make it unnecessarily hard to get back by making laws that said crews leaving had to be a certain percent English, before India was under the British Raj.

But when they were here, they probably lived in Limehouse. It would have been crowded and hard, in a climate they weren't used to, abandoned with too little money after they did the hard work required of the voyage over. A very different experience than the many Indian upper- and middle-class scholars or dignitaries who came to England for advancement, education or fun. But an equally important one.

And I have to see it. Experience it. Document it. For the historian in me, but also for the child of Indian immigrants.

"It is not safe," Leo says.

"Neither is a country estate for a governess, yet they keep going there."

"Fair point. But this is *really* not safe."

I roll my eyes. "We'll be fine. Because it won't be the first set of curious aristocrats coming to get something there they can't in West London. Or the first set of reformers trying to help without understanding any of the root causes of the problems, which spoiler alert, are policy based. They're used to you people."

"This is a bad idea."

Maybe. But I need to walk the same streets as my ancestors did. The first immigrants in a long line that led to my parents and then me. "You two can stay in the car...riage." Not a car. Cars exist right now but this isn't one.

"I am not letting you go in alone."

I roll my eyes but don't argue. It's probably the best I'm going to get. "Don't know how you're going to help in this situation, but all right. It's not like I can legally stop you from entering the area."

I get out my notebook and pen, ready to take notes on this trip. Leo raises an eyebrow when he notices which notebook it is.

"What? It's a good gift." I hold it closer to my chest in case he has any ideas about taking it back.

"I am glad you are enjoying it," he says neutrally.

I tune out the judgement coming from across me in the small space over our destination, letting my own mind gather thoughts and questions I want to ask people. I jot down some general themes and organize some open-ended questions while they're still fresh in my mind.

Since every witness to my time period is dead when I'm studying it, I don't do a lot of interviews. So I have no idea how I'm going to go about things aside from maybe finding a pub and offering to buy a drink to anyone who will talk to me.

Actually, that sounds like a solid idea.

I open the carriage window and hang my head out, clutching the side of the door in case it decides to get a wild hair and open while I'm halfway out of it. "Excuse me! Do you know the busiest pub in Limehouse?" I yell up at the coachman.

"Miss, you want me to take you to a pub? In the Oriental Quarter?"

I wince. That might be what the area is called right now, but I don't have to like it. Nor is now probably the time to explain why that's not the best. "Yeah. Like where there are people and food and alcohol."

"It's fine. Take us to a pub, please," Leo says from the opposite window. I can't see him because the carriage is in the way, but it's nice he's not arguing with me anymore about why this is a bad idea.

When I pull myself back into the carriage, I can plainly see on his face that he still thinks this is a bad idea, but he's helping. That deserves another giant smile. His eyes go straight to my lips at the movement, and I turn my face away before I give in to the urge to kiss him again, chaperone be damned.

But Leo isn't one to be ignored for long. "I missed you last evening."

"Yes. Her Majesty wanted to stay in for the night."

"Well. I had some interesting conversations. First, I spoke to the most well-informed gossips, and they knew nothing about Forsyth." I tense at the mention of the name. "And then I made some pointed remarks around the lady in question, and, well. I believe you."

"You told…them?" I look to Anne to make sure she isn't catching on to what we're talking about.

Leo shakes his head. "I was very discreet. I told her about a situation I heard about, involving someone else, and her guilty reaction confirmed for me what you were saying was true. Which means, what else you said must be true, too. No matter how absurd."

I breathe a sigh of relief that he believes me. It shouldn't matter, but it does, and I don't want to think too deeply about that.

Instead, I focus on the view outside the window. The streets are getting narrower now, and darker as the height and closeness of buildings cut off natural light. The smell is the same though: horrible. Apparently, that can't get worse. Noise, already a problem in the posh parts of town, increases along with the number of people out in the streets. We make more stops now, as the street gets more chaotic around us.

Then we stop for longer than usual.

"We're here. I think the Grapes will fit the bill," the coachman calls out to us.

"Excellent." I fix a confident smile on my face that I don't entirely believe and leave the carriage.

If I hadn't told the coachman where to take us, I would be shocked at where I started and where I ended up. Because even intellectually knowing there's a divide between the West and East Ends of London in the form of a truly obscene wealth gap, it wouldn't have been enough to prepare me for the change between my starting location and the destination.

It's like I'm in an entirely different world.

I nod and smile in greeting to the people closest to me, but power through into the pub. Leo, Anne, and his coachman following behind with much less enthusiasm.

A complete silence descends as almost everyone stops what they're doing to look at me; a silence as deafening as a scream when compared to all the noise outside. A sea of faces looks back at me. Everyone has on worn clothing, but the outfits themselves are a mix between South Asian, English, African and Chinese clothes to reflect the diversity of this neighborhood of London.

"Hello… everyone," I say nervously.

CHAPTER 19

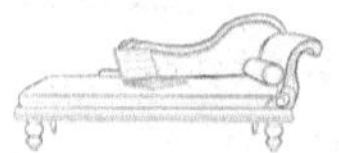

"You can say you want to turn around and leave at any point, and we shall go. You do not have to prove anything to anyone," Leo whispers in my ear.

"No. Everyone's just curious. Because we're being weird. So be less weird." I turn to the crowded room. I remind myself that I regularly lecture in classrooms and at conferences, but the overly critical part of my brain points out that they want to hear me, or have to for college credits they need to graduate. No one here needs to give me their time. And all my insecurities about making a scene and standing out well up.

Where are all my helpful notes? Unfortunately, not that helpful right now.

The truth is probably a good place to start. Well, some of the truth. The whole truth would be decidedly *unhelpful*. "I'm doing some research and I would appreciate if anyone not from England would speak to me about their experiences here. In return, we'll buy everyone drinks for as long as we're here talking to someone. Or for however long I have money; whichever happens first. We'll be over there." I point to an empty booth near the back windows, overlooking the Thames. "If you want to chat with us." I repeat the offer in Hindi, then Urdu, then Punjabi for good measure. "Anne, can you please pay the barman?"

I smile to the narrow but crowded room and make my way to a booth with faded red upholstery, heart racing at the thought that no one will speak to me. I open my notebook to a fresh page and get my pen out and ready.

I use the time to recover from my bout of assertiveness. Since it doesn't come naturally to me, it's a tiring experience. But looking at the empty book, ready to be filled with knowledge, helps ground me again.

We sit there for a few minutes in silence when I start taking notes on the room around me. The dark wood paneling of the walls, bar and furniture all give the pub more atmosphere than a BBC special on Jack the Ripper. The light isn't electric, so dim kerosene lamps illuminate the space while they blacken the walls around them with soot.

Slowly, the din of the bar starts to grow again, people deciding I'm not as interesting as they first thought I was going to be.

"They will not talk to you," Leo says when it appears that no one will.

"Everyone wants to be heard. They just don't trust us, and they have no reason to. Let's give it fifteen more minutes."

Time limit imposed, I write even faster. I get not wanting me here. I represent, to them, the part of society made of rich assholes who make their lives harder by needing their labor but cutting pay while passing laws to make it seem like they're the problem so they're unpopular with the public. Whose pay and jobs are also being cut. A tactic that will far outlive Victoria's reign, unfortunately.

Finally, just before my time limit is up and just as Leo is standing to put his coat back on, I get up again.

"Good afternoon, again. Listen, I know you've seen a lot of people like...well, us come by and make promises and not deliver, or condescend to you under the guise of charity, and I just want you to know I'm not promising anything. I can't. We can't. We don't have the power or influence. But I think you are all important, and I think your stories are important. You don't know how much I do. So the one thing that I can promise, is that I'll listen. Because everyone here has a life, has dreams, has likes and dislikes. And I want to hear them, because once upon a time my family were here, doing this work, in this town, and I never got to talk to them about what that was like. I want to listen to your story, I want to learn about my story, and I want to tell our story. And maybe I'll tell someone who can help. That's it. That's all I can promise."

Another silence, and I'm about to give in and collect my notebook when a man approaches me tentatively. He's older, his hair a wiry gray, and the wrinkles on his face showing his years. His clothes are middle-class, but worn, as if he hasn't bought new ones in a while. I sit back down with a relieved smile and Leo sits down on a sigh.

"Hello. Is it all right if I ask you some questions?" I indicate the chair across from me tentatively.

"Fine," he says in Urdu.

"Great. Thank you." I switch to the language as well. I open to a fresh page in the book and put on my historian hat.

"What's your name?"

"Rajab Ali."

"It's nice to meet you. I'm Meera Chopra. Can you tell me how you came to be in London?"

"When the British first came to India with the East India Company, they encouraged intermarrying among the company employees and local women. My family was one of these families. However, they later decided they did not trust the loyalty of these Anglo-Indian children, and so the practice was discouraged and there was discrimination against us. However, my family always passed down both of their identities, and I could read and write both English and Urdu. There weren't many opportunities for me in India because of my heritage, so I lied, said I was fully Indian, and got on a lascar group coming to London."

"How were the conditions on the ship?"

"Awful. It was so crowded. The European sailors had an amount of space they had to be allotted, by law, but we were given less. Diseases spread instantaneously in those ships, and we never got as good treatment, either. We weren't given fruit, like the European sailors were, and had different stores entirely; not as good ones. We weren't paid as much either. But it was worth it to get to London."

"What happened when you got to London?"

"I was able to find work teaching Urdu at a school to middle-class boys hoping to join the civil service in India. I was one of the few people who could read and write both languages, and I enjoyed the work. Although I think I would have enjoyed anything after being on a ship."

"What happened then?"

He sighs. "I was happy for years, had an established life here and earned good money, but then it ended. They decided to hire one of my former students to replace me. He never really understood the language like I did, but they wanted him and not me regardless. So I went back to India. As a passenger this time." He sits up straighter at that.

I smile. "That must have been better."

"Much." He smiles back at me. But then it fades. "But home didn't feel like home. I was away in England too long, and everything seemed off. I had missed my family, but home felt like a memory, and not somewhere I was meant to be."

"What did you do next?"

"I convinced my parents to come with me, and I moved back to London. I worked in a shop in the Limehouse area since I could speak to the sailors and the owners and saved enough money to open a restaurant here. Mostly Indian food."

"Congratulations! I don't know how long I'll be here, but I hope to eat there before I leave."

"I hope so too."

"Did you think you made the right decision, moving?"

"I think so. There weren't many opportunities for me where I was. There weren't a lot here, either, but my skills and experience were more useful here. I'll never know for sure, but I think I had a better life here. I still miss friends that I haven't seen in decades, but overall I'm happy with my life here. My family is here, and my children don't know any other home. But sometimes, I mention a place I loved in India, and they look at me in confusion. It's strange to think they know nothing of the place I grew up aside from what I tell them. I just hope I made the right choice, and they will have a more comfortable life than I had."

"You made sure they will." Just like my parents did. By way of plane and not ship, but they came as teachers, just like Rajab. He nods in acknowledgment and returns to the bar to take us up on the free drinks.

After him, more feel comfortable talking with us, and drinking with us. They don't tell me too much that I don't already know big picture-wise, but they add human faces and human details that are often left out of history books, since most books on the subject rely on English sources talking about them instead of their own voices.

Some came over as lascars, who were dumped in London when the ships were done with them, at times had no way to get home, and faced increasing hostility from English people. But they still took happiness where they could find it, because it is a very human urge to strive for happiness in the worst of conditions.

The people here have lives, people they love, jobs they enjoy. Babu met and fell in love with an English woman who he's currently married to. Hassan originally came to work at a country house estate up near York before they fired him. He got some partners and raised enough money to start a boarding house for Indians in Limehouse.

We speak to a royal who couldn't prove his title and who had to basically couch surf until people in the West End got tired of him, when he moved to Limehouse to live in Hassan's boarding house and is looking for work. Then there's the medical student who's studying in London and came to Limehouse to get Indian food that reminded him of home.

Some want to go back home but can't find a way back, while others like the opportunities they found here. But none had the same experience. Their treatment was decided by factors like their class, job, wealth, and who they were interacting with.

Their experience here and now is so different from the experience of early Indians I've studied in books, even from before the East India Company started taking India over. The early Indians could define their own identity here, because Britons didn't have any knowledge of them. I read about Emin, an early immigrant, who was constantly asked where he was from, and one confused Briton said that as long as he wasn't French, everything was fine.

Things changed, and became harder, after colonialism. An Indian identity was set by the government, and it involved making England the heroes, and India in need of their "saving," and "less than." As hard as it was, and as many people were miserable, many also had good lives here and were successful. Because no group of people's experiences are the same. Because history is complex and has so many nuances it can never be distilled into one sentence.

Leo relaxes enough to get food next to me, probably bored now that this has turned into long set of interviews in languages he doesn't understand. When they're in English, Leo looks interested in hearing people he'd probably never meet otherwise. Good. Maybe he can help. In Parliament.

Once the sky starts to get darker, Leo taps on my elbow. "We should probably head back now. Someone will be very mad if you do not get back before nightfall."

"You're probably right." I don't have to agree with a curfew to understand I don't want to be kicked out of the palace.

We get up to leave. "Thank you, everyone, for your time." A cheer goes up as we leave, since we've been buying drinks for the past few hours, and we're very popular around here.

"We're buying a meal for everyone as thanks," Leo says on our way out, dropping money at the bar to pay for it to a chorus of cheers.

"That's kind of you," I say as we leave the pub. "Can you pay for that?"

"As I keep saying: I am already going down. That amount was not likely to save me." Leo shrugs. "It was interesting hearing their stories. I never thought how hard…or how they lived…well, I just did not think about the lascars or other Indians at all, I suppose. Even though they are the reason for most things I touched today, from the linen of my shirt to the tea I drank waiting for you." At least he sounds chagrined by that. "And they come from the same place as Mother…" He trails off, probably thinking that but for a few twists of fate, he would have been in Limehouse and not in his English country estate. Or in India.

"Maybe you can introduce bills in the House of Lords to help?" It's changing the past, but he probably won't be able to get it passed anyway. And it's important to try.

"Yes." He's quiet. He keeps looking back to the pub, uncomfortable confronting his privilege. As most people are. At least he didn't lash out like people tend to.

We get back in the carriage and I immediately start looking over my notes. But then the setting sun and low light in the carriage makes me admit defeat and I close the book. I look up to see Leo staring at me.

He shakes his head. "Such a curious woman."

"Thank you for today. For bringing me here and staying with

me. And being generally accepting about my…curiousness." I remember last minute that we still have a chaperone and I can't say, *"Thanks for being cool about the whole time travel thing. I thought for sure that would scare you off. But it didn't. Must be that stiff upper lip those posters that haven't been drawn yet talk about."*

"You're welcome."

"Maybe tomorrow we could do another London day so we get seen out and about, and then the day after, we could go to Cambridge? Her Majesty's all right with you taking me, as long as I take Anne to chaperone."

"Let's go!" Anne says, still a little drunk from her day of doing nothing but drinking.

"We have a plan then. I know just where to take you tomorrow. You will enjoy it immensely," Leo says.

"And you'll be seen carting around a temporary royal ward, right?"

Leo rolls his eyes, like he's exasperated that I'm thinking about the deal. One of us needs to be concerned with him getting what he needs.

"Yes. I will take you to places other than my bedroom. There will be other people around to see us together." His voice is a little sharper than necessary.

"I'm just making sure you get something out of being my guide. I know it's a lot I'm asking."

"What about the pleasure of your company?"

"It's not enough." I hunch my shoulders by my ears, not wanting to list all the reasons I'm not enough. "My bank account isn't enough." Not only is it not enough, it's also in a bank that doesn't even exist yet.

"Damn the bank account!"

"You don't mean that. And my home is…" I look at Anne. "Far away."

Leo hangs his head in defeat. "We shall be seen by everyone. You will be happy to know I danced with multiple heiresses last night, at the ball you were not at, that had only mildly objectionable fortune origins. And with Miss Chilcott twice."

"That's good." Even though the churning in my stomach suggests my body thinks it's the opposite of good news. "But you should have called on her today." The churning gets worse when I keep pushing him toward other women. Acid fighting regret and whatever else is down there to make me as miserable physically as I am mentally.

"You can stop shoving me off on other women. I know exactly what is at stake here if I fail to make a good match. I look at my sister's face every day and answer her questions about what is going to happen to her if we lose the houses and if she needs to marry. I hear her worry. I even hear the worry of my tenants, wondering the same thing, minus the marriage issue." His voice rises with each sentence, leaning forward over the middle of the carriage to emphasize his words.

I sink farther back into the carriage cushions. Because I don't like Leo being upset at me. So I fall back into old patterns of retreat at a confrontation. Ones I thought I had actually been doing a good job getting over, since I've had to assert myself more here than I ever did at home.

"I'm only trying to help. The way you've helped me." Even though it's not easy to watch him be with other women when I'm this attracted to him. When I want to pound my fists and jump up and down, demanding he get a real job and sell off some shit and be with me.

But I'm not a permanent feature here and have no right to be making demands.

Leo deflates as well. "I'm sorry, I did not mean to snap. I do not like thinking about what I have to do. But you are right; it needs to be done. I should focus more on the task."

"So tomorrow we'll do see-and-be-seen things around London. And then we'll go to Cambridge the day after."

"Yes." There's the slightest hint of regret in his voice.

Which I ignore. If I can ignore the fact that it should be impossible to time travel and hang out with the Queen of England in 1895, I should be able to ignore the allure of the attractive man sitting across from me. Who I've already kissed.

It can't be harder than ignoring the fact that I'm living in one of my own academic journal articles.

Yet…it kind of is.

THE NEXT MORNING, I know what to expect with my callers. I grit my teeth and smile even though everyone in the drawing room is still staring at me like I know the location of Alexander the Great's tomb at a Classics convention.

It's been days. How are they still so interested in me? Although this may be more a result of no social media than my sparkling personality.

But Leo comes inside this time, now that he knows we have plans and I'm not a flight risk, which makes the circus more bearable.

He's born to do this, to charm everyone around him. They obviously know his family's scandal and should avoid him, but they still laugh openly with him, no sign of condescension or awkwardness.

Or maybe our plan is working that well, and a royal stamp of approval can override anything.

He cuts the length of visits down more efficiently than I ever would have, being firm but polite to everyone while he kicks them out of the room like he owns the palace.

Must be an aristocrat thing. They had to have some skill set, and it definitely wasn't working.

Soon after everyone leaves, he's rushing Anne and me into the carriage. I'm still a little dazed and a lot grateful at how much smoother the visit went with him by my side.

"Where to today?" I ask, shaking off the effects of being surrounded by too many damn people against my will.

"You are going to enjoy this. We are going to—no. It will be more fun to surprise you once we arrive."

"But I hate surprises."

"Who hates surprises?" Leo openly laughs at me.

"They're stressful. What if I don't like surprise? What if I don't adequately show how excited I am about the surprise? Then how do I reciprocate for the surpriser to show them they are just as appreciated? It's too much responsibility."

Leo laughs harder. "A surprise is for your enjoyment. It is not the beginning of a contract. Or a tactic for manipulation."

"Naive."

"Curious." But he says it with a wink this time. Because he knows exactly why I'm so "curious" now. "Tell me, how did Her Majesty react when you told her where we went yesterday? She did not lock you away, so I assume all is well."

"I didn't tell her." I performed verbal gymnastics to avoid telling her exactly where we went when she asked at dinner. I think she thinks we went to Hyde Park again, but I'm too afraid to ask outright.

We both look to Anne.

"And admit I let you go to Limehouse? That's more than my job's worth. And nothing happened anyway, so no need to tell," Anne says.

I smile at Anne, sure I'm growing on her, my curious ways and all.

The carriage stops in front of a row of terraced houses. On the other side of the street is a large green square, filled with leafy trees and birds singing a cheery hullo to us. Leo helps Anne and me out of the carriage and leads us to one of the houses in the row. It's a four-story house with large windows overlooking the street we're standing on, white stone covering a layer of brick that I can see on the fourth floor. On the third level, two classical statues of women look down at me and the street-goers.

I rack my brain, trying to think about where we are, but nothing around me gives me any answers. We're still in the fancy part of London; that much I can tell. "I give up. Where are we?"

"You will see when we go in. You will like it, though," Leo says with confidence.

"You can't know me well enough to know that."

Leo raises an eyebrow to taunt me. "Would you like to wager on it?"

"Didn't wagering get you into this mess?" I ask gently.

"Yes," Leo answers immediately, without taking offense. "But this is not hazard. I have done the work, researched the issue, and I am confident that you are going to like this. So confident I know I will not lose. It is not even gambling at this juncture."

His confidence is infectious and stirs a competitive side I didn't even think I had. "Sure, let's wager. What are we wagering for?"

"If I win, you must wear what I pick for you tonight's ball, without question."

"That sounds dangerous. And if I win—"

"Let's not spend too much time worrying about that. On the off chance you win, you can have whatever you want." Leo snags my arm and starts up the stairs.

"This is the sort of reckless tomfoolery that got you—"

"Speaking of reckless tomfoolery, the surprise is deep into the house, so I must request you walk with purpose through some rooms." I open my mouth to respond to that, but Leo keeps talking. "You can go back and look at them all you want, but the best part is the third room in. That is the one I want to see your reaction to. That room that will win me this wager."

Okay, so he does sort of know me even though we've only met a few days ago, if he knows I'm going to linger in the rooms.

I do love a good historic house (or just a house, as they would call it right now).

I don't know if that means he's a very perceptive man or if I'm very predictable, but either way, it makes me worry about the wager.

I'm beginning to think I'll be wearing whatever he wants me to, and I can only hope it's not Princess Leia's gold bikini or Princess Jasmine's turquoise crop top. My only saving grace is that neither of those things exist yet to give Leo ideas.

This is why gambling is bad. There's no such thing as a sure thing.

"Fine. We'll move with purpose to get to the special room of wonderfulness."

Leo opens the door and leads me through a wood-paneled hallway, then a nicely decorated room with a fireplace. I would love to see what period the pieces are from and the overall theme of the house, but Leo is firmly tugging me along. Forcing me to ignore all the furniture and sculptures on the way, like a monster. And there's a lot of furniture and sculpture to ignore here. Each room is packed with stuff. And I love stuff.

"But we're right here, I can take a quick—" I crane my neck back and slow my pace to soak in as much as possible while still technically moving forward.

"We shall come back." Leo doesn't sound mad or annoyed. More amused that I keep trying to ruin his surprise even after I agreed not to do this. "It has been there for decades, so it is unlikely that everything will up and disappear on us at this late stage."

"So you're saying there's a little chance?"

Then Leo stops. I don't realize it until a second later when his arm pulls me to a stop as I keep walking forward.

And then when I finally turn my head around, I gasp.

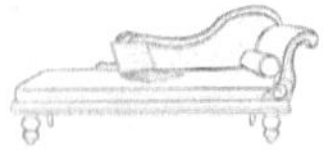

I have no idea what I'm wearing tonight, but I'm going to put it on with a smile. Leo deserves it.

"You like museums. So I thought you might like to see this one."

That is two understatements in a row. Because I love museums...and I love this. I'm in a crowded balcony overlooking a space topped with a dome letting in natural light. The light bathes antiquities, which fill in every inch of the space, lining the walls and even resting on the railing. Pieces of friezes and other architectural elements, vases and urns, as well as sculptures are crammed onto the walls. All looked over by a naked man with a fig leaf covering his bits, which is on the same level as us.

"You brought me to Sir John Soane's house," I say in delight. A place in London I've never had the time to visit since England has an embarrassment of riches when it comes to history and things to study, and this is slightly outside my time period.

"Yes. Architect. Neo-classicist. Passionate collector. Whose house is now a museum. I thought you would enjoy visiting since you liked the British Museum so much."

"Visit? I want to live here." I turn in a slow circle, taking in the art around me. "There's so much to study. I would never be bored!"

"It might not be exciting as this, but my old pile has a few things that might interest you. That you can see on the way to or from Cambridge."

"Hmm." I get my paper and pen out. I didn't bring the whole notebook because I thought we were going to do boring things, but I brought a few sheets, just in case I saw something I'd want to record. Big mistake, but better than nothing. "Shouldn't you have sold them off already?"

Wait. People do not like to be reminded of their problems. I should not have been so blunt. But with me distracted by this beauty, it slipped out.

"Probably. But we had the auctioneers in and they gave us an estimate of what we could expect to earn. The estimate was not enough to pay off the debts without also selling the house itself. So, I am trying the marriage route first. Maybe we can save it all. Either way, the creditors have been so kind as to give me to the end of the season."

"Ah." I look around and notice one thing that isn't here. "Not that I don't appreciate this outing, but…there's not a lot of people here. To see us." Just Anne, lingering behind us. Not close enough to be in the conversation, but close enough that I can't jump the man without being seen. Not that I should be jumping him, either way.

Leo wags a finger at me. "I have thought this through. If we are only seen at the obvious places, this might look artificial. But I made sure to pass the most fashionable places in London, and I brought the open-top carriage. We will linger over a picnic in Lincoln's Inn Fields across the road. And then tonight, everyone will see plenty." He sounds smug.

"All right. As long as you've got a plan." That means I can enjoy this museum without guilt. "Wait. Are you using your art collection to get me alone in your house?" But I'm not mad. It's actually quite considerate that he cares enough to pay attention to what I like and cater our outings to that. Even though this is supposed to be a deal that gets us both something, he's still making sure I'm enjoying it. It's sweet.

But I'm still going to tease him about it.

"No." Leo straightens up to the best posture I've ever seen in a human and not a wooden plank. He's affronted now. "I am a gentleman. I would never lure an innocent young woman to my home."

"Suuuuuuure. You just happened to discover my weakness and now you're trying to cater to it while you tell me about where I can find more of the good stuff. In your lair."

While Leo is sputtering in righteous indignation (and turning just the slightest bit red), I drag him (and Anne) back to the beginning and take my time inspecting every room of this museum. In his bequest, Soane said that everything had to be kept exactly how it was in his life, and the resulting museum is a fascinating look inside the mind of the architect. There's a room with models of classical buildings and a painting hallway with paintings hung onto large swinging panels, for easier storage.

And gargoyles. And an empty sarcophagus.

The upper rooms are less wild that the ones we saw in the beginning, and soon I'm releasing Leo and Anne, both yawning prodigiously, from the beautiful prison.

"Thank you. That was amazing."

"Excellent. I hope you can keep that attitude into this evening," Leo says.

"OH, HELL NO." I cross my arms over my chest, exuding stern negativity in the direction of my chaperone, like a nun seeing a dirty cartoon drawn in the margins of a Bible. "I'm not wearing that; it's absurd."

"Lord Basildon did make that wager with you. And win it." Anne holds up the offending garment. I don't know how she's doing it; with that much silk, heavy embroidery and pearls on it, the dress has to weigh a ton. "And Her Majesty approved. She thought you might like the Indian pattern on the skirt."

My complaints aren't so much with the admittedly very pretty gold and maroon design as it is with the width of the silk dress. Anne has multiple petticoats (one with actual metal hoops) next to her, and I'm to understand they're an "all" situation, not an "or" one. Together, they're going to add the width of four extra people to me—two on each side.

And don't get me started on the wig. It's very large, and the resulting height would qualify me for some basketball teams. Not good ones, as I still have no skills.

"If it helps at all." Anne's tone is aggrieved, wishing I'd stop making her job so hard. "Lord Basildon will be wearing knee breeches and silk stockings. And heels."

Leo finally told me exactly what we're doing tonight: going to a Georgian fancy dress party thrown by the Duchess of Devonshire. He said he had picked out the costumes, so I had nothing to worry about.

Clearly, he and I have different opinions on worry-worthy topics. Like right now, I'm worrying about how I'm going to get through doors, or into carriages. Or how many vases and glasses I'm going to knock over because I have no concept of how wide I am as a result of an ill-conceived bet with a man who apparently knows me better than I thought.

"Silk stockings, you say?"

"They'll shimmer when they hit the light, showing off his manly legs."

"Are you sure I'll be able to fit through doorways?" I give the dress another doubtful look.

"Yes. Devonshire House was rebuilt during the Georgian period, when this style of dress was popular."

I'm still skeptical, but a deal is a deal. "All right. Let's do this," I say with all the enthusiasm of a first-time sailor getting conscripted, against their will, to fight against France with Admiral Nelson.

Without any more complaints out of me (or at least a lessened amount of verbal complaints and some in my head while I physically comply), Anne gets me ready. Then she leads me to a drawing room where Leo is already waiting. He's looking out a window, but turns when I brush against a statue with my skirt and make it teeter precariously before it settles back down.

I'm so focused on almost destroying history, watching in horror and not being able to get closer for fear I'll knock something else over, that I don't see what Leo's wearing at first. When I'm confident I haven't destroyed anything, I look up at the person waiting for me.

Just like Anne predicted, he has on silk tights. I didn't even think I was that attracted to calves, yet here I am, lusting. Maybe we should bring back tights on men.

When my eyes travel up the rest of Leo, the lust doesn't go away, despite the fact that he's wearing a blue, gold, and cream outfit that might be louder than my dress.

And my dress is very loud.

When I get to his eyes, I find that they're doing the same thing, but they got stuck somewhere along my décolletage. I run through my emotions to see how I feel about that, and to my surprise, my lips curve into a smile. I'm flattered. And I was just ogling his calves, so I don't have the moral high ground here.

"Good evening." Leo bows in greeting and I do my awkward bow-squat since no one has actually taught me how to officially curtsy.

"Good evening…my lord."

"You look beautiful." And he looks sincere, not like when he throws out easy compliments to charm everyone around him into doing what he wants. I've seen enough of that in these past few days, all used to defend and distract from me, so I can tell the difference.

"Thank you. You look good too," I say softly.

I'm shy now. I've gone traipsing around London with this man, have told him that I'm a time traveler from the future, and sucked face with him, but now he's giving me compliments and I'd rather have to translate manuscripts from Old English in a windowless college basement than face the kind words.

Not that I don't like the compliment. No, that's not the problem. It's giving me very warm feelings that I am eighty-five percent sure aren't because of the bodice I'm wearing. But facing Leo and wondering if it's real or part of the ruse, wondering if it can ever be real since I'm such a novelty to him, and trying to remember how normal people react to compliments, is stressful.

But still, I'm going to write this in my notebook too. Because whatever reason made him say it, this is a moment I want to remember. It's not one that's worth historical note, not a moment that's going to make it into any articles or books. But it makes me happy and I want to record it.

"We should get going." We've been standing here staring at each other for what is probably longer than is socially acceptable, both in the Victorian era and in the modern one.

"Yes." The words jolt Leo out of the stillness we were in, and he rushes to me, offering his arm, which I take.

I don't know that I'll ever get over how nice it is for him to always offer me his arm. Yes, I can walk on my own, but it's so nice to have the connection to Leo when we're out. Like we're a unit, and also like he needs to keep touching me when we're together. It makes me feel wanted, which is not always something I always got back in the future.

Not only did no one want my research, but it seemed like no one wanted to date me, either. (To be entirely fair to the men of the present, I've been accused of spending too much time with books about the past to notice anyone, but that's just an opinion from my grad school roommate.) I've never felt like that with Leo, though. I might still mostly think he's more interested in how different I am than me as a person, but I don't doubt the intensity of his interest. And his interest makes me feel warm. It has me hoping it's because of me, and not just my novelty.

The carriage ride is uneventful and quick (with a slight delay as Leo had to figure out how to get my wide ass in the seat; the answer being making Anne sit with the coachman and making me kneel diagonally in the middle of the carriage), and too soon we're at Berkeley Square. Too soon, because I prefer being alone with Leo, even though that defeats the whole purpose of us spending time together.

"Ready for more balls?" Leo asks as he helps me out of the carriage, a suppressed smile letting me know he's thinking about our earlier conversation regarding balls. But if he thinks I'm going to back away from that, he doesn't know me as well as he thinks he does.

Or the new, time travelling me, at least.

"I'm always ready for balls." I leave Leo standing by the open door of the carriage, delighting in my foray into innuendos. They are fun; I can see why so many historical figures wrote them into the saucy letters to their lovers.

I hear his laugh booming behind me, getting louder as he jogs to catch up with me.

Leo grabs my arm gently. "That is because you are very curious. In the most excellent manner."

"Hmm. Wait until you suffer through this party with me before you make that determination."

"Nonsense. You are fantastic at a party," Leo says loyally, as the front door to the mansion opens in front of us.

"Don't put any money on that," I mumble as we walk through the house. Me sideways sometimes, because of my absurdly horizontal dress.

The excess here is enough to take me aback even though I

study pictures and descriptions of these houses. But it's a little more blinding in person; the gold and precious stones glittering even in the candlelight and early electricity. Every available surface is filled up with the same messages: we're better than you, we're richer than you, we have more taste than you.

And don't you forget it.

The message is conveyed with paintings, chandeliers, upholstered furniture made of the most expensive materials by the biggest names. And all with enough gilt to cover an entire herd of elephants, if it were morally acceptable to gilt elephants. I'm sure the owners of this house have tried.

Even the ceiling has elaborate golden molding, in case anyone looks up thinking they're going to get a break from being beaten over the head with the owner's wealth. The decorations are at the same level as the palaces I've stayed in, but I guess my mind expects that for monarchs. These are mere lords.

We keep walking past rooms that look dressed up for our visit, for us to only spend a few minutes in each, until we get to French doors at the back of the house. A trek that has me sweating in my dress because it weighs about eighty pounds, and because the walk is long, despite the fact that we're only in one house.

"Are you ready to help me find a wife?"

"Yeah. So ready." I grit my teeth, because of the uncomfortable dress and not because of the thought of Leo marrying someone else. A thought that has become more and more offensive to me the longer I spend time with the man. "I'm going to wingman the shit out of you tonight," I whisper under my breath.

Leo hears and gives me a strange look, but at least he already knows why. It's relaxing to know there's one person here I don't have to watch every word I say around.

Leo opens the door for me and I try to go through it, but get stuck. How I could forget I'm as wide as a basketball player is tall,

I'll never know. It's probably a testament to the human mind and what it can endure when it has no choice.

I turn sideways to enter while I reflect about how I'm getting used to the Victorian era. I've been lucky so far, aside from the constant, crushing anxiety of almost being found out, but I'm also a guest of the queen. As much as I'm hoping Cambridge will hold answers on how I get home, I need to acknowledge that it might not work.

If I'm here forever, I need to run away from this. Because they will find out I'm a fraud…and soon. Before that happens, I'll need to figure out how to survive without royal protection.

If I'm stranded here, I will use all my knowledge of the past to buy stock, bet on outcomes, and otherwise manipulate people into giving me money. Become a professional blackmailer. And if the universe didn't want me to interfere like that, or turn evil, it should have kept me in the right time.

But if I am stranded here, could I be with Leo? It's not fair to ask him to wait. By the time I resign myself to being stuck, he'll have his heir and be working on his spare. And even if we did start something, I could be torn from this world at any point.

"Shall we see the most wondrous garden in all of London?" Leo interrupts my thoughts, which have veered into the stressful again.

"Sure. Who doesn't like a garden?" Then I turn to see the "most wondrous garden in London" and wish I could crawl back inside and hide behind a naked Greek statue, where reality can't hurt me.

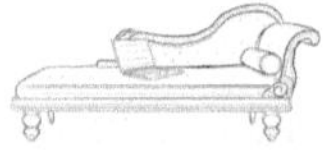

It's not that the garden disappointed.

It's as advertised. The space is lush, with winding paths framed with green hedges and plants to create pockets of privacy. Statues and water features are strategically placed every so often so that no one forgets how much taste (and money) the Devonshires have. And cutting-edge electric lights give the night a twinkling glow with dim bulbs emanating from lampposts, wall sconces on the exterior of the house, and bulbs hanging from branches. Like a beautiful beer garden with an eye for antiquity, which I would definitely frequent.

It's not even the crowd itself. Although I'm still not a fan, I've gotten used to giant groups of people all wanting to socialize with me.

It's one person in particular.

Charles is here. I've been doing so well avoiding him that I hoped he was a figment of my imagination. Or that he had to leave the country on business. Yet here he is, dressed like he belongs in the Georgian period, elaborate gray wig perched arrogantly on his head.

I stiffen next to Leo, but he must take it as general nerves and not person-specific terror because he urges me forward like he's a fan of exposure therapy. The movement, and the subsequent screech of my shoes on the patio as I try to stop the movement, draw too much attention to us.

Like the attention of Charles, who is now looking at me with a glare so full of intense dislike and suspicion that if England could weaponize it, they wouldn't have lost the American Revolution.

But emotional impact of his glare aside, he hasn't called out for some burly footmen to roughly remove me, so he hasn't gotten the letter back from India saying I'm a fraud. Point, me.

For now.

It does make me grateful for nineteenth century lack of instant communication. Even if I haven't been able to check social media for days, despite constantly reaching for a phone that isn't there.

Leo, smug in his self-confidence, strides forward like he's the damn Duke of Devonshire and owns this memorial to excess. He deftly avoids Charles, whether because he can sense that I don't like the man, he noticed the death glare Charles is throwing my way, or he just doesn't care about him, I'll never know. But I appreciate it.

Charles doesn't, and he looks even madder when Leo walks past him without stopping even though Charles is staring straight at him, clearly wanting to talk. I don't think it makes me a bad person to feel glee at the mixture of shocked, affronted anger on Charles's face, but even if it did, I can't stop it.

The giddy feeling doesn't last long. After one dance with me, Leo abandons me with my chaperone and the food table while he dances with heiresses. Doing exactly what I told him to do.

Leaving me vulnerable to the masses. The nosy, arrogant, terrifying masses. If I weren't in this dress, I could maybe climb over the fence. Well, with some help. Step one being someone giving me a foothold over the fence. Which will probably necessitate step two: someone bringing me a ladder to climb over, because the foothold won't help much.

Charles is the first one to sense I'm vulnerable and smell blood in the water, swimming through the crowd of people to attack me. He opens his mouth to say something, showing off his menacing teeth so I have time to worry about the attack before it comes.

"You came to the ball with Lord Basildon." His first salvo is a statement he means to be a question, inviting me to supply details.

"Yes." I don't elaborate. Because the more information I give, the higher the chance I say something that he can use against me. Or that could be proven a lie.

"That's unusual."

"Her Majesty can't take more time out of her busy schedule than she already has for me, but she's sent a chaperone. And she's very fond of Lord Basildon." A chaperone who has so far done nothing to stop anything from happening, which makes her the best chaperone in my book. Probably not in Victoria's, but I'm not telling.

Charles gives me a half-snarl in response, not liking the reminder that Victoria is looking out for me. "Her Majesty will know the truth soon. The response will come from India any day now. Will she be so fond of you then, I wonder?"

I quirk my eyebrow in what I hope is a flippant response. Because inside I am quaking over just that thing happening. "We'll see." I stare him directly in the eyes. He doesn't see what he wants to, which is the fear churning in my stomach.

But his relentless, bitchy politeness is waking up a part of me that I don't often use back home. The same part that stood in front of a group of strangers in a pub and asked them for help. The same part that is *done* with Charles.

"How is Lady Dumfries?" that wicked part of me asks. I smile placidly with the words. Who knew that pettiness was such a good solution to managing fear?

Charles straightens up immediately, his posture better than I've ever seen it. And since he usually walks like he has a stick up his ass, that's an impressive feat. "I am sure she is fine. I would not know the details," he says through gritted teeth. He abruptly turns around to find someone else to harass for the night.

This is information I can use when that letter comes in. Maybe I can get his silence long enough to disappear on my terms. I've already started the blackmail route, might as well go all in until I'm safe.

I can do this. I can survive; I *will* survive.

Leo comes back at that moment, when I'm high on my own abilities and have Gloria Gaynor stuck in my head. "Are you having a good time?" Leo holds out a glass of champagne for me, which I take, and then we start walking around the garden, Anne trailing behind us.

"I think I am."

"Good. We must be growing on you."

"Some of you more than others, at any rate."

"For my own happiness, I will assume that I am in the 'more' group rather than the 'others' group."

"Assume what you need to get you through the night." He is one hundred percent the person who has grown the most on me. But his ego, which is still so big even after getting knocked down by scandal and debt, doesn't need to be fed any more.

Leo laughs and shakes his head.

"How is your night going? Are we any closer to taking down your game?" I ask, lowering my voice so Anne doesn't hear about our plans.

"That sounds unnecessarily bloody."

"Minus the blood, it's an apt metaphor," I say over his laughter. "You've developed stratagems and camouflage." I point to myself, both the stratagem and camouflage in this scenario. "You've dressed for the hunt." Now I point at his cheeky calves and the gold embroidery on his jacket. "You've identified your prey." I jerk my head over the partygoers; his heiresses must be in there somewhere.

"And I have my weapon ready at the ready?" Leo asks dryly, getting into the spirit of the metaphor.

"Do you mean your..." I don't know if I'm allowed to say penis during this time period.

"My charm, Princess." He sounds scandalized, but he's also laughing so I have no idea. "What were you thinking was my weapon?"

Now we're both laughing. "Have I scandalized you again?"

"Yes. To the stocks with you, woman." His voice gets unusually deep when he growls out that last part and my lower body immediately clenches in desire. Okay, I can see why Queen Victoria fell bonnet over heels for John Brown when he called her woman. "Are all the women like you in this time you're from?"

I look around to make sure no one (Charles or someone who hates me and equally wants me to get taken down) heard that. When I'm sure everyone is busy and Anne is too far to hear our whispers, I reply. "Women have more freedom to be who they want. But in general, if a woman wants to talk about *penises*." I whisper the word, not because I'm ashamed to talk about genitalia but because I'm trying to keep a low profile over here. "She can. If she doesn't want to, she doesn't have to."

"That sounds not altogether unpleasant. People should be able to do what they feel is right without the public indignation. Especially when saying it doesn't harm anyone." With all the scandals in his family history, he is intimately acquainted with how harmful public indignation can be.

"It's not perfect. There are still people who think women should act a certain way and sexual harassment is still a big problem. But it's freer than here, mostly. Women can own property outright and have more access to education, jobs, and public spaces. They don't even need chaperones." Although even in this era, not everyone is confined to the ton's rules. Poor women who need to work do without chaperones, but the jobs they can have are limited. Richer women, on the other hand, have more access to education but are often limited in what they can do in public. And then there were a few, like Ida Pfeiffer, who travelled alone, damn the consequences.

He looks suitably impressed at the revelations. "How else is your home different from ours?"

That's a giant can of worms. "In too many ways to list. In ways that would probably be dangerous to talk about. Let's just say that technology keeps advancing at a pace that would shock you, even though you've seen the Industrial Revolution. And while women have more options for what they want to do in life, it's still harder for them than it is for men. And commoners get way more autonomy. But a lot of people still struggle to survive in ways they shouldn't, with the advances in technology and medicine." Then I add one more because I can't resist. "A title alone doesn't help much, but I guess it can still have some weight in certain circles." Not circles I'm invited to.

"Titles *not* granting their bearers with all the rights and privileges that come with them?"

I roll my eyes. Of course that's the one he focuses on. "It had to come to an end some time." My tone is unsympathetic. "It's about intelligence and hard work now. Or being cutthroat. Although some is still based on connections and family wealth. Okay, a lot actually still is, but in a different way." It's hard to distill an entire world of seven-point-six billion people into generalities. "But in general, there are more opportunities for people to have a chance at a good life than there is here, even though family wealth and connections still play a big part of the world."

Leo isn't comforted by that, if the sour look on his face is anything to go by. It makes me defensive. "Oh, come on, you can't sit here and tell me these people are any better than the people outside these walls. The people on the other side of this town. Everywhere has smart people, nice people, mean people, greedy people. These people here are just luckier than everyone else."

"Like me and my father. Him getting a fortune then wasting it away and abandoning his family. That's what you mean by mean, greedy people."

"I just mean a name or bloodline doesn't make anyone better than anyone else. I'm not a lady." I whisper the last part. "Does that make me less than the other people in this nicely decorated garden? Will your future marchioness be better than me because she married you and gave birth to the next marquess?"

"No, she will not be," Leo says immediately.

I look away, focusing on the intricate dancing in the middle of the garden oasis. "I wasn't fishing for a compliment. The point is she might be better than me, but it won't be because of her name or who she marries. Either way, I'm sure you'll be happy together."

"But if not for my name, what am I worth?"

"You can be anything, make your own worth. What do you want to do?"

"I do not know. I do not know who I am if I am not the Marquess of Basildon. I do not know what I have to offer beyond it."

"Because of that name you got a great education. So use it. What interests you?"

"I enjoy history. That was interesting in school."

"Hey, we have that in common! There's plenty you can do with it. You can write books. You probably have access to so many records, not just your own, but the records of your friends and acquaintances. You could teach. You could work a government post, probably, which would only sort of be related to history but would probably pay more. You could open your house up to tourists and charge for it, and teach about your family history!"

I'm done not trying to interfere with the past. The longer I'm here, the more my very existence is changing things. And with all the anxiety I have about being found out, getting home, and what I'll do if I can't get home, I can't think about the future effects of all this, too. Sure, I'll still try not to start a war or invent something that shouldn't be invented yet; I'll stay away from big changes. But I can help one person.

Especially when that one person is Leo.

"I suppose I could do those things. But none of them solve the pressing debt issues. The ones I have to solve before the end of the season or I will not have a home to live out of, or food to eat, while I pursue any of those other options. It is too late for me."

"It's never too late. I believe you could be a success at any of those things."

Leo shrugs, uncomfortable with the sentiment. "Perhaps. Ready for another dance?"

I down the rest of my champagne for courage and take his offered hand. I can't tell if I'm getting better at these dances, because every time I think I remember the steps to one, Leo drags me out to another one. He's always careful helping me during the dances, but it's clear I don't know what I'm doing. Lucky for me, no one expects too much out of me.

Still, it's nice to be touching Leo again. Even if it is through layers of clothes and gloves.

The rest of the ball is less exciting than the beginning, thankfully for my anxiety. People wander over and talk to us, curious about the courtship. We do a good job not giving anything away, sending the nosy people away with nothing they didn't already know.

And the attractions we're surrounded by! I don't know how they fit everything in, but there are tightrope walkers, a confident lion tamer (which was terrifying and sad since I have no idea how well that lion is treated), and an opera singer with an orchestra.

The night ends with a fireworks display. I have no idea where they're coming from, since we're in the middle of Mayfair, but I'm gonna chalk it up to rich people being able to move mountains if the mountain dares to cast a shadow that interrupts their garden party.

Leo stands close to me while the fireworks explode in the air, the bright colors reflecting on the crowd and their powdered wigs. If I were home, I would do what I want and tuck myself under his shoulder at the romantic scene.

But that's not my reality now, and I have a reputation to worry about. I also can't afford to get too close to Leo, someone who is not for me, despite how much I wish otherwise. So maybe the rules of the era are helping me a little, if they keep a little distance between me and the man who makes me feel more special than anyone has in the future.

After the party, Leo drops Anne and me off at the palace, walking us to the door and stopping there. Thanks to those societal rules, I don't get a goodnight kiss, or even a friendly hug, which I would very much like despite knowing they wouldn't help this crush I'm developing on the man.

Longing looks across a bumpy carriage ride are dangerous enough, but I can't stop myself from enjoying them.

"Shall I pick you up at nine o'clock tomorrow morning to go to Cambridge?" Leo asks.

"Right. To find a way home. Nine sounds good."

"Excellent. It should be a day trip by train, but if we do get late my family seat is there."

He has my attention. Because of my area of study, I do a lot of research on the English country estate in general. Knowing that I might see Leo's is like catnip to me.

This is actually *double* catnip to me, because I'm interested in his house as a historic artifact, but I'm also interested in the man himself and what the house can tell me about him.

At least I can comfort myself that I was into Leo before he offered to show me his family house, so I'm not stone-digging here.

"I'll see you tomorrow."

"Yes. Sweet dreams, Meera." He turns and saunters back toward his carriage, giving me a last look at those calves.

I didn't think hose would do it for me. And it's probably not the hose as much as Leo's legs. But I didn't know legs would do it for me either.

I'm learning so much about myself in the past.

CHAPTER 22

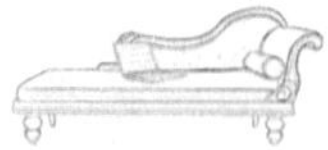

*D*espite not being a morning person (I schedule all my classes in the afternoon for a reason), I wake up excited. For two reasons: I get to spend more time with Leo and maybe find a way home.

But then I realize that one of those actions will put an end to the other, and that puts a damper on things. Because if all goes according to the plan, I'll be back home in the future, obsessively researching everything on the life and times of Leopold Clifford-Alston, Marquess of Basildon.

Who he ended up marrying. All the children he had with her. How he not only paid off his debts, but probably also refurbished his family mansion and gave it electricity. He'll have enough left over to keep a mistress in some row house in a semi-fashionable neighborhood, if he wants.

And with that thought, any excitement I had this morning flees. The sudden shift in emotions is a lot to take from someone already morally opposed to mornings, and I'm left in a funk I can't shake off.

"Are you ready for the trip?" Anne asks as she comes in the door, tearing me from my thoughts.

"Yes!" I throw the covers off to imitate the actions of a morning person, hoping the perkiness will follow. Like the therapists who say smiling can trick your body into releasing genuinely happy chemicals. Or that lying down and closing your eyes can give some benefits of rest, if you can't sleep.

"I've packed for you in case we have to stay the night, and Her Majesty is sending some money for you." Anne indicates behind her, where two footman are dragging a large chest.

"All this for one night?" Does the word *night* have a different meaning that scholars don't know about? Is it code for two weeks? Like fortnight, which took me too long to learn, and I only finally did because of historic romances?

"Her Majesty wants you to be prepared for any situation that could arise," Anne says defensively.

"She's very kind." I don't want Anne to think I'm ungrateful.

Anne nods and flutters around the room, getting me and my stuff ready for the trip. She's scarily efficient, while I'm focusing on preparing myself for how I'm going to feel when I see Leo again, black hair flopping in the non-wind like he covertly invented electric fans and made one of his servants follow him around with the prototype.

We get downstairs just as Leo arrives.

"Are you ladies ready for a trip to the countryside?" he asks when a footman opens the door for him.

He's got a genuine, careless smile on his face, and I'm struck by the fact that he always looks this happy. He's got more problems than even me…and I'm literally trapped 130 years and 5,442 miles away from my home.

But he's still enjoying things. Encouraging me to have fun, dragging me out of my shell when I just want to stand on the sidelines and observe, study, and record. And he's helped me more than he knows. I've stood up for myself more this trip than I ever have before. Whether it's because I don't have a choice since I'm in the limelight wherever I go here, or because I feel better knowing he's contractually bound to help me if it all goes to shit, it's given me a confidence I didn't know I had. Or maybe it's all of it.

"Are you all right?" Leo asks.

"Yes." I snap back into the moment with my own smile. "Let's go."

Leo's carriage takes us to King's Cross and I get to experience, once more, places I've been but only much later in time. It's a thrill I haven't gotten used to yet. The way that everything looks so similar, but then when I look closer, it's different. Here, the façade is the same now and in the future, but when we walk inside, I don't see the modern-style roof or the shops I'm used to. And the people! Since it's a place I've been, I expect to see modern clothes even though it's a Victorian building, but then I'm confronted with Victorian clothes and my brain takes a moment to catch up with my reality.

Leo sees me trying, and failing, to be chill. He gets something out of his coat pocket and extends it out to me. It's some paper wrapped around a pen and some ink. "We have some time before the train leaves. I know you must want to take notes."

I shyly take the tools. "Yes. I really do." I unfurl the paper and look around for something to write on. Leo, not done being my knight in shining armor even though I didn't go back to Medieval times, turns and reaches into his footman's bag. He pulls out a slab of wood and holds it horizontally in front of me, at around my chest height.

"You really thought this through." I give the compliment while my eyes and hands are busy on the scene around me and the paper in front of me.

"Although I am attempting to cut down on the gambling, it was a sure bet that we would need these items during our journey."

I blush, seeing his intense gaze out of my peripherals even

though I refuse to look at him directly. It's too much and I can't stop wanting to do bad things to him in a crowded Victorian train station. Things that would also be scandalous to do in pubic in 2025.

After I've filled up half the page, with Leo patiently holding up a board for me the entire time, I blow on the paper to dry the ink and fold it up to store in my tiny purse.

"Thank you." I risk looking up at him now, not strong enough to resist seeing his face now that my distractions are over.

He's got a half-smile, not annoyed or even mad that he's been my table for the last ten minutes. It makes me feel warm. And not just because I'm waiting approximately fifteen layers in this station among steam trains.

I clear my throat. "Is our train leaving soon?"

"We have time, if you would like to explore?"

"It's all right. I don't want to miss the train. We've got to get to Cambridge and find out what Andrew knows so I can get home."

Leo's smile immediately dims. What did that? I think back over what I said. Does he hate train rides? Does he hate King's College in some pointless college rivalry? Does he hate the countryside in general? Is he as disappointed as me about my upcoming departure? No, that's arrogance, thinking he cares about me as much as I care for him.

No matter how much I wish it was because he cares.

Leo leads us to a train and then into a wood-paneled train car with lush green velvet damask seats and matching curtains with dark wood paneling in between, and a small wooden table in one corner. This is nicer than the actual apartment that I live in, and it's a train carriage.

Ugh, eat the rich in any era.

I do support all the wood-paneling in the Victorian décor aesthetic. Something to keep in mind when I go back home, and if I win the lottery to fund a redecoration of my apartment.

The train rambles out of London and then beyond. I soak in the view as the city fades to countryside and sheep replace people, while green foliage replaces gray buildings covered in soot.

At some point, the train porters bring tea and set it on the tiny table, but we get to the Cambridge train station before I even finish my scone. What a shame, but also my own fault because I spent a lot of the first half of our journey documenting it. I wrap the scone in a napkin to save for later, shoving it in my purse with my notes before we leave the train. If I get crumbs all over the notes, well, it won't be the first time I find food stains on my own papers, including essays from students.

I'm nervous as we walk through the platforms. In the past few days I've been alternatively sure this is going to show me a way home and sure that it won't and I'll need to plan how to make my life here. And now it's here and I have to confront that today will go a long way to letting me know which one I'll be doing.

We exit the Cambridge train station, and I walk fast away from it, determined to get this over with so at least the anticipation will be over and I can start making plans for next steps. I don't get far before a throat clears behind me and I turn to see Leo, Anne, a footman and a pile of luggage a few feet from me.

"I have my carriage coming from the house for us," Leo says. Even though I'm a bundle of nerves, I force myself to stand on the street and wait for transportation.

"Do you want to write whilst we wait?" Leo gets the board out again.

"Actually, yes. Thank you." I shyly get out the writing tools and take notes, but my heart isn't in it this time with all the nerves coursing through me.

Still, my Leo-table is too nice to pass up.

Finally, the carriage arrives, even though it feels like I could have walked to the school faster than it took for it to get here.

Once in the carriage, my right foot bounces, the tapping as loud as a concert or a night club inside the small space. Despite how much everyone can hear how anxious I am, I can't stop it.

Leo tries, resting his hand on the knee of that bouncing leg. His touch helps a little initially, but the farther we get in town, the less it works. Maybe if he were touching my skin it would have been more effective. But with Anne here, we won't get to try it and see.

Then the carriage stops and I open the door with shaking hands. I don't know if this is the right stop, but I can't sit in here for any longer.

"Anne, you can stay here where it's comfortable," I yell behind me. Comfortable for me, because I don't want her around while I ask someone about time travel.

"But…" Anne says something else but I'm already out of the carriage. I'll deal with that fallout later, if she decides to tell Victoria.

I stride up the walkway to a beige stone neo-Gothic gatehouse, ignoring both the carvings on the gate and the porter that comes forward when he tries to ask me where I'm going. I keep walking through the open doorway, the giant oak medieval door open for my trespassing. I vaguely hear Leo behind me, saying something in his calm voice to the porter that makes the porter's voice stop.

Aristocratic nonsense. Useful aristocratic nonsense.

I look back quickly and see only Leo. Anne listened to me, or Leo said something to convince her to stay in the carriage, so that's one less thing to worry about.

I ignore stone carvings, historic figures and the soaring King's College Chapel with its beautiful fan vault ceiling to my right to focus on my task at hand. No time to take notes right now.

On the other side of the gatehouse, there's an oasis of stillness around a grassy courtyard. The noise of the street fades away inside the gates, and I don't see students running around, worried about being late to class or what they're going to do this weekend. Just one or two stragglers.

Now where would I be if I was a guy named Andrew, interested in time travel?

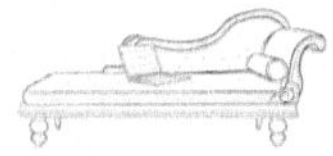

CHAPTER 23

"Do we know where we need to go?" Leo asks, a little out of breath jogging to keep up with me while running interference for me. He would have a rough time on my campus, where everyone is always in a rush. And there are hills.

"No." I look around. "That's the chapel." I point at gothic building I was studiously ignoring earlier. "I think those are mostly dorms." I point to the left. "And maybe those are classrooms?" I look straight ahead, across a perfectly manicured lawn with a fountain in the middle. I vaguely remember the college from a history conference I attended in the future.

"It's mid-morning. The students should be in lectures now. Shall we wander and ask people if they know where Andrew is?" Leo asks.

"That's the best plan we have."

A man walks by, looking at me half hungry and half confused, like I'm a steak dinner inexplicably cut in the shape of a Christmas tree.

"Maybe we should aim for getting out of here as fast as possible. These lads do not get a lot of female interaction," Leo says.

I roll my eyes. "Wait until the future," I whisper at him. "Schools are co-ed. Women everywhere. And we wear shorts. You can see ankles and knees and elbows and thighs and sometimes bellybuttons. And other times, we wear pants so tight you can see the outline of our butts. And you can just learn to control your base desires, because they are not my problem!" I poke him as my voice raises with each word, ending on a particularly intense poke. Then I walk off in what can only be described as a huff in any century.

Then the wind gets taken out of my sails when I don't see Leo walking next to me. I do need him before I apparently start a riot by existing. "Are you coming?"

Leo is as still as the statue of Henry VIII outside Trinity College just down the road. Now there's a man who would be happy with the state of fashion in the twenty-first century.

"Leo?" I walk back to him and poke him in his hard chest.

But I don't have time to enjoy his chest, just like I don't have time to take notes about this trip to Cambridge. Well, maybe I can multitask, if Leo is set on taking his time. I poke him again, this time shamelessly enjoying his muscles.

"I want to see the future. I want to see *you* in the future," Leo says, his voice rough. Imagining me in leggings he's never seen?

"If this man has figured out time travel, you're welcome to use it and see for yourself." I try to ignore how happy I get at the thought of him and me in the future, because we don't have time for that. There are too many complicated emotions around Leo, frankly, and if I start thinking of them, we'll never get moving. Like Leo isn't now, so I take his arm in mine and walk assertively forward with him.

He begrudgingly starts to move forward, stumbling a bit before he catches his footing. "Would you promise to show me what you usually wear?"

"Would it get you to move?"

"It might make it harder to move."

I laugh, surprised at the dirty humor from the aristocrat, even though I shouldn't be, knowing what they get up to. Every generation thinks they invented enjoying sex, or having fun with sex, and every generation is wrong. Maybe they all talk about it more freely than previous ones, but everyone does it.

"Did you just make a dirty joke at me?" We don't really have the time, but I can find some time for this.

Leo blushes, adorably. "I apologize. I should not be speaking like that to a lady."

I shake my head at him. "You have a lot to learn about women from the future. I'm sure some might be offended by the mention of an erection, but I feel that more would appreciate a good penis joke." Or at least I do.

He blushes even harder at me saying penis. Oh, this innocent baby angel face. How the world is going to change in the next hundred years.

"You don't have to worry about the wild women. They're far away," I say.

"If they are anything like you, I am disappointed to miss out on them. Even though I sincerely doubt they are exactly like you, because you are special."

There Leo goes again. Saying kind and perfect shit that makes me want to climb him like a thick tree.

He doesn't mean it. He can't. We've only known each other for a few days and he can't possibly understand me, or know how different everyone is in my time. I know him well enough to know he's not a complete rake, throwing empty compliments at me to get in my pants—or my pantaloons. But he is a bit of a romantic, and I think he's a little caught up in me being from the future. Shiny and new but nothing special if he ever took a trip to my time.

"Let's find this Andrew guy." Back to business.

"I do not particularly want my time with you to end. But if it will make you happy, we will find him." Leo raises his hand as if to touch my cheek but drops it before he makes contact when a student behind him drops some books, ruining the moment with the bang.

We enter the first door to our left and see more students in what looks like a lounge. With a bar.

Bless the English.

I still get intrigued looks when I walk into a room, but they barely register anymore with how many stares I've had directed at me since I've been here. I don't have to deal with this for much longer, hopefully.

"Let's talk to the most important person on the entire campus," Leo whispers against my ear as his hand pushes against my lower back.

"The professors?"

"The barman."

"Of course. What was I thinking, prioritizing the *teachers* in an institution of *learning*?"

"Precisely. You understand." Ah, so sarcasm hasn't been invented yet. "Excuse me? Do you know the student Andrew Huxley?"

"Could do." The man continues cleaning some glasses, less impressed than the gate guard was with Leo. Good, even if that does slow us down.

"Do you know where he is now?" Leo asks.

"Could do."

"Right." Leo slides some money across the lacquered wooden bar. "Where is he?"

The barman takes the money, more impressed with that than Leo's status. "Should be in lectures now. I don't know where, but he'll probably head back to his room before lunch."

"Which room is his?"

"Now why do you want to know that?"

"I want to surprise my friend," Leo says, pushing more money across the bar.

The barman takes it. "Room forty-two. I've helped him back to it enough times."

"How do we get there?" Leo asks.

"The rooms are all up the stairs." He points at a set of stairs with the glass he was wiping down.

"Thank you," Leo says, turning to the stairs.

With each step, my feet get heavier with the weight of what I want to find out on this trip. I use the time trying to think what I could do next to get home if this doesn't work out.

I can't Google time traveling and the people who are studying it. There's no subreddit I can look up to see what people are saying about the subject. I'll have to keep hounding different librarians, I guess.

We get to a plain white door with a neat *42* painted at eye level.

"Now we wait." I lean against the wall next to the door.

After a few minutes of silence, Leo stirs. "Have you thought about what you will do if Mr. Huxley cannot give us the answers we are seeking?"

"I always try to think of every possible scenario. I like being prepared, so yes, I've given it some thought. I need to find housing and a job. I could go to Limehouse, but Victoria might send someone there to look for me since it's the obvious place to hide. I could flee to the country, and maybe find work as a maid or a tutor, but I have no references, and how would I even know who's hiring? I think my best option would be to start making some bets. Small, so they don't get anyone's attention, but I do know when things will happen. And if that fails, blackmail is there, although I would feel bad about that, unless the person is bad. But nothing sounds particularly good. And nothing sounds as good as being home."

Leo nods but doesn't say anything. I wish he would. I want to know if he feels the same pull that I do when we're together, even though we're not only separated by an ocean, but also 130 years.

One could be circumvented by frequent plane rides, although that would get expensive.

The other is a little harder to deal with.

Would we live here or in the future? Would the universe even let us both back? And if we stayed, Leo would still have his money problems. If he left, his sister would be alone and vulnerable.

All of this becomes irrelevant if he doesn't feel anything toward me. Kiss aside, I could just be an interesting diversion. A curiosity to have fun with who doesn't think kissing someone is the end of the world, or an invitation to propose marriage.

"Whatever happens, you will prosper. Her Majesty enjoys your company. You are smarter than most people in this city. In this country. I would bet on you over anyone. If I were still betting," Leo says.

"Thank you."

"And if you did stay, I would be honored to show you more of London, of England, and of the nineteenth century."

I shake my head, denying not only the words but the feelings that the words engender in me. "If I do stay, Victoria will find out about me; I'll have to leave the palace and be on the run. And you'll be busy husbanding soon. Settling your estates with your heiress wife."

"I cannot imagine that as my life. Not anymore." Leo drills his eyes into me like I've got coal under my surface and he spent his last crowns on the mining rights.

"Just because you can't imagine it doesn't mean it won't be good for you. I couldn't imagine time travel or living in Queen Victoria's court, but here I am. And I'm going to make the best of it while I'm here." I shake my purse, indicating the notes I have in there. "If I go home, I can write about the time with amazing personal knowledge. And if I stay here, maybe I'll still write a book. Maybe 'fiction' about that future that will confuse scholars in my time. The governess who predicted the internet. And

Netflix." My eyes sparkle in mirth at the thought, a light spot in a stressful day. The longer I'm away from home, the less I care about changing the timeline. At this point, I'm just trying to survive.

"You are always thinking about the future." He shakes his head. "Not just the future as in the time you are from, but the future of what you want to do in life."

"It's comforting to have a plan. It's the responsible thing to do."

"You cannot plan for everything." He levels a look at me, referencing my unexpected time travel. "And great moments can happen when embracing the unplanned."

"I'm genuinely not against fun. I've had fun with you. But sometimes you just have to focus on the boring stuff, so you have space to have fun. Like your impending marriage. Once you propose, you'll get married and then you'll be set to enjoy life again."

Leo sighs. "I do not think there will be that much enjoyment after marriage. I would rather not think about that at all, actually."

Before I can harass him more into fixing his life, a man approaches the door, slowing when he sees us. This is it. This must be Andrew. Blood flows to my muscles in preparation for action, for finding out what he knows and what I'll do after.

Leo turns to see who stole my attention. "Ah, you must be Mr. Huxley."

Andrew slows to a stop, wary about the people at his door who know who he is. And where he lives, clearly. "Can I help you?"

I don't want to have the conversation out here, so I take the initiative to walk closer where I can whisper to him. "I would like to talk to you about a mutual interest we may have. Do you have some time right now?"

"I have classes in the afternoon."

"Maybe we can take you to lunch? It would be nice to get out of these walls for a few hours." Leo smiles charmingly.

"Who are you?" Andrew finds it easier than I do to resist Leo's charm.

Leo inclines his head. "I am the Marquess of Basildon and this is Her Royal Highness Meera Chopra, an Indian princess and Queen Victoria's ward."

"And what is this about?" He does look somewhat impressed by our credentials, but not completely swayed.

"It would be easier to sit and explain it all to you." And I still haven't decided how much to tell him. Prison or Bedlam are still on the table, if word gets around I'm claiming to be from the future, after I lied to the monarch about where I'm from and my family. I want to avoid that.

"No. I am not going anywhere with you when you have given me so little information about what you want." He opens the door, walks through it, and is about to close it again when I reach out to slap the wood, keeping the door open.

"I want to talk to you about time travel," I say, a last-ditch effort. I might want to protect myself, but I want to go home more.

That causes a change in his demeanor. He immediately straightens and looks at me with renewed interest, his gaze sharp as he searches my face and then Leo's.

"Well, now that is an interesting invitation. We can meet at the pub across the street. I'll just drop my books off in the room." He holds them up and turns to drop them off at his desk.

I sag in relief. "Perfect."

I share a look with Leo, but he's surprisingly stoic while I'm finally feeling lighter. I can't analyze his emotions in this moment, when I'm feeling so many of my own, but it's odd for the usually jovial man.

Andrew comes back out of his room and we walk out of the college and across the street to The Eagle, the pub where Watson and Crick are going to announce they discovered "the secret of life," or the structure of DNA. I mean, Rosalind Franklin discovered the facts that led to those two to figure out DNA and then you didn't credit her, but okay. It's still a piece of history.

The history of sexism.

And they do a solid fish and chips, I hear.

We order immediately and then fall into a silence until the food gets to the table. Now that we're at a place where I can get information, I don't know how to start. But I better, because Andrew is looking less than patient with the delay. Still, it takes me until we start eating to build up the courage.

"We got your name from a librarian over at Bedford College in London. She said you were interested in time travel and were doing some studies on it from a physics standpoint."

Do I tell him about me now? My hands start to shake and I hold off from giving that much information, my body clearly telling me not to.

"We're interested in the concept and were hoping to get your take on where the field stands. So…is time travel real?"

CHAPTER 24

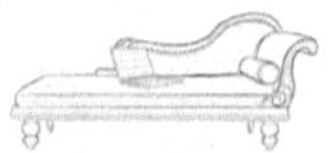

My hands, happy now that I'm not thinking of spilling all my secrets, shake less but don't stay completely still. I put them in my lap so no one else can see how much the answer means to me. Leo sets his hand on my clasped ones under the table, which does make them stop moving. Because I don't want to do anything that would throw his hand off.

"Oh, you're here to ask me? I thought you had some information for me," Andrew says, shoulders slumped in disappointment that we aren't here to give him the secret to time travel.

"Oh. No." Except that I kind of did it, but I have no idea how. "We want to know if it's possible."

"You know, I almost never get asked about that with a straight face. Well, in my spare time I am studying if the physics would allow such a thing to occur. Taking into account Maxwell's theory of light, and the…"

My eyes glaze over and my mind starts to wander despite this being potentially important information; I'm a historian and not a mathematician for a reason. But I smile and nod along like I understand what he's saying. I give him five minutes before I can't hear any more words that confuse me.

"This is all so fascinating," I say, interrupting him saying something about geometries of spacetime and the speed of light. "But we're mostly wondering about *how* this could happen. What the mechanism of time travel would be, if it was possible?"

Andrew shrugs. "I have never thought of it outside a theoretical possibility; I have only worked on the equations and the science. I am not to the point where I have thought about designs for a machine."

"But if you had to speculate." There's a desperation in my voice even I can hear.

"The machinery required would be quite advanced. Something with a large motor, if beating light is the key."

I jump in before he can start going on about the science again. "Fascinating. What about it being done without a machine?" I lean in closer.

Andrew leans back and gives me thirty seconds of consideration. Then he starts laughing at me. I give him a minute to let him get it out of his system, but he doesn't stop.

"All right, it's a fair question." Since I did time travel without a machine, I feel like the disbelief is unnecessary. Even if he doesn't know that, and maybe I won't be sharing if this is going to be his response. I would think that he would be more open to new ideas, considering he probably gets made fun of for studying time travel. "Can it be done?"

He shakes his head, still grinning. "No. You would need some sort of machine to facilitate the process. Otherwise, it is not physics; it is magic. Which does not exist."

Well, a puppy's unconditional love is magical, but I guess this guy is a science Scrooge.

I suppress the urge to throw my mushy peas at him. A difficult task since I don't want the mushy peas in the first place, and I can't think of a better way to get rid of them. But Leo might be able to read my mind, because he tightens his hand around mine as my thoughts get more violent.

I take some deep breaths and work on relaxing. "Have you heard any rumors of sudden time travel, maybe after some sort of unconscious experience?" He is still the person most likely to come across those stories, even if he doesn't believe them.

Andrew scoffs at me. But at least his laughter has died down. "No. That is the opposite of science."

"There are more things in heaven and earth, Horatio, than are dreamt of in your philosophy." I happily rip off Shakespeare.

Andrew looks at me like I'm a danger to him. Good. I could be a danger to him if I keep getting his condescending attitude. "It is not possible."

"Is there anyone else studying this? Maybe not from a physics perspective?"

"I would not know. And I have to get back to my classes. If that is all…" Andrew gets up.

"Thank you for your time." I slump back in my booth seat.

The hum of the busy pub at lunchtime fades away as I think about what this means for me. Even the feel of Leo's hands on mine loses its intensity as today sinks in.

I won't be seeing my family any time soon. I won't have a first day of class where all I do is go over the syllabus and try to entice my students' attention with the wildest parts of the course like I'm making a "This season on…" reel for a Real Housewives franchise. I won't get the relief of getting the last paper graded for the year. Or the excitement of getting an article accepted for publication, or seeing a student discover their love of history.

I'll never waste time scrolling through my streaming services to find something to watch, spending so much time on the task it's already bedtime when I finally find something.

I won't ever Google something again!

I start breathing heavily, my heartbeat doing a tap dance

against the back of my sternum as pressure builds in that cavity. Is this a heart attack?

Then Leo's hands are on my arms, rubbing up and down slowly like he can make my body's responses slow through the power of touch. As intriguing as I usually find him, this is too much for even him to distract me from. "Shall we get some air?" He tugs me up before I can answer, which is great because I don't have the capacity to respond.

I suck in deep breaths of the cool air when we leave the building. It helps a little. Enough so I can breathe again. Leo resumes his calming arm rubs tentatively, not knowing what reception he's going to get.

"I don't know what else to do. The only remaining path I have is to throw myself down every stairway I see in an attempt to recreate the original conditions of my time travel."

Leo winces with me at that thought. Yeah, it's not optimal. "There must be other options that do not involve quite so much bodily harm. And risk of long-lasting damage."

"There aren't," I yell in frustration, jerking away from his too-comforting arms. I don't want to be comforted right now. I want to be angry at the universe or the god of time-traveling that did this to me. I want to rage at the unfairness of me missing home and not even being able to be with the only person I connect with in this time.

We stand in silence for a bit and I think he understands that I need to stew in my feelings while still grasping in big gulps of the chilly air.

"We will get through this. You have people here who care about your wellbeing," he finally says.

"It's not the same," I whisper, most of the anger draining from me now. Leaving a giant, all-encompassing sadness. "You've all been very kind. But at the end of the day, you have your own lives to worry about. Eventually Victoria will know I'm lying to her. Soon, likely. Whenever the letter from Cooch Behar comes in. And I'll have to find out how to survive here. For real. Not this fantasy where I'm an Indian royal. And all of that is if I'm not arrested before I can flee."

Ugh. Jails in this time are *not* things I want to research first-hand. The mansions and museums are one thing. But the jails, with overcrowding, rampant disease and unhygienic conditions, unchecked corruption and lack of fresh air and light, I would rather pass on.

"Maybe you can start throwing me down any staircase you see. If I wimp out at the last minute," I say.

"No. I will not do that. And I cannot promise what will happen in a few weeks' time; I cannot even promise what will happen tomorrow. But we are in this together, and I will not abandon you. Not just because I have come to care for you. But, as you so enjoy pointing out, we have a deal. And all that work building both of our reputations will be for nothing if your secret is exposed. So, I will continue to protect you to the best of my ability until you are settled and happy."

He's so much more than I thought he was. He's kind, and considerate, and despite the fact that he loves having fun, he is not taking the easy way out right now. Because it would hurt me. What am I supposed to do with that? I already have too many feelings toward him that I shouldn't, and this isn't helping.

"You shouldn't," I say morosely. "You should cut and run now. Maybe be the person to tell everyone I'm a liar. Then you can save yourself. One of us should be safe. Just please let me know when you're going to do it so I can flee."

Leo shakes his head at me sharply. "I am a gentleman."

I can't help it; I laugh at that. *Gentleman* is a loaded term in the time when it applies to rich men with famous names behaving badly but everything is excused because of their titles.

"That is not quite the reaction I was hoping for, if I'm being truthful."

I wave my arms in front of me. "No. It's not about you. I know you'll help me; you're a good person. But you can't pretend the word *gentleman* has much meaning right now. They all have mistresses." Wait a minute. "Do you have a mistress?" I'm like a goldfish with my attention span right now.

I don't know how I feel about that idea. He's not married yet. Not even engaged, so it would just be a sexual partner. And in a lot of these marriages, both parties have their own...interests. Especially after a few kids. So he's within his rights to do what he wants with any consenting adult. And I certainly have no say either way.

"No." The answer is immediate. Sure. Well, that's good. "I cannot afford one."

My spirits drop. He just had to keep talking.

"But I suppose I can see your point, regarding gentlemen," Leo says.

"I don't want to be the reason you're harmed."

"You are not the cause of my problems; my irresponsible father was. And perhaps some of my own poor decisions, before I realized. You are helping me, in ways you don't even know."

I rub my hands over my face. "It's a mess."

Leo shrugs. "Life is unpredictable. Why don't we wait a few days before doing anything? You can spend the night at my family home to avoid London for a while longer. And then we can go back, and I will take you around all the places in London I think you will enjoy in a day of fun. For you. Because it will be filled with boring, important places that I would never willingly go to. And maybe some surprises." He looks more than a little wicked at the last part.

He gets a small laugh out of me, and then I take a deep breath in and out, trying to get out anything that I can't control, change, or deal with right now. "Thank you. Yes. That sounds like a nice plan. But—"

"We shall be seen by everyone who is anyone in London. In some of the locations."

Okay. So he can read my mind. He's been paying attention in the short time we've known each other.

"I'm still kind of hungry," I say instead of acknowledging how close we are. I barely ate when Andrew was talking, and I walked out on the food after he left.

"Let's go back in and finish our meal. Then we can go home."

I sniff. "Does it have a name?"

"Of course." Leo scoffs. "Do houses in the future have names?" He opens the door to the pub for me.

"Only the most pretentious ones."

"Ah." Leo leads me back to the table. "The house is called Alston Hall. Not very exciting."

"Descriptive, though. In that the home originally centered around a large room (the hall) that probably contained a hearth, and that it is houses Alstons."

"You make sound points. What would you name your house, if your future homes had names?"

"Oh. I live in an apartment complex. And I think any name might be bigger than my tiny apartment itself."

"Then you must name it something grand. For irony's sake."

I laugh, albeit weakly, remembering I have no way to that tiny apartment that I love. "So I should say I live in Chopra Castle? Or it's by the beach, sort of. Maybe Seabreeze Hall. Or Seasalt Cottage."

"Or Curiosity Manor." Leo winks at me.

"I think people would misinterpret what exactly goes on in there. To be way more interesting than it is."

"I think everything about you is interesting. And the place that made you must be fascinating indeed."

"It would stun you," I say, ignoring the fact that he complimented me and instead focusing on how he would react if he saw a plane. Because Leo being nice to me is too much to handle when my world is getting turned upside down. Again.

Because I genuinely thought I was going to find a way home today. Naively, since I had no evidence, but I *hoped* I was going to find a way home. So fervently that it became an expectation in my mind.

After we finish the meal (including dessert), Leo escorts me out into the English rain. "You came all the way here. Do you want to see King's College Chapel whilst it is right there?"

I sigh. "Sure. That sounds nice." And it does, despite my less than enthusiastic tone.

Leo leads us back across the street to the gatehouse I so confidentially strode through this morning. I'm much more subdued this entry, and the gate guard looks relieved as he tips his hat to Leo.

We walk across the front court and with its immaculate grass and statue of the college's founder Henry VI, and enter the chapel from a side door. My eyes are automatically drawn upward to the soaring ceiling with its intricate fanned vaulting made of limestone. Brightly colored stained glass brings color into the wooden and stone space, the beautiful colors bouncing off the black and white tiled floors.

I pull Leo deeper into to the Gothic chapel, under the rood screen separating the nave from the altar, engraved with Henry VIII and Anne Boleyn's initials. I hope my fate here is a little less...behead-y than hers.

Past the screen, I sit in the student seats behind the choir pews. Leo takes the seat next to me, so we're both huddled in the dark brown seats, feeling tiny in the eighty-foot-high chapel.

"This is almost exactly the same as when I visited. You know, in the future," I whisper to Leo, the stillness demanding lowered voices even though we're the only ones here. "Except maybe the stones are a little less worn."

"All the changes you have spoken about, but this stays the same?" Leo asks in surprise.

I nod. "Almost completely, aside from some electrical upgrades you can't really see anyway. Other historic buildings have been torn down, and some have shifted their purpose. Some have completely gutted interiors, some have different furniture and decorations, and some only have minor changes. But this view we're seeing now is almost exactly the same as the one I saw over a hundred years from now. And it's one people have seen for hundreds of years before us. It's seen wars and the admission of women into the university and monarchs rising and falling. Democracy spreading. And it's still here." The words and the feel of history under my feet calms me down a little. Grounds me.

"I never thought of history like that. Of a building like this, and about who would see it in the future."

"I stand there in over a hundred years," I say softly, mostly to myself, squinting at the altar as if I can see myself on that future date, a tourist with camera out, admiring the stained glass. I had come with Luis, who was visiting the King's College professor he was dating. Will I ever get to see my friend again?

The light-filled space that has stood since the 1500s lends me some more of its peace, helping release the last of the panic I felt in the pub and the hopelessness I've felt since. Something about this building enduring, and the connection I now have with all the people who've walked through these doors, past, present, and future, helps give me not only calm but strength.

The building is as much of a time traveler as me, albeit with a different method.

I lean my head on Leo's shoulder, no one around to stone me for being a slut. Leo shifts until his arm is around my back while the other takes off my hat. Then he maneuvers my head so it's tucked more firmly into his chest. I take deep breaths and let the scent of his earthy soap calm me just like the building did.

"I'm glad you're sitting here now," Leo whispers against my hair.

"Yeah. I am too," I whisper into his starched coat. And it's true. Mostly. Despite how much I want to go home, I'm glad I get this moment with Leo.

Despite whatever the future holds for me.

CHAPTER 25

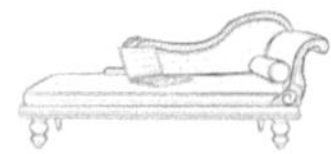

*L*eo's mansion isn't far from Cambridge. The same carriage that took us from the train station to the college meets us there again, with chaperone, and sweeps us away into the green countryside.

We amble through an open metal gate, the iron a little rusted, but still grand because of the scale and the intricacy of his family crest displayed on it, and Leo nudges my foot with his. "If you would like to look out the window, the best view of the house is from right here." He sounds tentative...maybe nervous? Of how I'll respond to his house?

It's historic. I'm going to enjoy it whatever style, size or interior decoration scheme he has. While still thinking that the wealth required to build it is inherently unethical. I'm contradictory like that.

I stick my head out of the window as I was so gently implored to do. At first the wind catches my hat, pushing part of it down over my face, and some of its feathers firmly into my mouth.

I swat at the impractical garment and spit out feathers, only succeeding at the task when I rip it off my head entirely. I quickly forget about my internal tirade against the centuries-long irritation of women's fashion when I see what's in front of me.

It's beautiful. The three-story, English Baroque, beige stone building has two wings protruding forward from a central building. Like the house wants to give me a giant welcoming hug, and I want to hug it back. Rows of tall windows wink at me in the afternoon sun, and in the middle directly in front of me, a giant dome watches over it all.

Small statues (but probably still huge since I can see them from this far away) line the top of the house. Famous Alstons and Cliffords, most likely. Making an army of family members watching over and judging their descendants. And their guests.

The carriage moves up the drive to the front entrance, where the staircase starts wide and then narrows to a grand door. The façade has built-in columns that span the height of the building, ending in a triglyph and metope frieze on the top to rival the Parthenon, with a pediment in the middle, above the frieze. I want to see what the carved scenes on the metopes are more than I want my next meal.

I try to find out now. By leaning farther and farther out the window until my entire torso is out of the moving carriage. Strong hands grasp my waist before I can fall out of the vehicle onto the hard, unforgiving ground below.

Although with all my layers, I've never been more ready for a fall.

Surprisingly, all these layers don't do much to dull my response to Leo's touch, and I can feel the solid strength of every one of his fingers digging into my waist. Causing my heart to beat louder than the sound of the eight horse hooves trotting along the dirt road. His fingers should feel like manacles trapping me, but instead they're protective, like he wants to make sure I don't hurt myself when I'm lost in my curiosity.

"I take it you approve?" he asks wryly from behind me.

"It's amazing," I say with reverence. "Can you hand me my paper and pen?"

"Not until you get back inside. But I promise you can have all the time you want to explore. As long as you do not fall and crack your head open right now. Then you will only get to see one room, and it will be whichever one has a doctor inside it."

I consider ignoring Leo. It's pretty out here. And so perfect I half-think I'm imagining it, but as long as I don't blink or look away, it can't disappear. But the hands at my waist are getting more insistent about my return, so I give in with a sigh and let them pull me back into boring safety.

"It's beautiful," I say to Leo.

Leo puffs out, accepting the praise even though it's clearly meant for an ancestor I don't know who built it, and more importantly, that ancestor's architect.

"This level of wealth is still unethical," I say, just in case his ego gets too big and crushes and/or suffocates Anne and me in the small space.

"Can I enjoy the happiness it gives you since I personally have no wealth?" His chest hasn't deflated at all, my volley unsuccessful in managing his ego.

"No. Still unethical, what with your tenants doing all the work."

"Well, wait until you get to the ocular excess that is the interior. And as promised, for your reentry into the carriage." Leo presents me with my own notebook and pen, which he must have asked Anne about since she had it last time I checked. He bows over the materials as he extends the gift, presenting it with all the gravity of the formal court world he's a part of, even though I'm no one and we're talking about a journal.

Apparently, aristocrats only have one speed.

That doesn't stop me from taking the book from him, even though he does get an eye roll for his pomposity. He winks at me, letting me know the exaggerated movements were done for my effect.

I open the book and write down my first impressions and badly drawn doodles of what I'm seeing, leaning my head out of the window but keeping all other body parts in the vehicle, as instructed. I comply more out of fear that Leo will touch me again and send me into a haze of lust so thick I'll be stunned into accepting that I'm a Victorian now, than of fear of falling and physically injuring myself.

Leo patiently waits when we get to the front of the manor, giving me an extra ten minutes to finish my notes even though I keep lying to him and saying I only need another minute. This is the house of a half-Indian marquess after all. It's important to record so I can analyze it later. Even if it's just for myself.

His "of courses" get less and less credulous as time goes on, but he doesn't pressure me to finish so we can go inside. And he doesn't even have a phone to stare at while we wait.

That should be an example in a chivalry book.

Finally, my last "One more minute" is true, and I close the book. "All done." I realize I'm also holding Anne up as well. "Sorry, everyone. Time got a little away from me there."

"This is your trip. For whatever you want or need."

I nod, acknowledging I heard the sweet not-a-rake, but not wanting to verbally respond since it would be a mess of giggling and infatuated looks.

Leo accepts that as a response, getting out of the carriage and then turning around to help me out. Heaven forbid I try to get out myself. It would probably cause chaos and the fall of the Empire, like if those ravens at the Tower of London went away.

Wait till I tell him it's going to fall anyway.

Not that I would. Even though I've relaxed my paranoia about ruining the future by sneezing at the wrong time, I shouldn't give away that piece of information; it's too big. No matter how satisfying it would be to tell it straight to Charles's smug face.

Instead, I take Leo's hand with a smile. My smile gets wider as I get a closer look at the house behind him. Not because it's better, it's just less complicated than the man in front of me.

The door swings opens and Leo's employees flood onto the stairs, seamlessly moving around us to deal with the carriage and our luggage.

A man who I assume is the butler approaches Leo and gives him a bow. "My lord. How good to see you again so soon after your last visit."

"Thank you. Apologies for the lack of notice. We did not make the decision to stay until today."

"Whatever you need, my lord. Your room is being prepared right now."

"Excellent. Let's set up the Rose Room for our guest, as well as a room for her chaperone."

Albert inclines his head. "Of course."

"And call Mrs. Garnett to come and give our guests her famous tour."

"Of course."

"Perfect. And arrange for dinner after they are done with the tour."

"An early dinner then, my lord?"

"It will not be the way this woman takes a tour."

I'm distracted from sketching his pediment by the words I'm not sure are an insult or a compliment. Leo's face doesn't reveal anything other than a slight amusement. "Thank you?" There. That covers my bases.

"I 'eard ye needed me?" An older woman with a warm smile and a deep Scottish brogue walks up to us, wiping her hands on her apron.

"Always. This is my guest, Her Royal Highness, Princess Meera Chopra. Of India. And this is the woman who raised me, Mrs. Garnett." He gives Mrs. Garnett an affectionate nod, and then says, "Can you please show her around? Feel free to tell her all the salacious details of our history."

Mrs. Garnett claps her hands. "Ah. The things ye don't usually let me tell the polite tourists. This'll be fun."

"He's already told me about the origin of the family title," I whisper to Mrs. Garnett.

"Then he's already taken my best story! There're scones in the kitchen and some fresh preserves. Go." She swats Leo away from her. "Let me give this tour in peace. For yer special friend you've brought home, quite suddenly." She eyes me like she would rather hear the salacious story of who I am and why he brought me here.

"This tour might be a tad bit different. I expect she will have loads of questions about everything and want to stop and take copious notes along the way. Please indulge her."

"Then we'll take our time, so you can ask all the questions ye want. We'll start in the hall."

The interior of the house is as stunning as the exterior. It looks like the Carrara marble quarry threw up inside the main hall, with blindingly white columns, statues and busts all popping against the beige limestone walls. The marble competes with the bright colors of the paintings, both on canvass and the murals in the dome. Which in turn in is competition with the furniture, with its gold details, embroidered fabric and intricate carvings.

And that's just the hall. The rest of the rooms are more of the same, except with the addition of silk damask wallpaper so the walls aren't bare.

Mrs. Garnett is as lovely as a tour guide as she is a person. She even uses the time when I'm writing notes to order us snacks, which means some poor footman follows us around with a tray of delectable baked goods and tea. I don't know how I'll go back to touring house museums without this service in the future.

Mrs. Garnett does tell me some good stories, like the secret passageway the second marquess used to get to his mistress during house parties. And the time he thought he put her in the blue room, but she was in the yellow and the earl's wife in the blue room was only too happy to see a young, nearly naked marquess walk out of her giant fireplace.

I could think of another marquess I would like to see, naked, at my secret passage.

And wow, I did not mean for that to sound like that in my head. But also, maybe I did.

Leo has turned me into a sex fiend. Not a comfortable discovery to have while standing next to a warm, maternal-type, figure. The same maternal-type figure who raised the very marquess I'm lusting after.

In between moments of extreme lust, Mrs. Garnett gives me some great stories about this pile and the family who owns it, and I get great notes and less good (due to a lack of skill on my part) sketches.

This house is amazing. But that makes me wonder why I haven't already heard about it. The thought brings my mood down, because there's only one reason why I wouldn't have heard of a house this nice, with a collection this significant.

It must mean Leo, or his descendants, don't turn around the debt situation. And then the house must get destroyed, either by the natural process of decay making ruins or a fire sped along the process, the art and furniture scattered among the new rich industrialists. In the period right after World War II especially, a lot of country houses were abandoned and demolished due to lack of funds of the landed gentry, who were not prepared to keep up with a changing world.

Will my presence have changed that for him? His house information hasn't updated in my head, as if I had learned it in school. But maybe I'm exempt from the effects because I'm not in the future when the change happened? Time travel is so complicated.

"Thank you for your time, Mrs. Garnett. For showing me around the house." I subtly reach out my hand for some money from Anne. One of the (few) perks of service in these country houses, which is otherwise a difficult job, is that some employees gave tours to "polite tourists" (rich people) who come to see the houses, and they got paid tips.

"I'm not taking anything from such a close friend of Leo's." Mrs. Garnett folds her arms across her chest, giving me the most unfriendly look she's given me thus far.

"Well Anne isn't Leo's close friend. And you showed her around too. So take it for Anne." I know how much they both get paid. Not enough. She and Anne are going to take all the tips I can get Victoria to give me.

Mrs. Garnett begrudgingly takes it. "I'll show ye to your room, and then whenever yer ready, ye can come down for dinner."

She takes us to the Rose Room, with beautiful pink floral wallpaper and a giant painting of a pair of lovers behind a rose bush that looks Rococo. Anne, not impressed with Leo's house as I am (living at a palace has really desensitizing her to excess), bursts into action once we get into the room. She opens my trunk and gets out a dress for dinner that I didn't even know we packed. And makeup toiletries I was also unaware of. That probably have lead in them.

"We're just having dinner with Leo…er, Lord Basildon." Right. No first names. What a disaster what that would be, familiarity between the sexes. *hardest eye roll to ever roll eyes* "He knows what I look like without all of this." I wave my hands about to encompass the items on the table.

Anne efficiently gets me to the vanity without responding to that, by luring me with my own notebook and promising I can take notes while she works. She gets no complaints from me after that. Well, little complaints. She is trying to apply poison to my face.

Once Anne's made me "presentable," Mrs. Garnett appears out of nowhere (probably those secret passages) to take me to the drawing room.

"There's only the two of us. I don't think we need the entire drawing room to dinner procession," I say. But the room is nice. It's the room designated for the women to gather, so it's done in pastel colors, with a pink rose wallpaper, light green upholstered chairs, and wide windows partly obscured with light green curtains.

Mrs. Garnett gives me the same response Anne did. Not a verbal one, more ignoring my strangeness and lack of social propriety while sitting me on the couch with a drink in my hand.

"It is no use arguing with Mrs. Garnett," Leo says as he walks into the room to sit next to me on the couch. "She is always right," he whispers in my ear.

When he's done whispering, he stays close, his eyes hot on me as they linger.

"Now why would ye whisper that last part?" Mrs. Garnett says, sighing like someone who has dealt with a lot of Leo's shenanigans over the years. "Anne, come have dinner with us down in the servants' hall." Mrs. Garnett tugs Anne toward the door.

"But I should…chaperone—"

"They'll be fine." Mrs. Garnett allows no argument as she drags Anne out of the room. And then closes the door on the rest of Anne's argument.

Leaving us alone in a room plucked from my literal fantasies.

CHAPTER 26

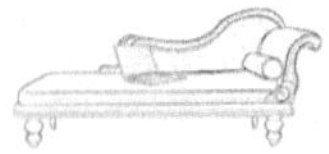

$\mathcal{I}$ clear my throat. "Your house is beautiful." I don't share what I realized on the tour, mostly because there's a chance I'm wrong. There are so many country houses in the United Kingdom; maybe I just missed this one. And maybe what we're doing, putting him closer to the monarchy, will make a difference. I'll get zooped back home and I'll wake up knowing all about the historic, famous, wonderful Alston Hall.

I'll probably get back home and realize it was so important I wrote an article—no, I'll have written an entire book about it and about the half-Indian marquess who turned around a family's fortune—Leopold Clifford-Alston. And he did it ethically! Well, I guess that depends on how one feels about beer and marrying for money.

The universe will push all sorts of unwelcome knowledge about his family into my head. Like all the kids he had with his beer heiress. And how he got so rich he was finally able to afford a mistress after all.

But I don't need to tell him any of that.

"Your face went through quite a lot of emotions in a short period of time. Some of them not as happy as others."

"No. Only happy thoughts," I lie, which I've gotten so good at in the past week. "It's a stunning house." There, I even ended with something a hundred percent honest.

"I am glad you like it. You appreciate it more than I ever have." He looks around, maybe trying to see it like I do. Not as a family home, but as an expression of hundreds of years of history, with all of the social and political pressures and changes, culminating in the phenomenon of the English country house.

"I have a different perspective. I could never look at a place like this and see a home," I say.

Leo quirks an eyebrow. "Why not? It might be missing some of the most recent domestic innovations until I obtain the money to renovate, but it is a good pile of bricks."

"It's perfect. But in my time, most of these houses are museums or hotels or event spaces. A much smaller number are family homes, and even fewer have the original families living in them."

"We already get some visitors; letting in more of the *hoi polloi* sounds terrifying."

"But you can charge them! Solving your money problems as well." It maybe isn't fair to suggest it, since the houses don't become full, organized museums until 1960 at Longleat.

Tigers will be involved. Because apparently, if you can't get people to visit you for the history or art, why not open a zoo in the middle of the English countryside?

But I don't care as much about timeline continuity, not when I could potentially help Leo. Plus, Hampton Court had been open to the public since 1838 for a shilling. And this is the time when country house tourism is rapidly increasing with the invention of railways and cars, changing from rich people seeing other rich people's homes to everyone traveling and seeing history. Some of the houses are open in an informal way for anyone who wants to visit, with the housekeeper giving tours, and some even have other infrastructure like buses and inns to facilitate travel to the house.

So I'm not giving anything away, even if the practice of visiting these houses doesn't become a large, formal business model until later.

"I do not think it would make a difference at this juncture."

Looks like the timeline is safe. "I'm just telling you what happens in my time."

"Have you visited my house in your future? What happens to Alston Hall?"

Why is he so much more perceptive than I originally thought? He's supposed to be a rake, damn it. "I haven't seen every house in England, and not Alston Hall. So I can't tell you its fate."

"But you study us…if anyone would know, it would be you."

"Thank you for thinking I'm good at my job, but there's plenty I don't know yet. That's the point of studying and learning. And some things are hidden to the future, especially by the people I want to study themselves. I didn't know that your mom was an Indian woman living in England, and she is my specialty." Maybe I can write about her when I get back. Do deeper research now that I know what I'm looking for. Maybe some of the family documents survived, but no one has bothered to read them. Plus everything I've learned about her from Leo.

"Hmm." He doesn't believe me, but he lets it go.

We fall into silence. "Really beautiful house." If I keep repeating it, maybe I won't have to move on to any other uncomfortable topics.

"So I've heard. I will get you a guidebook from the village before we leave. Someone wrote it for the occasional tourists we get, and I am sure you will enjoy it."

"Thank you, that sounds really interesting." More silence. "I especially liked your library."

"I've noticed you like libraries."

I lick my lips nervously at the reminder of what we did in the last library we visited. It doesn't help that Leo remembers too, his eyes locked on my lips.

"Have you read all the books in there?" I ask as an attempt to distract him from thoughts of our kiss.

"I have opened some of them."

"What a waste." But at least he's looking at my eyes again.

The butler comes into the room, saving me further. "Dinner is ready."

"At least we don't have to worry about the social hierarchy of who goes in first. With just the two of us," I say as I take Leo's extended arm.

Leo snorts. "You are clearly the better of us. You should go in first with me trailing sadly behind. Far behind. You will be on the dessert course before I even arrive."

"That seems excessive. Let's call it a draw and walk in together."

"How egalitarian of us."

"Must be the first time you've tried equality on."

"I shall choose discretion at this juncture."

Phew. No more talking about what happens to his family home, even though I think he has deduced why I want to avoid the subject. He's too sharp. Must be all those expensive schools he went to. If only they taught him how to make money.

We walk through the ceremonial procession-way connecting the two rooms, and into the dining room, with wood paneling making the room darker than the light, airy pastels of the drawing room. And more intimate. An ironic word since the table in the middle of the room is giant. Like it could hold thirty people, easily. And it's got silver centerpieces and flowers decorating it like all those people are coming tonight.

In reality, it'll hold only two. The head of the table is set for dinner, as well as the place to its right. At least we aren't going to sit across from each other, a mile apart, yelling about how good the food is for the rest of the night.

Leo approaches the head setting. I think he's going to sit down, since he is the Lord of this Manor and all. But he doesn't.

Instead, he pulls the giant wooden chair away from the table and looks at me expectantly.

I raise an eyebrow. "I get to be at the head?" I sit down before he can change his mind and banish me to wherever the commoners eat.

"I told you; you are better than me." His smile is more genuine than his charming one. Wider. More teeth and more crinkling around his eyes. A little less performance and a lot more real.

"I'll take your word on that." I sit down and Leo takes the seat next to me while the footman comes in and serves the first course, a soup.

"I am looking forward to taking you around London tomorrow. All the sites you spoke about wanting to see, plus a little surprise in the evening I think you will enjoy."

I sigh, putting my spoon back down. "But I have to face reality sometime. And figure out what I'm going to do when...if..." I stumble over the words, then clear my throat and try again. "*If* I can't get back."

"Yes. You are very responsible. But you've had a shock, and I think you should not think about it, at least for the day. With me. In London. The problems will still be there the day after."

"All right. It will get us seen, at least. Which you still need." I level a look at him. "And it'll only be fair since I dragged you away from London in the height of the season for this." For nothing, it turns out.

"If that is what it takes, I heartily agree that I am owed a day with you."

"Good." I cheers him and take a sip to seal the deal.

"Is there anything in *your home*"—he looks around furtively, clearly not used to the cloak and dagger bit—"that you will not miss?"

"Something I won't miss?"

"I do not wish to make you sad remembering all the things you are potentially giving up, but maybe you will be happy to leave something behind." He takes a deep breath and the smile falters. "For example, if I was in in your position, I would be happy to leave my debt and start anew. I would probably still end up in the same mess, but I want to know who I would be without all of this. The expectation, the title, the inherited debt. Just me."

Oh, Leo. The man I've gotten to know would figure it out. The way he's been rescuing me, taking care of me, and making me happy. He would be fine. "I think you'd be able to make it."

He inclines his head in thanks. "But that is a dream. Here, I am responsible for all of this. For everyone." He encompasses the room and the footman bringing the fish course. "And I will not disappoint them."

"Responsible, yes. And you had great opportunities. But you also inherited a mess. I appreciate a good education, especially in classics, but maybe they should have given you some business courses. And everyone in your class thinks that working is evil. Something to look down on and it would make you less of an aristocrat. That's a lot to go against, especially when you're young." I can't believe I'm trying to make an aristocrat feel better about his life. This time travel must have scrambled my brain. Or Leo—I think *he* has scrambled my brain. "What could you have done with all that?"

"I should have watched the ones everyone was making light of. The people who were investing, the barons in trade. Anyone in trade." I wince and he backpedals. "Never the East India Company, though."

"Yeah. But you'll get through this." Maybe. I don't know, and that lack of knowledge is killing me, even though initially I thought it was refreshing.

Leo shakes off his melancholy, smile back on his face. I wish it were that easy for me. Unless he's just shoving it all down and one day he'll explode. Not ideal. "No more stalling. What will you miss the least?"

"I guess if you're making me answer..." I look to him to confirm that he's making me, and he nods encouragingly. "I will not miss the bullshit parts of my job."

"What are those?"

"Well, I want to study and write about Indians in England, especially in the Victorian era, but my department head keeps trying to get me to publish on other subjects in this time, saying I would get more success if I kept to other, mostly whiter parts of history. And I usually give in, writing both the articles I want and the ones they want. More of the ones they want. Because it's easier, and I don't have security in the job yet."

"I cannot imagine you giving in to anyone. You are so strong. The way you stand up to Forsyth and everyone here."

"Well. You should work on your imagination. Because it's hard to rock the boat. When I first met you that night, I thought everything was fake. It was easy to be forward with you all because I thought none of it was real. And then I realized it was very real, and I had no choice but to stand up to Charles since he wanted to have me arrested."

"I think this was always you. It is hard to change your entire personality at a moment's notice."

"You're wrong. You've seen a very different version of me because of the circumstances. You should have seen me when one of my undergraduate professors at university berated me in class when I asked questions about Indians in England because I was curious. He said it was 'unnecessary to advance the discourse,' and that they weren't 'significant parts of history.' Now I know that was most likely because he had no idea about the subject. But it made me not want to ask the questions about what interested me. Well, that and people's eyes would glaze over when I talked about it. So I learned to be quiet about it, doing my own research in my free time."

"But was that not a history classes? Why would they not be interested in the subject?"

"Everyone goes into history with their own ideas about what it is, ideas that can be formed by popular culture, which can get it wrong, or previous scholarship that has since been disproved. And people don't like leaning things that go against their world view. Like the views that English history is white, or that brown people couldn't have happy lives in English history."

"That is absolutely wrong. London is a cosmopolitan city." And he would know.

"Obviously. But people ignore things they aren't interested in. The problem is that the same narrative gets told again and again and the general population seems to genuinely think that European history is all white. Just because others haven't been studied as much and there's an absence of evidence, people take that as evidence of their absence. But hopefully that will change. One day."

"I might not spend any time in Limehouse, but even I acknowledge it exists."

"Then you're more progressive than the average American in 2025. Congratulations."

"That seems like a poor reflection on your time."

"All right. Calm down the judgement, *my lord*. You're more progressive in *limited* ways."

The entree comes next, roast beef with vegetables, Yorkshire pudding and gravy.

"It may be small comfort, but you are obviously right. Last year we had three diplomatic delegations from India came and spend the season with us. I do not know if they got what they came for, but they socialized in the highest circles while they were here. And a few people stayed. I am not saying it is easy for Indians, but there are plenty of people who are happy. Me, as evidence. And some that are rich. Although I am not evidence of that."

"They probably didn't get what they came for." The delegations often came to get an increase in their pensions or just to get their pensions enforced at the contracted amounts. The same contracts that transferred rulership to the British, in exchange for what was supposed to be a pension. Pensions that magically got smaller after the contract was signed. Royal groups sometimes went to London to appeal to the Crown directly instead of the British government in India, but it didn't help much usually.

"Anyway. That's the thing I won't miss about h…home." I get choked up at the end of the sentence. "And now I won't have the opportunity to change anyone's mind."

"Ah. This is not helping as much as I had hoped it would."

Sweet man. "It was a nice idea."

"That did not work in execution?"

"I think it's going to be really hard for a long time. But you're right, too. I have options and some friends here. I'll be all right."

"I do not think you believe the last part," Leo says gently.

"It's hard to believe it now. But if I keep saying it, maybe one day I will believe it."

We eat in silence for the rest of this course, and through most of the dessert course of fruit, cakes, souffles and meringues. All very casual, and the completely appropriate amount of food for two people. If one of them is fancy.

After dinner, Leo offers to walk me to my room. Probably a good call, since one tour is not enough to get me acclimated to this house and its numerous hallways.

"Thank you again for bringing me to Cambridge," I say as we get to my door.

"Before you try to make me a knight in the Order of the Garter, remember that I am getting something out of our arrangement as well."

"Right. Royal connections for your heiress hunt." I hate Miss

Chilcott and her beer and money. For absolutely no reason that I can substantiate, other than Leo wants to spend the rest of his life with her. Knowing my luck, she'll be smart and kind too.

"That too, I suppose."

I look up at him in surprise. "What else is there?"

"You. Spending time with you is a pleasure all on its own, without the need of any secondary benefits."

"You can't say shit like that, Leo." I give him a half-hearted punch to his shoulder to emphasize the point, but not to make him go further away from me.

I like him where he is. Maybe he could even be closer.

"What? The truth?" He obliges my thoughts and gets closer, his voice getting lower.

"Did they teach you all this charm at Eton? Maybe from the Cambridge days?"

He nods solemnly. "Yes. Right about when they taught us Plato's *Symposium*. When Aristophanes told everyone his thoughts on the origin of love."

"There were three types of people." I pick up the story, whispering as he moves closer. "A man and woman connected, back-to-back, and two women and two men, joined in the same way. And Zeus thought they were getting too big for their giant, conjoined britches and cut everyone in half and scattered them across the globe."

"And love is finding your literal other half," Leo finishes. "Maybe some of the matches were sent to different times, as well as different places." Leo reaches out to tuck back some of my hair that had escaped Anne's elaborate hairdo. He tucks it behind my ear, grazing the top of my ear in the process. Heat pools, warm and liquid and viscous, low in my belly as my head shifts to get closer to his hand.

Hie eyelids lower to half-closed as he sways a little closer to me.

"Maybe." He still hasn't retracted his hand, and I'll agree to almost anything as long as he keeps it on me. The other joins its friend and both move down my neck, until he's wrapped his hands around it, caressing the skin with his thumbs.

That's it. I'm no Victorian about sex. Not that they even followed the propriety they liked to talk about so much.

A lot has gone wrong this week, but tonight, I'm getting what I want.

Who I want.

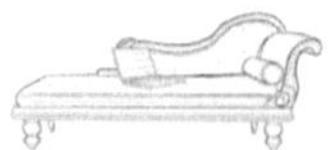

"*D*o you know where my chaperone is?" I ask suddenly.

That takes Leo aback. Physically, unfortunately for me, as his hands drop. "She's most likely in her rooms in the servants' wing. Do you need her now?"

I curse my own awkward-ness as he takes another step back.

But this is the new, forward, Victorian Meera, so I grab his hands and put them back where I want. No subtlety involved. No suppressing what I want because I'm afraid of how other people will react to me.

He doesn't resist. Always a good sign.

"No, I don't need her." I say it as emphatically as I can. "I want to make sure no one is in the room behind this door. Because I want to go into it and spend approximately an hour getting out of all these damn clothes, with you. And then I want to become one person with you. Just like Aristophanes said. And I want to not traumatize Anne while I do it."

Leo is so still I worry this became a superhero movie instead of a time-travelling one, and a villain has frozen him with a freeze-gun. Right before potential coitus, the bastards!

But new, forward Victorian Meera isn't done trying for what

she wants. I step closer to Leo and close my eyes while I raise up on my toes, hoping I land on his lips.

Before I make contact, Leo proves he wants this as much as I do, his hands tightening on either side of my neck as he pulls me forward until we're touching from chest to knees. Still with too many layers of clothes on, but it's a start. I don't have time to enjoy the new position before his lips meet mine, and my world shifts.

It's not just a metaphor for his kisses, which *are* world-shifting, but also a literal explanation of what's happening. His strong arms lift me up a few inches off the ground. Just enough so he can move us back to my door. He shifts me again, this time to one side and to one arm, as his other opens the door and lets us into the room. I feel his erection against me and spend all my energy focusing on arching against him, each stroke making my vagina clench.

Unlike the last time I entered this room, when the only thing I was thinking of was taking notes for my research, my mind is now completely on Leo. Still taking notes, but only in my head and just for me, about what his body feels like against mine, what his lips taste like (dessert and whiskey, the last things he consumed at dinner—my new favorite combination), and how my body melts against his in reaction.

More instinct than intelligence, a big departure from how I usually operate, I start tearing at clothes, pushing when I encounter buttons and pulling when I encounter knots. Leo makes a noise, not appreciating the haphazard approach to peeling back his layers of clothes and gives us some distance.

But I'm assertive now, so I close the distance again.

Except Leo is an aristocrat, not used to his will being thwarted, even by a woman who just discovered assertiveness. So he deftly and firmly turns me around, pushing me against one of the columns of the four-poster bed. He starts pulling at the fastenings on my back, shedding layer and layer with speed and efficiency, showing more than a passing acquaintance with the garments.

As he works behind me, I feel lighter and lighter as I get closer to undressed. He *finally* gets to the last layer, a chemise. I ignore how ridiculous I must look in that garment and focus on him. Lucky for me, this isn't the Elizabethan times, and men's fashion is somewhat the same as in 2025, albeit complicated 2025 clothes.

Still, he must not have faith in my skills and knowledge, because he starts taking off his own clothes. I rush to help, figuring four hands have to be better than two. But mostly our hands clash and tangle unhelpfully, so I give up and get rid of my chemise, shoes and stockings while Leo performs a striptease for me.

Not one that he's aware of doing. And thankfully he's not taking an entire song to get naked, because I don't think I could wait a whole three minutes.

In less time that it would take for Ginuwine to sing "Pony," Leo is naked. He advances on me and pins me back against the column that my front got acquainted with earlier, this time even more affected by the cool, lacquered wood behind me.

Leo kisses me again, hands roaming like he's going on his second Grand Tour, this time on my body. Trying to help him get to Italy faster, I climb the man until my legs are wrapped around his waist and my getting-wetter-by-the-minute folds are rubbing against him.

He groans against my neck, his arms settling around my back. I like the feeling of being enveloped by him. I feel vindicated in my assertiveness. Unlike all those other times that I tried to assert myself and was shot down, here I went after what I wanted and now I'm drowning in pleasure.

I also feel cared for and cherished, in the way he holds me so close. I haven't been alone here in Victorian England. Not really. Leo's been helping me, and Queen Victoria in the form of housing, food, clothes, and Anne. And Anne herself, who has allowed me privacy when I needed it. But I still felt alone. Years and miles away from my home, I've felt lonely being the only future person in the past.

But right now, I don't feel like I'm alone. Leo's body is a warm and safe weight surrounding me. He's here with me, and he won't let anything happen to me.

He sucks on my neck while his hips thrust. My body reacts at his closeness, back arching, fingers clawing and hips aggressively chasing his penis, which teases me but doesn't enter me.

He *finally* gets bored of teasing the sanity out of me. He tosses me on the bed and my world shifts again. And then it doesn't stop after that, as his strong hands drag me to the edge of the bed and then spread my legs.

His erection slides against me, this time getting closer to going inside, shocking me with pleasure but also reminding me of something. "Condoms! Do you have a condom?"

Leo raises his head to look off in the distance, dazed. He doesn't answer, so I slap lightly at his chest, a light sheen of sweat already forming.

"Anything?" We can work around it if not.

"Yes." He nods. "I do. I will just be a moment." He's breathing hard when he says the words and it takes him a second to get up. A compliment to me I suppose.

Leo disappears, naked, out of the door before I can stop him. I hope all his employees are already tucked in for the night, because that would be quite the sight for them. Or maybe they're used to this kind of behavior.

Above me, the canopy, a rich pink cloth with gold embroidery, glints in the low light. I sigh, still barely believing that this isn't all a dream. That I'm experiencing history quite this... physically.

Before I can panic too much over having sex with someone in the past, Leo comes back. Still naked, but no longer looking dazed. Instead, he's triumphant, like he single-handedly just beat France in one of the thousands of wars England and France have fought over the years. And he's holding what vaguely looks like a condom, but already stretched out.

He is a fan of the animal-skin condom. Great.

I wish I knew less history. Not in general, but just for this moment I wish I knew less. Like if I didn't know, I could pretend that was a rubber condom.

While I'm remembering the unfortunate history of the condom in my head, Leo is putting it on and advancing on me. Then he's back on top of me, caressing my thighs as they encircle his waist again. Quivering thighs that apparently don't care what the condom is made of.

Then he kisses me, and I fully don't care anymore. Because I'm not thinking of anything but his mouth, gently exploring mine, the light dusting of hair on his chest tickling my breasts, and his warmth now between my thighs. I also forget all the stress and problems I have, to focus on having fun with this surprising rake.

Hell, if he keeps this up, I'm going to forget my own name.

He gently thrusts in. Shallow at first and then deeper as my body shifts to accommodate the new intrusion. I writhe under him. I want more because he feels amazing and more of an amazing thing can only be more amazing.

Or maybe wanting less because what Leo makes me feel is a lot to take at one time. Especially from someone who spends more time reading about historic figures' sex lives than having one of her own.

He keeps thrusting, groans becoming harsher and more guttural.

"Are you close to orgasm?" he asks, voice more growl than his usual aristocrat cadence.

"Sure." I've never come with a man before. Sex has still been enjoyable. I just can't orgasm with a partner the same way I can with my vibrator. But this is definitely the most fun I've had with a man.

Leo stops and I groan at him in frustration. The movement makes my body move toward him and Leo thrusts once more before being still again. "'Sure' does not sound very confident."

"Well, I'm getting further away now." I don't want to talk about this. I want to keep doing what we were doing, the only sounds our grunts of pleasure and not this inquisition.

"Tell me what you want. What you like." He nuzzles my ear after he asks the questions. The motions are sweet but the words are an order; I have no idea how he combined the two.

What do I want? For him to be quiet. And to do more of what he was doing.

It was one thing being assertive and grabbing him earlier; it's different to talk about sex while I'm having it. I'm in no way that comfortable being vulnerable.

"Do what you were doing." I squirm more under him, hoping that will get him back on track.

"But that was not working for you like it was for me. What do you do when you are alone?"

He's really going to make me be assertive Meera...*again?* During sex? This is becoming more effort than it's worth. Ugh, that's a lie. It is worth it.

"If I show you, will you keep doing what you were doing?" Showing will be better than telling.

"Yes," he answers instantly. "Do you need more space?" He starts to retreat and I clamp my thighs around his torso.

"No. You can stay there." I want him closer. It'll be easier to do this if I can't see his face, and the feel of his body is a nice distraction.

I slide my hand between us and start to play with my own clit. Leo leans up on his hands to watch, but I can see his face too clearly while doing something too private, so with my other hand I drag his head back down until he's kissing me.

I get wetter, keeping up the movement until Leo starts moving again.

I didn't think I would be able to get in the same headspace as when I masturbate, with the same lack of inhibitions, but I slowly start to relax and enjoy the pleasure as I touch myself. And feeling Leo inside me as I play with my clit is even better than when I'm alone, slowly causing a familiar tension in my body.

As the tension builds, Leo's hand slips between us and he takes over for me, his fingers rubbing my clit the same way my own just were. Having him touch me, in the way that I've just shown him I like, gives me so much pleasure I moan into his shoulder, clawing at his back in case he thought about stopping.

"Are you getting close now?"

"Yes," I breathe out. No tepid (and lying) "sure" this time. My entire body feels tight, like it's strung on a bow.

"Good," he growls against my lips. The word pushes me over the edge, throwing me into my first orgasm with another person. He follows me after a few more thrusts and then collapses next to me after a last kiss to my forehead.

Without any more words, thankfully, he gathers me in his arms. His breathing evens, letting me know he's asleep. I guess he's spending the night in my room.

It's a good thing I like him.

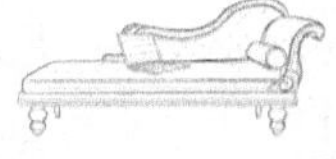

"I've ruined you."

This is a fun way to wake up. Especially since I've been ruined, in the sex-shamey sense of the word, since freshman year of college. I could also do without the regret in his voice.

I had what was the best sex of my life, and I don't need it ruined with his regret.

"I think I need breakfast before we get into this." Except let's not get into it after, either. How about we get into it around 2025? I can explain the patriarchy to his headstone. I get out of bed naked, not really wanting to stick around if he's going to be this depressing.

"We should get married?"

I freeze in the act of pulling my chemise over my head, blood running cold at the thought of making a permanent step to a life here. Which would be admitting I'm never going home.

Also, and this is a small but important side note, I don't love that phrasing. *Should* is reserved for all sorts of things I don't want to do, like I *should* eat more vegetables. I *should* exercise more. I *should* go to bed at a reasonable hour and not stare at my phone until I've lost all chance of getting my recommended sleep hours in. And then he makes it a question to boot, which is just insulting.

The bigger point is that I can't marry him because I'm from the future. The petty reason is that I'm mad he isn't more excited about the prospect of marriage to me.

He would be so lucky to be married to me.

The level of confusion needs to be buried under a full English breakfast. I don't think that includes baked beans yet, which is a tragedy, but I think I can still get eggs and sausage out of this. They can keep the cold kippers. Oh, maybe he'll have kedgeree. They'll be spices in there I can relate to, even if the Brits do have their own take on the Indian dish.

Yes. I can think about food. It's better than wanting to kick Leo right in his pale and shapely butt. Incidentally, the main body part I can see as he gets out of the bed and tries to find his clothes.

"I shall need to obtain a special license from the archbishop, but I believe I have enough pull and enough funds left to get it without much issue."

"We aren't getting married!" I yell out. Okay, I'm not getting food before we have this conversation. I was so hopeful for the delay. And the sustenance it would give me. "We don't need to get married just because we had sex."

"I shall do the right thing."

"The right thing is to feed me breakfast. And then we'll go back to our lives. Me trying to get home to mine, you trying to save yours."

"But we had intercourse." Leo looks at the bed as if there's still evidence there that he can see. Or like he's imagining us doing it in that spot again.

"Yes. But you've had sex before and you haven't married any of those women."

"But…" Now his eyebrows are drawn low over his eyes. "It is different."

"It's not. I'm not a princess or lady or whatever. I'm not even a knight's daughter. And I'm poor. This won't ruin my reputation any more than the fact that I'm lying to the queen will. Less, probably. Even if I stay in this time, I won't be in the *ton*. So, no worries. It's been great. But you have responsibilities."

"You are right," Leo says with a sigh, instead of the denial I thought he would keep throwing at me. "Those responsibilities are not compatible with me doing what I want to. And I cannot be like my father."

Ouch. I have never been this livid at someone agreeing with me.

I think the hit to my head did more damage than just sending me back in time. I think it knocked the common sense out of me and left it in the future without me.

"Good. I mean, yeah." I rummage around my trunk for clothes to wear today. It's not like I could put them on myself after I get them out of the luggage, but it's something to do while Leo escorts himself out of the room.

Leo grabs my arm as I walk back to the bed, his strong grip closing around my forearm and immediately sending me back to last night, in the best way.

"Though I wish I could have what I want." His eyes bore into mine. So much heat being conveyed that I clear my throat in response.

There's no doubt that he's talking about me being the one he wants. No looking over my shoulder to see who he's talking to. He wants *me*.

"I know. I wish…" There's too much to articulate. Too much that can't happen. I settle on the most general phrase I can. "I wish things were different."

"I shall send Anne up to help you get ready." Leo slides his hand down my forearm until he gets down to my fingers. Which he then raises to his lips, in order to kiss the back of my hand.

And then he's gone, while my hand stays up where he left it, hovering in the air.

I'm glad he didn't push on the marriage front. I don't know that I would have been able to keep saying no to him.

And that's terrifying.

~

THE TRIP back to London is uneventful. Somber, too. A lot of far-away stares outside of carriage and train windows. Even Anne feels it, and she's probably disappointed that she failed in her chaperone duties. A fact she could tell right when she walked into the room.

I've spent the morning avoiding thinking about what gave me away.

At the palace, I give Leo an awkward goodbye, waving at him since I don't think awkward side hugs are acceptable yet.

I get back in time for lunch with Queen Victoria and her daily lunch curry. I'm so exhausted from the nighttime activities it's very hard to keep track of what's going on, and I'm glad Charles didn't come to visit. Abdul is bad enough, giving me slight side eye when I let some slang slip. Lucky for me Victoria thinks it's some "Hindoostani" which is really Urdu, that she hasn't gotten a chance to learn yet, and doesn't question it.

"How was the trip?" Victoria asks.

"It was really good, thank you. I got to see so much of the English educational system. Quite impressive. I'll have plenty to report back to Suniti Devi on things she can implement in her school." There. Everyone loves being complimented.

It works, and Victoria spends the rest of the time talking about India with Abdul. I nod a lot but keep actual contributions down since I only have tangential knowledge about India during this time.

Then I get some time alone in my room. No callers, no

monarch and no Leo. No Anne, even. I open my notebook and go back and forth between adding notes and observations from my trip and brainstorming more ways to get home.

But now I have to give serious consideration to knocking myself out. I haven't even tried it since the first day, because making myself unconscious seems like a poor decision. But there might not be any other way.

Whether or not the time travel works again, my time is nearing its end. The letter proving I'm a liar should be arriving soon and I should be gone from the palace before that happens. I could go to Limehouse first and get a room at one of the boarding houses until I figure out my next steps. Although it is the obvious choice, it may be crowded enough to provide some protection.

Then maybe I'll try America, in Victorian times. Home, but not. I can steal something from the palace to fund my travel and new life there. Call it reparations so I don't have to feel bad about the theft.

But Leo did want to take me out on a cheer-up day. So I'll refrain from giving myself a brain injury for at least another day. It would be rude to leave the time or the country when I've already made plans with Leo, is all.

Okay, decided.

One more day. Then I leave.

THE NEXT MORNING, Leo picks me up early and comes with a present. He hands me a bouquet of roses, which gets him a smile and a genuine thanks before I hand it to Anne. I don't know where the flower vases are in this palace, but I don't think Her Majesty would appreciate me putting flowers in one of her many Sevres vases.

Then Leo hands me something else, a twinkle in his eyes that he didn't have when he gave me the flowers. I open it, and gasp in excitement. It's the cutest, tiniest little notebook with a small pen to match. The notebook is a beautiful brown leather, with a floral pattern embroidered on the front.

"I know you will appreciate these flowers." He points to the notebook cover. "More than the first ones. And that you might want something a little smaller for our touring today."

"I do." I hold the treasures closer to my chest. "I mean. The real flowers are lovely, too. It was very kind of you to bring them for me." Wherever they are.

But I'm not handing this notebook off to anyone. I tighten my grip just in case anyone tries to take this and put in some water.

"Where are we going today?" I ask.

"The places that you talked about wanting to see. Mostly. With one surprise at the end of the day."

"A surprise?" I groan.

"I know how you feel about surprises, but you know how I feel about surprises. I want to see your face when we get there. I think you will appreciate it, in a way that no other woman that I know would."

"Cryptic." I let him have it for a second. Then my natural impatience wins out. "Is it a museum?"

"Maybe in your time. But no, it is not a museum now."

I look around to make sure Anne hasn't gotten back from putting the flowers away. She's not in sight and the footman is too far away to hear me, so I relax. "Hmm. In my time, we have a game called twenty questions. One person chooses an object, person, or place in this case, and the other people get to ask twenty yes or no questions and then try to guess what the item is. Can we do that? To guess what my surprise is?"

"You may ask one question an hour until we go there. It is not twenty, but you are smarter than the average person, and I do not want you to guess it too easily."

"Agreed. Is—"

"You have already asked your first one, and I have answered. About it not being a museum."

Drat. So I have. "All right. That's a start."

"I will tell you where we are going now—the Palace of Westminster and Westminster Abbey. This is going to be a busy day, so if you want to skip something or end the day early, it is all up to you. I will not be offended. I want you to have a good day."

"Oh, you sweet summer child." I pat him on the shoulder. "I always travel like I might never go back to a place so I have to see everything all at once, exhaustion not allowed until the end of the day. So I will happily go anywhere and everywhere you can stand to take me."

"And we need to leave your chaperone behind. Hence the flowers." Leo gets up and urges me to do the same, checking to see if Anne is coming back yet.

"I'm in." I'm still not used to having to have a chaperone, so I don't mind ditching her. Even though she's been nothing but nice to me. Didn't even snitch about that whole sex thing. But I'll be gone soon, so even if she tells on me now, it won't have much effect.

"Excellent. Just remember, the longer you stay, the more I can show you." Leo takes my hand and kisses the back of it as we walk quickly to his carriage, smiling so earnestly I swallow back the truth.

Because no matter what happens with my temporal location, I won't be with the sweet man next to me.

CHAPTER 29

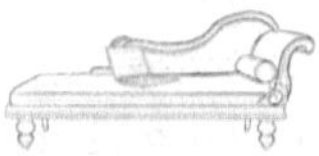

"It's been an hour. Does the place have food?"

Leo sighs and keeps walking through the halls of Parliament. "No. Well, there may be some, but it is not the main purpose of the location. I personally cannot remember if I have ever eaten there."

I write that little tidbit down, even though the question didn't narrow anything down.

Most of Westminster is the same as it is in modern times, but the real treat is that I get to eavesdrop on ministers, unfiltered, and watch them work in Victorian times. Boy, do they have opinions on the Factory and Workshop Act being debated this year. Although the opinions are largely as expected (rich people hate it), the real gold is the bits of their personal lives they talk about when they should be discussing legislation.

It's fantastic. The notebook is certainly getting broken in, pages already filled.

Leo lets me sit in the House of Lords throne where I order him around for a minute before I get nervous that someone will see me on here and behead me, and he makes out with me in the House of Lords Library.

Because libraries are our place now.

Unfortunately, we're interrupted in the library before things can get really good by a dour-looking man in a robe who doesn't see anything scandalous but disapproves because he can sense we're having fun. We shuffle past him, giggling like schoolchildren caught by the headmaster. I'm laughing so hard Leo has to physically pull me along.

Next on the list is Westminster Abbey, which I enjoy seeing without the velvet ropes keeping the public back. I take liberal advantage of the freedom, rushing to document every bit of the areas I couldn't see in 2025.

There's no kissing there, which is probably for the best.

"Hour's up," I whisper at him. "Are we going to a play?"

"No," he whispers back. I make a note as we leave the church. "I imagine you are hungry now. Will you take your tea with a hint of intrigue?"

"Intrigue? Yes, please." I tug at his arm, speeding up to get to his carriage faster.

"Would you like more information before you commit fully? Intrigue tends to involve danger."

I scoff. "I'm with a Peer of the Realm. I somehow think I'll be all right." Or I could bear the entire brunt of the punishment, but I'm banking on Leo protecting me with his aristocratic cloak.

"Hmm. We are going to take tea at White's."

I gasp and stop in place. "White's? No-girls-allowed White's? With the betting book and the *no girls allowed*? That White's?"

"Yes. I am going to throw a cloak over you and pretend not to hear any questions about the entire situation. I have also enlisted the aid of friends to get through most of the enforcers. They think this is quite the jape."

"There's going to be enforcers and disguises and annoying the patriarchy?" I smile so wide my cheeks hurt at how perfect this tea is going to be. I wish I had a giant poster that says *Girls Rule and Boys Drool* that I could leave in the sitting room to really stick it to them.

"I thought you might enjoy it," Leo says as he throws a cloak over my head, dampening my image but not my enthusiasm.

"This dress is really obvious. We've got a lot working against us," I say, muffled by the material.

"We are relying heavily on my friends in this scenario."

"Did you promise to buy their drinks?"

"For a fortnight. And they can certainly drink, so please derive as much pleasure as you can out of this."

I don't tell him how irresponsible it is. Considering my time with Leo is limited, I don't want to waste any of it being responsible. Or lecturing Leo about spending his money.

"I'm going to enjoy this more than any place a man has ever taken me." I can't even get into White's in my time; I'm still too woman-y for those losers.

The carriage ride is short, and then Leo is walking me past the famous bow window where Beau Brummell judged passersby. I don't gawk at it like the tourist I am because Leo's striding through the door with a confidence that I've never felt in my life, not even with how assertive I've been in the past week. I try to emulate it, not wanting to be the weak link in our subterfuge.

He even nods cheekily at the doorman. And when said doorman gives me a closer look, an entire group of carousing men tumble into the building from behind us, pushing me farther into the masculine space.

And boy, does it want me to know it's masculine. Like a very insecure person, it pushes stereotypical manliness in my face at every turn: wood paneling or plain walls, only minimal crown molding, paintings of stodgy men looking sternly down in case I had the nerve to be a woman (oops), and dark wood tables covered with newspapers. Only some red leather chairs and a flirty chandelier break the theme.

It smells like smoke and musty newspapers, and I've never

been more grateful for the future ban on indoor smoking than right now, as I cough in this hallowed space. It may be better to take it all in with my other senses.

I dip into the morning room and take a seat at Beau's famous window. I put my nose in the air and give Leo my best British accent. "Look, old chap. Look at this unfortunate soul who has the temerity to wear paisley. Paisley is so last season, I say."

Leo rolls his eyes and leans against the wall just outside the window. Leans very seductively, although that may just be because I find everything he does seductive. "I do want you to enjoy your time here, but we might want to hurry if you want to see as many rooms as possible and take tea."

"Good point." I get my notebook out and take notes as I spread my lady-ness on everything. "Look, I'm getting girl on EVERYTHING." I sit in a few chairs to maximize my presence and caress a few tables in defiance.

"Yes. Everyone is going to wonder why it smells so lovely when they get in."

The rest of the building looks surprisingly plain. I guess the main draw is no women, and they don't need to try hard with the decoration.

There are a few men lounging around, chatting and reading the newspaper, who give us only a cursory glance. I guess they really do take privacy seriously. And anytime someone gets a little more curious, or looks at us too hard, a hoard of rowdy men descends as a distraction, drawing attention and disapproving looks their way.

"Can I see the betting book?" I whisper.

"Yes, you can." Leo leads me to another room, with a book open in the middle. It's too high for me to read comfortably, and before I can be sad about it, Leo appears at my side with a few books. My mother would slap me for standing on books because it is very disrespectful to do in Indian culture, but I'll apologize to them after.

It's worth it, because the bets are a treasure trove of information! Betting how long a drop of water takes to get down the window, how soon Lady Marquette will get married, whose son is going to reach five feet first between two lords, and how soon it'll be before the widow Lady Alfred takes her first lover.

Nothing logical to bet on, like sports. But clearly superior in my opinion, because it shows everyone loves petty drama and gossip, even if they pretend to look down on it.

"What's the wildest bet you've made here?" I ask as I peruse the bets.

"I do not bet here. I take my pleasure watching my friends get invested in the contents of the book in front of you, but I do not want to become like my father so I try to stay away. To limit my gambling, at least."

"Responsiblest rake ever," I say under my breath but not really that quietly.

"Pardon me? Someone responsible would never take you where I am going to take you later today." He sounds so genuinely affronted I can't help but laugh at him.

"Ah-ha! It's somewhere rakish!"

Leo looks chagrined. "That is one of your questions."

"No, it is not. It was freely offered information that I didn't even have to work for. Now, about this rakish place—"

One of his friends saves him by appearing with a tea tray, complete with sandwiches, scones and pastries, and all the requisite tea equipment.

"Better than having one of the staff bring it. So you can have a chance to enjoy it with less chance of being thrown out," Leo whispers in my ear.

"This is the most fun we have had in ages." The friend lingers after he sets the tray down on a table. "But you have been having more fun than us, haven't you?"

The man leers at me, and I'm more impressed he can be into me when I'm covered in a shapeless clock than angry. Leo wouldn't let anything happen to me. Because he's a good man. And because the Queen of England would be cross with him if he did.

What is my life?

"Leave. Now." Leo sounds firmer than I've heard him, and I look up from pouring some tea. Because that tone is working for me. The friend backs off with a smirk, leaving us alone again. "He is more acquaintance than friend."

We enjoy the tea for a while, Leo relaxing again to charmer and not enforcer (which also works for me, because everything about this man works for me), before we're interrupted again. By another one of his friends, I assume, since Leo isn't worried.

"You two might want to hurry. People are starting to get suspicious," his friend says, then leaves us alone again.

"Oh, damn. I was hoping we would have longer," Leo says.

My mouth is too full of scone being drowned down with tea to respond. I hold up a finger, signaling I will answer eventually. When I'm not busy inhaling delicious, tiny, illicit, sandwiches, made more delicious with how illicit they are, and soaking in the atmosphere that only a handful of other women have seen. "It's all right. This has been amazing."

Despite the urgency of getting caught, I take the time to stuff food in my pocket and take notes. I then take a beat longer and pull Leo down to kiss him. This being one of my last days, probably my very last, with Leo, I'm not going to have many more opportunities to do this.

I'm going to miss him so much.

Leo is surprised at first, standing still and not responding to the kiss. Then he hears a noise outside the door, which spurs him into action. The action is to try to bring me in closer, just as I try to pull away and run so we don't get caught.

Leo makes a sound of frustration but moves to the door after me. He quickly jogs in front of me and leads us out of the building, a sputtering Englishman scolding after us.

I laugh in exhilaration, making it much harder to run. We burst out into the afternoon, the cool air helping me calm down. Leo keeps us moving until we turn around the corner, collapsing against the brick wall to catch my breath.

"That was so much fun," I wheeze out.

"Good. I am glad you enjoyed it." Leo peeks around the corner to see if we're being pursued. He must not see anything because he leans back against the wall with me.

"Is the next place going to involve this much crime?" I ask.

"Do you want it to include illegal acts?"

"Well, I'm already doing illegal things by lying to the crown, and we just infiltrated White's, so maybe I should be a bit more circumspect? So as not to push it."

"Where is the fun in that?"

Fuck it. I won't be around long enough for all my crimes to matter. Or if I am caught, what's one more crime to add to the list? "You're right. I'm game for wherever you want to take me."

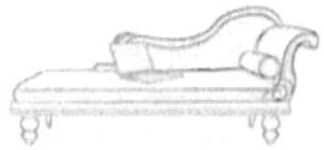

"I admire your spirit. But we will not do anything too scandalous next. In the evening, however…" A damn tease, Leo doesn't finish the sentence.

"I get my question now. This mysterious, rakish, illegal event, is it something athletic?" I don't know where else to go with the questions, if it's not a restaurant, dinner party, or a play. I don't think it would be another ball, but that's an option.

"No. I suppose some do complain it is hard on their body after extended periods of this activity. But it is not meant to be athletic, in the sense that it is done for the purpose of exercise or there are competitions for it. At least no official competitions, although many do tend to brag about their ability to participate in this type of activity for extended periods."

"Hmm. Evasive, strange answer to a simple yes or no question. Is it sex? Are you taking me to a nice place where we're going to have sex?"

Leo, bless his Victorian heart, blushes. "No. And that is two questions," he mumbles. He leads us to his carriage, telling the driver where we're going in a whisper I can't hear.

"All right." I throw my hands up. "You know, Victorian pornography develops a bit of a reputation in my time."

"You don't have…pornography in your time?" He stumbles over the word, because of all that Victorian training of repression with the "fairer" sex. Absurd.

"Oh no, we definitely do. In a way that is more accessible than you could ever imagine. We have devices where you can carry all the porn in the world in your pocket and watch it whenever you want. And we've got books, pictures, paintings, and video, so you can choose your own adventure in the medium."

Leo looks shocked and I giggle, but also hope this doesn't break any more time travel rules. Not that the universe has punished me yet for breaking the rules, which I'm sure I have at this point.

"It's not just a pornography machine," I clarify when he still hasn't spoken. "It has *all* the information in the world. Or at least a lot of it. And a lot of lies too." Anything someone has posted to the internet. "And it just happens to include pornography."

"You live in a truly wondrous time. Advanced technology. Educated, assertive women. And a freedom of sexuality."

"I thought you'd like that. I mean, it's still complicated and there are some who are less progressive. Victorian morality is kind of making a comeback in some ways. But in general, there's more freedom for people to decide what they want their rela-tionship with sex to be." I don't feel the need to tell him that I've been more assertive here than I ever was back home. But the parts about education and pornography are still the truth, and he's probably more concerned with those anyway.

"I can understand why you want to go home so urgently."

"There are good things here too," I say shyly, refusing to look at him. "Things that I will miss when I leave." *People* I will miss. Leo-type people.

"But you still want to leave?" He asks the question softly, like he's as afraid of my answer as I am of giving it.

"I have to." I don't want to get into the debate again for something I'm so conflicted over. Because in reality, I want it all. I want my home and I want my Leo. And I don't see how I can have both of those things, or even one of those things, at this point. I try to change the subject. "Where are we going now?"

"This next activity needs a small caveat," Leo says carefully.

"What? How bad is it that you need to caveat it? Why are we going if it's bad?"

"I am not taking you here because I approve of anything that happens in this building—"

"Then why do I want to go?"

"Allow me to finish. I think the scholar in you will appreciate what you are about to see. But it is going to make you, the person, angry. So please get your book out, and please do not hit me with it."

I get the book out. "I make no promises. But I will keep your warning in mind."

"That is all I can ask."

We chat for a while, Leo loosening up, until finally the carriage stops and he goes back to looking nervous.

"Where are we? We were traveling for a while."

"Earl's Court."

Earl's Court. 1895. "Shut up. Are you taking me to the Empire of India Exhibition?" I stare at him for a few seconds while he stares back at me. So still, like he's a bunny and I'm a hawk and he doesn't want to risk moving and catching my attention.

He's a hundred percent right. I will hate it personally and be very interested in writing about it.

Organized by Imre Kiralfy, the burlesque and spectacle producer, the exhibition is meant to show scenes of Indian past and present, from landscapes, history, food, animals, art and industry. With an emphasis on how *Britain* was responsible for any good that comes out of India.

It's going to be educational to see the way this British exhibition tries to shape an Indian identity, for Indians in England and those in India. And what they say about themselves as they try to shape other identities.

It's also going to be infuriating. Because these are actual humans they're fetishizing and condescending in there. Some maharajas even acted as patrons, which seems even more messed up after the Crown took their authority but let them keep a meaningless title with a pension that the government decreased whenever they felt like it.

Leo relaxes now that I'm not raging. I look up at his too-handsome face, wondering how he got to know me so well in such a short time. By paying a lot of attention, I guess. My heart aches inside my chest, wanting so badly to tell him how I feel, but knowing there's no use. In fact, it will make everything worse.

"You're right. And it's a good choice. Not a good thing, but something I need to see," I say instead of what I want to say. Which is, *I love you. I don't know how, since it's a terrible idea. I've spent more time reminding myself of all the reasons I can't love you, but nothing is convincing. I'm so in love with you.*

But that wouldn't help anyone.

Now Leo's smiling. "Thank god." He opens the door. "Shall we?"

I nod, not speaking because the only thing I want to do is to yell over how much I love him. Since I can't do that, silence is the better option.

He leads me to the exhibition space, a Mughal-inspired building erected specifically for this exhibit. Which means a lot of domes and multifoil arches. Inside is booth after booth of what England thinks India is, including food vendors and Indian craftsmen that fit their narrative.

We wander the stalls, and, as expected, England is taking credit for anything positive that happened in India, which is not great. If anything, it should really be called the British Exhibition, because it says more about them than India: their priorities, their interests, and their rewriting of both past and present to fit the colonial narrative.

Leo takes me on the Great Wheel, a giant Ferris wheel that looks down on the exhibition space. They're still a new invention, so it takes a lot of trust to get on this one, and I clutch Leo's hand the entire time, our connection hidden by my cloak.

It's not enough contact, but it's all I can have.

After the ride, we go back in the exhibition building for some Indian food. I can't complain about its authenticity, because it's cooked by legitimate Indian chefs and the spices they brought with them. I eat a lot, because it's closer to home than the dishes Victoria's chefs make, and I'm missing my mom's cooking. Just like I'm missing my mom.

After I eat my body weight in Indian food, Leo extends his arm and I take it without any reservation. He walks us to the Empress Hall, the theater space built specifically for this show, "India: A Grand Historic Spectacle."

"There isn't much written about exactly what is in this show besides 'elaborate costumes and songs and dances,' so this is interesting for me. From an academic perspective." The racism will not be interesting, personally.

"Just remember how much I've evolved since I met you."

"Noted."

The curtains start to rise, cutting off further conversation. And then the spectacle begins. Even with the wonder of television, movies, and even Broadway, it is quite the spectacle from a purely entertainment/technological standpoint. The backdrops and costumes are vibrant and elaborate. And there are lots of song, dance and even mime numbers.

But everyone is played by an Englishman, including all the Indians. And the play focuses on England being the heroes, saving people in need of their "civilization" efforts. Ew.

At the end of the show, they get a B for presentation, F- for content. As a professor, I have many comments on how they could improve the historical accuracy without sacrificing entertainment, but I left my red pen in 2025. Lucky them.

After the historic spectacle, which is light on history and heavy on spectacle, is over Leo leads me back to the carriage.

"Indians actually had a lot more leeway in defining themselves before the British Raj. There was nothing like this then, back in the 1600s," I say.

"What changed?" Leo asks.

"Empire. Once the East India Company shifted from trading to taking over and then the British government started taking over as colonizers, they had to paint Indians as less than, of needing their rule. To justify stealing people's land and their homes and their rights."

"I never thought of it like that."

"The exhibition is more than entertainment. It's a piece of propaganda and is making two national identities: for England and for India."

We fall into silence and my eyes run over Leo's face, memorizing it in this particular light. I've already done the same for his face in the morning light, the afternoon light, Westminster Abbey light, and carriage light. I've only got a few more times of the day left to add to my collection of memories before I'll have hoarded them all. For those lonely nights. Wherever I end up. Whenever I end up.

Leo notices my open staring and clears his throat. "It is not over yet. I hope you are awake enough for this, but if you are tired we can reschedule for another night. I want you to enjoy this fully."

"Not a chance." Not only do I want to find out where we're going because he's been talking it up all day, there won't be many other nights for us, even if my chest aches at the thought. Not that he knows that. And I won't be enlightening him. "I drank some chai at the exhibition just so I would be caffeinated and ready."

"You are game for adventure. I admire that greatly about you."

His compliment tugs at my heart, which has already had too much action today, from the euphoric realization that I love him to the immediate emotional punch that I won't be able to have him. "I get one more question, right?" I ask, even though I'm no closer to guessing where he's taking us than I was this morning.

"All right; I shall risk it. One more before we get there."

"Do you go there often?" I smile at the pickup line that isn't a pickup line for another hundred years. And not even a good one at that.

But if I only have one question and we're heading there anyway, I might as well use it to get more information out of Leo about himself.

"I used to go, not often, but more often than I do now. Which is hardly ever. Both then and now, it was somewhere to go if friends were going." I see a light red appear on his cheeks, and I commit it to memory too. Under: Leo in the early evening light, with a blush, in a carriage.

I'm so screwed.

I shake my head to focus on his answer. That's a lot of hedging. On the slight chance I wasn't ravenous to know what Leo has been building up all day, now I'm even more curious.

Leo tries to distract me from the inquisition, getting out a basket with some food he brought for the long, fun day. He thought of everything.

"I think I'm still full from what we ate at the exhibition."

Leo pushes the basket at me anyway. "You may want something in your stomach before the evening's activities."

I warily take it. "All right. If you say so." I take a tentative bite of some bread. "Is alcohol going to be involved?"

"Only if you want it to be. But best to be prepared either way."

"Hmm…alcohol, scandalous crimes, young men carousing—"

"I know you possess the intelligence to easily guess the answer. And I can see you are getting close. But since we are almost there, it may be more fun to allow surprise to have the final say?"

"I can't turn my brain off, but I'll try for you. You may want to distract me in case my brain doesn't get the message and tries to deductively reason against my will."

"Shall I tell you about all my glorious stories of my travels?"

"Oh yes! But tell me more about the *inglorious* stories, please."

Leo shakes his head at me. "Curious woman. But all right. I will tell you all the stories about my travels that I thought were not fit for a lady."

"I'll even ignore the fact that you just said that, in the spirit of charity." But breaking my promise almost immediately, I glare at him for the sexist sentiment.

Leo spends the rest of the trip telling me about his "educational" trips around Europe, visiting France, Germany, Italy and Greece. Educational in the sense that he ate great food, drank all the wine and had flings more often than he saw history. He does mention the art he bought and commissioned on his trips, some of which I saw in his family home.

Since I can't turn off the historian in me, I take notes while laughing at his stories, multitasking. He's living proof that an Indian person could live well in England and be happy. Just like Sophia Singh, walking her dogs in Hampton Court Palace where she lives and getting involved with women's suffrage and the Indian community in London. Or Catherine Singh, falling in love with her governess Lina, and living with her in Germany until Lina passes. Or Frederick Singh, living the life of a country gentleman, with his love for English history and membership in antiquarian societies.

And that was just one Indian family (possibly the most written about). There were countless students, ayahs, lascars, teachers, professionals, princes and more who made their home in England, with various degrees of struggle and happiness.

Because everyone had a unique experience, and it is naïve to think none of them could have had happy lives.

Then the carriage stops and Leo trails off in the middle of a story involving a marble tiger, an Italian countess, and a thousand-year-old Roman tomb. I want to hear about the rest of the story, but I want to find out where we are even more.

I reach for the carriage door handle and Leo covers my hand with his, stilling my movement. I tug at his hand. "You've been building this up all day. I want to see it. Now." I'm going to explode with curiosity if I don't get to find out soon. It's my job and nature to be curious, as Leo points out, and I can't contain it.

"I know. In a second I will let you out. Before you do, in case I misjudged and you feel uncomfortable or do not want to stay, we shall leave immediately."

"You're making it so much worse."

"All right, all right." He lets go and then pushes my hand out of the way gently to open the door for me. He gets out first and then turns to help me out.

I don't know what I was expecting when I stepped out of the carriage, but it wasn't where we are. Maybe I expected a wild circus, or a...a...I genuinely didn't even know what to think with all Leo's cryptic hints. Sex dungeon, maybe?

But we're back in the Pall Mall area, on a quiet street, with quiet, beautiful Georgian architecture looking back at me, white townhouses connected in a seemingly endless row of carved facades. This is *not* what I expected.

"Are we going to a ball?" We've had a lot of those in our short acquaintance. More than I ever thought I would go to.

"Would I have spent all day teasing this specific plan just to take you to another society event?"

"Maybe?" I hope not, though. I don't want to waste time with Leo being nervous and on guard with society vipers.

"Your low opinion of me notwithstanding, I did not do that."

I take his arm before he extends it, hoping to get past my lack of faith in his planning skills. He has given me the perfect day so far, and even if this ends up as an aristocratic musicale where the poor debutante has no skill despite having Victoria's favorite musician Felix Mendelssohn himself teach her, I will listen to the unfortunate screeches with a smile. Or a grimace, that I hope passes as a smile.

"I'm sure I'm going to have a good time." But the tone is less sure, because where am I?

"Hmm," Leo mumbles, but refrains from defending himself. Which either means he acknowledges that this is going to be a letdown, or it's so amazing he's not worried about my doubt.

Either way, I'm about to find out. Leo leads me up to the anonymous building, opening the door with no fanfare.

The smile freezes on my face as I walk in.

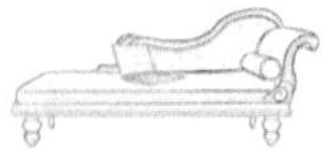

I'm in a hedonistic fever dream. I almost walk out the door again to confirm I entered into a staid Georgian townhouse. Who knew this would be a portal to debauchery?

The air is smokey, which isn't great for my respiration, but I'm distracted by the loud mass of bodies crammed into the space. Mostly men, and some women, crowd the entryway laughing, yelling and stumbling over each other, like I walked in to an elegant, costumed frat party. People are about as drunk as a frat party-goer. And I think I see a couple making out.

After all the balls I've been to and the propriety shoved down my throat, I might be a bit scandalized. Or at least a little surprised.

"Where are we?"

"A private gaming hell," Leo whispers in my ear. He's joined the spirit of getting closer to members of the opposite sex than is usually allowed, and his breath tickles the hair by my ear.

He nudges me along, probably to stop me from looking like the tourist I am. We move into the next room, this one set up with tables. More people jostle and joke around them, playing cards and hazard. There's more room to breathe here, but it's still crowded.

"This is not the most captivating part," Leo yells in my ear. He's loud but I can still barely hear him over the roars of excitement and disappointment filling the room.

"It's pretty good." More proof that everything edgy we think we invented has already been done.

Leo smiles and keeps tugging me along. He takes me up the stairs, the din of noise lessening as we get farther up. "This may not be the most elite gaming hell I could have taken you to, mostly because women are not allowed in those."

I give him a dirty look and he throws his hands up. I roll my eyes. "I'm not mad at you. I'm mad at the entire situation."

Leo nods. "But this one in particular does let women in. It is also run by a barely respectable widow, and caters to a wider swath of society. It is the most interesting gaming establishment I could have taken you to."

"A barely respectable widow?" The best kind, I think everyone will agree.

"And we are going to speak to her right now."

I gasp, getting my mini-notebook and pen out of my purse. "I'm ready."

Leo knocks at the closed door at the end of the hall and opens it after an "Enter" comes through.

"Lady Jane." Leo bursts into the room and approaches the white woman sitting at the desk, who is reviewing documents. She's wearing red silk, with one or two less petticoats than me so the dress hugs her curves a little more. She's more fashionable than me with my older, borrowed dresses. Her gray hair is done up and she's wearing more makeup than is entirely proper.

There are two large white men in the room, who stand up as Leo approaches her, ready to do violence to him for nearing her.

"Basildon," the woman greets him warmly and accepts his kisses to the cheek, motioning for the men to back down.

"Looks like business is doing quite well."

"Despite you lot trying to close me down in Parliament, and then showing up on my door step the same day you try to pass laws on vice and gambling." She shakes her head at him.

"Lady Jane, I would never vote for those monstrosities." He puts his hand on his heart for sincerity.

"Hmm." The elegant woman looks at me. "Who is this?"

"Indian royalty," Leo says with a wink over his shoulder at me. "Her Royal Highness Meera Chopra, of the Cooch Behar royal family. And this is the infamous Lady Jane."

"Bringing me royalty? You must want this place to succeed."

"I may not be the best advertisement. You might want to hold off putting me in the brochure," I say.

"You speak strangely."

"I travel a lot, especially in America."

"Ah, they are strange there. Welcome to my establishment."

"If you're not too busy, may I ask you some questions?"

She jerks her head back on a laugh. "You come to my den of sin and you want to *talk* to me?"

"It's so impressive, what you've built here." I wave my hand behind me to encompass her domain.

"Leo has brought so many of his friends here, and they've spent so much money, that if one of his friends wants to talk, we can do that."

"Great." I get out my notebook and start the interview, wishing my phone had come with me. I could use the recording app for all the fantastic information I'm getting recently.

Lady Jane is open with me. Her great-grandmother ran an aristocratic Faro house, back when they were in fashion in the 1790s. It was acceptable for women to play in private houses while men played at their private clubs. But people started to be more concerned with the morality of gambling, especially after the French Revolution and the growing middle class who disapproved of the vice. For women, it was increasingly associated with a loose sexuality, because how dare women have fun? And without men—unacceptable.

More laws against private gaming houses shut down a lot of the Faro Ladies, but Lady Jane's family kept running a small gaming house after. When Lady Jane inherited it, she built it up to where it is now.

I could have listened to her talk all night, but she has to do actual work, so Leo tugs me away. He leads me back downstairs. "Did you enjoy the talk?"

"So much." I smile at him.

"Good. Now maybe you can enjoy the gaming hell itself."

Before I can ask what he means, he leads me to a table with gentle tugs and pushes until I'm in the seat.

"I don't have any money," I whisper to him, trying to stand back up.

Leo puts his hands on my shoulders to keep me at the table. "I shall fund you. I am sure you will be more responsible with it than I ever was."

"I'm not going to lose your money." I resist even though the dealer is starting to give us the stink-eye for delaying the game.

"You have an opportunity that no other scholar gets. To not only see the past, and hear it, but to taste, smell, and touch it. To experience it fully by living it, and gaming is very popular right now. So, enjoy it."

"All right, but only a few hands so I can say I've played at this badass woman's gaming hell. Then that's it."

Leo shoves money at me and I shove half back at him, ignoring his protests. Later, before the night ends, I'm going to make him promise to propose to Miss Chilcott. He needs to get engaged before everyone realizes what a fraud I am, hurting his reputation.

I take an extra a few seconds to caress Leo's face. Standards of behavior seem to be a lot looser in this establishment, thankfully, and I'm going to take advantage by touching Leo as much as I can before the night is over.

He leans into the hand and covers it with his own, planting a kiss on my palm. Then he nods at the table, while motioning for wine to be brought to us.

Two hours later, I'm giddy. And tipsy.

"This is dangerous." I lean into Leo, who has stayed by the side the entire time, as I gained and lost and gained a small fortune. A small fortune for me, since I had very little money to my name to begin the night with, and none with me. I'm able to pay Leo back his stake, with interest, and pocket a respectable amount of guineas to help when I flee.

It's so Leo, helping me through this entire journey. Without any thought for himself, or how he really should be saving his damn money. I still don't even think that wealth accumulation is a good thing. But maybe he should accumulate enough to save *one* of his houses. The rest can be museums.

"It's very dangerous. But you appear to have good luck."

"I'm stopping here before I push that luck."

Leo doesn't make any bets himself. He watches me, cheering me on to make my own bad decisions. But he refrains from putting any money down on the table.

Because he really is the most responsible rake ever.

"You don't want to keep playing?"

"No. I'm done for now." I clutch my purse closer to me so I won't be tempted to put more money down and potentially lose it.

"Would you like to return home or continue watching the revelry here?"

"I want to stay." I don't hesitate even a second. He might not know I'm leaving soon, but I do, and I don't want to miss a second with him. I need to build an entire lifetime of memories from this day.

They'll have to be enough.

"Let's people watch." I don't want to think about my lonely future. I'll have an entire lifetime to be sad about losing him; tonight I'll enjoy him.

I entwine my hand in his, feeling very twenty-first century. Besides my giant dress, lack of phone, and the shitty lighting. But the couples in this house are getting friskier the later it gets. Women sitting on laps and even some canoodling.

I think we'll be good with some hand-holding.

Leo knows people here, and we stop and chat when we run into them. Well, he chats, and I pump them for information. While also enjoying their company. Because I can multitask.

I do wait until they're gone to make notes about our conversation. I'm not completely unfit for social interaction.

We wander back upstairs to get away from the heat, the noise and the crowd, which has only increased as the night goes on. We find an alcove set back from a balcony, where we can sit and watch the hedonism below with some peace. Nice for me, because I'm used to studying history, not living it, and it's kind of exhausting to be on the other end of it.

"You don't want to be downstairs among the revelers? That's not very rakish of you." But I'm glad. I like pushing close to him in a crowd, but I also like being in our own little world of two. Where I can look at him as much as I want. And touch him when I want.

"Madame, are you doubting my credentials?"

"No?" But then I see the glint in his eyes. An intriguing glint that I want to see more of, and I change my answer. "Yes. I think you lied to me the first day when you said all you wanted to do was have fun." There. Gauntlet thrown.

"All I want to do is have fun. And I stand by my stance. However, I have learned some consequences are not worth momentary pleasure. A lesson all hedonists must learn eventually."

"So you're an ex-hedonist?"

"I most certainly am not. I can do hedonism with any of these children downstairs. And for longer, because I've learned how to do it with stamina."

"Okay." My tone is purposely as patronizing as I can make it.

He leans toward me assertively, like he can will me into thinking he's a wild child when I've seen the hints of responsibility he tries to hide.

"I shall prove it to you."

CHAPTER 32

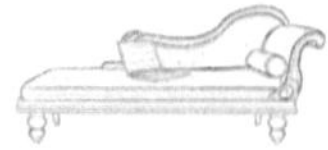

"What are you going to do?" Whatever Leo is planning to do to prove his stamina, I wish I had my phone so I could photo-document it. Or that I could have photo-documented any part of our relationship to look back on later. But especially now, when Leo looks a really attractive mix of confident and sexy and mischievous.

And fun.

He doesn't answer with words. He leans forward and grabs the ankle closest to him, raising it into his lap. I tilt my head at him, not expecting that move. He maintains eye contact with a hint of a self-assured smile as his hand slides under the many layers of my dress, caressing calf, knee and thigh along the way.

Is he going to—oh god. Yes, he is.

With the background chatter of a hundred rakes downstairs, Leo slips his fingers past the slit in my open drawers. Damn unintentionally sexy Victorian underwear that is supposed to be for me to use the bathroom without getting undressed. Not for… this.

But this is better.

I grip the seat of the wooden bench we're on, knuckles

turning white as I bite my bottom lip to keep the moan in. Not that anyone would hear it over the sound of partying below, but it's hard to rationalize through things when Leo's touching me like this in public.

I just barely keep the moan in, but as Leo's fingers find my clit and stroke the wetness he finds there, I can't stop my heavy breathing. My chest fights against the corset restraining me, and I get a bit out of breath the more his fingers play me like an instrument, eliciting sounds I didn't know I could make.

Guttural, primal sounds.

More grunts than words; more sensation than coherent thought.

As my body focuses on the bundle of nerves between my legs, the rest of me loses its ability to function. I slump down, bringing my other foot up to the bench to spread my legs and give him better access.

He follows my slumping body down, pressing his erection against my leg as his fingers increase in speed rubbing my clit. Soon that's not enough for him, because he slips all the way off the bench. I lean up on my forearms on the hard surface to see what's happening, but don't see him. Because he's already disappeared under my skirts.

His mouth replaces his fingers, licking my clit with as much precision as his finger was employing seconds before.

My body likes that too much and defeats my good intentions to keep quiet. A moan escapes as I get closer to orgasm, feeling the familiar tightening take over my entire body, straightening and straining every muscle.

Before I get my happy ending, Leo pulls away from under my skirts and reappears to sit on the bench. Now my groan is one of frustration.

I'm dazed by the abrupt loss, but with the newfound confidence of Victorian Meera, I go after what I want.

I start unbuttoning everything in front of me: coat, pants,

vest, shirt; anything that even loosely resembles a button is getting tugged on. His penis is in clear agreement with me, hard as a rock when I brush against it in my frenzy to undress.

"Hold on one second, love." Leo flattens his hands on mine and I still.

"But I don't want to." I pout. Not proud about it, but that's my response to a lack of Leo.

"I want you, too. But I was told I wasn't a hedonist, and I have to prove myself."

"I take it back. You're the most hedonistic hedonist to ever hedonism in the history of the world. I'll fight anyone who says different."

"I am not sufficiently convinced that you have changed your mind." Leo stands up and takes my hand, urging me to do the same.

"You make my legs jelly and now I have to walk on them? This isn't hedonist stuff; this is torture."

"Hmm. You will not think that in a minute."

We only get as far as the railing in front of us. My legs are still wobbly from what Leo was doing, but they hold for the journey. He sets my forearms on the rail, giving me support as he crowds behind me until I'm bent over at the waist and looking down. There's no one under us, since the balcony overlooks an empty hallway.

But I can still hear the crowd of people somewhere under us, out of sight but also too near. A few steps in the wrong direction, and they'll see me hanging off the side of a railing, still clothed but breasts straining against my bodice, bouncing as Leo thrusts against me.

"But the people…" I break off on a moan when Leo grabs me around the neck on one side and bites into the other side. He holds me in place with a giant hand while he kisses the spot he just bit.

"No one comes back here. But we'll stop if you want. Find somewhere more private." Leo's front is thrusting against my back while his hand and mouth make me care less and less about getting found.

"No." I don't want to wait for however long it'll take to get to a private location. It would waste too much time, which is already a limited resource.

And it's kind of hot. Plus, I'm confident now; I *can* do anything I want, and *will* do anything I want.

"Here. Now." I arch back into him, while rolling my hips to rub against his penis.

"Thank god," he groans.

He slides down my body, scooping up my dress until I feel a breeze coming from behind. Not a big one, because I'm still covered in layers that are at the same time too much and nothing at all. Because despite the number of layers I have on, once Leo gets past all the petticoats and dress, there's that open slit.

Leo fiddles with his clothes behind me, and then his hands are on my waist, where he tilts my hips back and up. He presses into me from behind, the heavy weight of my skirts thrown over his forearms.

Finally! I sink deeper onto the railing, which pushes Leo in farther. Now he's the one to moan while I smile at the thought that I affect him as much as he affects me.

He thrusts firmly into me, my body more than ready for him after the way he worked it earlier. He keeps up the pace until I'm fairly certain the railing is going to break.

I'm also fairly certain I won't care. Unless I go down with it.

Leo shifts until one of his hands reaches my clit, rubbing to get me back to where I was before he pulled away on the bench. It doesn't take long until the same tightness takes over my muscles, my entire body on the edge before he pushes it right over with his clever fingers.

I come with a loud moan, and Leo belatedly covers my mouth to cut off at least half of it. He isn't far behind me, coming with a particularly deep thrust. He buries his head into my neck to muffle his groan.

As we both catch our breaths, still leaning on the railing, I'm impressed with how the thin pieces of wood continue to hold up.

Breathing finally calmed down, Leo moves away from me, testing the railing one more time by pushing against it, this time to get up. I turn over, one hand on the railing since my legs are still a bit wobbly.

Leo deals with the condom he must have put on when I was facing away from him, conscientious hedonist that he is, and he tucks everything back into place.

"Have I sufficiently proven my hedonist credentials?" His words might be smug, but his breathing is still choppy, letting me know I'm not the only one affected.

"It was an adequate showing. But I think if we wanted to make sure it wasn't a fluke, we should try a few more times. So I have more evidence to support the finding."

He laughs, kissing me. I can taste myself on him, and even though I'm tired, and immensely satisfied, I still feel stirrings.

"Just give me time to rest, Your Highness, then I will be happy to provide all the evidence that the scholar requires to make a determination on my hedonist status."

"Still calling me my fake title? Even after fucking me over a railing?"

"*Especially* after fucking you over a railing. I am a gentleman."

"I must have missed that chapter in the gentleman's handbook."

"Well, we would not let a woman read it." He winks at me so I know it's a joke.

"Jerk." But I laugh at him.

"Come now, I need to return you home."

The words tear into the perfect moment I've created by ignoring reality.

Because I will be going home soon, or finding a new home. But it won't be with Leo, which means we'll be over soon.

But I still have a couple of hours left of today. And I'm not going to give any of them up before I have to.

CHAPTER 33

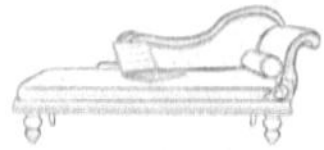

"Leo, get up!" I shake him awake.

I accidentally took more than my few hours allotment. Leo brought me back to the palace after our fun in the gaming hell, but I wasn't ready to say goodnight, so I snuck him in. It was surprisingly easy, and probably a national security concern. Not my concern, but someone's.

There are so many secret passageways in the palace that people have used for a variety of reasons through history: to sneak women in, so they don't have to see their servants, and to do shady political things. Secret passageways that people wrote about in their diaries, waiting for someone who has made a career of reading such documents.

But I bet they never thought an Indian-American commoner would be the one to use them to sneak in some aristocratic tail.

We took a quick nap before Leo woke me up and went for a more naked round two. This one slow and drawn out, a contrast to the quick coupling in the gaming hell. He was supposed to leave after that last time, after a quick cuddle. Where I was just going to shut my eyes for a minute to enjoy his body against mine.

But we both fell asleep and now it's morning and there's a knock at my door. I hope it's Anne, who has been very chill up to this point. If it's anyone else, I'm screwed literal hours before I was going to flee anyway.

"Leo! You have to leave. Now!" I shake a bit more vigorously this time. My voice raises, but still stays low enough so everyone doesn't hear I snuck a boy in past curfew.

"Hmm. Perhaps we should stay for a few moments longer."

"You don't have a few moments longer." I've moved on to outright pushing now, and he's getting closer to the edge of the bed. He's going to find out that the floor is a lot less comfortable than this bed. And getting there via a fall isn't going to improve the experience.

Leo finally gets up, not as worried about getting caught in a strange woman's bedroom. Of course he isn't. He'll get a wag of the finger and a congratulatory wink, and the label rake attached a little firmer on his name. Meanwhile, I'll be completely banished from polite society.

To be entirely fair, I am already planning to self-banish from polite society, but it's the principle of the matter.

"A peer of the realm always has a few more minutes for pleasure."

I snort at the joke but keep pushing his chest that is puffed out in fake self-importance. "Whatever. You still have to go." I'm so flustered by the urgency that I've given up worrying about introducing slang into the lexicon a little earlier than it should be.

I just need to find a cottage somewhere where I can be alone so I won't have to worry about the timeline after I leave. I can write articles about people of color in the Victorian period just so people can find them later...and probably still ignore them. Despite it being a firsthand account. I still haven't figured out how I'll pay for this cottage or the food I'll undoubtedly need, but that'll be a tomorrow problem.

I do have some money now because of Leo's gambling adventure. But that can only go so far.

"What...ever?" Leo asks.

I give the final push, which sends Leo over the edge. He lands with a grunt, but he was able to twist and stop the fall with his hands. It's fine, there's a rug on the floor and I did warn him about the urgency.

"No time! You get dressed and I'll distract whoever is at the door."

"There's someone at the door?"

"Yes. That's the source of the knocking that's currently happening. That you're ignoring." I get up, wrapping myself in a robe, and move to answer the door before whoever it is gets reinforcements. It's a good thing I remembered to lock it when we got in, or this morning would have been even more disastrous.

I unlock and crack the door open a little.

"Good morning. Shall I get you ready for the day?" Anne asks, apparently not wanting to talk about the fact that I ditched her yesterday and am acting suspicious today.

"Yeah. Um. Could you please coordinate a bath for me?" There. At least the palace has plumbing so multiple maids don't have to haul heavy buckets of hot water up the stairs. But it should distract Anne enough that she goes away for a second while I figure out the guest in my room situation.

"Shall I get you clothes to change into?" Anne motions like she's going to enter the room and I grip the door harder.

"Don't worry about them. I'll bring them when I come."

"If you like." Anne looks confused that I haven't budged to let her in.

"Thanks." She turns to get the bath coordinated. "And thank you for everything you've done to help me in the past few days. You've made this stay special." Both in taking care of me and in hiding my more wild moments from Victoria and everyone else.

"Are you leaving soon? Should I pack your things?"

Bless her, I think she's forgotten I don't own anything. Well, nothing beyond a costume dress and some notebooks. "No. I just want to tell you that you are amazing at your job."

"Thank you."

I nod, and then flinch when I hear Leo drop his shoes from behind me.

"Oh." Understanding floods her face. Whelp, she knows Leo is here. But will she keep that close to the chest is the real question?

Then she surprises me with a nod and a wink. "I'll get that bath started for you."

She might be cool with this, Victorian morality being a hang up of the middle class and aristocrats, but I'm also sure that everyone "below stairs" is going to know about this before the day is out.

There will probably be a working-class version of White's betting book set up to bet on who it is. Or everyone will know it's Leo because he's been calling on me daily. And I'm not exactly subtle with my feelings.

"Thank you." I shut the door before I reveal anything else.

"Are you ready?" There's a secret passageway/backstairs for servants at the end of the hall, so we don't have to get Leo far. We just have to do it quietly, and quickly.

One of us (Leo), isn't adequately grasping the severity of the situation. Because he is not being quiet, and he is not being quick. I'm vibrating with nervous energy around him, amazed that he can remain so calm right now.

"I am almost dressed. I was thoroughly used this past evening, and I need time to recover."

I snort. "There was mutual using." The new me in the past takes the time to correct people when they're spouting bullshit.

"Hmm. I do not remember. Maybe we should try again." Leo grabs me around the waist and pulls me in close, nibbling on my neck, his vest forgotten on the floor. "I promise to pay attention this time."

"You don't even have a notebook. How will you take notes to study?" But I'm not trying very hard to get away from his warm embrace. Because my body would go into full-scale revolt if I tried.

"I procured your notebook. I could get another one if that is the only thing between me and heaven." One arm firmly around me, the other snakes into my robe, loosening as it goes.

"Go get your notebook and we'll talk." Regaining some control over my wayward body, I push him away. Not a strong push, and one that he listens to out of courtesy as opposed to the strength of the movement.

I immediately regret it when his arms drop, but I remind myself that the stakes are a lot higher when you get caught with a man in your room in 1895. They're even higher when you're already lying about who you are, and where, and when, you come from.

I got my last night; I should be happy with the extra time. But all I want is more. All my worries about "one more night" not being enough were completely founded. And there's nothing I can do about it now. Except hold those memories close, hoping they keep me warm on the cold nights to come and don't just make me sadder about what I lost.

The cold nights which will be literally chilly if I can't get back. They don't invent a heating system that I can afford for a while yet.

While I'm mourning the loss of something that was never really mine to begin with, Leo finishes getting dressed. He gives me a quick kiss, surprised when I grab him around the neck and deepen it. Surprised, but I get no complaints from him. He wraps his arms around me again, responding to the kiss.

Until we hear a noise in the hallway.

I tear away. "You've really got to go this time." I cross the room to open the door, investigating what the noise was.

I don't see anyone, so it may have just been the palace trying to tell me the man has to leave. With all the intensity of a special ops human, I motion for Leo to come while keeping a lookout.

"I am going home to change, then I shall come calling again. One more kiss." Leo kisses me one last time. Not that he knows it's a last time. Just like he didn't know last night was a last time.

"No. I have bath time! I'll see you later." Never. Well, I may stalk him from geographically or temporally afar. But he won't see me, if I can find a modicum of self-control.

"I will see you soon," Leo says. And then one more kiss, because we're both liars about quantities of kisses.

I watch him escape through the same passage we used to get him up there, standing in my door a few extra moments in case he wants to come back for just one more surprise kiss. But although he turns to give me a jaunty wave, he's gone without any other fornication.

I hear footsteps down the hall and turn to see Anne coming toward my room. "The bath is ready."

"Excellent. Thank you. For the bath." And for the distraction from thoughts about Leo.

After I'm clean and dressed, I'm left alone again for breakfast. Alone with my thoughts, which are half trying to figure out how to leave, and half being sad about Leo.

I've already snuck out of the palace a few times, and I don't have a lot to pack. My notebooks are in a small bag at my feet, but I couldn't get back in the dress I came to the past in (Anne said I couldn't possibly wear an evening dress to breakfast, especially one that was out of fashion, and I decided it would be too suspicious to argue). I'll just pay the fee for a lost dress if I ever get back to the future.

As for the dress I'm about to steal, they won't miss it. With all that wealth. There we go, this dress is a reparation for the Koh-i-Noor. And boy, am I getting the short end of *that* stick.

I have some money tucked into my corset, and I'm ready to flee at any moment. Probably should have already fled, but it's scary. To leave the palace, and Leo, to go into the unknown. Alone.

But I should have a good meal first, right? It only makes sense to flee on a full stomach. I can't think of a plan if I'm thinking about meat pies. It's just logic.

Now my stomach is filled, maybe even overfilled since I'm eating to procrastinate, and my second plate is clean.

Okay. It's time to leave.

I reach for my bag but stop before I touch it. But what if it wasn't? What if I could make it work with Leo here? He's titled; I've got boundless knowledge about the time. Maybe we could make it work.

And I love him. The thought of leaving him is paralyzing me, even if I know it is the right decision.

I'm still sitting, unmoving, when Victoria glides into the room. "Hello. How are you this morning?"

I get up, stumble into a curtsey, and then my butt slams back onto the elaborately upholstered chair. "Good morning, Your Majesty. I'm doing well, thank you. How are you?"

Victoria sits down and a very attentive footman puts a plate in front of her before she's all the way in her chair. "Much better now that I've decided we're going back to Osborne today. London and Buckingham have never been the same since Albert." The queen gets a faraway look on her face. Sad and wistful at the same time.

Then my sympathy fades to the background when I realize what she just said. *We're* going to Osborne.

Well, that's going to make it harder to flee.

CHAPTER 34

"I should stay behind. You've done so much for me; you should relax at Osborne and I'll stay out of your way." Permanently out of your way.

"Nonsense. You can't stay here alone. Who will take care of you?"

Me. Myself. I. Take your pick, lady. Also, all the staff that will still be here will make sure I don't starve or steal anything.

This is part of the past I'm not so eager to be experiencing. I would much rather only read about this in a book.

"It's really fine. You work so hard already, I don't need to be one more thing you have to worry about." I don't try to change her mind about independence and women's capabilities. She's a lady monarch; if she doesn't think other women can be as capable as her, nothing I say will help.

"Anne is already packing for you and will make sure your things get on the carriage. You shall come with me after I finish eating."

There's not much leeway there. I peek over to the open door and potential escape route. But since I've gotten here, activity has exploded in the hallway. Footmen are running around, getting ready to move the queen's household. Apparently, this was decided last-minute.

There's too much activity for a quiet escape now. I don't know if Victoria has issued orders to keep me inside, but now isn't the time to figure it out.

"Do you want to write a letter to your marquess? A footman can tell him where you have gone when he comes to call, but it would be better coming from you. Men do get offended so easily," Victoria says.

"Oh. Yes. I'll write that letter." Except now Victoria has me thinking about Leo and how at some point, he was going to come back here, hopefully changed out of yesterday's clothes and some unlucky footman was going to tell him that I left without saying goodbye.

I think he'll be disappointed. He hasn't said how he feels about me, but he must care beyond a fuck buddy. He keeps coming to call, taking care of me, and helping me get home. And failing that, he took me on a sightseeing day he didn't have to, just to cheer me up.

So he'll be at least a little hurt that I abandoned him without notice. The thought of him hurt, and me causing that hurt, makes my own heart ache. And that is on top of me already not feeling great at the thought of losing the man I love.

But it's too hard to tell him my decision. And I don't want him to talk me out of it. He might be able to do. If anyone or anything here has a chance of convincing me, it's him. I already kind of want to make a home here with him myself, so it wouldn't even take much convincing from him.

Victoria takes the decision out of my hands by calling for some paper and a fountain pen for me, so concerned about Leo being disappointed if I left. When a footman brings the requested materials, I start writing. Maybe I do owe him a goodbye. A written one, to do the bare minimum.

Leo,

I'm sorry I'm not telling you this in person, but I'm leaving. And now I'm sorry that I wrote that so abruptly—without easing you in. But I don't know what to say to soften those words, and the effect that they may or may not have on you.

I'm going to Osborne first with Her Majesty. Then it'll be time to find a way home.

Thank you for all your help while I've been here. It's no exaggeration to say I wouldn't have been able to do this without you. You've given me protection, joy and occasionally wisdom. You've made my time here perfect.

I hope you find what you need to make your life perfect. Because you've come to mean a lot to me.

Even if you are a hedonistic Lord of the Manor.

I'll miss you.

Meera

"Ready with the note." I hold up the folded paper to find Victoria's plate clear and her looking at me in amusement. How long was I working on that? Probably a long time, because I had to stop multiple times to keep the tears back and compose myself. And then the pauses to figure out what to say.

She shakes her head. "Young love. We can invite Basildon to come with us, if you would like?"

"No!" Victoria looks taken aback by my vehemence. "I wouldn't want to disturb him. He has a lot to do in the city." Whatever lords do.

"We shall be at Windsor before you know it. I do not know when we will be back in London, but Windsor is no long journey for a persistent man like Basildon."

"Yeah. I'll see him before I know it." If I get home, I'm going to Google him, first thing. Even before a shower with adequate water pressure/temperature or a long Netflix binge. Even if I have to purchase an entirely new phone in modern London to access the internet to do it.

And if I don't make it back, eventually I'll take to a life of in-person stalking. From afar, though.

I hand the letter off to a footman, resisting the urge to edit it within an inch of its life like I do with the articles I submit to academic journals.

Should I have tried to ease into telling him I was leaving? Should I have told him how I feel, not just hinted at it? Should I have used that em-dash?

The footman is already out of the room before I can call him back to implement some of those changes, and Victoria is commanding me to follow her out to her carriage.

Maybe the Isle of Wight is where I should be. The universe spit me out there. Maybe it wants me to live there. Or maybe there's a magic portal there to get home, like there was to bring me here.

A girl can hope. Even when she's not entirely sure she wants to leave Leo anymore.

～

LATER THAT EVENING, we arrive at the Isle of Wight, and Osborne House is just like I remember it, but I'm a lot less confused and only a little panicked this time. And a lot more confident. I've outwitted an entire royal court for this long; I'm prepared for anything now.

Not dealing with my feelings for Leo in a healthy way, but anything else. Luckily, I don't have to deal with any crises, and it's a quiet night at Osborne House.

The next morning, Victoria leaves me to do her work and her lessons with Abdul. I'm at a loss for what I need to do. For the first time since I've been in the past, I have no callers or Leo, no idea what to do, and too much sadness and hopelessness that can't be pushed down with a cup of tea.

I'll still try, because even sad tea is better than being sad without tea. Which is why I've drunk approximately seven cups of the liquid comfort in the past twenty-four hours that I've been at Osborne.

They don't solve any of my problems, but I'm very well hydrated.

"Good afternoon." Anne walks into the room, probably relieved to find me where she left me for once. I can't have made her job easy while I've been here.

"Hello. Can you sit with me? Have some tea?"

"Oh, I couldn't."

"Please do. It's very quiet here." I didn't think I was incapable of being alone. When I'm not teaching, I spend plenty of time by myself in the library or at my apartment. But it doesn't feel like I'm alone because I'm busy grading, researching, or writing, or I can turn on music or the TV. Not really an option here. Not that there aren't music devices, but the music here isn't exactly Sabrina Carpenter.

"It would really help me if you would sit with me for a bit," I say.

"I know it must be hard without your young man."

"No—yeah." What the hell? I have no pride here to protect. "I've gotten used to having him around." And maybe it isn't the biggest lie. Anne might think I'm crumbling because I haven't seen my gentleman caller in a day, but I am sad that I won't see him ever again. Close enough.

Anne gives me a knowing look and sits down.

"Let me pour you some tea. And I'll call for more refreshments," I say before she can answer.

"I can do it."

"No, it's okay. You sit." I could easily give up cooking and cleaning, but not doing anything for myself for this past week has been strange.

That's another thing I read about in my scholar life that is wild to see in practice: the British aristocracy's relationship with labor, and how a mark of the aristocracy and gentry was how little manual labor they did, including even dressing and bathing themselves.

But to see, to *experience* it, when I've lived in a modern world where I put my pants on one leg at a time, and by myself, is unsettling.

Anne, who I already know is great from all the times she's ignored me doing objectively abnormal things and ignored when I fled from her chaperoning, is wonderful company. We drink what feels like all the tea in the Isle of Wight. And I only think of Leo a handful of times. Maybe a dozen. A baker's dozen, at most.

"I've noticed you like to see the sights. Maybe you would like to take a quick trip into town before dinner? It would take your mind off things. And then as soon as you know it, you'll be back near London and seeing your Lord Basildon daily," Anne says.

I ignore the entire last part of her sentence. "Yes. I would love to see a bit of the island."

"Excellent." Anne nods at me encouragingly, and we set off after she calls for someone to take the tea dishes.

On the way to town in the royal carriage, the salty sea air whips past us as the horses pull us closer to our destination. Seagulls squawk around us, adding to the idyllic beach village ambiance.

When we stop, I step out, and I'm in the prototype for the perfect English seaside town. There are cottages with thatched roofs, adorably painted doors and windowsills with just the right amount of scuffed paint to make it look rustic, and artfully arranged hedges and flowerpots.

Brightly colored signs vie for my attention, in case I wanted more tea, some food, or alcohol. One even wants to help me rent a bathing machine, which can roll me from the sand into the sea so men don't get the chance to see even a hint of my skin while I enjoy the bracing, cold, sea water.

I hear waves crashing against the beach, the ocean out of sight behind the village cottages, and take a deep breath of salty seaside air. I could live here; it's calming. I could find a nice life here when I flee Victoria. I still don't know what I would do here, but that can be a task for another day.

"What would you like to do first?" Anne asks.

"Is there a bookstore?" Maybe there will be something there that can distract me from the drama in my own life.

Anne nods. "Right this way." She starts walking in one direction, when we hear a yell that stops us in our tracks.

"Meera!"

I turn, the blood rushing from my face when I see who it is.

CHAPTER 35

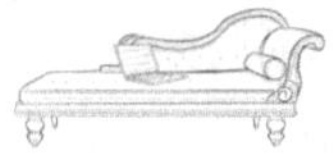

"*L*eo. Hi."

Those are the only words I can get out. Not *Why the hell are you here? What are you doing here? Do you know how hard it was to say goodbye to you once? Then why are you making me do it again?*

Those words would have been way more helpful.

Leo moves toward me, rushing from his own carriage. He stops just short of me, like he was going to hug me before he remembered we're in public. And in a sexual repressive nightmare where people can't hug, because heaven forbid men and women touch genitals through a combined eleven layers of clothing.

The absolute scandal.

"I am so glad to have found you."

I firmly tell the part of me that lights up at the words to stuff it. We are not supposed to be seeing him again; this is not part of the plan, nebulous though it may be. "What are you doing here?" I don't even try to infuse my voice with the warmth or excitement at seeing him. I'm not going to encourage the perfect man who's hurting me right now. Even if it's not intentional.

"I received your letter from the footman. I wanted to see you again before you..." Leo looks at Anne. "Well, I wanted to see you again."

Anne is giggling off to the side, like this is the most romantic thing she's seen. The hero tracking down his heroine when she's dragged away by a forceful guardian who doesn't care that she's interfering with true love.

Only the heroine is from the future and the guardian is trying her hardest to matchmake us.

I quickly change plans from the nice, quiet bookstore day to deal with this. "Let's take a walk on the beach."

Anne leads the way, and then falls back so she can chaperone from a distance, giving us some privacy. I don't want privacy! The last time we had privacy, we fucked on a balcony. Privacy gives me leave to make terrible, wonderful, bad-for-me decisions that I enjoy a lot in the moment, but only make it harder for me in the long run.

"What are you doing here?" I ask again when we're firmly on the sand, the water and seagulls I heard earlier much louder now and giving our conversation further privacy from Anne.

"You said goodbye, Meera. Did you expect me to accept that?" His voice is uncharacteristically sharp and I look up at him over the rebuke.

I glare back at him, immediately in defensive mode. "You knew this was always going to end. Whether it's in a letter while I'm swept away by a head of state, or I disappear into time, or I watch you get married to your rich heiress from afar. This was always going to end. So I don't know why you're here right now, doing inadvisable things to change the inevitable." I slap him on the chest with my small purse. He's lucky this isn't the future when I carry around my huge work tote, with laptop and books and a spare sandwich, just in case.

"Damn the rich heiress!"

"What's your plan here? We're going to get married?" I lay on as much sarcasm to the question as I can, so at least one of us will believe this is a bad idea. "You're going to lose your home and your sister will be carted away to relations, or she'll get a job as a governess, which she'll hate because you rich kids are terrible. Or she'll get married to some monster. And Queen Victoria will probably pay for our wedding, but I don't know where we're going to live after that. And while owning all the land and making people work on it while you steal the majority of the profits isn't great, you're probably better than a lot of the alternatives of this time, so all your tenants will be screwed with a new landowner. And *then*, when everyone finds out I'm a liar, we can both go to jail. Is that what you want? A honeymoon in Newgate?"

Leo, to his credit, lets me get all that out without interrupting. And then he waits a little longer.

"Well? Do you have something to say to that?"

"I love you."

"No." A tear leaks out of the corner of my eye. "I disallow it."

"You disallow my love for you?" Leo smiles tenderly, not at all affected by my edict.

"Yes. It is forbidden. I have forbidden it. You can't."

"But I do."

"Shut up!" I cover my ears. It works for toddlers, right? The if-I-can't-hear-it-it-isn't-true method of approaching life.

He gently takes my hands and tugs them down from my ears, then doesn't let them go. "I love you," he says again.

"Why?"

"Why? We've gone from 'You can't' to 'why'?"

"Yes. Why?"

"Because you challenge me and make me better. Because you are fun and genuine and intelligent and unlike any woman I have ever met, in the best way. I cannot imagine being with anyone else."

I sigh.

"Is there something you want to tell me?"

"No." I scowl at him for emphasis.

"Anything at all?"

"No. Well, there is one thing. You can't love me." But my voice isn't as sure as it was before.

"Anything *else* you would like to say to me?" His voice is patient, like he has all the time in the world. But time has always been our issue.

"I can't love you either. Especially because you're such an irritating, problematic person. You have benefited from unearned privilege and it's infuriating. And you both don't take things seriously, and also sometimes are *too* responsible and it really interferes with me putting you in the box of useless hedonist. And you're also kind of considerate, remembering what I like and using that to make me happy. Who does that? I don't like it even a little bit."

Leo opens and closes his mouth. "I must admit, I was not expecting that response."

But I'm still on a roll. "And you haven't let go of my hands. And I can't stop thinking about you when we aren't together. I shouldn't be here, and at any time I may have to leave. But I don't even know if I even want to. I'm thinking about giving up the internet and air conditioning and planes, just to be with you. And you don't even know what those things are. It's confusing. And I don't like being confused."

"I have never told a woman that I love her, but I do *not* think this is the usual response."

"This is what you get!" I'm yelling now. I finally snatch my hands back. "And you only like me because I'm different, but if you were able to come back with me, you would see I'm not special. Then you'd regret telling me you love me."

"Impossible."

"How would you know? You've never met anyone like me, remember. I'm *curious*."

"I do not know that there is anything I could say to sway you right now. You would have to trust that I know my feelings; you would have to trust *me*. And over time, you would see that your trust was rightly placed."

"I don't have time!"

"You have now. I am not asking you to stay here for me; I do not know if that is even possible. I do not understand time travel. And I do not know if it is fair to ask you to give up such wonders even if it were a choice. But at the very least, I would like to spend every moment you are here, with you."

"I'm not marrying you."

He smiles at me tenderly. "That is all right. Because I have not actually asked you to marry me."

I cringe at that reminder. "Fine. Just so we're on the same page. I guess you can stay."

Leo grabs my hands again, and this time pulls me into a hug. "Kind of you to let me stay on this public beach."

I breathe in his scent while I wrap my arms around him, because he's here now, and so am I, and I'm savoring every moment of it. "Oh, shut up." But there's no heat there now. "Aren't you supposed to be all in love with me and in too much awe to sass me?"

"I am in love. I have not received a hard hit to the head."

"Great." But I'm not mad. I wouldn't have given up sassy Leo for anything.

Anne clears her throat behind us, closer than she's been during our conversation. She closes the rest of the distance until she's standing next to us. We break apart, still too close for propriety, but less likely to shock any delicate Victorians who walk by. "We should get back to Her Majesty. It's almost dinner and she'll wonder where we've gone. Lord Basildon, will you be joining us?"

I don't take my eyes off Leo while Anne is talking, so I catch him look at me in question.

"Yes." I deflate. "Leo, er, Lord Basildon will be joining us. As long as that's all right with Her Majesty, of course."

"I'm sure it will be. You know what a romantic Her Majesty is."

We walk back to the carriages, where Leo gives his coachman instructions and then gets in our carriage.

I still haven't told him that I love him, too. He's taking the lack of news well, smiling at me tenderly on the ride back to Osborne while I scowl at him. Stubborn lord of the manor.

Doesn't he know what's best for him? Living an uncomplicated life with the beer heiress, for one. Ignoring women who lie to monarchs and say they're from the future, even if they do happen to be telling the truth, for another.

We get to Osborne House and head to the drawing room to wait for Victoria. She doesn't take long, lighting up when she sees Leo.

"Basildon! I was not expecting this." Victoria greets Leo warmly, offering her hand for him to bow over as her eyes sparkle in matchmaking success. Anne was right; the queen is a romantic. "Albert would have done exactly the same thing." She pats his cheek when he stands up out of the bow. Then she turns her eyes on me. "It's quite the suitor you have here."

"See? Her Majesty, bestowed with a higher-than-average intelligence, knows I am an exemplary specimen."

I've seen peacocks during the height of mating season, with full plumes of shimmering feathers, that strut less than this. His ego is going to be impossible to live with now.

Not that I'm going to be living with him.

"For an equally exemplary lady." Victoria, mother of nine children, tries to keep the peace between us. I lean around the voluminous skirts of the monarch and stick my tongue out at Leo from behind Victoria's back.

"Did you hear that? I'm equally exemplary. Her Majesty says so."

"Yes. I agree," Leo stage whispers at me.

Victoria giggles like an elementary school student who just found out there's going to be a field trip to the zoo, instead of a woman who's buried two loves of her life. "Come on, children. It's time for dinner."

We make the procession to the dining room, slightly ridiculous when there are so few of us, but the British do enjoy their traditions.

I can't pay attention to the luxurious dinner, my eyes repeatedly wandering to Leo. So much that I almost spill soup all over my borrowed dress, but save it at the last minute. It takes everything in me to stop myself from telling Leo that I love him. I don't know if that will make it easier or harder for him when I leave, but now that I've accepted that Leo loves me, I want him to know that he's loved too.

By the end of the dinner, I've succumbed to the fantasy that it can always be like this: being with Leo, enjoying his company, laughing with him. Maybe I won't be leaving at all. Maybe we can do this. Victoria and Leo are talking animatedly about something, and I might just want him so bad that I'm willing to justify anything, especially after he told me he loved me, but we can make this work. He's close to the queen; she'll help us.

I know about the past. I can help him make money, and a title will still shield both of us from a lot, after a marriage. Maybe we won't be living in London, but we can be happy in the countryside. Or have a perfectly happy life in London, just not invited to pointless balls, which is also fine. We can start a charity for the lascars that actually understands their needs and helps them, and Leo can use his position in Parliament to make life better for people here.

We can figure this out. If we work hard enough, we can do this.

And staying away clearly isn't working; I keep dragging my

feet on leaving and he keeps following wherever I go, making us both miserable in the process.

There isn't really a good time to tell him about my epiphany (and about my love), though. Not when Victoria is talking about India. What would I say, *Actually, a lot of people there are being mistreated and they aren't that happy to be colonized, and also Leo, I love you?*

That seems like a lot.

I can't when dessert comes out and it's a strange and slightly terrifying jelly mold that is five layers tall and jiggles in a precarious manner. *Please pass me a piece of the jelly dessert that moves as no food should, and also, I love you.* No, that won't work.

Not during our after-dinner entertainment, either. *Victoria is quite the...interesting singer. I love you more than she loves India.* That's not the best comparison.

Having something I need to tell him, but not being able to find an appropriate time to do it, is putting me on edge. I'm going to burst, like a balloon that was already full at the beginning of dinner, but that keeps getting air pumped into it whenever Leo does something that makes me love him more.

I need to release some of that air, or love, in his direction before I burst.

Aside from being an overfilled balloon, the evening is nice. Pleasant. Calmly enjoyable.

So I'm not prepared for the interruption that plows into the drawing room just as Victoria starts singing her third song.

"I have it!"

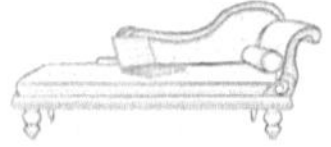

Charles bursts through the drawing room door like the water out of the geysers at Yellowstone: violently, loudly, and creating a mess that could burn me if I stand too close. In his hand is a letter which he waves back and forth with an expectant look, like we should know what's in it and should look suitably impressed.

"A piece of paper?" Victoria's voice is cold. "You interrupted your monarch's lovely evening to show me a paper?"

"Your Majesty, I apologize for the interruption." He gives a belated bow, but his eyes lock on mine on his way down, gleeful in a menacing way that makes me look for every exit in this room.

Shit. Charles has been suspicious of me since I got here and I can only think of one thing that would put that look on his face.

He has proof I'm a liar and a fraud, taking advantage of the monarch next to me.

I mean. There may be other things to put an evil grin on *his* face: extracting record profits out of India, colonizing some other unsuspecting part of the world, stealing the voice of a young ingenue via a contract containing unfair terms.

Standard villain stuff.

But the evil grin is focused on me, so I'm going to make an educated guess and say this is about me. Which means I need to get back to an exit strategy. And after I just decided to give Leo a chance, too. Because a large part of my most recent plan was to be a marchioness *before* the letter came. Or at least talk to Victoria before she could get the news in this way.

There's no chance she'll want to protect me, or us, if she hears the news from Charles, made to look even worse than it is, without us easing her into this.

I slide away from Leo and off the couch. Charles, who has been glaring at me since he started to bow, hurries out of the movement so he can get back to pointing and accusing.

"I knew all along she was a fraud and now I have proof!" He shakes the all-important paper again, in case we forgot how important it is to the moment.

"That is quite an ugly accusation to make towards my guest. And so late in the evening." I don't know if she's madder about the accusation or the timing, but I don't wait to find out.

Instead, I go on the attack.

"I have never been so offended!" I develop a bit of an English accent, as it is the best accent to show deep disdain in any given situation. I stalk toward the man who interrupted the serenity of my unexpected and very wanted time with Leo. "To insult my character, nay, my parentage, in this manner is inexcusable. I was led to believe that the English were a civil people." I barely contain the snort at that assertion, considering what they're currently doing in the world. "But this is beyond the bounds of decency. I am a guest in your country, and in this residence."

Each word brings me closer to Charles, and to the door into the hall behind him. Leo, who hasn't exactly realized what I'm working up to doing, is laughing at my dressing down of the Secretary of State.

"I do apologize." Victoria is glaring at Charles. "You may

return to your room while I listen to what the very rude government official has to say."

That won't help; he's telling the truth and probably has the letter from the Cooch Behar court to prove it to everyone in this room. But she has given me a way out of the room that isn't just running away.

"Thank you, Your Majesty. I am certainly not going to sit here and listen to this slander."

I move quickly, not at a run yet, but as close as I can be without making it obvious to the entire room that I'm fleeing in guilt. I don't look back as I fast-walk to my room, hearing Charles yelling after me and Victoria yelling at him.

I get the bag with notebooks and money, grateful that Charles or Leo didn't follow me up (for very different reasons) and that I didn't bother to unpack this bag after arriving here. Maybe Leo still thinks he can intercede on my behalf and make it all better, but it's too late to help now.

In all these layers, I flinch with every step I take and sound I make. I try to hold my breath to minimize the noise I make, attempting to channel a graceful, sneaky cat but probably sounding more like a heavy-breathing, clumsy bulldog instead. Who is rustling an entire fabric shop worth of clothes.

My muscles tense even more when I get closer to the drawing room door. I don't know if they stayed in that room to talk, but the eerily quiet house isn't helping my already paranoid mind and I imagine them jumping out at me from behind every corner and large cabinet.

I wish I had been nosier and done some more investigation of the house before now. Because I'm sure there are other ways to get out besides crossing where everyone still probably is, but I don't know what they are. Since there's nothing else I can do about it, I begin to cross the dining room's open doorway.

"There she is! I knew she would try to leave, now that we know she is a liar and a criminal!"

Verbose motherfucker. I abandon all pretense of sneaking, hiking up my dress and petticoat with one hand, the other tightening on my bag with books in it, and start sprinting.

Or as close to sprinting as I can get. Me, who hasn't run since the sadists who were imprudently allowed to teach PE in middle school made me run the mile. Without ever doing any training or exercises that would actually improve my running time.

But I never had a stuffy, racist aristocrat running after me back then. A shame, because this motivation is working to get me what will probably be my fastest mile time ever.

However little preparation I have for this footrace, it seems that Charles is even less ready. At least I have to walk around my hilly college campus every day to get to the lecture hall from my parking lot. Charles looks like he's carried everywhere by his chairmen.

I'm running to the front door and freedom, but Charles calls out to the footmen there, who move to block my path. I don't know if they're listening to him or just confused at the sudden, yelled instructions, but I don't wait to find out. I immediately turn to my left and head toward the main wing of Osborne House, where the public rooms are.

I push through the first door I come across at the end of the grand corridor, which leads to the back gardens of the house, running blindly into the poorly lit space. The sun, betrayer that she is, leaves me to help people on the other side of the world who probably aren't even fleeing for their lives.

And leaves me to navigate the rapidly darkening garden.

"Meera!" Leo calls out for me, but I don't stop or look back to see where he is. It's too hard, and will lead me to do something I'll regret, like staying and dealing with the consequences of my lie, ruining both of our lives.

Leo's yells get closer, and he must be in better shape than all of us, because he overtakes Charles and catches up to me, when he visibly slows down to match my pace. And where did he get all this athleticism?

"What's happening?" He's not even out of breath. Ass.

"Charles…knows…lying…fleeing." Each word is forced out through a chest too tight, through lungs that are punishing me for taking precious, life-giving air from the act of breathing while running to form unnecessary words.

"Stay, Meera. Stay and marry me. I'll make this right with Her Majesty. And we will work to support ourselves. Really do work, to get my family out of debt. It will all be okay. Just choose to stay. Choose *me*."

What, is he going to recite Shakespeare's complete works next? We get it, his respiratory system is functioning at an optimal level.

"Can't…" I push out. Meaning both I can't stay and I can't talk right now. No matter how much I want to do both.

"Stop…running. Footmen…coming," Charles yells, just as out of breath as me. At least that's something, in the slowest foot chase in history.

I ignore them both and focus on the darkness in front of me. All it will take is a stumble or one trip, and then I'll have a chance to break free. I could either run onto the beach which I can follow to a town, or directly into East Cowes. Either way, I should be able to find a place here or get on a ferry to London, and then disappear into history.

I'm so consumed with avoiding the men behind me and planning the life in front of me, that I don't notice I'm at the top of the steps that brought me here and began this entire adventure. Since I don't notice they exist, I definitely don't notice the ledge of the first step.

The one that my right foot rolls right over. I have a moment where I teeter on the edge, and Leo reaches out his hand, in slow motion, to try to stop the inevitable.

"I love you, Leo," I yell out as my body loses the battle with gravity and rolls down those stairs, tumbling head over feet, a flurry of dress and petticoat and a bag that I clutch against my chest.

Not this again.

CHAPTER 37

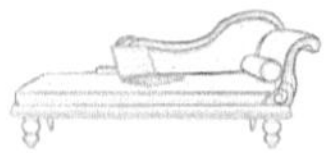

I should have been more specific on *who* I wanted to trip. I understand that now; I was ambiguous, and the universe acted accordingly.

I lie still at the landing in the middle of the steps, where the staircase changes direction. I don't bother getting up until the world stops spinning. And until the pain stops hammering at various body parts enough that I can do something other than breathe through it. If the pursuers want to drag me up and carry me back into the house to arrest me, they're going to have to do the heavy lifting.

Literally.

But as the pain recedes, light filters in through my consciousness.

And it's *wrong*.

The light has suddenly gotten better, even though it appears to be later at night than it was just before my fall.

And there's no arrogant marquess or douchebag government official chasing me anymore.

"No. No no no no no." My hand lands on my bag when I try to push myself up, so I absentmindedly grab it along the way.

Fully standing, I stretch out the kinks in my back from my second fall within a week. I am too old for this. And for being thrown from time to time, without regard to my plans, hopes, or the feelings I've developed.

I limp gingerly up the stairs, trying to rub my back but not getting much out of it through the heavy corset. Something I wish had stayed in the past.

My heart sinks further when I get to the top of the stairs. Everything looks exactly the same as the conference event I was at before taking my first trip. Loud music over speakers entertains a crowd inside the house, and as I go inside, I hear laughter and yelling. I walk into the Durbar Room and see people in modern replicas of Victorian dress, but none in the real deal, and none of them are the people I want to see.

Even irritating Charles would be better at this point, so long as he comes with Leo on the side. But I'm never going to see Leo again, and that makes my lips quiver as I process the implications of that fact.

Was it real? Did I get knocked out from the fall and dream the entire thing? It is something I would imagine. But no. I clutch the bag close to me, filled with my notebooks from the past, and give my dress, a loan from Victoria, an affectionate pat.

"Did you change clothes, Meera?" Heather walks up to me, a little drunker than she was before I left the party, approximately a hundred and thirty years ago.

"What?" Who gives a shit about my wardrobe choices? I just lost the love of my life. *Shit.* The love of my life is dead. He grew old with his beer heiress, probably, or maybe he decided Americans were to his taste and went after a Vanderbilt, or an Astor, or maybe a Rockefeller. And he had children and lived an entire life without me, dying in his family home, surrounded by love and family and friends. All in the span of the few seconds it took me to fall down a set of stairs.

And I'm just someone he met once upon a time. With a wild story and strange ways.

I want to stomp my foot and shake my fist and punch the universe right in its face. And cry. A lot.

"Your clothes. They're much nicer than they were earlier. You should have just worn these all night," she says.

I narrow my eyes, finding a target for all the heartbreak of losing Leo and frustration over not being taken seriously in my field. Frustration that I let build up for too long without doing anything about it. There's no time like the present.

"You're wrong." She looks taken aback at my vehement defense of the rented costume. "Not about this." Obviously, a princess's dress is better than the dress I rented for fifty pounds. And shit, I'm going to have to pay the lost fee for that, on top of everything else.

But I need to focus. "Your continued belief that European history is as white as a group of polar bears sitting on the snow in the Arctic, despite multiple primary sources showing that all of Europe has been in contact with people of color since antiquity, is historically inaccurate and frankly, lazy scholarship. Unless you want to forget the Romans and Carthage, or Alexander the Great and India. And that was just the start, leading to millennia of travel and interaction. The fact that you think people of color would never explore is rooted in racism.

"And sure, maybe they weren't a majority, but they existed. And maybe they didn't start coming in larger numbers until the 1500s, but they did come. They laughed, cried, made fortunes, lost fortunes, survived, thrived, failed, made homes in new lands, and returned home. And you don't get to dismiss that because you don't bother to look deeper. I'm not even asking you to study it; you're clearly not the best person for it. But *you* don't get to tell *me*, an actual expert in the field, that people of color didn't live full lives in English history."

That off my chest, I finally take a deep breath. Heather is

staring at me, eyes wide and mouth open in confusion and maybe a bit of weariness.

"So, I just wanted to say that. Because of what you said earlier." I don't wait for another reaction, not sure that there's anything she could say that I would want to hear, or that would change anything. "Now if you'll excuse me, I need to Google something. It's an emergency."

I walk toward the coat room, needing to at least do a quick search of Leo before I explode from curiosity.

"Hey, there. Are you feeling okay?" Luis slides up to me as I walk, keeping pace with me. But not too close. Like he doesn't want to be next.

Great. Everyone in the field will hear about this soon.

"I'm…okay." Not great. I've returned home, which I was trying to do the entire time I was in the Victorian era. But now I'm away from Leo and that sucks too. "I just need my phone."

He tries to comfort me, because it is apparently obvious that I need it. "I'll get you some wine for when you get back."

"Thank you. But I think I'm going to call it a night." I won't be fit for company whatever I find out about Leo.

"Okay. Text me if you want to grab food before our flights back."

"I will." Then I hug Luis. I might have lost the love of my life, but I gained back all my family, my friends, and Wi-Fi. It'll have to be enough. I don't think it will, but it'll have to be.

The coat room is where I left it this time, and I get my coat, purse and phone back with a desperation that the poor coat check person is probably unused to seeing. I don't wait until I get back to my room to start the search. As soon as I pull the phone out of my purse, I type in Leo's name in the internet browser's search bar.

Walking while reading, I exit the door and scroll through the options. He doesn't have a Wikipedia entry, which is annoying, but I guess makes sense since I hadn't even heard about him before this in my research. Not everyone in history is written about and remembered, not even aristocrats.

As the event organizers direct me to one of the waiting shuttles back to the hotel, I keep scrolling past the other search results. Some mentions that he existed and was a marquess, but nothing about his life. Or if he got married, which is what I really want to know.

Come on, internet. Don't fail me now; I came back for you!

Also my parents, obviously.

I try searching for his house, and a website to visit the building comes up first. Apparently, it's a museum now. But it's not as in depth on the history of the house as I would hope. It goes in depth until Leo, and then just talks about his sister's family. About a year after I was there she married a wealthy duke and they had three children. They were unfashionably in love and even age appropriate. Whatever happened after I left, at least Leo's sister seemed to be happy.

After more research, I find that the house is owned by a private trust, called the Alston Hall Trust, but that's not super helpful, as there isn't that much information on it either.

"Ma'am? We're back at the hotel," the bus driver says.

I look up and finally notice that we're stopped in front of the hotel, the lights of the bus on, and the door open. I have no idea how long he's been sitting here waiting for me to notice and get out.

"Sorry. Thank you." I rush out of the bus, anxious to get my laptop and its research opportunities. Maybe I can make an appointment with the trust of Leo's house to see the records, if they have any. Or they could be in the local records office for the county.

The trail is not cold yet, and school doesn't start for another month. I have some time and nowhere to be. My finances aren't going to be as excited about the research expedition, but I'll manage, staying in hostels and eating an unadvised amount of

Gregg's sausage rolls, which will be delicious, if not exactly healthy for me.

"Miss Chopra," the front desk employee yells after me as I cross the lobby. "We have a message for you."

"For me?" There was nothing on my phone. I check again as I walk to the desk. Who would know that I'm here but doesn't have my cell number? Maybe it's someone from the conference I don't know well. We're all staying here.

"Here you are." He hands me a sealed envelope. It's small, and has my name written on it in the fanciest script I've seen used for my name.

"Who is this from?" I tap the envelope on the counter.

"They didn't leave a name. But someone came while you were out tonight and left it. Looked like an accountant or lawyer type."

I have no idea why any English accounts or lawyers would want to leave me a letter, but okay. Did some family not like what I wrote about them? Am I being sued? Damn it, now I need to find an attorney here, and they wear wigs...how can I take that seriously? Oh, but maybe I could get more of their records out of discovery and write another article about whoever is mad. Maybe a book this time, with all that access.

I open the envelope and start walking to the stairs again. Then I stop in the middle of the lobby when I see the letterhead.

The Alston Hall Trust.

I'm so shocked I almost drop the paper and my phone on the marble floor of the hotel. And then I almost drop them because someone bumps into me from behind. Okay, it may be my fault for stopping in the middle of a walkway, but still, driving rules say don't follow someone so close that you can't get out of the way if they abruptly stop.

So I think we can all agree we're both equally at fault.

We apologize reflexively to each other, because the woman is British and I've been in England too long.

Then I detour from my room to find a chair in the lobby. I

can't wait for however long it'll take to get up the stairs to the fourth floor in this heavy dress, or a very slow ride in a very tiny elevator.

Finally, out of danger of being knocked over by people walking, I start reading.

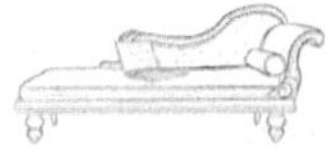

Dear Dr. Chopra,

I hope you're enjoying your time in our country. I am one of the attorneys responsible for the care and management of Alston Hall. In that capacity, I have been asked to extend the invitation to you, to come visit the estate.

I am currently staying on the Isle of Wight, so if you would like to accept the invitation, simply call the number listed below, and we will make all the arrangements for a visit.

Regards,

David Maynard

The Alston Hall Trust

What? I get up and make a circle to look around the lobby, wondering if I'm being watched right now. How do they know I'm here? Why do they want me to come to the house? To Leo's home. Who asked them to invite me?

Maybe Leo left me a letter, and instructions to find me when he knows I'm in England. To let me know he had a good life. Maybe he left some historical insights or an old book; he knows how much I would love that.

But I can't ignore that the only other way this could have been more tailor-made to lure me to a kidnapping would be if they had included the promise of English bulldogs, primary sources of the Indian experience in England, or one of those elaborate milkshakes with pieces of cake to top them off. So even though this may be how I get kidnapped, I'm calling that damn number.

My fingers shake as I type the number from the letter into my phone. I realize too late to do anything about it that it's almost midnight and people with good work-life balance, especially Europeans, might not answer their phones after hours, but I can't stop myself any more than I can resist getting a side order of fries whenever it's a possibility.

But someone answers the phone, although he does sound tired. "Hello. This is David Maynard."

"Uh, hi. Sorry about the late hour, I just received your letter. This is Meera Chopra."

"Dr. Chopra, so lovely to hear from you! Please, don't worry about the time at all." Now the voice sounds alert.

"I was surprised to get the letter. What is this about?" A very delayed self-preservation instinct finally rears its head, pushing me to get some information before I cheerfully hop into the windowless van full of my personal catnip.

"I can't go into the details over the phone. There are things I need to show you and give you."

"Right. But I don't know you. And I don't know what the Trust would want with me. I have no connection to it." Well, not one that I can explain to you. Not one you would believe.

"That's fair. I have a very specific set of instructions and can only request fervently that you visit the house. We can make all the arrangements for you and send a car. It will all make sense at Alston Hall."

Mysterious. And since it's in my job and nature to be curious, I'm going to make the irresponsible choice. "Can I bring a friend?" I do have a little self-preservation. Not enough to not go, but still, it exists.

"Yes, of course. I'm not trying to kidnap you."

"Haha." He gets a forced laugh. "I would never think that." Or at least I would never tell you I thought about it. "Let me check with my friend if he's available and then I'll give you an answer?" Frankly, I'm going regardless, but I will not be letting them make my travel plans if I'm going alone.

"Splendid. Please call or text when you know, and I can arrange everything."

"Will do. Thanks." I end the call, then stare at the phone for a little bit longer. Then I make another call.

"WHY DID THEY CALL YOU AGAIN?" Luis asks me the next morning, too bright and too early, as we wait outside the hotel for a car to pick us up and whisk us away to Alston Hall.

"They were sparse on the details." So sparse they provided no details. "What if they read something I did and want me to look at their archives? The family did have an Indian member, and subsequent part-Indian members and I am an expert in the field." Probably because there's so few of us studying it.

"We're heading into the English countryside, in a car driven by a stranger, and we don't know why exactly?"

"Yes. Where's your sense of adventure?" And this is Leo's house. I would never say no to Leo's house, no matter how sketchy the invitation.

"I'm a historian. The only adventures I like are the ones I can read about."

"Then this will be good for us. Give us a better perspective on the adventurers that we study."

"It's a good thing I scheduled some extra time in England." Luis gives me a look that suggests he isn't swayed by my arguments, but he's going so I don't go alone. And because he wants a free ride to get closer to his boyfriend at Cambridge. But I need him to stop asking questions, because I can't explain to him why this particular invitation isn't as random as it seems.

"Thank you. You're my favorite and this will be reflected in your Christmas present this year."

A sleek car pulls up to the hotel, and the driver gets out. "Dr. Chopra?" he asks.

"Yes. That's me."

He reaches for my bag. "Mr. Maynard is meeting us at the estate, and I will take you to the hotel near the house to drop your things off and freshen up if you would like. Then it'll be on to the house."

"Sounds good."

The driver puts our luggage into the trunk as we get comfortable. Soft leather seats greet us, with drinks in a cooler and a host of buttons letting me know I can control every part of my experience in this car, from the lighting to the temperature of the seats.

"Explain to me *again* what's happening right now." None of the excess has escaped Luis's attention.

"I'm getting your trip to the English countryside paid for, along with a night in a fancy hotel with a many-starred restaurant you can enjoy with your boyfriend. Because of my wonderful historian powers."

"Those aren't a real thing. But I can't argue with these snacks." He rummages in a box on the floor, getting out some salt and vinegar chips. Thankfully, the chips stop the questions that I can't answer.

Five hours, one ferry ride, too much traffic, and a stop for lunch later, we pull up to a hotel. After an efficient check-in and time to freshen up, we get back in the car, my body protesting the confinement after its recent freedom.

It's gotten later, even though the sun is in no danger of going down any time soon (thanks, summer in England). We pass cars leaving the estate as we drive through the welcoming gates, me for the second time, and past an almost empty parking lot.

Then we're at the house, and I almost create even more questions in Luis's mind by crying, but I hold back the tears. Because I don't know how to explain crying in reaction to a museum that I said I had no connection to.

But I can't stop my heart from aching as the numerous windows wink at me in the bright sun, welcoming me back. And then it aches at the thought that the building is still there, but the lord of this manor, the man I love, is long gone. The only comfort I can get is walking the same hallways and rooms that I walked with Leo, and seeing the same furniture. If it hasn't been sold or replaced by now.

I didn't realize how much I would be affected by seeing the house again, or I would have prepared for it better.

Luis breaks into my thoughts. "It's a nice pile."

"Yeah. It really is."

The driver pulls up to the main entrance. "Mr. Maynard will meet you inside the house."

"Thank you."

I get out of the car, walking up to the impressive façade and trying not to remember the last time I did this, while Luis follows behind. The front door is cracked open and I push it the rest of the way in.

"Dr. Chopra! I'm so glad you took us up on our offer." An older British man, outfitted in too many items made of tweed, just in case we had the nerve to mistake him for a city dweller, welcomes us into the building. He's got a large smile on his face, projecting affable grandpa.

"Well, I'm very curious to find out what this is all about. My family was so excited when I told them where I was going," I say, so he knows that people know I'm here. They don't, because I didn't think of that till now, but that would have been the smart thing to do.

"Let's not waste another moment. We'll borrow an administrative office to have our meeting."

He leads us up the stairs, and to the right. Even though this house is giant and I have a terrible sense of direction, I do know that a left at the top of the steps would have taken me to the Rose Room. I swallow and force myself to turn away and follow David in the opposite direction.

"Please, have a seat." David sits behind a Victorian desk and indicates the Louis XVI armchairs in front of it. We do what he says, but I sit a little closer to the edge than normal, wanting him to get on with it already. "Would you like some refreshments?"

"No," I say as Luis says, "Yes."

"We'll eat after," I say to Luis. But right now, I want to hear and see whatever David has for me.

"Are you sure you don't want to be alone for this?" David looks at Luis.

"No, it's fine." I don't even want to wait the time it would take for Luis to leave the room.

"Then let's get to it." David shuffles his papers around on the desk.

Ahh, more stalling. Stop torturing me!

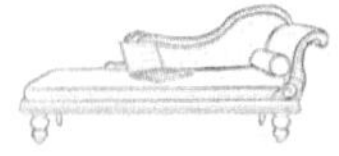

David clears his throat. "In 1897, the Alston Trust was formed, and Alston Hall was transferred into it. According to the trust documents, the home and all the furniture and décor are to be kept intact and open to the public, for a small fee. This property wasn't entailed, so the marquess at the time was free to do it."

Two years after I left. Leo would have been marquess then. Did he do this?

"The trust is administered by my family's law firm. My great-grandfather was actually the nephew of the marquess at the time, and the first administrator."

I perk up even more, searching the face that I mostly ignored before. This is Leo's family. Well, Lydia's direct family line. But in his face I can see Leo's nose and jaw, softened a little in age but still there. An age I never got to see on Leo.

I'm staring with a little too much intensity, if David's throat-clearing is any indication.

"And in the trust documents, there were instructions to open a letter in January 2025. This year. When we did, we found a legal document inside, as well as two sealed letters." David chooses this moment to pause for dramatic effect, looking up at us to make sure he has a rapt audience. He does. A thousand percent, he does.

"And?" I ask when he doesn't follow up.

"The document leaves the primary management of the trust, as well as the head curator position, to you. Meera Chopra. An American historian who is supposed to be visiting England in summer of 2025 for a conference on the Isle of Wight. Although she may or may not disappear for some time, or be difficult to track down. But when we find her, on or after the last day of the convention and not before, we are to tell her about the position."

"What?" There's an echo, but it's not my hearing; Luis is just as shocked as I am. I'm going to have to explain some things to him later, and I'm not sure if I'll tell the truth or how he's going to take it if I do.

"You are the current lady of the manor. Or at least the curator of the manor." He smiles at me. I guess he's not mad I'm apparently taking the business right from under him.

"But I don't understand," I whisper.

"It is a lot to process. My peers at the firm and I were shocked when we heard the news as well. But we read our own letter and read your published works, and we understood. There's a letter for you as well, which we very much had to restrain ourselves from opening. But never fear, I have guarded it securely." He hands me the letter, looking eager at the prospect that I'll open it right now and he can get a peek at it. For all his restraint.

"Can I have a minute, please? Alone. To read this." I direct that to both men in the room.

"Of course," David says, but he looks disappointed at the development. "How about I give you a tour of the house?" he asks Luis. "I'm not a historian, but I have grown up hearing stories of this house."

"Sure." Luis looks equally disappointed, but they both leave without snatching the letter from my hands.

I turn the document over in my hand, feeling the weight and texture of the paper. It looks old. Like a letter from Leo in 1890s old. He managed to get a letter to me. And also give me his house, apparently.

Charming, responsible hedonist of a man.

The historian in me rears its head and I grab some latex gloves from a shelf before opening the letter. But that's the last concession I make before sliding my fingers under the wax seal, opening it with a deep breath.

Meera,

Hello. It has been some time since I last saw you. Or maybe it has not. However much time has passed, for you or the world, I need you to know that I miss you desperately, and I love you. I have never experienced as much pain as I did when I saw you fall down those stairs. Except for the moment immediately after, when I went down to the landing and you were not there.

I knew then what it must mean. The same kind, mischievous universe that brought you to me got cruel in her old age a week later and took you away. I am glad you found a way home, to your family and your wonderous inventions, even if you had to leave me to do it.

I know you will have some questions, my curious love, and I shall try to answer as many of them that I can think of here.

Forsyth went half-mad after you disappeared. He was sure he saw you fall but then could not find you. He told everyone you had disappeared right in front of him, and Queen Victoria told him to cut back on the liquor.

You would have liked seeing that. And seeing his face after.

She assumed you had gotten away and Forsyth was too embarrassed to say he was outrun by a woman. She blames him for running you off, even though she did read the letter. She felt quite foolish at first, and maybe more than a bit angry. Maybe it was best you left when you did.

But she did relent. She quite enjoyed your time together and missed you more than she was angry. She swore Forsyth to secrecy, so your good name is intact, if you even find yourself in our fair country again. In our fair time.

And now you are probably wondering about the trust. A wise woman told me that it was all the rage to open your house to the public for their general amusement and intellectual enrichment, and for the purposes of separating them from their hard-earned coin. So, as this estate was not entailed, it was possible to enter it into the trust and open our doors, and hopefully keep them open until your special time.

The same wise woman also told me who wins the first auto race in France. So I broke one of my rules. I bet every last cent we had and some that I could borrow from a lender who had not heard our dire financial straits (I had to go all the way to Manchester!) on who would win. He was not favored, so when he did, we won rather a lot of money. It was enough to put down generous initial payments to creditors, and we're paying the rest through the fees we get from the house visits. I have a job now! I give tours and the public absolutely adores me! And I manage the trust (that part is less fun), which is set up to make sure this house survives.

The newspapers are calling us poor and bad ton for charging admission, neither of which is a lie, and also maybe because of the zoo I had put in (I do remember everything you told me). But after Lydia had a bit of a faint at the idea, she is just glad she can buy dresses that are in fashion, the same season they are in fashion.

And Lydia got married, to someone who makes her happy and who is quite titled, so you see, your association has only helped this family, and not just because of the gambling tip. She even has a little one, and I am a proud uncle. He is the smartest baby to ever be born, and I will not hear any disagreement on that point.

Lydia has already agreed to continue running the trust and museum after I'm gone, and to have her children run it after that. I told her the truth about you, and even though I think she thinks it is a work of fiction or that I am a candidate for Bedlam, she agreed to humor me and pass the estate and knowledge of what happened on through her family, per the trust conditions.

The title will go into abeyance upon my death, but so be it. My only concern in this time has only ever been Lydia, and as she can inherit the house, she will be fine. She also has her own money and title now, and frankly, duchess outranks marchioness, so I do not care what happens to it. Titles are useless anyway, haven't you heard?

If this house museum survives to your time, I can think of no one else I would want to run it. Your intelligence, curiosity, inventiveness and strength are exactly what it needs.

It is what I need too.

Which leads me to my next bit of news, one I know you will be angry at. I haven't married, nor do I plan to. Now that we've temporarily saved the house and have a long-term plan, there is no need.

There is no one for me here. I cannot ruin someone else's life by marrying them when all I will ever be able to think about is you. I cannot hold someone close when all I will be able to think of is holding you.

So even though I cannot hold you, I hope you will walk my halls and feel protected and cherished by them. Even though I cannot watch you thrive, I hope the same paintings I pass every day and the chairs I sit in now witness your beautiful smile.

I have never wished for ghosts to be real until now, so that I can see you, in your scandalous modern clothes, competently ordering around an entire army of adequately paid museum staff, inviting guests into our home the same way you would have if you had stayed, and we would have gotten married.

Because it is our home. Even if we cannot enjoy it together.

I have kept my bedroom blocked off of the museum spaces for you, whether or not you take the position. You can stay here for as long as you want.

I cannot force you to remain, of course; the trust can carry on if you refuse. But knowing you might one day be lady of the house will have to be enough to get me through the rest of my lonely life, however long it may be.

I love you, curious one. I hope your life will be as happy as you have made mine.

Leo

September 8, 1897

Postscript: Check under our bed for a surprise. And the hallway of Indian portraits at Osborne House for another. I'll be going to the unveiling there next month.

I'M glad I sent everyone away, because I can't stop crying. The tears I forced back earlier, too busy yelling at Heather and trying to find out what happened with Leo, fall freely now.

I don't think about all the history he changed—his stately manor being the first to open to the public on a large scale, his bet and sudden fortune, his not getting married.

I just think about how much I wish I was still in 1895.

One thing's for sure: nothing can stop me from taking this job.

CHAPTER 40

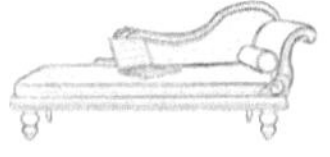

One Month Later

"Have we ordered the new magnets for the gift shop?" I ask.

"Done," my hyper-efficient assistant, Mary, says as she consults her tablet.

"Which new scones are we going with for the tearoom?"

"We're divided about fifty-fifty on that. We'll need you to break the tie."

How difficult my job is. But someone has to do it. "And did the curator from Longleat House let us know about the items for loan?"

"They are signing the contract for the exhibition as we speak."

"Excellent." Then they're not too mad we took their title of first stately house in England to open to the public on a commercial scale. Not that they *know* we stole that particular title. But I think they can sense it, and that's why they made negotiations for my "Indians in the English Country House" exhibit items slow and painful. "Thank you for your hard work, Mary. Why don't you take the afternoon off and get started on your weekend early?"

"Are you sure?"

"I'll be here if anything comes up. You enjoy." I never thought I would be this happy to live at my job. Especially since Leo made sure the trust has been updating the house, but especially my room in particular, with all the modern amenities, including a modern, en-suite bathroom, recessed lighting, and Wi-Fi. And a very expensive heating/cooling system. Someone even added a TV and a small kitchen in the room next to me, as well as a washer and dryer.

But no one has been allowed to touch the furniture he picked for me, except to clean it and preserve it.

After Mary leaves my office, I pack up my large tote and head for my room. I may still work, but I can do it in a historic, four-poster bed, under an embroidered floral, silk canopy. Surrounded by, I hope, the ghost of Leo. I don't know, since he hasn't made himself known to me, but I like to pretend that he's still here. I certainly talk to empty rooms like he's here.

I take the long way around, passing through the rooms that are open to the public on my commute home for the day. I like hearing the responses of the people visiting, too. Some in awe, and some so mad that this much wealth was able to be accumulated at one time while so many go hungry. I get both reactions.

Then there are some who were dragged by their more history-minded traveling companions and have very little interest in my house, as I've come to see it. That, I understand less.

But none of them have ever been as vocal as the commotion I hear when I'm passing through the library.

"You can't sit in the chairs, sir." The guide's voice sounds panicked, loud and with a hint of a shake to it, and I pick up speed to follow the direction of the sound, ending up in the sitting room.

"Do not tell me what I can and cannot do in my own home. I

shall sit wherever I damn well please." The voice that responds is British. Posh. And familiar.

"You don't live here. No one lives here, except Dr. Chopra. It's a museum. Are you a period actor no one told me about?"

"We'll get this all cleared up in a second, and my guest will *get up* for right now." That's David. I didn't know he was coming up to the house today.

David stops by for tea every now and then, sometimes for business for the trust or the times he helped me with immigration things and sometimes just to chat. He never really believed his family stories until I showed up, when it became a lot harder to doubt them, and he had so many questions about his ancestors and my experience. We've really bonded over him being the only one I can talk to about my trip. He's even brought his older brother, the man who inherited the dukedom that Lydia married into. But he always calls first.

"Can I help—" I stop where I am, waves of shock rooting me to the floor. I hear my tote drop, but faintly, like it's happening in the distance.

Because Leo is standing in front of me, in full Victorian suit, sitting on my chaise with his arm thrown over the back, his ankle resting on his knee.

My hands cover my mouth to press in the scream welling up in me. It's a mix of joy, and disbelief, and a deep hope that I haven't manifested his image through sheer loneliness and being surrounded by all his shit.

But I'm not making this up, because other people can see him. They want to get him off the couch. Where he's sitting, smiling arrogantly at me like he...like he owns the place.

I lower my hands. "Is this..." I can't get out the rest through my shaking voice.

"Why don't we go to your office?" David picks up my tote and slides it back over my forearm to rest it on my elbow.

"David?" I focus on him instead of the vision in a full evening suit sitting on my chaise. "What?"

"Let's get you both in the office." David gently turns me around, and then less gently grabs Leo by the arm to get him up.

I walk through the halls, not seeing the extravagance around me for once. I turn my doorknob, forgetting I locked it, and have to rummage through my bag to find the keys, which have disappeared into the black hole of my purse only to reappear after I've spent a good thirty seconds searching for them.

"Is this real?" I collapse on the seat closest to the door. Leo takes the other one and David hovers by the door, which he closes behind him.

Leo quirks an eyebrow. "The woman who travelled to Victorian times is confused when I travel in the opposite direction?"

"It's really you." I feel pressure in the back of my eyes, getting emotional as I lift a hand to tentatively cup his face, making sure he's real one more time.

"This conversation probably doesn't need me. I'll go. Call me later and I'll help sort out the legal details." David opens the door and slides out.

"It's really me," Leo says, ignoring David altogether.

"I thought I'd never see you again."

"I thought the same." Leo turns his head to plant a kiss on my palm.

It breaks the dam, and I rush from my seat into his lap, running my hands all over his body and planting kisses all over his face.

"But…" Kiss, kiss, kiss. "How?" More kisses. I restrain myself to his cheek so he can answer and I don't have to stop. But I can't restrain myself from moving to the corners of his mouth.

"I mentioned in the letter that I was going to Osborne House to see the unveiling of a portrait. Actually, did you find the surprise I left you?" Leo's voice is muffled, what with an Indian-American woman smothering him with a lot of pent-up affection she never thought she would get to unleash on the object of that affection ever again.

But now I get to.

"Yes. Loved it."

Leo had a portrait of me commissioned. I don't know who he got to do it or how it looks so much like me, but I love that he wanted a reminder of me around. It's hanging in my room, because it would be hard to explain why I'm hanging a Victorian painting of myself over the library fireplace.

"Victoria had a painting commissioned of you. Two actually; one she kept and one she gave to me. Because of how obviously sad I was when you left."

"What?" That makes me pull back, eyes wide in terror at those ramifications.

"Oh, yes. You made quite the impression on Her Majesty. Not even Forsyth's proof could change her opinion for long. And he did try after you were gone. She said you must have had good reasons, and either way, you were a citizen of her empire who needed help."

"Well, I don't like that bit, but I appreciate her defense."

"She had the portraits painted, from a court painter who had seen you at events. With help from Her Majesty and myself for the details. She was convinced your breasts were smaller than they were, but I set her straight." His eyes track directly to the breasts involved in the controversy.

Yeah, he's going to be seeing them in a second. In this office, if it comes to it.

"So, you were at Osborne House?" I do need him to finish this story first. But he's still a little distracted by my boobs.

He clears his throat. "Yes. For the official unveiling, even though she sent me my copy in advance since she knew how much I missed you. Then I got quite emotional seeing you again. Her painting is quite large, larger than the one she sent me. And accurate, after my advice on your décolletage."

"Yes, we get it. I have boobs."

"Boobs?"

Oh, yeah. There's a lot I need to update him on. Things I was trying very hard not to say when I was in Victorian England, but now I've slipped right back into old patterns.

"I was upset." Leo gets back on track without the modern English lesson. "And I enjoyed some of the drinks provided for the party. And then before I knew it, I was intoxicated. And, perhaps this was related, but I fell down the stairs in the garden. Then I woke up in this time. Did you know Osborne House is a museum now? With guards who get mad when you are in the garden after closing. Intoxicated, still. I did not realize what happened until it was too late. Until I demanded to see Queen Victoria."

"Do you have a court date? Do we need to get you a National Insurance number? We need David back to coordinate everything." I look to the door and think about getting up, but Leo tightens his hands around me.

"David is the one who rescued me. The guards thought I was lying when I told them exactly who I was, quite truthfully, might I add." Leo sounds very aggravated at the fact. "They sent for the constables, who took me to a very strange-looking jail in a very strange conveyance. I told them to contact the trust, hoping it still existed, and thankfully they did, even though I did not know the address. But everyone has telephones now, did you know that? They were such a novelty during my time, an expensive one. At any rate, the constables used theirs and David came to the constabulary to free me. He said he would get all the necessary documents for me. And that I was a 'period actor' whatever that means."

"Your great-great-nephew or whatever, is a fantastic attorney." I've seen the trust's books; this house museum is doing well.

"Meera, have you been in a car? I've been in cars in my time, but they are *nothing* like these."

I snort. "I lived in Southern California, so yeah, I know what a car is. Wait till I get you on a plane."

"What is a plane?"

"I have a proposition for you," I say instead of answering.

Leo quirks an eyebrow and I smooth my hand over it, still half not believing he's here.

"What is it then?" Leo asks.

"I'll show you, former Lord Basildon, I'll show you everything you need to know in this time. But first, I have a question for you." I get off his lap to squat down in a kneel.

"Absolutely not. No matter what century I am in." Leo grabs my arms to halt my progress and slams down hard on his knee, getting to the ground first. "Meera, I love you. I crossed time to get back to you. Will you marry me?" His eyes are tearing up a bit, and I don't think it's love driving it. I think I'm going to need to introduce him to ibuprofen first and foremost.

"No. Because I was asking you to marry me first. Because I love you." In case he didn't hear me while I was yelling it at him during my fall. "I'm so glad that the universe sent me to you. And then you to me. Even if I have no idea how this all happened. And woman can do anything in this brave new time you're in."

"This will take some getting used to. But when in Rome." He shrugs. "Yes, I will marry you."

I launch myself at him, taking him down for the second time in a minute.

He grunts when he lands. "I'm in for a curious adventure, aren't I?"

"The adventure of a lifetime. Even if no one will ever believe it happened."

And then we don't talk for some time.

EPILOGUE

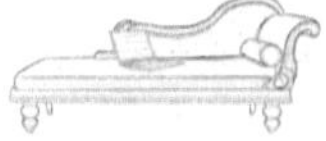

"What about LordBasildon@gmail.com?"

"That's not even accurate, because the title went into abeyance," I say, yawning as my fingers hover over the computer keyboard. It's been exhausting giving Leo a crash course in the twenty-first century, but satisfying having him and my family in the same time. I'm working on getting them to move so we're all in the same place, but asking them to leave Southern California weather for the British rain has been…a process.

Leo's been adjusting as well as can be expected. He's fascinated by every new technology he sees, and it's been a special experience seeing this all through his eyes. I already hugged various appliances in appreciation when I returned from my time in Victorian England, but seeing him interact with all the things I've mostly taken for granted (well, up till my trip) has been fun. I think his favorite item has been the streaming services. The "plays" on demand have kept him enraptured far into the night, many nights. To be fair, that would probably be my favorite too.

Although he is still shocked every time women wear shorts, kiss their partner, or have jobs. Shocked, but not mad at it. He loved the first time I wore leggings in front of him. So much that we did not make it to our errands that day. And he certainly loves being able to hold my hand and kiss me whenever he wants. All without a chaperone watching over my virtue.

It hasn't all been wonder and excitement and love though. I know he misses his sister and family and friends in the past. He's been getting to know his descendants, which has been wonderful, but they won't ever replace the sister he grew up with. Sometimes I'll find him staring at the paintings in the house of Lydia and his family, and there are a lot of them even for nobles, as if she knew he would need them one day. I've also caught him hunched over the tablet I got him, absorbing every bit of information on them that he can find. He says he doesn't regret giving it all up for me, and I have to believe him and hold him a little closer when he gets melancholy.

We're planning a trip to California soon, which should be fun and terrifying (for him). But maybe seeing my family, and feeling the welcome and love they already have for him, will help a little.

"What about ILoveGamingHells@gmail.com?"

"That's too '90s. Both 18 and 1990s."

Luckily, David set up all the important administrative details that make Leo exist in this time. Apparently, they've been preparing for something like this for a while, and I don't want to know how, but David had everything sorted more efficiently than I thought possible.

Leo's enjoying his work, which is the same one he had after I left the past. He's giving tours, quickly becoming our most beloved tour gide, helped by his first-hand knowledge that no one is supposed to know about, and large reserves of charm. His hedonist side makes sure that no tour is boring, and he might already be planning a ball or two to raise funds for the museum. Although I do keep having to tell him to stop sitting on the chairs in front of the public; it sets a bad precedent.

I'm enjoying my work as well. We've been doing a deeper dive into his family history, and I might be cheating a little asking him about his mom for my next book, but my sources can't get any better than that. Even if I do have to fudge the truth about where exactly I got the information from. Running the museum has been so rewarding as well. There are no museums dedicated to the history of those with Indian heritage in Britain, so adding the information to our tours has been amazing, and makes us stand out so much.

"How about LeoLovesMeera@gmail.com?"

"How about we stick with a classic, Leo.Alston@gmail.com?" I enter in the information and pray someone hasn't already taken it.

"Boring, but all right." Leo waves his hand at the computer screen. Introducing him to the computer was fun. He couldn't figure out scrolling at first, and thought there was a demon in my computer. He's adjusted, and we're still getting packages from his first online shopping spree, weeks later.

"Settled." I click the button to create the account. "And Meera loves Leo, too." I lean over and kiss him, technology forgotten for a while.

It has been a wild adventure.

And as much as I love studying Indians in English history, nothing beats living with my very own historic artifact. Even if it means there's one less Indian in the Victorian period.

I'm not going to lie to you, this book is mainly a product of spite.

After hearing so many times that there couldn't be any people of color in western history, and if there were, they had to be enslaved or poor laborers or otherwise have miserable lives that could never be the subject of a romance novel, I snapped and did what any angry nerd would do; I Googled some stuff.

And through books, articles, and even someone's PhD dissertation, I found out there were more people of color in the last six hundred years of English history than even I had assumed.

And then I wrote a romcom about it.

It turns out, the role of people of color in England is too complicated to distill into a single sentence. Because the experience varied depending on the era they came, their status, gender, wealth, location, religion, and who they were talking to on any given day. Some were happy, some were sad, some were rich, some were poor, and there was a lot of in between cases. Some hosted parties for royalty, while others were forced into poverty just miles away, and some studied law somewhere geographically in between the two.

There were a few liberties taken with my work of fiction, but some things are true: there were Indians in Britain, especially in London, from the palaces to the docks. Victoria had a soft spot for Indians. Not only did she act as godmother for several colonial subjects, she had a strong friendship with Abdul Karim (the Munshi), who started out as a servant and became a confidant so close, one of the first things the new king did upon Victoria's death was to burn all the letters Victoria had sent to Karim. Victoria stood up for Karim again and again against the very vocal protests of her own court, to give him honors such as land grants and present him to kings. That is why I think she would have helped my very fictional historian when she found her way to Osborne House.

Sophia Singh and Victoria Davies Randle both existed, and both benefited from Victoria being their godmother, both socially and financially. Indian royals often visited Britain, whether to socialize, or to litigate their pension agreements with the Crown or other legal matters. The lascars are real, as well as their difficulties in getting back to India and in settling into life in London if they couldn't or didn't want to return to India. There were also many biracial children, half-Indian and half-British, because the East India Company encouraged their soldiers to marry local women. The experiences of these biracial children also varied, depending on the same set of circumstances that influenced the experience of people of color in Britain, with the added circumstance of their two heritages.

I had fun inventing this story for my hero and heroine, but there are plenty of real-life stories that are waiting to be discovered, and hopefully more to come as scholars continue to dive into this previously ignored area of research. If you want to read more about Indians in British history, or general British history, I've included books I read to help me write this book.

Fisher, Michael H. *Counterflows to Colonialism: Indian Travellers and Settlers in Britain 1600-1857*. Permanent Black, 2004

Bance, Peter. *Sovereign, Squire and Rebel: Maharajah Duleep Singh and the Heirs of a Lost Kingdom.* Coronet House, 2009.

Basu, Shrabani. *Victoria and Abdul: The True Story of the Queen's Closest Confident.* Bloomsbury, 2010.

Mathur, Saloni. *India by Design: Colonial History and Cultural Display.* University of California Press, 2007.

Fidler, Ceri-Anne. *Lascars, c. 1850-1950: The Lives and Identities of Indian Seafarers in Imperial Britain and India.* 2011. Cardiff University, PhD dissertation. https://orca.cardiff.ac.uk/id/eprint/55477/1/U516542.pdf

Hoffenberg, Peter H. *An Empire on Display: English, Indian, and Australian Exhibitions from the Crystal Palace to the Great War.* University of California Press, 2001.

Foreman, Amanda, and Lucy Peter. *Queen Victoria's Buckingham Palace.* Royal Collection Trust, 2019.

Tinniswood, Adrian. *The Polite Tourist: Four Centuries of Country House Visiting.* The National Trust, 1989.

Girourard, Mark. *Life in the English Country House.* Yale University Press, 1978.

ACKNOWLEDGMENTS

Thank you to Mackenzie Walton for your amazing edits on this novel. You have not only made this novel stronger, but you have made me a stronger writer.

Thank you to Ink and Laurel for the stunning cover that I can't stop looking at. It completely captures the story, and is a work of art.

Thank you to my husband for proving that romance heroes aren't just a fantasy, for always supporting me, and for always being willing to listen to me venting about the latest adventures in publishing, even if half of what I say about it sounds made up.

Thank you to my mom and dad for your love and support. Not everyone gets as lucky as I do in the parent department, and I'm grateful for that. I can't imagine the person I would be if I didn't have you.

And thank you to the readers! All the people above helped me write this book in some way, but there would be no point if it weren't for the wonderful community that loves books as much as I do. And for each of you that have picked up these books, I want you to know it means the world to me.

ABOUT THE AUTHOR

Suleena Bibra has read romance in one form or another since she could pick her own books. She occasionally branches out to other genres, but really, what's the point if there's no kissing? She also loves to laugh, which probably has to do with her dad putting Monty Python on whenever her mom wasn't looking.

Suleena studied art history in college and loves to travel every opportunity she gets. A bit indecisive, she has worked as a museum intern, lawyer, workers' compensation adjuster, and private investigator. Author is best, though, so she can continue living out a bunch of other careers without changing out of her pajamas.

Suleena writes RomComs heavy on banter, shenanigans, and aggressive whimsy. She spends the rest of her time annoying her stubborn, but adorable, bulldogs (who also double as her particularly lazy writing assistants) with her love and watching copious amounts of reality TV.

IF YOU ENJOYED AN AMERICAN
DESI IN QUEEN VICTORIA'S
COURT, CHECK OUT MY
NOVEL, THE ROAD TO GRETNA!

What better way to escape reality than going on a reality show that combines The Amazing Race, Love Island, and Pride and Prejudice?

Naomi Richmond is hoping an ocean is far enough away from her overbearing father. She's chosen London and built a life there with a job she only dislikes about a quarter of the time.

Nate Williams is perfectly happy where he is, and his dissatisfaction with his job is so low it can't be quantified numerically. Unfortunately, his boss (and Naomi's father) is asking him to do something that might make him start to hate Mondays: convince Naomi to come home.

Nate arrives in London at the same time Naomi receives an offer that intrigues her as much as Nate does: be on a reality dating show, where the contestants will pretend to be Regency aristocrats eloping to the famed Gretna Green. Nate is sure it's his job to stop this, but instead, he ends up on the show with her. Now Naomi is trying to make a name for herself while Nate is trying to make sure she doesn't do anything to embarrass her father, and they're both trying to fight the attraction they feel for each other. On camera.

Tune in whenever you find this book and watch Nate and Naomi find themselves and each other, on The Road to Gretna!

Available now in ebook and paperback at your favorite retailer!

CHAPTER 1

Naomi

"I need five Red, White, and Blue Margaritas, please!" I loudly request over the music, in the dimly lit basement restaurant that has become our spot.

Bubba's serves what English people think American food is, mostly burgers and hot dogs with small American flags stuck in them, like we conquered processed meats. The walls are covered in American license plates and pictures of American treasures like the Lincoln Memorial and Dolly Parton, and on special occasions, like today's Fourth of July celebration, they get a real American band. Or four English guys with a banjo.

It's become a second home for us.

I hadn't expected this weekly meeting of Americans to turn into a regular thing. All because of a chance meeting at the American food aisle, where Zara and I almost came to blows over the last Lucky Charms, to her introducing me to her friends at a "real American diner" in the heart of Kensington (which was decidedly unreal), I clicked with these people. In two years since, they've become family.

"Can I have an order of the chili dogs, but can I have that with a side of sadness that you lost us in 1776?" asks Zara, a Southern Californian who works on reality shows.

James looks at her pityingly. "Oh, love. We watch the news. We're good with that particular loss."

"Well, you also lost our ancestral homeland of India," I say. Well, not Lucy's. And I guess it's only half mine.

"I'll get you those chili dogs." James, our favorite server, is used to us by now and only engages with us half the time.

"Chili dogs for all, James," orders Jaya, an Indian-American castle publicist (publicist for cultural heritage sites) who always looks glamorous. I met her through my PR agency when we worked together on an assignment, and when I found out she was from San Jose and homesick too, I invited her to our group.

"Did we miss anything?" Lucy, a white mystery writer from Los Angeles, approaches our table and then sits down across from me.

"She means did you order us drinks? And I need drinks after dealing with Madame." Dev exaggerates a posh English accent when talking about his (least) favorite person, his boss's daughter. Dev's an Indian-American curator at a big, extravagant, historic house in the countryside and is originally from Southern California. He drops down next to Lucy. They both knew Zara from before I ran into her on the day that is now known as Marshmallow-gate, since they all grew up in Artesia. Zara and Dev were dragged to the same temple against their will one Saturday night a month when they were teenagers, and Zara and Lucy went to high school together. They reconnected when they found out they all lived in London, through social media.

"We have food and drinks coming and we will acknowledge signing a declaration to be independent later. But right now I want to hear Zara's news." I turn to Zara, refusing to engage with anyone until I hear what caused all those cryptic, maybe happy texts we've been getting in the group text today.

Zara, resident reality TV producer, builds the drama before she answers. "Well…"

"Out with it, or Naomi's gonna have a small cardiac event." Dev's not wrong.

"It actually involves Naomi, just a little…"

"Okay. I will haunt you forever if I expire from this cardiac event before I find out the news that you have kept from me. Since eleven a.m. this morning." I take a sip of the patriotic margarita that appeared in front of me. "Thanks, James."

He squeezes my shoulder and leaves us to celebrate our centuries-old victory over his ancestors. No grudge present.

"I got a job on a new reality show filming here in England!" Zara finally tells us. We're all out of our seats in a flash, crowding around her in a giant group hug.

Zara's had a hard time since she was fired from her first job in London. She's been looking all over the world for the next opportunity, and in the meantime doing temp jobs. And moving in with me, who very much appreciated the split rent. And living with my best friend.

She was even considering going back to the States, but she didn't want to go back as a failure, especially because of whatever happened to make her leave Los Angeles (which she still refuses to talk to me about and I refrain from circling around her for the information like a hungry shark that smells chum in the water because I'm a great friend).

"You lot might have won your independence, but you don't even have universal healthcare," an Englishman drunkenly slurs at us, mistaking the reason for our happiness. Which is rich coming from someone who's enjoying our patriotic margaritas so much.

"Way harsh! And this is unrelated to George Washington, the deeply flawed man who nevertheless kicked your collective tea-drinking asses," Jaya yells back.

"How is this related to me, though?" I ask when we finally disband the group hug.

Zara grabs my hands, probably so I can't escape when she gives me the news. "Well. The thing is. One of my first jobs as this show's field producer is to fix a problem we're having with a contestant pulling out last minute, and the showrunner now hating all the back-ups we had planned."

I get an uneasy feeling in the pit of my stomach, guessing at where this is going, and assuming the worst, most embarrassing outcome of this conversation.

"And I started describing you to my boss, and he sort of loved the idea of adding an American, specifically you, and wants to know if you can join the cast?" Zara gets the request out in a rush, so fast it takes a second to process it.

"Wait. What? Me? Why?"

"I described you because this can be good for you. I know you're thinking about starting your own business as a publicist, and this could be great exposure for you. You can get your name out there. Manage your own post-reality show buzz, or a fellow contestant's, and show everyone how great you are at the job. And then famous people from everywhere will want to work with you."

It would be an amazing opportunity. I've been working at the PR firm for two years, getting promoted from intern to assistant, and I love it. But there's not many opportunities since the company is so small right now.

And my dad keeps badgering me to come home. He's that Harrison Richmond, of the New York Richmonds (ew, I know, but an accurate portrayal of how he sees himself) and he has very firm opinions on how I should live my life.

At his company. Living at home. Becoming a mini-him. A terrifying prospect.

He thinks if I'm just getting coffee and arranging schedules for very little money, I should be doing it for the family business.

He's even offered to put me in the marketing department. But I can't work with him. He treats me like a spoiled princess, like any actual work might break me. Anything from doing my laundry or getting my own groceries.

And I let him. Because it's easier to give in than fight over chores. And I hate doing laundry.

Every time I get geographically close to my parents, I let them take over, and I regress to an entitled teenager. But I don't want to be that person. I want to earn my accomplishments. I won't say I'm doing it by myself, because I didn't refuse the financial help for school and some living expenses. I may have pride, but I also need to eat, despite how unfair that is to people who don't have my safety net.

But here, unlike in New York, at least no one knows who I am. I even go by my mother's maiden name, Patel. Every success I have, I'm confident I earned.

Unlike the time in sixth grade, when Dad saw I got a C on an essay, and he went down to the school, yelling and badgering teachers and administration until I got a B on it. And I know I deserved the C. I completely forgot about the assignment until the last minute, when I word vomited something onto the page so I wouldn't get an F.

I worked harder after that, because I didn't want to be known as the person whose father comes and saves her all the time.

But the clamoring from Mom and Dad to come home has gotten louder, and since I'm now in possession of two shiny degrees, undergraduate and graduate, it's harder to push them off. Dad sweetens the job offer every time I see him, and it's getting harder to resist, because I can be weak.

I've talked to Zara about the issue. And about the fact that if I started my own business as a publicist, a successful one, then my parents would see that I can and should be on my own. Bonus: I would be able to afford to live on whichever continent I damn well please.

But still. A reality show?

I love the genre. But they edit those for maximum drama, so I'm sure it's going to lead to some embarrassment. And I don't want to think about what my parents would say if they found out. Which is why I wouldn't tell them till after filming, like the mature adult I am.

"C'mon, leprechaun. I need this, but I think it'll be really good for you too," Zara says, unfairly using the nickname she gave me when we first met, arguing over that box of Lucky Charms.

"I am only seven inches shorter than you, giant," I say without heat, a regular argument for us.

"Do it!" Lucy says. "I wanna be famous adjacent."

"You're the famous author. We're already famous adjacent. To you," Jaya says.

"I'm not famous. But if you want to mention my books on the show, that would probably be really helpful for me paying rent in the future." Lucy wags her eyebrows at me.

"I haven't agreed to do this." I remind the table. "What's the show even about?"

"I can't actually tell you that. It's sort of a dating show, mixed with a little bit of competition. A cash prize at the end." Zara is hedging. "You could use the money to start your company."

"A dating competition show? Do you want me to be on Love Island?" I'm both terrified and excited about that prospect.

"You wish. No. But it's similar."

"You did say you wanted to get out there and meet more men," Dev, usually quiet during our conversations, says.

I glare at him. "How dare you remind me of my own words? At the most inopportune moment?" It's true, though. I have been avoiding hooking up with the many attractive, accented men I meet on this island. But I've been busy.

And no one quite matches up to a certain man. Who is now an ocean away from me and probably doesn't care about the distance, because he definitely doesn't think about me as much as I think about him.

Dev looks at me neutrally, like he always does when we overwhelm him with our combined personalities. Just like I imagine a little brother would if we were all his big sisters. But he got dragged into this circle of friendship years ago and we're not letting him go.

"To clarify, you want me to sign on to a show where I don't know any of the details, and give an anonymous corporation the rights to portray me however they want on TV with no privacy restrictions?"

"Yes. But if you come in tomorrow to sign a non-disclosure and do some light interviews, they'll give you more details before you have to sign on for good. And there'll be scones." Zara looks so hopeful.

This has the potential to help us both. Or, you know, ruin my PR career before it even starts, forcing me home to an Upper East Side mansion with my tail tucked in between my legs in failure.

I take a sip of American freedom juice and answer, "Fine. But if I look like anything other than an intelligent, professional woman, you have to buy me unlimited Lucky Charms for the rest of my life."

www.ingramcontent.com/pod-product-compliance
Lightning Source LLC
Chambersburg PA
CBHW030920300726
48970CB00001B/252